Buying the Virgin
Box Set Four

'The Virgin and the Masters'
The Continuing Tale of Charlotte the (Ex)Virgin
And Her Two Masters
In a Story of BDSM, Ménage Erotica

This Box Set Contains

Book 17 - The Virgin and the Masters - Part 1
Book 18 - The Virgin and the Masters – Part 2
Book 19 - The Virgin and the Masters - Part 3
Book 20 - The Virgin and the Masters - Part 4
Book 21 - The Virgin and the Masters - Part 5
Book 22 - The Virgin and the Masters - Part 6
Total Approx 84,000 Words

Author: Simone Leigh

Part One

A Continuing Tale of (Ex-)Virgin Erotica, BDSM and Ménage with Two Masters and *More......*

Part Seventeen Of
The 'Buying the Virgin' Series

Author: Simone Leigh

The Virgin and the Masters
Part One

Charlotte

Sitting in my room, the small private space that I call my own, in the house I share with seven other students, my phone beeps. It's an incoming message, from Michael

"Purchase completed fifteen minutes ago. Your Home awaits you."

*****

Fumbling, as I balance my bags in one hand, door keys to the lock in the other, I step into the hallway of the student house.

As I tramp upstairs, a voice floats down from the top floor; Marie. "That you, Charlotte?"

"Yup," I shout back.

"You've got visitors.... They're up in the kitchen here. I made them a coffee while they waited."

I don't get visitors. There is only one possibility. Racing upstairs, I dash into the kitchen, and, yes, it's them, my Master and Michael, both grinning wildly.

"Surprise!" says Michael. He sweeps me into his arms, swinging me around, kissing me on the mouth.

My Master, more circumspect, touches me on the shoulder, kissing my forehead. "Hello, Charlotte. Lovely to see you."

"Mas.... James! Michael..." Suddenly conscious of Marie's stare, I say. "Oh, Marie. This is Michael, my fiancée and... James.... his friend. This is Marie, one of the other house shares."

Marie is looking at Michael with far too much interest for my liking. "Ah.... the mysterious fiancée at last," she says. "We've been wondering what you'd be like... Can't say I blame Charlotte for keeping to herself so much when I see what she's saving herself for...."

Michael says nothing. With his blond, blue-eyed, good looks, he always draws attention. My Master sucks in his cheeks, looking amused.

"Come on downstairs," I say. "We can talk in my room. It's a bit quieter there. Thanks for making the coffee, Marie."

"Oh, *no* problem." She eyes Michael, all too obviously, and he pointedly fails to notice.

Down in my room, with the door closed behind us, and now with privacy, my Master wraps his arms around me, holding me tight, his mouth opening over mine. His kiss is long and slow, and when he finally pulls away, he remains close, his arm pulling me in at the waist. "We've missed you," he says.

"I've missed you too. Why didn't you tell me you were coming? I'd have at least made sure I had some chairs for you to sit."

"We thought you would enjoy a surprise visit."

With the three of us in my mini-flat, it becomes obvious how small it. It's fine just as my study room; a bed, a desk, bookshelves, a chair, wardrobe and built-in drawers, but now, my Master sitting on the single chair, Michael sits on the end of the narrow bed as I put on the kettle. Then I have to go back up to the kitchen to find a couple of extra mugs.

Returning with the borrowed cups, I make coffee. Michael comments "Snug. You might swing a cat in here, but it would have to be a small cat."

"It's fine. I only use it for working and sleeping. The kitchens and bathrooms are shared."

Music thumps through the floor, the base turned up too high, and from the kitchens above, chairs scrape across the floor. "It's a bit busy around here, isn't it." says my Master. "How about we go out somewhere? A restaurant perhaps? That is, if you've not yet eaten, Charlotte....?."

"No, I've not eaten. And yes, I'd love to go out with you both. It's been so long. I know it's only been a few weeks, but it feels like forever."

"And...." continues my Master... "If we're not interrupting anything important." He head-points my books and notes, open on the desk. "We did choose Friday night, hoping you would be free?"

"Oh, no. That's fine. I have until Wednesday to hand that work in."

"You're not going out anywhere with the other students?"

"No, I don't really go out. I'm here to work."

Michael purses his lips a little at that. My Master looks bland. He continues, "Good, and later..." he lifts my hand, kissing the fingers..." A hotel room perhaps? We thought you might like to celebrate your new home?"

"I'd love that, but, er.... but I don't have anything really to wear for going out in. I only brought jeans and tee-shirts and everyday sorts of clothes."

"That's alright." says my Master. "We brought some of your other clothes along. They're in the car. And um, perhaps you should have a shower first? You smell of machine oil."

I laugh. "Yes, at college today, they were showing us how to use a lathe and a milling machine."

Michael snorts. "Is that what you'll be expected to do when you're working properly? In an actual job?"

"No, but you're expected to have some idea of how a machine shop and a tool shop work, and that means I come out smelling of machine oil...."

"James is right. You need a shower. Why don't you get cleaned up and changed, and we'll wait upstairs? It's a bit crowded in here...." He sees my hesitation. "Don't worry. I'm sure James will keep me out of Marie's clutches."

I laugh, realising how silly I'm being. ", I think she's expecting her boyfriend, Pete, along this evening."

"Another student?"

"Yes, he's on the Aeronautical Engineering course."

While my two Lovers wait upstairs in the kitchen, I shower and wash my hair, put on some make-up and check out the clothes they have brought with them. A classic 'little black dress' and high heels, and I feel ready to take on the world.

Teetering slightly - living in jeans and sneakers, I am out of practice at walking in heels - I go upstairs, to find my Master and Michael chatting with some of my housemates. Kylie and Sandra are there; Caroline too, and a couple of the boyfriends. Michael is drawing attention from the girls and my Master looks amused. Pete is there, his back turned to me as he stirs something in a pan; Marie's cooking is awful, and Pete usually cooks for both of them.

As I enter the kitchen, all eyes turn to me, and Pete glances around, then does a double-take as he sees me. "Bloody Hell, Charlotte. I didn't realise you had legs under your jeans, let alone legs like that."

Then he realises what he has said, and blushes apologetically at Michael. "Um, sorry. didn't mean... Not used to seeing her like that. Usually, she's just one of the boys...."

"Is that right?" grins Michael. "You've seen a side of her that I've missed then."

*****

My Master has booked a room in a very expensive hotel. As we step into the lobby, all polished glass and brass, expensively perfumed air washes over us. Light classical music whispers into the background.

"Shall we eat in the restaurant?" asks Michael. "Or use room service and have it in privacy?"

"Oh, I think I'd like us to eat in our room," I say. The chance of time alone with my Master and Michael is not to be missed.

Michael smiles, his face sunny, then hooking one arm through mine, waves me towards the lifts with the free hand. My Master joins us, then taps the button for the penthouse.

"Um.... isn't this a bit expensive Master?"

He looks smug. "Director's privileges. This is a Haswell hotel. The suite's not occupied right now, so we have it for the evening, the weekend if we want it."

The suite is gorgeous, with thick, plush carpets, fresh flowers on the coffee table, and a vast window, which overlooks the panoramic view, and leads to a terrace.

"Can you order the food please, Charlotte." says my Master. "I'll have steak, rare, with salad."

Michael is inspecting the suite, checking out the bedrooms. "Same for me," he calls, thumb pointing one of the rooms. "This one I think."

Peeking inside while I order the meals, I grin. "Looks good to me."

Michael waggles his eyebrows at me. "I'll get that jacuzzi filled, shall I?"

Half an hour later, pushing my plate away. "That was good. You can live on pizza, but sometimes a proper meal is what you want."

Michael looks up, his expression disapproving. "You're not eating properly?"

"Well, it's not easy there. There's eight of us sharing the kitchen, plus boyfriends when they're there, and it's difficult to cook anything complicated."

Michael is unimpressed. He doesn't like it when I say anything that suggests I am not living well. "It's not complicated to make a decent salad with a good mix of ingredients, or an omelette, or...."

"No, it isn't, but there's not a lot of space in the fridge for a good mix of ingredients."

He's not happy, and I change the subject, not very subtly, by worming my way into his arms. He knows exactly what I'm doing, but, as I press myself against him, he can't maintain his air of stern reprimand, which melts into a smile. "Ah, Charlotte. You always win don't you...."

And now, my Master is there, behind me. I kiss Michael, then turning, reach to kiss my Master. We all three know where this is going, my Master, Michael and I, ready to make love together....

They take me by the hand, leading me to Michael's chosen room....

*****

Michael

She is so beautiful, standing there between us, James to her fore, me behind. My hands on her shoulders, I rest my face over her head, scenting her hair. James, with an arm around her waist, pulls her in close, controlling her, as he does, and as she loves. Kissing her, his mouth wide on hers, I hear her gasp, feel her body shiver as she responds to him.

Behind her, slipping her waterfall of copper hair to one side, I slide down the zip of her dress, feeling the fabric ride her silhouette; her perfect breasts, the curve of her waist to hip, and as the dress falls away, her scent billows over me, almost an assault. As I nibble at her neck, the soft skin behind her ear, her head flings back against mine, and she swings her face back to me, trying to kiss, as she croons her growing arousal; sheer honey to my swelling cock as it presses to her through my jeans.

James drops to his knees, holding her at the hip, his face nuzzling into the vee of her legs as he tugs at her panties, sliding them down to leave her naked to us. Slipping a shoe between her feet, I push her ankles apart, allowing him easier entry. She staggers, but I support her, holding her under the arms as James parts her pussy lips, working her clit with his tongue.

Shuddering and moaning, she rocks against me, struggling with her balance, so, James glancing upwards at me, I eye-point sideways to the bed. We learned to read each other years ago. He slows-blinks an agreement, kisses the copper of her loins, then, as I turn her to face me, he stands, his hands sliding up her beautiful pale skin.

Fully upright, he takes her again by the waist, yanking her backwards to the bed, pulling her off her feet. Off-balance, she drops, gasping, to land where he sits on the edge, cradled in his arms. Her wild green eyes are wide, feral with excitement, a touch of red blushing up her pale cheeks. James hooks his ankles under hers, parting her legs, and I drop between her knees, her gorgeous pussy open to me, glistening with moisture, pungent with her arousal.

Her pussy lips are bright pink, swollen and wet, and I scissor them open with my fingers, sliding back the hood of her clit with a thumb to expose her. A couple of fingers inside her, and she clenches around me, arching her spine, almost hissing through clenched teeth. My cock twitches, wanting to be inside her.

I take her labia in my teeth, tugging gently, and as her hissing turns to whimpering, my balls tighten, my jeans growing tight. Looking up, I see James pinching at her nipples, nipping them hard. I lick over her clit, circling it with my tongue. Her hips quiver and James tightens his hold on her, curbing her movement.

Dipping lower, pulling her wide open with my fingers, I lap out her pussy, savouring the tangy taste of her, salty and lemony as her heated cunt trickles into my mouth.

Jeez, but I want to fuck you....

Deepening my reach, I swipe out the rim of her muscles with my tongue, feeling her clutch at me, her whimpers becoming wails.

Time to up the ante....

Licking long slow strokes the full length of her vulva, from pussy, through her lips, and over her clit, I exchange glances with James again, then stand.

He heaves her up towards me, letting me catch her. Then, as he repositions himself back on the bed, kneeling upright, I pick her up, placing her, facing me, but on her knees between his.

Reaching around her, he takes her arms, locking them behind her. Wrapping his hand into her hair, he arches her backwards, then with his knees, forces hers apart. She is held, restrained, every muscle straining as she pants, her breasts and belly heaving, skin gleaming with perspiration.

You love it when he controls you don't you, Baby...?

Her knees splayed, hips thrust upwards and outwards towards me, thighs open, her foxy hair glistens as she grows wetter, her thighs slick with her own juices. Holding her green-eyed gaze, I reach for her clit with a single finger, touching her nowhere else. As I circle it, winding spirals into her flesh, her mouth opens as she moans, lips parted.

James watches over her shoulder, straining her tighter, his eyes soft as she responds to his embrace, her cries growing sharper. My hard cock pulses.

Is he hurting you Babe...?

... if he is, you like it...

Slipping two fingers between her pussy lips, I delve deeper into her, thrusting with my hand. Her flesh is hot and swollen, her juices coating my hand as I finger-fuck her. Pulling out, I suck my fingers clean, tasting her. Then, coating myself in her again, I push fingers into her mouth...

"Lick yourself off me, Charlotte."

She obeys, wide-eyed, pupils huge as she sucks my fingers clean.

I love it when you look like that. when you look up at me and I know that the only thing you want right now, is me inside you, fucking you senseless.

Then plunging my hand deep and hard into her, I hook my fingers forward, scraping at her inside, and she screams, bucking and jerking, or trying to.

James tightens his hold on her once more. She can't move; simply trembling in his embrace as I probe deeply, my thumb pressed against her clit.

"Oh God, fuck me. One of you, please fuck me." Her voice is broken, breathy.

I pull back, eye-pointing James to take her. Once again, he pushes her to me, releasing himself from behind her, then as he rolls to one side, my hand to her chest, I push her down again, flat on her back, legs splaying. James drops between her thighs, lifting her at the hip with his hands. I push a pillow underneath, arching her, raising her to meet him, as he presses his face into her sex.

James settles between her thighs, kissing her lips and clit and pussy. He glances up, locking eyes with her for a long second. I see both their faces, and I know adoration when I see it; his, narrow-eyed, restrained; hers, wide-eyed and open. Then he locks his mouth around her cunt, lapping and licking at her.

I watch her face, looking down on her as her arousal spirals ever upwards, first her breasts and neck flushing pink, then further, up and over her cheeks. And now, her eyes lock with mine, those eyes; sometimes grey in the dusk light, sometimes sea-green, under the sky and the sunlight. She reaches for me, fingers touching my face, tracing my mouth, my cheeks.

"My Golden Angel...." she whispers.

Angel, Baby? Yeah, I'll be an angel for you, but the demon in me wants you too......

I lean into her touch, kissing her fingers, willing her to orgasm. I love to watch her climax.

Come for me, Baby....

Her lips parted, panting, a fine sheen of perspiration over her skin, her lovely pale skin, now blushing red all over.

I bend to kiss her breasts, taking a nipple between my lips, feeling it harden between my teeth, pebbling into my mouth as I nibble at it, biting just hard enough to make her gasp and react.

She gasps, arching her spine, presenting her belly, raising her hips, juddering as James teethes on her clit.

I'm going to fuck you to screaming soon......

Her hair spread around her, spilling over the sheets and the pillows, she looks to me, her eyes glazed, tits scarlet with lust, glossy with sweat, nipples hard.

"I want you inside me," she says to me.

How can I not smile? Because I know that she doesn't just want my cock inside her pussy.... She wants *me* inside *her*....

Inside you? I want to drown myself in you...

James pulls away, sitting on the edge of the bed, watching, his penis, rock hard, twitching with his pulse.

Charlotte lies there, her green-eyed gaze pulling me in, knees akimbo, arms outstretched to me, in invitation.

Oh God, I've got to get my cock inside you....

Shucking my jeans, I roll on top of her, pressing between her warm thighs, my balls tightening, pulling in as I test her entrance.

Her hands around my neck, one sliding up into my hair, nails biting into my skin, she stares, dreamy-eyed, up at me, her eyes wide pupilled, black against jade.

I push a little inside her, gauging her wetness, her readiness for me. She whimpers, arching her spine further, reaching for me with her hips, spreading her thighs wide, giving herself to me. Pressing in my cock-head, feeling it skim by her ring muscle, she clenches around me as I penetrate her, letting her swallow me.

All she wants, right now, is for me to fuck her.

I withdraw, completely, then again, press inside, slowly, delving into her heat.

James sits beside her, looking down, fingering at a nipple, pulling and rolling and tweaking. Every so often, she yelps and jerks as he pinches hard, her pussy clenching around me, and I want to simply let go, shooting into her, while she screams under me.

Jeez... hang on to your control man... you're not some fourteen-year-old....

I ram in hard, hilting myself inside her, then again, and again, loving the noises she makes; wailing, as I fuck her hard, her pussy tightening around me with each thrust.

She spirals up towards climax, shuddering and shaking. I meet eyes with James, he tilting his head slightly in signal.

All the time, pressing hard inside her, I hold her tightly around waist and shoulders, holding her to me, and I roll, taking her with me, so we lie side by side.

Still working her inside with my cock, feeling her flesh heat and tremble around me, I present her to him; her curvy ass, that perfect rear....

She knows what's happening. As James lubes himself, and then her, I whisper. "Alright, Charlotte? Both of us?"

Her breathing is heavy, rapid. She doesn't speak, simply nodding, before I feel her holding her breath, as James guides his cock into her, first testing her a little, once or twice, before gradually pressing inside her. Her body freezes against mine, tensing; her only movement, her breathing and a shiver at her hips, as he presses inwards. She quivers against my groin, tightening around my cock as James works himself inside her, taking her ass.

I'd love to do that, fuck you there.... but I want to see your face, Baby.... When you Come, I want to watch you Come....

Her heart pounds against me, banging through her chest to mine

Are you okay Babe? Really okay?

She is so wet, her moisture seeping down over my thighs, wetting my skin. She smells of lust and sweat and sex, and of James, and me.

I want to fuck you until you scream, and lie with you in a puddle of sweat and cum and sensation....

James starts to move, thrusting slowly, gradually, and she rests between us as I match his rhythm. She lies still, passive, simply taking us both within her.

All my worries, all my concerns, just vanish when I can bury myself in you, be consumed by you, swallowed by you....

I start to thrust harder, my tempo increasing. James matches me, his eyes brushing with mine as we mutually fuck/make love/ shaft/love this woman that we share, that is so much a part of the both of us.... She lies between us, her moans synchronised with our movements, her body commanded by both of us, her heart and soul ours....

She is gazing at me, wide-eyed as the day she first met me, when James had taken her virginity only a day before. I reach to kiss her, awkwardly from our conjoined position, but our lips meet, and I penetrate her mouth with my tongue, as my cock penetrates her warm, wet, welcoming cunt.

And now she is mine also...

This woman we both love...

And the Rush is coming...

The pressure begins, in the base of my shaft, balls tightening, migrating upwards to pressure my cock-head, intensified in the rim and at the tip.

All my senses filled with her, I pump hard, extending/ accelerating the glorious build-up of sensation, the coming of the Rush

My hips locking, I spill into her...

Riding the adrenaline, heart drumming, vision blurring, I slam my first shot into her, flying high, firing hard. My cock twitches another load into her. She's screaming something, but I don't hear what, as, with a final shudder, I pull out, to fire over her belly.

She's so close herself. As my vision clears, her head flings back, to rest by James' face. He's controlling himself, hovering near, but his eyes slide sideways to watch her as, her beautiful eyes screwed shut, mouth wailing open, she convulses, howling her orgasm between us. I'm still inside her, and her cunt spasms around me and, I think triggers James, as with a groan, he drops his face to her shoulder, grinding himself into her.

James grunts, juddering against her, pressing into her ass, before, with a gasp, breaking free, to lie on his back staring upwards, sweating, breathing hard....

She's not finished. Still riding the wave, she is all but collapsed against me, eyes closed, forehead resting on my chest. She breathes shakily, occasionally jerking spasmodically and whimpering with the after-burn of orgasm.

Holding her, supporting her, I withdraw my semi-flaccid cock, then lower her to the sheets, where she lies, panting, as I bend to kiss her breasts, then her lips.

She wraps her hands around my neck, fingers sliding through my hair. "Thank you." she murmurs.

James looks up at me briefly, then sideways to her, smiling. She returns his gaze as he, also with one hand on a breast, kisses her lips.

We lie together, he to one side of her, I to the other, in an extended moment of quiet. I encircle her, and she rests in my arms.

*****

Elizabeth

I answer the phone.

"Hello?"

"Hi, Beth. It's James. Is Richard there?"

He sounds tired.

"Hello, James. No, I'm sorry, he's not, but I'm expecting him soon. Can I pass on a message for you?"

"Um, no not really. It's just that I've got the printouts with me for the projected costs on C-Site. I'm on my way back from checking out some of the suppliers. Could I drop them off with you there on my way back? It's easier for me than going to the office tomorrow."

"Yes of course. Are you alright? You sound done in."

"Yes. It's been a long couple of days. I'm rather tired."

"Would you like to stop for dinner when you get here? You'll feel better with a meal inside you."

"That would be great, Beth. Thanks. I'll be there in about an hour."

I ask Ross to set an extra place for dinner. James is co-director with my husband Richard on his City Renovation Project. They've both been working all hours. It's no wonder he's tired.

James arrives an hour or so later, looking washed out. I'm concerned about him. Normally vigorous and active, he is clearly doing too much. Settling him into an armchair by the fire, I pour him a brandy, rather a large one.

"Nice to see you, James. Are you well?"

"Yes, I'm fine. Just tired. There's a lot going on." He stretches out long legs, rubs the back of his neck.

"And Michael? Is he alright?"

James grins, looking more himself. "Michael is busy knocking down walls, rebuilding walls, replacing roof struts, laying floors and generally fighting dragons on Charlotte's behalf.... I've never seen him happier."

"This in this house you're renovating between you? Up in the mountains?"

"That's right."

"I'd quite like to see it sometime."

"You'd be more than welcome. Mainly Michael's trying to get at least part of it fit to live in by the time Charlotte gets back at Christmas. He wants to welcome her *Home*." He rubs his nose, looking sceptical. "Personally, I think we might all be living under canvas."

"It's that bad?"

He rocks his hand back and forth. "No, not really. The house itself is a shambles right now, but we can always live in the hotel section for a while. It's just that Michael's trying to get *that* open as a Spa Hotel, so it would be better if we can treat it as a building site, so the workmen can get on with the renovations and upgrades there, and it can start actually earning some money...."

Richard arrives home, looking every bit as tired as James. I manoeuvre him into the opposite armchair by the fire, pouring him a brandy too, topping up James' while I'm at it.... At least Ross is cooking, so it will be a good dinner. And Richard seems pleased to have some company for the evening. I sit with them but try to retire into the background. I want to hear what they have to say.

"I'm glad you're here, James," says Richard. "How's Charlotte? Have you spoken to her recently?"

"She's fine, yes. We talk every day or so, and we called by her digs last week, Michael and I."

"She's doing alright at college? Working hard?"

"Working very hard. 'Driven' I think is a better word. She doesn't seem to have a social life at all, judging by what her housemates were saying. She has some extra exams in a couple of weeks; with her having changed course from last year, there's catch-up work to level her up with the other Engineering students. So far as we can see, she does little but work and sleep."

"Well, I'm sure that she'll enjoy herself when she's back with you at the end of the semester."

James sucks in his cheeks, saying nothing, but there is a gleam of humour in his eye.

"Um, James," says Richard, with a touch of hesitation. "There *is* something I wanted to discuss with you, about Charlotte."

"Oh?"

"It's to do with that home she was in, Blessingmoors."

James sips his brandy, looking wary. "Mmm...?"

"I was talking to Will..."

"Will?"

"Will Stanton, Police Commissioner.... The investigation on that place was never fully closed, although it has been semi-dormant for some years. During the original inquiry, they caught, convicted and imprisoned a number of the gang-leaders responsible for trafficking the youngsters, but they couldn't get convictions on all of them, due to lack of evidence..."

"So....?" Now, James looks worried.

"So.... they would like to interview Charlotte. Take her through things again, in more detail. Show her photos of the men concerned. See if she can give a positive ID on any of them, or any more information. They're trying to get convictions. Especially as there is reason to believe that some of the parties concerned may still be involved in trafficking. They might want Charlotte to stand as a witness in Court."

James closes his eyes, pinching the bridge of his nose. "I've been worrying that something like this might come up. When do they want to talk to her? I can't break that kind of news to her in the middle of her term, and certainly not when she's got exams coming up."

"Perhaps when she's back at the end of the semester?"

"That would be better timing, yes. And she'll have Michael for support then."

"Michael?"

"He's better at this sort of thing than I am. When things get emotional, I sometimes... over-react. Michael's a rock. She'll need him."

Richard gives him a long look. "Over-react?"

James doesn't speak at first, then, 'Let's just say that Michael deals with some things better than I do."

"Things alright between the three of you? It must be difficult sometimes to.... um.... achieve a balance?"

Again, James speaks slowly, clearly choosing his words. "Things are fine with the *three* of us. I suspect that the difficulties you imagine, are not the ones that actually matter between us. Certainly, *balance*, as you put it, is not a problem. Michael and I are very different people, and we interact with Charlotte in different ways."

Richard continues his probing.

Is he pushing his luck, asking things like this?

"And you and Michael?"

James raises an eyebrow. "Michael is my closest friend. He has been for years."

I decide that it is time to interrupt.

"And how is Charlotte herself?" I ask. "After what happened over Summer? Finally coming out with everything that happened to her as a child...."

James sips at his brandy. "She has nightmares."

"What sort of nightmares?"

"Being trapped in the dark. Running.... I'm not much good for her with that sort of thing. Michael is much better..."

"But of course, Michael is not with her at University."

"No, he isn't. Which is why I'm not willing to discuss anything of this with her at all until she's back with us at Christmas."

"Did she always have nightmares? Before the Summer?"

"No, not before then, or at least, not while I've known her...." He stands, pacing up and down. "Look, I understand why the Police want to talk with her but give us a little while after she gets back at Christmas. Let Michael and I have a few days to help her let off some steam, relax a bit..."

"Work hard. Play hard?" My husband eyes are crinkling at the corners. He has seen for himself, at one of the clubs, how the threesome 'let off steam' together.

James rubs the back of his neck, suppressing a smile, "Something like that, yes."

I interrupt again. "And we could go out together, Charlotte and me. No offence, James, but she needs some 'girl-time' too, and she doesn't seem to me to have many female friends."

"That would be great, Beth. Thanks, and.... you're right. The girls she shares the house with all seem to be on other courses, so she doesn't really mix with them much. And the other students on her own course are almost exclusively male, so them, she keeps at arm's length to... er...."

"... to avoid misunderstands? Mixed signals?"

"Mmm. Yes."

"No problem. We'll go shopping one day. I'll call by the office and collect her from there."

Richard smiles. "With, hopefully, no repeat of what happened the last time you took Charlotte shopping?"

James chokes on his drink. I try to sound prim. "Charlotte was defending me when she hit that lout. It was a pleasure to see him go down."

SIMONE LEIGH

*****

Charlotte

I drive up the mountain, returning 'Home', and wondering what I will find. I know that Michael has been working hard at the renovation ever since the sale went through, but the house was a complete wreck, and I'm not sure if I am going to have a roof over my head for Christmas.

But the drive up the mountain is so beautiful. Climbing the steep, winding road, I drop to third gear, then to second, skirting around tight corners, and occasionally pulling in to let some idiot pass me at lunatic speed. I just want to amble *Home,* and enjoy the spectacular views; the glory of the forests, the lake, the plant life that scrambles, wild and beautiful, everywhere around me.

And I look forward to being together again with my Master and my Lover, no.... my *fiancée*, for a few weeks until I return to college after Christmas.

As I turn the final corner, the hotel hoves into view, looking good already. Paint has been freshened up, windows replaced, signage installed; 'Life and Beauty', doubtless to partner with Michael's 'Life and Fitness' brand in the City.

But from here, I can't see the house. It sits behind the hotel, hidden by trees and a rambling, overgrown garden.

Michael knows I am coming, of course he does. But I didn't give him a time, or phone ahead. He and my Master surprised me at my student digs. I want to surprise him here. Parking up, I go looking for him.

Where is he?

Walking through the hotel, a variety of workmen are there, plumbers and electricians by the looks of them. From upstairs, across the house and down in the basement, there is a cacophony of banging, clattering, hammering, drilling.... It is *deafening*....

I snag the nearest man in an overall. "Have you seen Mr Summerford?"

He looks at me oddly. Of course, he probably has no idea who I am. "I think he's out back somewhere, Love."

As I walk through, one of them shouts after me. "Careful out there. It's not safe everywhere."

The gardens at the back are still an extravagant mess of unpruned roses, rampaging brambles and nettles, overgrown trees and forgotten lawns, but a clear path has been hacked through, so I don't have to navigate spikes, stings and thorns in quite the same way as I did on my first visit.

I can hear chopping.

The old house, when I reach it, has a kind of roof; tarpaulins sheeting over to keep the weather out, while old struts, trusses and timbers are renewed or repaired. Floor joists are missing entirely, apparently removed *en masse* for replacement, and so, as I stand on the ground floor on plain stone flags, I look up into a wide roof space, or at least, what would be a roof space, if there were a roof.

I still hear the chopping, and I follow the sound.

Passing through the kitchen; at last.... an area that seems to be a functioning room. An add-on to the main house, it has a tiled floor, a ceiling and, looking out and up, a roof too. There is a door beyond, perhaps leading outside, and another to... who knows where? A scullery perhaps? Tables and chairs gather around an old cast iron range, set into an inglenook, and blazing with heat. A single, unlit, light-bulb dangles from a cord in the ceiling. I flick a wall switch in a mood of experiment, but the bulb remains firmly off.

An old stone sink looks antiquated but functional. Checking the faucet, the water spurts. Of course, once of a time, the kitchen was the heart of many houses, and so this is now.

Despite the ruin and dilapidation, it is quite beautiful.

The sound of chopping is loud now. I follow it through a back door and outside, into a shed area where, despite the December chill, stripped to the waist, jeans tightly belted, and skin gleaming with perspiration, is Michael, my Golden Lover, bringing an axe down on a timber block, splitting it to firewood. As each piece splits, he repositions it and strikes again, gradually reducing slices of tree-trunk to useable firewood.

He doesn't notice me, and I simply stand quietly, watching him, enjoying the view. As he swings the axe, in a long arc over his head, muscles ripple and play under his tanned skin. His blond hair is slicked down over his head with sweat, and his brow furrowed in concentration, as he targets the wood with the blade, splitting it, then tossing the stove-lengths onto a growing heap to one side.

He looks like a god. My bronzed, blond Apollo...

And I gaze on, for the sheer pleasure of watching him move, male beauty in motion, sheer poetry.

Having reduced one tree core to usable pieces, he moves to pick up the next, placing it on his timber anvil. And now, he sees me, his face lighting up.

"Charlotte!"

Dropping the axe, he strides over, sweeping me into his arms, his eyes alight.

"I didn't hear you arrive. I was trying to have everything ready for you."

"I can see that." I grin. "Looks like you've got the house toasty warm for us."

"I wanted you to come *Home*." His expression is a puzzle; longing, love, hope, enthusiasm, sadness. "I wanted you to.... to have a place to call your own."

And then he is on me, his arms encircling me, his mouth fastened on mine.

I love him. I want him. And my body wants him.

He breaks the kiss, looking down at me, a speculative look in his eye. "Yes?" he says.

My heart pounding - I have seen too little of my Golden Lover in the past few weeks - I cast an eye over our surroundings. "Um, yes, but *here*?"

He grins, beckoning me with his eyes.

"Er, no, not here...." Taking me by the hand, smiling all the while, he leads me back into the kitchen, opening the unidentified door I spotted. And beyond is....

The chamber is basic in the extreme; four walls, a ceiling and a bed. But a fire burns brightly in a hearth, on the wall to the rear of the kitchen range when I think about it, and there are candles *everywhere*. Only one or two are lit, but Michael moves around the room with a taper, lighting one candle off the last, until light glimmers golden with candle and firelight.

The bed is huge and thickly blanketed.

"I couldn't get the house properly ready for you," he says, apologetically. "I wanted to, but there simply wasn't time. But I was able to get it to the point that we can eat, and sleep and make love."

The room, bare though it is, is beautiful. And I see from the hope in his eyes that he wants me to like it.

"It's lovely," I say. "Um.... have we a bathroom?"

He hesitates. "You see all those trees and bushes out there?"

I've got to pee outside?!?

Then he cracks out laughing. "Gotcha!" And I laugh too, wondering how much of a joke I am laughing at.

He straightens his face. "It's not great," he admits. "But you can walk right through to the hotel and use the bathrooms there if you want to. Or there's an old privy out the back. I'll have to dig a new pit for it though until we get some proper plumbing in."

"Right.... Um... A shower?"

"Did you see the tin bath hanging off a nail in the kitchen?"

This should be interesting....

"Hope you're happy roughing it for a bit?" he asks, anxiety in every word. "I so wanted it to be perfect for you, but...."

Words won't do for this. I step close, flowing into him, my fingers in his hair, my lips on his. "It *is* perfect. You're here. I'm here. And...."

"Yes..." he says. "James will be here too, later."

Then he stops to kiss me, and the world is a warm and wonderful place.

Despite the fire, the room is chilly. "Don't get cold. Get into the bed," he mutters, his voice husky. "I'll just go bolt the door. Don't want any interruptions."

By the time Michael returns, only a minute or so later, I have peeled off layers of winter clothes and am between the sheets, having found waiting for me, half a dozen hot water bottles.

He smiles, sheepishly. "It'll be warm enough once we're both in there."

I lie back, watching him as he undresses, unbelting his jeans, shrugging them off to climb between the sheets with me.

He looks embarrassed. "I'm sorry. I should have been able to shower first," he says.

"Don't be silly." I stretch out a hand to him. "You've been working, hard, on building our home. You're fine." And he is. He smells wonderful, of hard work, clean sweat and warm masculinity.

My Golden Lover....

"It's too long a time apart from you. I just want to touch you. To be inside you." he whispers.

"And that's what I want too."

His lips lower to my breasts, slowly, tantalisingly. His skin is cold, but his breath scalds across my skin, my nipples puckering. His arms, one around my midriff, one about my shoulders, pull me in tightly, contouring my curves to his harder, muscled body. Again, his fingers are chilled, sending a *frisson* scampering up through me and drawing a warm response from deep inside my core.

His nails, rough and hard, dig, point-like into my spine, drawing little gasps from me and sending my pussy into a liquid meltdown.

His body is sleek and hard against mine, his erection pressing against my thigh. I feel electrified, heady; and the tremor inside me brooks no denial.

"Inside me. I want you inside me."

His blue eyes are intense, lustrous in the candlelight, wide-pupiled as he moves to sink his cock into me. Already wet for him, more than ready after our long parting, I spread myself wide, willing him inside me. I know that, always, he fears that I love only my Master, not him

"I want you. I love you. I've waited for you." I murmur. "Make love to me. Fuck me."

His eyes widen, and as he slowly penetrates me, I move to take him, swinging my hips to meet him, to match him, as gradually, he presses inside me.

His face lying on the pillow by mine. "Charlotte...." He almost breathes the word....

He moves within me, slowly at first, to a rocking rhythm, which I match, meeting him. This is lovemaking at its most simple. Two people, one within the other, the meeting of flesh, the meeting of souls; my Golden Lover and I, as we rock and love and fuck our way to climax.

He thrusts harder, more forcefully, and again, I match him, swinging my hips up to take him as deeply as I am able. His cock ramming into me, balls banging against me, our bodies colliding, slamming, each against the other....

He is shuddering, sweating. I know he is struggling for control, to hold himself for me to come first.

And it won't be long....

Orgasm, coiled within me, quiescent, for too long, strains for expression. With Michael's cock within me, stretching me, filling me, my pussy quivers and wells. My thighs tremble. My belly shudders....

And my climax unfurls and surges, rising through me, rippling in waves as, crying out, I grip onto Michael, fingers digging into his skin, winding into his hair. As I arch and strain against him, he holds me tight, his own climax close.

Almost as I relax, he groans, dropping his face to my chest, sighing as he spurts into me.

After a few seconds, still deep inside me, he pulls himself up onto his elbows, looking down at me.

He is dripping with sweat. Casting around, he is looking, I think, for a towel. There isn't one, and he settles for wiping his forehead on the sheets. "I'll definitely be prioritising improving the facilities," he comments. He looks worried. "Can you handle this?"

"It's great," I say.

He looks sceptical.

"No, really. It is." I stroke his face. "As long as we're all together, it's fine. It looks as though we have all the necessities. Anything else can come later. And I can see how lovely it's going to be."

He flushes with relief. "Glad you feel that way. I wasn't sure how my bride-to-be would react when she saw that she'd be living in a building site."

I shrug it off. "I've lived in worse."

He turns serious. "So, you have."

Time to lighten the mood....

"Want to give me the guided tour? I couldn't look inside the house before. It was too dangerous. It looks as though you have it all opened up now."

His smile blossoms. "I'd love to. Um, get plenty of clothes on. It's cold out there..."

*****

My Master arrives. I stand outside as he pulls up, and he smiles as he sees me. Stepping out of the car, he wraps his arms around me, brushing his lips against mine.

"Welcome home," he whispers. "Um, not too private here, are we?" Looking around, curious faces are watching us through the hotel windows, various workmen looking out.

To Hell with them....

We walk, hand in hand, through to the house. During the day, I have done battle with the kitchen range, effectively enough to produce a decent casserole. If I stick with 'one-pot cooking' we should eat well from here. The three of us sit, sharing a meal, over wine and candlelight.

My Master glances up. "When can we expect electricity?"

Michael rocks his hand. "I'm hoping we'll have it for Christmas." Then he looks over at me. "Sorry Charlotte. I just couldn't...."

I cut him off. "It's perfect. Don't worry about it. We're together. That's the main thing."

He smiles and settles, wineglass in hand, simply watching me, gazing at me as though there is nothing else in the world to look at.

After a while, it becomes a bit embarrassing. "Um, I'm not going to dissolve if you look away, you know."

My Master snorts a laugh. "You'll have to forgive him, Charlotte. Michael has worked every waking hour on the house since the day he got the keys. He's been looking forward to your arriving here."

I reach out a hand to each of them, holding fingers. "Me too. I did as much work as I could back at college so that we could enjoy being together."

I see that eye-lock thing they have, their eyes meeting, and I *know* that I'm about to be fucked six ways to Tuesday....

And Michael's only just......

Then my Master looks at me, his lips curved in that almost-smile of his, and jerks his thumb towards the bedroom. "In there, I think, Madam."

The bedroom is warmer now, the heat of the kitchen range percolating through the wall. I stand next to the bed, sandwiched between them.

Michael looks down at me. "Strip," he says.

Strip? He's never put it like that before.

"Strip?"

My Master leans close. "Michael wants to get his cock into your mouth, and I want to fuck your cunt, so.... strip."

And my pussy floods.

Their eyes meet again. Both smiling, they look smug, having obviously pre-arranged this between themselves. I could neck them when they do that, but my pussy is growling for attention, and they both know it.

Business-like, I strip, pulling off layers of pullovers, removing boots, jeans and thick socks. Neither of them makes a move, or touches me, until, as I stand naked before them, suddenly they lunge, grabbing me by the arms, and they pull me, shrieking with laughter, onto the bed.

Michael pinning my arms over my head, my Master produces rope from his pocket, tying my hands, tethering me to posts of the bedhead.

Has he had it there all the time?

Of course, he has....

Wrists bound tight to the bed, I am pulled back down the mattress, the two of them tugging me at the ankles until my arms are stretched taut, and my belly and thighs tremble in anticipation. My breath is already shaky, and my pussy is going into overdrive.

I want to be fucked.......

......again....

Naked and immobilised, I watch them as, standing at the end of the bed, where I can see them both, they undress, each looking down at me; my Master with his non-smiling smile, eyes crinkled at the corners, Michael, soft-eyed, his smile, very white against his tanned face.

My tall, dark-eyed Master strips off his tie, removes cuff-links, unbuttons his immaculate white shirt, and peels it off to reveal his long, lean torso. Well-muscled and firm, tight-waisted, with a fine scattering of dark hair over his chest, that narrows to a tight line leading below his belt, he kicks off shoes, peels off socks, then pauses for Michael, my Golden Lover.

Michael also watches me as he undresses, his blue eyes holding mine as he pulls a thick sweater and undershirt over his head, and off. Not so tall as my Master, but more heavily built, he is broader in the shoulder, his muscles, strap-like, his abdomen flat and well-defined.

Both stripped to the waist, bare-footed, they gaze down on me, making me wait as I quiver and gasp.

Michael pulls something from his pocket; a black silk scarf. I have seen it before. He uses it as a blindfold.

Yes, they planned this together....

Pulling a pillow behind my head, he props me up a little, then binds the scarf around my eyes. "Not too tight?" he murmurs.

"No, I'm fine, but please.... don't make me wait too long...."

He chuckles, pressing a finger to my lips.

Blind now, I must take my cues from other senses. Michael is still close to me; his clean scent of pine and spice washing over me in waves as he moves. He straddles my chest, massaging my shoulders and breasts with strong hands, working my neck and head with his finger-tips.

My Master parts my legs, opening me at the knee and thigh. Fingers peeling my pussy lips apart, his hot breath washes over me, and I would writhe and wriggle, but with Michael's weight pinning me, I cannot move.

Fingers broach my pussy, testing my wetness I think, then withdraw. There is a pause....

One of their non-speaking conversations...?

Yup.

Michael moves from atop me, lying alongside instead. He nibbles at a nipple, sending electric dancing along nerve-endings to tantalise my clit. Simultaneously, teeth tug slowly at my labia, and a finger penetrates my back passage.

I am *so* ready for this. Despite my earlier tumble with Michael, several weeks of almost complete abstinence have left me primed. Already ascending a short spiral to orgasm, I smile to myself at the thought of how much of this the three of us will be doing over the next month.

"That's a nice smile," says Michael softly. "We must be doing something right, eh?"

I can barely move, but I reach with my face, trying to find him, and his lips meet mine, open-mouthed, his tongue sliding over my teeth.

As we kiss, his fingers pluck and tease at my puckered nipples, and my clit is being gently tortured by another warm tongue.

Hips a-tremble, my pussy begins to shudder, the heat within blooming outwards into orgasm and... it stops....

The tongue withdraws, the mouth leaves mine, and my nipples are abandoned.

And my orgasm recedes and fades, leaving me twitching and panting.

And the two of them go silent, for a long count.

Just as I am beginning to worry, I am touched again. Michael's hand, palm flat to my belly, slides south, fingers winding through my wet curls until one presses over my clit. His mouth settles once more over my breast, his teeth be-devilling my nipples.

A tongue probes into my pussy, deeply, wiping out inside around the ring of muscle, and to the rear, I am ass-fucked by a single finger. At all my most sensitive points, I am worked and probed and ....

The sheer tide of sensation is irresistible, and my climax rises again, my core vibrating upwards to a pulse......

And, once more, it stops.

Oh, God....

Feverishly panting now. "Hey, Guys. C'mon. I need to come..."

There are only two soft chuckles in reply. My breath judders as, once more, it begins. I am losing track of who is doing what. Fingers wind circles around my clitoris. More fingers probe and scrape within me at my g-spot. Now, there is something inside me to the back, vibrating, sending ripples through to my aching cunt. My hips judder and jerk under this assault of sensation.

Again, my tormenting orgasm wells, hot and pulsating from within. Straining now against my bonds, my whole body taut with the desire for orgasm.... and.... and.... It stops. Even the vibe is quickly removed.

I could weep with frustration.

"Oh god, please, let me come. Let me come."

My Master's voice, smooth as cream. "Ask nicely." There are other sounds.

Undressing?

"Please, Master. Please. Let me come." My pussy is gushing hot, my thighs wet with my own juices, the sheets below me, damp. My whole body is quaking now with the *need* to come.

He doesn't reply immediately. Then, "What do you think Michael? Do we let her come yet?"

"Not yet. I think we can do another round or two. I'm enjoying watching this. Charlotte...." He briefly kisses my lips.... "You look fantastic. I want to watch you quiver a bit longer yet. Then, I'm going to put my cock in your mouth, and, whatever you don't swallow, you're going to get over your face and tits. And I think that James would like you *really* liquid, for when he has his mouth wrapped around your cunt when you *do* come.... When we *let* you come...."

My pussy convulses again at his words, and again the heat of an open mouth descends over my entrance, licking away my juices. Michael's fingers... I *think* it is Michael's fingers, flick and flutter over my clit.

Moaning loudly now, all trace of self-control gone, spine arching, I raise myself on shoulders and feet, trying to get some relief. The tongue delves deep inside me. My clit and pussy and ass dissolve together in a frenzy of sexual sensation. My orgasm rises again, and this time there is no stopping it. This time, it is not to be denied....

I think they know it. This time, there is no cessation. Michael slides my vibrating nub between his fingers, kneading it, circling and plucking and flicking. My Master, his hands supporting my upraised hips, sucks and laps and mouth at my molten cunt until....

Screaming, I orgasm. No holds barred, my climax spasms through me, in a tsunami of fire. The sheer intensity of it robs me of breath, and my howling wail wavers loudly and softly as I snatch at the air.

I am still riding the wave as the blindfold is snatched from me, and my Master, bending me all but double, legs pressed back against me, my knees hard against my chest, plunges in, ramming hard, his body as deeply within me as is possible.

I howl the pain and the ecstasy of it. He is himself volcanically aroused, his cock huge within me, stretching me wide, as he fucks me hard.

He seizes my chin, fingers holding my face tight, pulling my face to his as he kisses me roughly, almost violently. His mouth pressed against mine, he spasms and groans, first grinding against me, then repeatedly ramming hard into me. His eyes wild, he pulls out and away from me, lying to one side, panting.

And now, Michael is there, pushing his cock at my mouth. Again, he is already huge. Our earlier tryst has had no effect on his readiness. His cock-head streams over my lips as I open to take him in. There is no question of my working him. I simply wrap my lips around my teeth and let him face-fuck me, the ridge of his cock riding over skin slippery with sweat and saliva and pre-cum. My jaws ache, stretching wide to take his girth. He smells of heat, and lust, and sex; the pungency of his groin washing over me as he brings himself to climax in my mouth.

I feel it coming. He pauses, trembling, one hand gripping his shaft. Through my chest, the tension in his thighs grows and then, with a grunt, he spurts, hot, briny cream coating my tongue, before he pulls out, covering my face, splashing into my hair and over my neck.

Still shaking, he drops to all four over me, his still seeping cock resting on my neck.

"Jeez...." he mutters.

"I'll second that...." comes my Master's voice.

"If that's what a few weeks' enforced abstinence gives, then perhaps it's worth it."

"Um... Guys." I say. "Any chance....?"

They both burst out laughing. "Sorry, Charlotte," says Michael, untying my wrists. "We're forgetting ourselves aren't we."

My Master tosses me a towel and I wipe myself down. "Um, Michael, Master. Are we able to have a bath or a shower here?"

Michael grins. "I was joking about the tin bath. Yes, we can use the hotel facilities. In fact, sensibly, we need to set ourselves up in one of the rooms there over Christmas, at least for everyday purposes. We can come here when we want to be cosy by the fire, or if we want some privacy."

He leans over to kiss me, wiping away a little of his cum that I missed. "You *do* like it here?"

He needs reassurance. "Stop worrying. I *love* it here." I stroke his face. "We're going to be so happy."

"Yes, we are." smiles my Master. "By the way, did I mention that we have visitors tomorrow?"

"No, who?"

"Richard and Beth wanted to have a look at the place. Um, I think they're as intrigued as much by our living arrangements, as by the house itself, but anyway, they'll be dropping by tomorrow morning to have a look at the place."

"Great!" says Michael. "Our first guests."

*****

The car pulls up, chauffeured by Ross. Richard steps out of the back, walking round to open the door for Beth. He is wearing a suit. She is beautifully dressed, wearing an expensively tailored gown and high heels. Her hair and make-up are immaculate, her nails polished, and she moves like a ballerina. Everyone always tells me that we look alike, but seeing her arrive, wearing my jeans, sneakers and three layers of woollen sweaters against the cold, I feel like an ugly duckling.

Michael groans. "Oh, God. Look at the state of her. You did warn them that we're living on a building site, didn't you?"

My Master clicks his tongue. "I did, yes. but some people don't take a hint." Then he pastes on a smile. "Beth, Richard. Lovely to see you. Do come in."

*****

Michael gives them the guided tour, my Master and I watching from afar. It *is* Michael's project after all. Richard seems deeply interested in everything. Beth oscillates between fascination at the work and the building, being appalled at our living conditions, and dumbstruck at how to cope with her high heels over the broken floors and mud.

She used to be a hotel cleaner herself. Surely, she's not forgotten all of that?

But, however out of place she looks, Beth still looks beautiful. I heave a deep sigh.

My Master glances sideways at me. "Something wrong?"

I don't really know how to express what I'm feeling. "She's such a lady, isn't she? So elegant. I always feel clumsy around her. She's always well dressed. She dances beautifully. She never looks less than perfect. I just wish I was a bit more like her."

He looks amused. "More like her? Charlotte, you are *matchless* just as you are."

*****

We sit together in the kitchen, the five of us, Michael pouring into a teapot from a kettle, using an old rag to hold the handle.

Beth suddenly leans towards me, peering down.

"Charlotte, whatever happened to your hands?"

Embarrassed, I try to cover my hands, wringing them together as though one hand can hide another. "Um, I was in a foundry for a couple of days. Then we were in a metal and ore processing plant, drawing tungsten bar down into wire. They use graphite as a lubricant. It gets everywhere..."

"Everywhere?"

"Yes, *Everywhere*.... I've not managed to clean up properly yet."

"But your nails...?"

"Oh, yes.... I was polishing up a sample in the metallurgy lab. Er... My fingers were numb with the water coolant, and I took off my nails and fingertips on the polishing wheel… I didn't actually notice anything until I saw the blood on the wheel…"

My Master laughs. "I did exactly the same thing myself, as a student…"

"Sounds painful," comments Richards.

"Oh yes. It is," he says. "You don't feel a thing when it happens, but once your fingers warm up afterwards, it hurts like billy-oh, eh Charlotte? It happens, once, to most students who spend any amount of time in a metallurgy lab."

He's right. But still, I sit with my hands hidden.

*****

"Would you like to come shopping one day next week, Charlotte?" asks Beth. "There's me and a group of the girls having a bit of a get-together."

"Yes, you should go, Charlotte." says my Master. Michael nods agreement.

I hesitate. "Come on," says Beth. "Why not join us? Get yourself out, somewhere a bit more civilised for a few hours."

"Um, maybe. Let me think about it."

A few minutes later, Beth excuses herself, Michael directing her through to the hotel to find the bathrooms.

Richard sits, silently drinking tea from a chipped mug.

"Charlotte, why so reluctant to go with Beth? You got along rather well with her, I thought?" asks my Master, after Beth has left the room.

"Yes, I do. but she mentioned her friends being there too. I don't think I'd fit in very well."

Eyes rolling at me, he pulls my hands out from between my knees, turning them over, examining both sides, looking at my stained palms and broken nails. "If it's bothering you, why don't you get yourself a professional manicure? I'm sure Michael would be delighted to have you using his facilities at the Centre. In any case, you hardly lead the same kind of life as Beth. You can't expect to..."

Richard breaks in, looking puzzled. "Charlotte, why are you trying to compare yourself with Elizabeth? Yes, she behaves like a lady. I expect it in my wife, and she knows it, but I also know, that *you know* how she and I met..."

I blush. "Er... yes, she did tell me, that evening we had rather a lot of wine together."

I glance sideways at my Master. He looks intrigued but obviously doesn't want to speak out of turn. Richard follows my gaze, pauses, then turns back to me, with a lop-sided smile.

Pointing a long finger at my Master, "You didn't tell him?"

"Um, no, well, it seemed a bit personal. I didn't think you would like it if I started gossiping about you...."

Richard bursts out laughing. "And all this time, James, I thought you knew." He nods me to my Master. "Feel free to tell him. After all, I know how you two met. But apart from that, keep it to yourself. Yes?"

"Yes, of course."

My Master sounds irritable. "Knew what? Charlotte?"

"Er... How Richard and Beth met. Er.... Beth...."

Richard holds up his hands. "Spare my blushes. Wait until I'm not around before you tell him. Elizabeth and I need to be going anyway. Do meet up with her and her friends in the City next week, Charlotte. Get yourself a change of air."

We see him out to his car, where Ross is sitting, eyes closed in the driver's seat, listening to music. Michael and Beth join us after a minute or two, Beth looking as fresh and beautiful as a newly picked daisy. As they drive away, we wave them off.

My Master swivels to me, eyes crinkling. "Spill the beans, Charlotte." Michael frowns in puzzlement.

"Um.... Beth was working as a maid in the hotel, cleaning the rooms. I think it was the one where you had the apartment. It was hot one day, and she used the shower in the Penthouse, where Richard was staying. He'd gone out, but he came back early and caught her in his shower, um, naked.... then.... er.... he tied her to the shower and um..."

My Master creases up with laughter. "I get it. No wonder he was so relaxed about you and me."

"There's a bit more to it than that."

"Really?"

"Er.... He offered her a contract, and she accepted. She was um... *at his beck and call*, if you know what I mean, and in return, he funded her through college and trained her up."

My Master sobers up. "You're kidding? So, when he knew that I'd *bought* you...."

"Yes, he was comfortable with it once he knew that I went into it willingly. Because he did essentially the same thing with Beth."

Michael is shaking his head, arms folded, a broad grin on his face. "I *definitely* think you should cultivate your friendship with Beth."

*****

"Charlotte, can we talk about something?" My Master's face is serious. Michael is here too, and I can see by his unhappy expression, that he knows what my Master wants to discuss.

"Is something wrong, Master?" My heart sinks. "Have I done something to upset you?"

"Oh, no. No." he says hastily. "No, nothing like that. But.... we wanted you to have a couple of days here, relaxing before we mentioned this to you." He swipes a hand through his hair. "Um, why don't you sit down."

He waves me to where Michael is patting the seat of the chair next to him. As I sit, he takes my hand, holding it tightly.

Beginning to feel really anxious, "What is it? What's wrong?"

"It's about that home you were in as a child, Blessingmoors ...."

My throat tightens, and I stare at the ground.

My Master hesitates, but then, "The Police still have the inquiry open from the original events there. They are trying to collect evidence on some of the original gang-members that ran the operation, but who they never succeeded in convicting at the time."

Michael, holding my hand, is all but squeezing the blood out of my fingers.

Breathe......

"Okay, so....?"

"They would like to interview you; ask you some questions about events there, have you look over old photographs to see if you can identify any of the people involved.... Could you do that?"

Collecting my scattered thoughts, "Why are *you* asking me this? Instead of the Police?"

"Haswell is friendly with the Police Commissioner, who knows that he has a personal interest in you. And of course, he asked me. Everyone thought it would be better coming to you this way, rather than your getting a phone call out of the blue from some stranger. I said.... Michael and I said.... we would ask you, on condition that it waited until after your exams, and once you were back here so you have some moral support."

Breathe......

"It's Richard who is asking me to do this?"

"Yes."

Breathe......

"What happens if I identify someone? Someone they want?"

"If it comes to it, and they have enough evidence, they'll ask you to stand as witness in court."

"What do you think, Charlotte?" asks Michael softly. "Could you do it....?" His beautiful blue eyes are soft with concern. "......Stop the same thing happening to someone else that happened to you?"

Yes, that's the clincher, isn't it....

"Yes, I'll do it," I say.

My Master voice is startled. "You're sure? I thought you might want to think about it for a while?"

"No. Michael's right. It needs to be done. If I can help, I'm in. Now.... Um.... 'S'cuse me." And I dash out, to throw up, outside, into the bushes.

*****

I enter the conference room in the Haswell Building. It has been chosen for my interview to provide me with familiar surroundings, rather than asking me to attend a police station. and yes, I do feel more comfortable, knowing that my friends are only on the other side of the door. My Master, Michael, Beth and Richard, are all gathered in the next room.

A thin-faced man, with nondescript sandy hair, stands to greet me.

"Hello, Jennifer. Do sit down. I'm Officer Corby. I've been asked to conduct your interview today."

I sit. "It's Charlotte. Not Jennifer."

"Ah yes, there was a note about that." He pencils a couple of words into the margin.

I don't care for the look of the man, Corby. He has an officious, I-know-it-all-and-better-than-you look about him.

"Thank you for coming in today, Charlotte, and for agreeing to this interview. I do understand that it must have been difficult for you," says Corby.

"That's fine. I'm happy to help if I can."

"Of course, yes. Now, about Mr James Alexanders...."

What???

"I'm sorry." he continues. "I know this is going to be an uncomfortable discussion for you, but we have the records from the auction house, listing him as your... buyer...."

"What's this got to do with anything?" I demand. "I thought I was here to talk about what happened at Blessingmoors?"

"Yes, that is *one* of the topics we would like to discuss with you. But also, we would like to discuss Mr Alexanders' involvement with the auctioning of young women..."

"I'm not willing to discuss that. It's private business, between the two of us."

"That may appear to be the case to you, Ms Conners, but the investigation into that auction house, and the circumstances surrounding it...."

"Are you trying to pin something on James Alexanders?"

"He is listed as the buyer of a young woman...you... for purposes of..."

"He did nothing I didn't agree to. He didn't hurt me, and he's done nothing wrong."

"Miss Conners. We want to take proceedings against all the buyers...."

I stand, my chair scraping back behind me. "No! I'm not saying another word. This is *not* what I came here for." Turning on my heel, I leave the room, seething with rage.

"Miss Conners...." The man's voice trails out behind me. "Miss Conners...."

*****

The Virgin and the Masters

Part Two

A Continuing Tale of (Ex-)Virgin Erotica, BDSM and Ménage with Two Masters and *More*......

Part Eighteen Of
The 'Buying the Virgin' Series

Author: Simone Leigh

The Virgin and the Masters
Part Two

Elizabeth

The door slams open from the conference room, and Charlotte, red-faced, clearly furious, strides out. "We're going home." she snaps at Michael and James.

They both look baffled. "Charlotte? What's wrong?" asks Michael.

She whirls on my husband. "Mr Haswell, I'm sorry, but you told me that this was about Blessingmoors. *Not* about some kind of witch-hunt on James."

Richard looks perplexed. "What...?"

James' head swivels. "Sorry, Charlotte?"

"They're trying to pin something on *you,* about the auction house and what went on there..."

James says nothing, lips pressed tight, staring at the floor. Corby comes into the room after Charlotte.

"Miss Conners," he starts. "I understand that you're upset but...."

"Upset?" she hisses. "*Upset?* I've been brought here under false pretences." She glares at Richard. "Nothing was said to me about any attempt to attack James. And if you think I'm going to help with that, you can all go to Hell!"

I have never seen Charlotte like this; utterly enraged, red-faced and panting. It seems so unlike her.

But is it?

The lioness defending her pride?

My husband interrupts her. "Charlotte, please accept my apologies. I did not know of this either. And I would certainly not have had any involvement in it if I had known."

Corby breaks in, his tone officious. "Mr Haswell, I am simply doing my job..."

"No, you're not," says Richard, flatly. "This is not what was discussed as subject matter for Charlotte's interview. Excuse me, I have a phone call to make."

"I really want to talk with Charlotte here..."

"Well, you're not going to. Now, *sit down* while I make my call." He jabs a finger at a chair.

He picks up his phone, taps a key. "Francis, could you get hold of Will Stanton for me please; ask him to call me back urgently. Yes, immediately if possible."

At the mention of the Police Commissioner's name, Corby looks suddenly uneasy. Richard puts down his phone, addressing him.

"Charlotte is quite right to be 'upset'. The circumstances of how she and James met are well known to us all, and there are *no* outstanding issues. It is strictly a private matter between the two of them. *You* were invited here to interview her regarding the Blessingmoors investigation, a topic which she finds very difficult to discuss, and it was only with reluctance that she agreed to it. You have gone well past any possible remit you had, in what you have done so far."

His phone rings. "Hello? Ah, yes, Will. Thanks for calling back... Yes, she's here. Yes, so is he. We're having some difficulties I'm afraid...." He holds Charlotte's gaze for a moment, then alternates to James'. "I understood that the object of this interview was to learn anything that Charlotte could offer regarding the Blessingmoors' investigation. Instead, it's opened with an attempt to blacken James Alexanders' name regarding the business with the auction house... Yes, that's right... Yes... I'll pass you over to him."

He passes the phone to Corby, who puts it to his ear, then recoils as a voice blasts down the line at him. Pale-faced, he turns to

Charlotte. "It seems that Commissioner Stanton prefers that I only question you regarding Blessingmoors..."

Charlotte says nothing, simply staring him down.

"Perhaps we could return to the other room and continue our discussion?"

"No," she says. "I'm not discussing anything with you. Or with anyone else, for that matter. I want an assurance that no attempt is being made to damage James before anybody gets another word out of me."

Richard raises his eyebrows, but hands steepled under his chin, says nothing.

Corby protests. "Miss Conners, I assure you...."

"Forget it." she snaps. "And I want it in writing. And until I have that, you'll get no cooperation from me." She nods to Michael and James. "C'mon. We're leaving."

My husband calls her. "Charlotte, wait.... Please."

She looks at him, her face lowered, but there is nothing subservient or submissive about her. Regarding him from under lidded eyes, she softens a little. "Alright, Mr Haswell. Since it's *you*...."

He tilts his head in acknowledgement, then turns to Corby.

"I'd like you to leave, *now*. We'll rearrange the interview for another day, and with another officer."

Tight-lipped, Corby gathers his papers from the conference room and leaves.

Richard pauses, weighing up his words, then turns to Charlotte. "I promise you that I knew nothing about that."

She nods. "I believe you, but you can't give the guarantee I'm looking for, can you?"

He shakes his head, glancing over at James. "No, I can't."

She shrugs. "As I said, they'll not get a word out of me right now. I don't know where the Police thought they were going with that line of questioning, but until I have something in writing regarding James, that's it."

Richard nods thoughtfully. "Fair enough. I'll get back to you when I've had a word with Will."

*****

Charlotte

My Master's phone rings. "Yes? Oh hello, Richard. What can I do for you?" His gaze slips over to mine. "Yes, she's here... I'll pass you over."

Wordlessly, he hands me the phone, then stands, arms folded, eyes downcast, but obviously listening in.

"Hello, Richard."

"Hello, Charlotte. Listen, I've been talking with Will Stanton about what happened the other day. He's not very happy, but there are protocols he must follow. The business with Jasmine Hardacre and her treatment after the auction opened a whole can of worms. Regardless of what the auction house promised regarding protection of the girls involved, clearly it didn't happen, and the paper-pushers have responded by trying to attack anyone who had any involvement at all."

"So...?"

"Will has your document prepared, guaranteeing immunity to James regarding the matter, and he is happy to give it to you, but he wants to talk with you first, face to face, so that he is covering himself. If he can discuss it with you in person, and you reassure him that James did nothing wrong, did not in any way abuse you, I don't think there will be any problem. Are you prepared to do that?"

"Yes, I am."

"Good. In that case, I was going to suggest that, rather than an 'interview', we all simply meet at my home, say for dinner, and make it all much more informal. Will can ask you whatever he needs to, and you will have James and Michael, and for that matter, me and Elizabeth, on hand, if you need moral support. How does that sound?"

"It sounds fine, Sir. I'm quite happy to do that."

"Good. Pass me back to James please."

I return the phone to my Master, who nods a couple of times, then gives me a squeeze around the shoulders. "Tomorrow night, their place. Six pm."

*****

Elizabeth

We all sit over one of Ross' excellent dinners. After the hash made of Charlotte's 'interview' by the paperclip counters in the Police Department, Richard believes that an informal setting will be much more likely to produce a positive response from Charlotte....

And I agree with him.

Charlotte, seated at the table, obviously enjoying Ross' starter of immaculately cooked sea bass with buttered caper sauce, is flanked to either side by Michael and James, on one long side of the table....

.... Ye gods... but that girl's got something. Her living arrangements might be unusual, but when I see James, with his aggressively alpha, protective stance, and Michael, with his angelic blond hair and glorious blue eyes, I can see why she has chosen it...

And, glancing at Michael, that 'Angel' has a dirty halo.... He holds my eyes for the briefest of moments before looking away...

.... some of the possibilities do fairly boggle the mind.

I keep my smile to myself, placing my hand on Richard's.

Will Stanton, Police Commissioner, and Richard's friend of some years, sits at the head of the table, where he can command the scene, but not sitting directly opposite Charlotte, is not too confrontational.

Over perfectly presented roast lamb in mint, he starts the conversation.

"Hello, Charlotte. I'm Will Stanton. I'm an old friend of Richard's here, and firstly, I wanted to apologise for what happened the other day. It was not done by my authority."

She nods a, slightly frosty, acknowledgement.

"For the record, although when the business of the auctions first came to light, Richard here was....um... economic with the truth," He glances askance at Richard, ".... about the identity of someone he knew, being one of the girls involved; since then, we have spoken at length on the subject, and it appears to me, that in your case, all went well and there are no criminal charges to pursue..."

Charlotte says nothing, her face flat, expressionless. Dinner plate forgotten in front of her, she sits bolt upright, arms folded. James is similarly blank-faced.

Will appears to realise that he has some ground to cover before getting much response from her. He continues. "May I ask you some questions regarding the circumstances, and the outcome of your involvement in the auction?"

She nods. "Yes."

"You entered the auction of your own free will?"

"Yes."

"You were in no way coerced?"

"No."

"Why did you choose to enter the auction?"

"Because I needed the money, and it was a better rate of pay than standing on street corners."

Richard looks suddenly away, hiding a smile. James apparently finds the portraits hanging over the fireplace deeply interesting. Only Michael doesn't bother to hide his grin, apparently delighted at Charlotte's *modus operandi*.

After a deep intake of breath, Will continues. "And after the auction, you were contracted to one James Alexanders? Who if I am not mistaken, is sitting next to you right now?"

"That's right."

"And he did not abuse you, or take advantage of the situation?"

Charlotte pauses. "He had *paid* to take advantage of me, but he in no way abused me, and at all times, he was very clear that I could stop anything that was happening by simply saying so."

"What would have happened if you had drawn a halt to proceedings?"

"Um, I suppose the contract would have been void, and the money would have reverted to him."

Will pauses, I think, finding the interview difficult. "Charlotte, for the avoidance of doubt, you were happy with the outcome of the contract you entered into, and you have no complaint to make relating to it?"

"That's correct."

He nods, pencilling a note, then, producing a large brown envelope, slides it across to her. "You will find the immunity document you requested in here."

She opens the envelope, taking out the document, examining it carefully, then, passing it to Richard, says "Mr Haswell. I don't have a lot of experience with legal documents. Does that look okay to you?"

Richard looks startled, but takes the paper, looking it over carefully for a couple of minutes, then passes it back to her. "Yes, Charlotte. That looks fine to me. James is covered against anything relating to the auction house investigation."

She nods, relaxing a bit, unfolding her arms. Will regards her, chin resting on his fist.

"You don't like the Police much, do you Charlotte?"

"Not much, no."

"Why not? I think there's more to it than this misunderstanding over James."

The folded arms are back. "Because on the half dozen or so occasions I ran away from Blessingmoors, every single time, the Police caught me and took me in, and regardless of anything I tried to say to them, delivered me right back there to have the shit beaten out of me."

Will rubs his lower lip thoughtfully. "So, why did you agree to help us at all?"

"Because Mr Haswell asked me to."

Will looks startled. "Mr Haswell? Richard here?"

"Yes."

"What has he to do with it?"

"I owe him."

Richard doesn't look up, instead, paying close attention to his lamb in mint.

Will continues. "And you pay your debts?"

"I do."

"Do you think this pays your debt to Richard?"

"Nope. I reckon I owe him a bit more than this."

Will pulls a document wallet from his briefcase. "So, Charlotte, about Blessingmoors, I have your file here, taken from the records on the premises at the time it was closed down...."

She looks uneasy, shuffling in her chair. Michael's hand snakes out, taking hers.

Will continues. "I have to say that it doesn't look too good. It says here that you were in trouble numerous times for all kinds of petty crimes.... shoplifting."

"I'm not a thief."

"That's not what it says here." Will waves the file he is holding.

"It's still not true. How can I have been a shoplifter when they never let us out?"

"So, you've never stolen anything from a shop?" Will raises an eyebrow, looking sceptical.

"Well, yes, I did, but it was when I was trying to run. I was a kid. I had no money. I had to eat..."

He says nothing, simply nodding as he writes a note in the margin.

"Drugs...."

"I've never touched drugs."

"Not ever?"

"Not ever."

He leans forward. "It is known Charlotte, already, that Blessingmoors was rife with drugs. No-one's going to hold it against you."

"It hardly matters. Yes, they were there. And no, I never used them."

He sighs, then scribbles in the margin.

"Assault on a warden? On several occasions?"

"Um, yes, that bit *is* true." She hangs her head, looking shamefaced.

"What were the circumstances?"

"Sometimes they were trying to... you know. Other times, it.... just kind of burst out of me."

"When you say, 'You know'.... you are implying sexual assault?"

"Um, yes. But I always fought back, and.... I didn't look like much then. It always ended up with one of the other girls.... or boys.... getting it instead. They'd just lock me up for a couple of weeks."

"I also have it here, that you were reported earlier this year for assaulting a customer in 'Francesca's' tea rooms in the City? Although the charges were later dropped...."

"Yes, that did happen, but...."

Richard interrupts. "On that occasion, Will, I know personally of the circumstances. Two drunken louts were trying to...press their attentions on Charlotte and my wife. Charlotte put up a spirited defence on Elizabeth's behalf."

Will says nothing, but pencils in another note.

"Your school records have you listed as disruptive, and a bad influence..."

Now my Master interrupts. "But Charlotte loved school. She's told us about it herself..."

"Er, that was the school when I was with my foster family. Yes, it was great there. The school at Blessingmoors, no, I didn't do very well."

"Why not?" asks Richard.

"Um, bored really. They had no books to speak of, and never tried to teach us anything beyond basic reading and writing. I'd got all that by the time I was six or seven, so after that they were just trying to make me sit in a classroom, staring into space all day."

Again, Will writes a note. "And the last thing I need to ask you about Charlotte, is that according to our records, you now co-habit with two men, Mr James Alexanders and Mr Michael Summerford?"

She flushes. "I don't see what that has to do with anyone else?"

Will sighs. "The point Charlotte is that I am trying to establish if you are a credible witness."

"Sorry?"

"If we take your testimony and it leads to anything, we will have to go through the courts. The people we are dealing have a great deal of money from their.... trade... and can afford the best of legal representation. If you have the kind of character that a lawyer can simply discredit in the eyes of a jury, then we are wasting our time, and I might as well *not* put you through a lot of pain."

There is violence in her eyes at his words, but her voice is level.

"And you think I am a non-credible witness?"

"I'm not sure. If you can eyeball a solicitor and say that you only stole because you were a child, and you were hungry. Or that your personal arrangements are none of his damn business, then you should be okay. Do you think you can do that, or would you be intimidated?"

"If I have to, yes, I could do it.... Mr Stanton?"

"Yes?"

"Is there anything else in that folder?"

He glances at it. "Like what?"

"Anything *earlier*?"

He stares at her for a minute. "Yes, there is. You would like to see it?"

She whispers, her eyes big. "Yes."

He pushes the file to her, sliding it across the table. "Here, take a look through it while I talk to Richard here."

She picks up the file, Michael's eyes following her all the time.

*****

Charlotte

I look through old papers, riffling through, seeing snatches of words, phrases...'Ward of the court'....', ...taken into care....', '...single parent deemed unfit...'

....and stapled to the paper, an old photograph, tiny, curled up at the corners and badly creased.

A woman looks out at me; young, pale-skinned and red-haired. Her eyes are badly shadowed. She looks ill. On the back, a name, "Michelle Conners."

*****

Elizabeth

After a few minutes of talking quietly with Richard, Will turns back to Charlotte.

"Charlotte... Miss Conners?

She holds a small, very dog-eared photo in her hand, her eyes glossy. "Yes, Mr Stanton? And it's okay. It's 'Charlotte'." Her former antagonism has vanished.

Will hesitates, looking at the photo in her hand. "Thank you, Charlotte. And it's 'Will'."

She nods, smiling. He continues. "Charlotte. I can't give you that file, but there's no reason I can't have it scanned and copied for you, including the photo, if you would like?"

She sucks on her lips, her voice small. "Yes. Please."

"Do feel able to talk some more?"

She nods. I notice Richard nodding, discreetly, to Ross, a quiet gesture telling him to fill Charlotte's wine glass. Michael's hand, I notice, is back, holding hers.

James said that he's her Rock....

Will speaks. "Charlotte. You have mentioned that sometimes, the children you knew at Blessingmoors would simply disappear, taken away. Can you tell me any more about that?"

"All I really know is that at about fourteen or fifteen, we just didn't see them anymore. We were told that the older ones were moved on, to another home, for seniors, but we never ever heard back from any of them."

"None of them?"

She shrugs. "Not that I ever saw."

"So, for your purposes, the older teenagers simply vanished?"

She nods, then stares at the ground.

"What about the younger ones? Did they ever disappear?"

"Sometimes, usually if they'd been beaten hard. We'd be told they were taken from the Infirmary to a hospital, but sometimes, they didn't come back."

James interrupts. "You told me Charlotte, that you were in the Infirmary on one occasion?"

"Yes, I'd run away, again. I was always caught sooner or later, and the Police would bring me back...." She stares at Will for a moment, who blushes and looks down. ".... We were always beaten for running away. That time, yes, I ended up in the Infirmary. They told the Social Worker I'd been drinking and taken a fall down the stairs...."

"Did children ever disappear from the Infirmary itself?"

"Well, the kids would go in there sometimes, and we wouldn't see them again, if that's what you mean."

"And you have no idea where they went?"

Charlotte is silent, staring down. Her breathing is quickening, her face pale. At first, I think we have lost her, but then, her words visibly being forced out....

"You know there were cellars there, right?"

"Yes, we know about the cellars. The whole premises were, of course, searched at the time, before it was demolished."

Richard interrupts. "When we took the building down last year, the cellars were filled in and covered over, as part of the rebuilding program, both of them."

Charlotte looks up. "*Both* of them?"

"Yes, both of them."

"Richard, there were *three* cellars in that place...."

*****

Michael

"Charlotte, you don't have to do this."

"I think I do."

I hold her hand as we stand together at the demolished site of the old Blessingmoors institution. Now a wasteland of rubble awaiting redevelopment in the new City Project, the only pointers to the old buildings are the road layout and a few hard to identify pillars and gateposts. Nonetheless, we believe we are standing on what was once the threshold of the Blessingmoors building.

Charlotte is pale, even more so than usual, and her hand, as I hold it, is clammy. James is here, his face a mask, as he stands, hands in pockets, simply watching, but his eyes follow her everywhere as she steps over the rubble.

The others; Haswell, Stanton, and a variety of investigators in white paper coveralls, also stand by, watching.

"I'm sorry," she says. "I just don't recognise any of it. There's nothing *here* to recognise."

"Perhaps with your eyes closed?" I suggest. "Start at some known point and see if you can walk in the dark? Keep hold of my hand. I won't let you stumble."

She doesn't speak, simply nodding as she licks her dry lips. She turns to Haswell. "This was the front entrance?"

"Yes."

Then, closing her eyes, gripping my hand tightly, "I'll try. I was smaller then, of course. And it was a long time ago."

Stepping forward. "There were three steps, up into the hallway." I steady her as she walks.

She continues. "There was a door here." She indicates ahead. "Then a corridor and another door." Eyes still closed, she opens invisible doors, walking through unseen halls.

She waves to one side. "That's a staircase, up to the dorms."
Stanton is beside us now, examining some old document. I glance at
him, not liking to ask. He holds up the sheet; a tattered floor plan. As
Charlotte speaks, he is comparing her words with the plan, nodding
agreement.

We walk a little further. She indicates the other way. That's the
corridor to the kitchens. Two of the cellars came off from there. I
think one was an old coal cellar. The other was just general storage."

Stanton nods. "Yes, we know about those."

She hesitates, her face churning.

"What's wrong?"

"I can *smell* it.... It's got to be just in my head, but I can smell the
place."

"What does it smell of?"

"..... dust, the children, disinfectant, cabbage.... I don't know. It's
just how it smelled. I'd never thought about it before, but it feels
like...." She pauses, swallowing hard.

"You okay?"

"Yes."

"Want to take a break?"

"No. I want to *do* this."

We keep walking. Everyone is with us now, walking quietly
behind us as Charlotte continues her blind walk in the dark.

She waves vaguely ahead of her. The main stairs were here.
Upstairs was the staff area, where they lived. I was never up there. I
think they had bedrooms and a common room, but I never saw it."
Then she veers to one side. "But there was another door here, by the
side of the stairs."

Stanton looks puzzled, looking at his plan. "Are you sure of that,
Charlotte? It shows a blank wall here."

She nods, vigorously. "I'm sure. The door was sort of under the stairs. You would only see it if you knew it was there. But it led to another cellar, the one they used as a punishment room."

"Alright," says Stanton. "You've done enough." Then he turns to me. "Get her out of here." Waving over to the white coveralled technicians. "Geophys, over here."

I pull Charlotte away, nodding James to join us. "C'mon, we're leaving."

Charlotte resists. "You're not staying here," I say. Still, she hesitates. "Charlotte, I'll drag you off if I have to. You're not staying here."

"And I'll help him," says James.

Reluctantly, she comes with us.

"Let's go to the Centre," I say. "You can have a swim, and I'll give you a massage."

Finally, she nods, really looking as though she agrees.

"I'll join you in a while," says James. "I want a word with Haswell and Stanton."

*****

Ten minutes later, I lead Charlotte by the hand into the Centre; it's time the staff met my fiancée. If nothing else, it might persuade Tracy to stop making cows eyes at me. She was never in with a chance, and lately, she's been a bloody nuisance.

"Do you mind if I use the gym first?" asks Charlotte.

"Of course not. Use anything you want. Let's get you some gear."

I point her at the shop front. "Pick out what you want." She chooses trainers, jogging pants and a top. I add in the kind of heavy-duty sports bra that a girl with her figure needs, and a swimming costume. "Female changing rooms are over there." I point. "And the gym's through there. I'll see you there in a few minutes."

By the time I've done a quick round of the staff, and checked if anything needs my attention, Charlotte is already in the gym, jogging on a treadmill, upping the speed as I watch.

"Everything alright?"

She nods, beginning to perspire as she warms up, so I join her on the next machine, jogging along to keep her company. She increases her speed again, breathing more heavily.

After a few minutes, I see James walking by and wave him in.

"Just give me a shout if you need anything," I say. As an afterthought, I put a bottle of water on the shelf in front of her. Charlotte nods thanks, again turning up the speed, and I leave her with it.

James nods towards her. "She okay?"

I rock my hand back and forth. "Running off nervous energy I'd say. I'll give her another ten minutes on there, then I'll get her into the swimming pool and give her a massage afterwards."

As we watch, she turns up the speed yet again. Dripping sweat, she pounds the treadmill. Chest heaving and face red, she's going for broke.

"Is that a good idea?" asks James.

"Within limits. As I say, I'll give her a few minutes to burn off some stress, and then wind her down. Why don't you go for a swim, and we'll join you in a few minutes?"

He nods, heading in the direction of the male changing rooms.

Charlotte is still hammering away, so walking over, I reach across the control panel, setting the machine onto a cool-down program. As the track slows, I grab her wrist, feeling her pulse and counting.

"Two-twenty beats a minute. You're over-doing it. Time for you to ease down a bit."

For a moment she looks furious, but then washes a more polite expression over her face.

"Sorry. You're right."

"Shower off. Let's go for a swim. James is already there."

In the pool, she dives in, cutting the water cleanly. I follow. James, seeing us, breaks off from crawling lengths, to swim over and join us.

Finally, I see her tension dissolve. The last time the three of us shared a pool, we were at the beach house. On more than one occasion, we had sex together in there. James flashes his brows at her, suggestively, and she smiles brightly, looking much more herself.

"There's too many people around for us to use the pool as you might prefer," I say to her. "But, in the massage room, we'll be quiet." Again, she smiles, eyes soft now. "Have a swim and then...."

She launches herself into the water, swimming slowly and easily in a relaxed breast-stroke.

"You're taking her for a massage?" asks James.

"Mmm, yes. You joining us?

He pauses. "No, I think I'll leave you with her. She needs your touch more than mine, right now, I think."

I say nothing to this, no need to be tactless. Instead, I push off from the edge to join Charlotte. She flashes me a smile as she realises I am swimming beside her.

After a dozen or so lengths, catching her eye, I wave her out of the water. Pulling myself up on the side, I lift her out as she reaches a hand to me.

Tracy, I notice, sitting in the lifeguard's chair, is looking daggers at her.

My manner cool, "Something wrong, Tracy?"

"Um, no."

"Then you should be watching the pool, shouldn't you?"

She flushes, turning back to watch a party of schoolchildren getting their weekly lesson.

*****

Back out in Reception, showered and dressed, Charlotte finger-combs her damp hair. I take her by the hand again, leading her to one of the massage rooms, turning the key once we are inside. I want privacy now.

"Take your clothes off," I say to her. "Lie on the bench."

As she stretches out, on the white be-towelled massage table, I pull another towel over her. She doesn't speak, simply watching me, wide-eyed, with an air of waiting.

In a silent mood, Babe? Perhaps, with all you have to think about right now....

"Lie back. Relax." I sit, perched on the edge of the table next to her, my hands flat to her belly "Now, would you like a massage or a *massage*?"

She writhes, stretching and smiling, her green-grey eyes intense. "I think I'll leave that to the masseur."

Relaxing back, she lies framed by her sea of red hair, her skin very pale even against the white towel, spine arched, knees slightly akimbo. She gazes at me, lips slightly parted.

Jeez....

My cock twitches, balls pulling upwards.

I want to fuck your face, Babe.... Get my cock into that beautiful mouth.... Spill over your tongue and watch you lap it up....

Locking with her eyes all the while, I oil my hands, rubbing my palms well to warm up.

I start at her feet, manipulating the toes, gliding through to her ankles before working her calves with the heel of my hand.

Her breathing is slow and deep....

Do I do the whole thing....?

.... let's see what she wants...

Moving upwards to her thighs, I work the muscles deeply as she begins to tremble, a shuddering that rises from her pelvis, transmitting through her flesh to my fingers....

And I can almost *see* her growing wetter....

Should I take the towel away....?

...No, not yet.... make her wait....

I skip to the far reach of her body.

Still sitting with one hip balanced by her on the bench, pressing the pads of my fingers against either side of her temples, I circle the skin behind her ears. Skimming behind to the base of her skull, I lift her slightly at the neck, and she arches into my massage/caress. Sliding up into her hair, I work her scalp, all the time her breathing deepening, and now, quickening....

I'll make you gasp soon, Baby...

Her eyelids begin to flutter. "Don't relax *too* much," I say.

She opens her eyes again, slightly showing her teeth in a semi-smile...

Time to fire up....

"Look at me..."

Her head resting back, her eyes widen to meet with mine again.

I move down to her shoulders, kneading through to her muscles with fingers and thumb, bending to nibble at the delicate skin of her neck. Her breath hitches and she turns, reaching up to kiss the side of my face, her hand sliding into my hair to pull me to her. Open-mouthed, I kiss her, and she moans softly, her fingernails digging into my scalp.

Jeez, but these pants are getting tight....

Fuck the massage....

I drop to her breasts, skimming the skin with the palms of my hands, mouthing at a nipple. I suckle gently, and it puckers and tightens between my lips, hardening when I nibble. She whimpers softly, beginning to pant, both hands tightening around my neck and shoulders.

I slide away the towel, leaving her naked for me, thighs parted in invite, her skin gleaming from the oil. I glide a palm down across her stomach, over the vee of her thighs. She is already warm and damp, curls glistening, labia swelling with her arousal....

If I can arouse you, Babe, you're not feeling too bad....

Pushing my fingers in further, she is slick and warm. Testing her pussy, she quivers under my hand as I briefly finger-fuck her.

I stand back, shucking off my jogging bottoms and tee-shirt. I don't want to do anything complicated; just get inside her, fuck her, remind her that she's loved.

The bench is narrow for two of us, and I'm careful as I settle atop her. Her thighs part wide for me, inviting me in, then wrap around me. Her arms swing around my shoulders, pulling me close.

I slide my arms under her, lifting her a little, pulling her into my embrace. As I ease my cock inside her, she moans gently.

"Shhh...." I murmur. "We can't be too noisy here."

She nods, smiling dreamily.

You just want me inside you, Babe, don't you?

She feels tight and slick and warm as I move slowly within her, not yet thrusting, but working up her arousal. She sighs and trembles, rocking gently with me, matching my tempo as I begin to move more powerfully.

Will you come, Babe? In this state of mind?

I don't think so....

No pressure then....

I don't think she even wants to climax. She simply needs the closeness. All the while I work her body, fuck her with my cock, her eyes are open, gazing into mine.

She reaches to kiss me. "My Golden Lover." she murmurs.

Where did you get that from, Babe? No-one ever called me that before you....

I come suddenly, unexpectedly. The pressure straining at the base of my cock, balls abruptly tight, I spurt into her, once, twice, her tightness around my shaft increasing as she contracts around me, I think deliberately, as she feels me come.

Vaguely conscious that her fingers are twisting into my hair, I pump a final shot, before collapsing onto her.

Realising that I'm crushing her, I pull my weight away. "Sorry. Didn't mean to come so soon. Are you alright, Charlotte?"

Again, she doesn't speak, simply kissing my face.

Yeah.... she's fine now.

"Let's go find James."

*****

Charlotte

I look through endless photos, some in old books, some on databases. I flick pages, click websites; weary of seeing blue eyes, brown eyes, scars, black hair, long beards, goatee beards, clean-shaven, bald, sharp-eyed, dull; hundreds of them. On the laptop, I set the gallery of strangers to 'Slideshow' and let it simply play, one face after another, flicking past every few seconds.

Michael comes in, bearing a tray of mugs. "Coffee?"

"Oh, lovely. Yes, thanks."

He peers over my shoulder. "Nothing?"

"Nope. I'm not even sure now, I would recognise someone I knew. It was so long ago. I was just a kid, and.... and I think I'm going blind looking at this lot."

"Is it just random strangers they're showing you?"

"I don't think so. I think they're suspects in people trafficking cases, but there's so many of them."

Something familiar flashes by my peripheral vision, and my head pivots back to the screen. "Whoa...."

I stab at the keyboard, reversing the slideshow. What did I see?

The previous face is still a stranger. I don't know it. I click back again.

And the familiar stares out at me, from years past; older than I remember, but still the same face. The forehead is higher, hair greyer, but the same cold, deadpan eyes stare blankly out; no emotion there, the gaze of a monster.

There *are* monsters in the world, and most of them look like real people.

"You know him?" asks Michael, his voice flat, careful.

Feeling sick. "I did. A long time ago."

"At Blessingmoors?"

I nod. "He wasn't one of the regular staff. He came by occasionally, and he'd leave taking the older ones with him. We would never see them again."

*****

Stanton says "We know who and where he is, but we've never managed to pin anything on him. If we pulled him in, do you think you could pick him out of a line-up?"

"I think so, yes."

*****

"It's mirrored glass. They can't see you."

I stare through at nine men; similar heights, comparable faces, easy to confuse. But I have no doubts.

"That's him." I point.

"You sure of that? You don't want to think about it?"

"No, I'm sure. That's him."

*****

"You were quite correct, Charlotte, and quite sure of yourself. We would like to show you some more photos now, of people known to be associated with this man. Are you comfortable with that?"

"That's fine."

*****

Several hours, and *pints* of coffee later, I have five more faces for them. Stanton seems.... *delighted* is the wrong word, given the context, but certainly very pleased.

"Charlotte. I can't thank you enough. With your evidence, we have enough to put a case together and take this to court. Our only problem is that we know the locations of two of them, but not of the others, so we can't simply bring them all in."

*****

Michael

Breakfast at home: over toast, juice and coffee, Charlotte's phone beeps.

She barely looks at it, obviously knowing what the tone is.

"S'cuse me," she mutters, vanishing into the bedroom, leaving her phone on the table.

James' eyes meet mine, his expression quizzical. I lean over, looking at her phone screen.

"What is it?" he asks.

"Mmm... Calendar Reminder.... 'Take your pill.'"

He nods, looking thoughtful. We sit in awkward silence for a few seconds.

"You think she wants children?" he asks.

"Not sure. Certainly, she's not mentioned it, so I'm guessing she's not interested right now. In a few years, who knows?"

After another pause.... "And, do you?"

"It's a big house..."

James stares into space, looking pensive.

Time to take the bull by the horns.

"James..."

"Mmm?"

"For the avoidance of doubt.... If Charlotte *should* fall pregnant, I will adopt, in the womb, any child she bears..."

He glances up for a second, no more, then drops his eyelids in acknowledgement, looking happier.

*****

Charlotte

Down in my small office in the Haswell Building, nothing else being asked of me just now, I am busy with a college assignment. There is a knock.

"Door's open..."

A familiar face appears. "Hello, Charlotte. They told me you were down here. I was in the area, so I thought I'd call by."

It is Daniel, originally introduced to me by my Master and Michael for one of our 'parties'. However, he blotted his copy-book the last time we met, by making an unsubtle attempt to tempt me away from my two Lovers. He has not been invited to my company since.

And I am not comfortable with him turning up, unbidden, in my office; just the two of us.

"Hello, Daniel. What can I do for you?"

"I thought you might like to go out for a drink this evening? Or dinner perhaps?"

"No thanks. I'm busy."

"Another evening then?"

"No. Daniel, you *know* that I'm with James and Michael. I don't fool around." I hold up my left hand, displaying my ring finger with its twinned bands of yellow, red and white gold.

He tilts his head, looking at me askance. "*You don't fool around?* The last time I met you, you were *fooling around* with three of us. And the first time, as I recall, there were five of us."

"That's different. It was with James and Michael. If you want to play, you have to ask them."

Very uncomfortable now, I gather my text and notes together. "You'll have to excuse me. I have an appointment in a few minutes." I'm lying, and doubtless, Daniel knows it. I squeeze by him out of the office, making my way up to the canteen, where I can work in a more public place.

*****

"You've missed a bit."

"Have I?" My Master peers sideways in the mirror, and I stroke his face where a little stubble has escaped his razor.

"Ah, yes. Thank you."

"You seem nervous?"

He rocks his head one way and the other. "I'm always a bit edgy when there's a meeting with the Thorntons. Thornton Junior is a bit of a firebrand, and I'm still the new boy, seniority-wise."

Finishing his shave, he buttons on a shirt and puts on his tie. He's all fingers and thumbs. After watching him, three times, trying to get the tie straight, I turn him at the shoulders, undo the tie and re-knot it for him."

"Who *are* the Thorntons, Master?"

"They're Haswell's major shareholders in the City Project. Thornton Senior runs the show from their end. Thornton Junior thinks he does."

"Richard has the larger shareholding though?"

"Yes. Jaye Thornton, the son, wasn't happy about it apparently, but his ego was appeased by quite a lot of the Project being named after his father."

I laugh. "The famously fragile male ego?"

"Mmm. Perhaps." His smile is wry. "Interesting you should put it like that. Apparently, the idea to do it that way came from Beth."

"Are you a shareholder?"

"I am now. It was part of the directorship deal. Haswell likes to have all his associates on board one way or another."

"To keep all the interests aligned?"

"Yup."

"And you *wanted* it that way?"

"Of course I did. Even as a minor shareholder, it's worth a great deal of money.... After all, I have a wife *de facto* to support." He gives me a half wink.

"I think you would have wanted it anyway, Master, with or without a wife; *de facto* or otherwise."

He flashes eyebrows at me, grinning, but then turns serious. "You'll be fine, Charlotte. You have me, as well as Michael. And that's before you've even started earning properly in your own right. You're never going to be short of money again. You can *choose* your life, rather than having it thrust upon you."

*****

Up in Reception, my Master vanishes into his office to fetch the files he needs for the meeting. I am about to leave for my own office when Richard flags me down from the Conference Room.

"Charlotte, don't disappear. Fetch your notebook. I want you as Meeting Secretary for this one."

I follow him in, along with the rest of the attendees, trying to identify the Thorntons. I assume that they are the two men, one elderly, one much younger, who sit to one side of Richard.

Another man, whom I don't recognise, starts to seat himself several chairs away, then sees me. He looks again, very unsubtly checking me out. I look away, but he moves from his original seat to the one next to mine. He does not, however, sit in it.

Instead, he perches on the edge of the desk next to me. He's good-looking, in an oily sort of way, but his smile is pasted on, fake.

"Well. Hi there. You're new, aren't you?"

"Fairly new, yes." I make a show of arranging my notebook, ready to take the minutes. and trying to display my be-ringed left hand.

He slides closer to me on the desktop, and I lean backwards, "And what's your name again?" he asks, his voice oily. "I didn't catch it."

"That's because I hadn't given it. And it's Conners."

Still smarmy; "No, I meant your first name?"

"Ms." I snap.

He holds out his hand, still with his fake smile. "I'm Ewan."

Reluctantly, I take it, shaking briefly. His hand is damp.

"Nice ring," he says.

"Isn't it?"

Thank God! Surely, he'll take the hint now?

"Would you be interested in lunch later?"

He notices my ring, and still, he asks?

"Yes, I'd be very interested, but not with you, thank you."

Finally, flushing, he backs off, seating himself a couple of chairs away, further along the conference table, his expression angry.

Have I overstepped the mark? Richard must have heard the exchange from the top of the table. I see him looking at me over his glasses.

"Are you ready, Miss Conners?" he asks.

'Miss Conners'? It's always been Charlotte before.

"Yes, I am, Sir."

"Fine. I think almost everyone is here.... Ah James, there you are...."

*****

When the meeting is finished, my Master accompanies the Thorntons out. "I'll see you at lunch then, Richard."

I am about to leave myself when, "Charlotte, a moment please."

Oh, Hell. Am I in trouble again....?

"Yes, Mr Haswell?"

Again, he looks at me over his spectacles, this time sucking in his cheeks against a smile. "I just wanted to say, Charlotte, that I appreciate that sort of thing puts you in an awkward position. I did consider blasting him myself. His behaviour was very inappropriate. However, I think you will do better by, for the most part, fighting your own battles."

I let out my breath.

Hadn't realised I was holding it....

"You look relieved?"

I dance from one foot to the other. "Thought I was in trouble again for a minute."

He rubs his nose. "Not from me Charlotte. You handled it rather well I thought, left him stinging. But, *trouble*? You're going to have that kind of trouble to deal with all the time."

"Er, didn't mean from you actually. From... er...." My eyes trail out of the office.

Richard follows my gaze. "From James? Sorry, but he's going to have to learn to deal with it too...."

*****

I curse, muttering to myself as my laptop hums and flickers. Obliged to twiddle my thumbs for a while, I startle as I look up.

My Master leans against the door frame, smiling down at me. He looks elegant in his suit, which fits his long frame well.

"Aren't you several floors away from your zone? The Directors' Empire is on the Fifth Floor if memory serves."

Sucking in his cheeks, "Oh, just thought I'd wander down and sexually harass some of the minions... one of them anyway. Problems?" He nods down at my laptop.

"It's just decided to run an update, right when I was in the middle of something. Everything ground to a halt...." Exasperated. "Did you have this problem as a student?"

He snorts in laughter. "Computing has moved on a bit since I was a student. Home computers weren't even envisaged then. They taught us on the university mainframe; Fortran, using punched cards..."

I gape. "Punched cards? You're joshing me..."

Shaking his head, laughing, "No, I'm perfectly serious. We had one piece of work, a test-piece, writing the program for solving an equation by iteration. It meant breaking down the steps and individually punching the cards. It took me *hours*. Then my 'friend' decided to nudge my elbow and I dropped the lot. They scattered everywhere.... I had to do the whole thing again."

"Couldn't you just sort them back into order?"

He rolls his eyes to the heavens. "Imagine trying to sort out a pack of playing cards, but there's no pictures, just holes in the cards giving you a code for what the picture is..."

I burst out laughing. "It puts my problems into perspective, doesn't it?"

"Indeed, it does," he says, smiling, then his face turns serious. "Listen, Charlotte. I came down here because there's something I need to talk to you about..."

He sounds worried.

"Master?"

"I've been talking with Will Stanton. He's concerned that with you giving evidence against the traffickers, but some of them still being at large, you may be.... at risk...."

"I know that. But I took it on board when I agreed to help..."

"Yes, but...." He is clearly uncomfortable about what he has to say. "....... they would like you to stay close by for the moment, so you can have protection."

His meaning begins to penetrate. "Close by? You mean, here? They don't want me to go back to the University?"

"That's right."

"But I can't *not* go back. I'd miss lectures. I'd get behind on my work.... After everything I did to get there...."

"We'll sort out some other arrangements," he says. "I don't want you away from here until this whole thing is sorted out, one way or another."

"But Master, I *got* to go back."

"*No*, Charlotte. You don't. I don't want you to go. And you're not going, for now at least. And that's the end of it. I expect you to obey me in this...."

I look away, swallowing hard.

"Was that a yes?"

He holds my chin, making me look him in the eye.

"Is that a yes?" he repeats. "You will not try to return to the University until we have made arrangements for you to be safe?"

I don't speak. I try changing the subject.

I eye him.

He hesitates. "What's that look for?"

"I thought I was going to be sexually harassed? I'm not feeling very harassed so far...."

"Is that right? I might just push this door closed and spread you on the desk...."

I can't suppress my grin, nor he. I see the slant to his eye. He knows that I'm trying to distract him, but he goes for it.

We stare at each other, neither looking away. Clicking the door locked behind him, he stands over me, then grabbing me by the wrists, pulls me upright and into his embrace.

Kicking the chair away from behind me, he pushes me up against the wall, pulling my arms above my head. I slam backwards, he, grabbing a fistful of my hair. My hands flat against the plaster, I accidentally bang the light switch, which blinks on, then off once more as my fingers knock it off again...

Leaning in close to me, he presses my wrists tight against the wall. "Don't move," he mutters. "You want harassment? Let's see what we can do..."

Carefully, so as not to disturb the order of anything, he lifts my books and notes from the desk, placing them on a bookshelf, then places my laptop next to them.

The desk cleared, he seizes me again by the wrists, swinging me around, pushing me rearwards down onto the desk. All but atop me, still stretching my arms over my head, he presses me down at the chest with the heel of his hand. "Are you going to stay like that, or do I have to tie you?"

My breath juddering. "I'll stay, Master."

There's a gleam in his eye as he pushes my skirt upwards around my waist, displaying my panties, already staining dark with my arousal.

He stands up straight, taking off his jacket. "Now," he says, looking down, dark-eyed at me, "Do I lick you out first, or just fuck you where you lie....?"

".... Too good an opportunity to miss...." he continues. Then, kneeling at the end of the desk, between my legs, he swings my feet over onto his shoulders, pressing his face into my panties. I hear him breathing in, scenting me, his face nuzzling against me. His fingers slide behind the fabric, scissoring open my lips, presenting my clit to his teeth as he nibbles at me through the fabric.

I squeal and buck. Immediately he stands, removing his tie. Binding my wrists together with the tie, he stretches my arms back down the desk, attaching the other end of the tie to the desk legs. Then, quickly pulling my panties down, he stuffs them into my mouth. "Exciting as it might be, this is not the place to start making noises and get caught *in flagrante*..."

Then he resumes his position, kneeling between my legs.

Now, with free access to me, he pulls open my lips and pussy, double-handedly, stretching me wide, the thumb of one hand pushing back the sheath of my clit. For a moment or so, he pauses, breathing warm over my exposed sex, then, very delicately, he traces the outline of my clit with the tip of his tongue.

Trying hard to remain still, to remain quiet; nonetheless, I moan through my stuffed mouth, my hips shivering and jerking.

He continues his work, lapping at my twitching bud, sending sweet pleasure stabbing through me. Continuously working me, he slips a finger into my pussy, which clutches at him in response, then a second finger, and a third.

Now with his mouth wrapped around my clit, he sucks at me, circling all the time with his tongue, and the fingers rub up inside me at my sweet spot. My spiral up to climax is rapid, and the juddering of my hips quickly turns to the pangs of orgasm, blooming out in a slow vibrating wave from my fluttering pussy. It flows in waves, over my thighs, my belly, to wash over my calves and ankles, breasts and neck.

As I arch and cry out, muffled through my gag. He plants his mouth over my pussy, fucking me with his tongue, swiping around the inner muscles as I spasm and gush into his mouth.

As I relax, he rises, unbelts, unzips and releases his erection. Leaning over and into me, he plunges in deep. Lying atop me, thrusting hard, he pulls the pants from my mouth, kissing me hard, open-mouthed, then claps his hand over my lips.

I want to move with him, to take him into me more deeply, but my position is awkward, feet dangling over the end of the desk, and I can gain no traction. Instead, I must simply lie here, passive as he fucks me.

His eyes meet with mine, and he smiles a bright, white grin before, teeth clenched, he groans, and head dropping to my chest, he presses hard against me, juddering as he spills inside me.

He lies still, when outside, in the corridor, is the sound of a vacuum cleaner. Quickly, he stands, rezipping and re-belting, then unties me, and while I adjust my clothes, he replaces my papers and laptop on the desktop.

Just as we both sit, either side of the desk, my Master's eyes crinkling in amusement, there is the sound of a key in the lock, and the cleaner opens the door. "Oh, sorry Charlotte," she says. "I'd not realised you were still in here. I'll come back later shall I?"

"No, it's alright. I was just finishing for the night."

I close my laptop, ready to leave, but I still have my problem. *Not to go back to University?*

*****

Waiting for my Master to finish talking with Richard, again I wait out in Reception, reading a textbook.

I should set up a tent here....

My Master sees me through the internal window, tapping a 'Five minutes' signal on his watch to me.

And now, Daniel is here again, standing over me. "Hello again, Charlotte. Our paths seem fated to cross."

Truly uncomfortable with him now, I shuffle up the couch, trying to distance myself from this intrusive man. "Hello, Daniel," I say, head-pointing into my Master's office. "I'm waiting for James. If you're looking for him, he's in with Richard."

He ignores my words, instead glancing over at my book, mouthing words to himself....'Computational Fluid Dynamics...' Those are long words, wouldn't you say?"

Needled; "No, I don't think so. *Patronisation;* that's a long word, I would say."

He fails to take the hint, continuing blithely on. "I wondered if you'd thought again about coming out with me?"

"No, I told you. I'm not interested."

He seats himself close to me, too close, and I lean away from him. "Hey, c'mon. You enjoyed my company. I know you did. We could get together some time, couldn't we?" He touches my arm, stroking it slightly.

"You'll have to ask James."

"I don't need to ask *him* surely? You can decide for yourself."

"I *have* decided for myself and I said, 'No.' I mean it. Now leave me alone."

"You were happy enough to have me bang you before. Don't you think you're giving me mixed signals? Playing hard-to-get?"

"No. I don't give mixed signals. And I don't play hard to get either. I play, or you don't get me."

Daniel, with his back to the window, has not seen that Richard, glancing up, has noticed what is happening, and is muttering something to my Master, who twists around to look. As he sees Daniel, he scowls and stands.

Stepping out into Reception, he does not look happy. "Hello, Daniel. Something I can do for you?"

"Just chatting to Charlotte here."

"Yes, I can see that." Lips pressed hard together, his eyes skim over me......

Jeez...I'm going to get it off him later...

"Leave her alone, Daniel. Was there anything else? No? Then, Goodnight." His expression is severe, the message clear.

Daniel shrugs and leaves, trying to catch my eyes as he goes. I look away.

"Has he been bothering you?" demands my Master.

"Not much, no."

"Not much? This has happened before?"

"Er... yes, a few days ago."

"Were you planning on telling me about it?"

"If I told you about it, every time some guy comes on strong, we'd never talk about anything else."

His eyes narrow.

Oh, shit.

"Is that right?" He turns on his heel and returns to the office.

*****

Later, driving home. "Master. Are you angry with me? About earlier today, with Daniel?"

"No. It wasn't your fault. I could see that you were not encouraging him...."

Relief

".... however, I have dispensed with Daniel's services."

"You've sacked him?"

"Yes."

"You didn't have to do that. He wasn't bothering me. I'm quite capable of saying 'No'."

"He was bothering *me*. You shouldn't have to keep saying 'No'."

I stare down. "You *are* angry with me."

He glances sideways at me, then relaxing, he smiles, taking my hand and giving it a squeeze.

"No, Charlotte. Really, I'm not. You will have to forgive me. I'm in unfamiliar territory when I suffer jealousy over you. You're right. With your looks, you are bound to draw male attention. I can hardly hold it against you, especially when I can see you refusing it."

I stare out of the window.

Let's hope it stays that way......

*****

Back home, despite my Master's words, I am expecting a reaction.

I am not disappointed.

He stands over me, an arm to either side of me as he leans against the wall, caging me with his body. If I were not sure that he loves me, I would be intimidated.

"My first choice, to remind you how to behave, and who you behave with, is to strip you naked where you stand, slam you up against the wall and fuck you 'til you scream...."

My pussy floods...

He bends to nibble at my neck, whispering ".... And my second choice is to say something like that to you to get you aroused, then carry you to the bed and make love to you."

Wow.......

His smile is gentle as his lips brush mine, so softly, fingers caressing my hair. As I lean into the kiss, his arms sweep around me at head and waist, pulling me in close. The kiss is long and leisurely, slow and coaxing, his stubble scraping slightly against my skin

My Master does not often make love to me. Usually, we fuck, and hard, but now, the mood is upon him, and his touch is tender and passionate. He is such a beautiful man, but seldom does he show me this side of himself. In this mood, I see his soul.

His fingers in my hair, he trails kisses down my neck. He smells sweet and musky, a clean masculine scent that always sets my blood pumping. Fingering the tie of my bathrobe, he unravels it, pulling the robe apart. Stooping to kiss the top of my breasts as the garment falls open, he takes one nipple between fingers, and the other between his lips, sucking gently.

I am trembling now, my fingers stroking through his hair as he loves me with his mouth, my nipples crinkling to tight peaks. Then standing upright in front of me, he slides the robe away from me entirely, leaving me naked before him.

He cups my large, slightly pendulous breasts, lifting them a little, almost as though feeling their weight in his hands, before, reaching up into my hair again, he removes the pins and clips that hold it under control. He finger-combs my long locks to fall free, still a little damp from my shower, loosely about me, tumbling over my shoulders and breasts, to drop by my waist.

His dark eyes are all but black, pupils wide. Still without electricity in our home, our lighting is from candles. His lean face is cast to chiselled shadows by their flicker.

He doesn't move, waiting, I think, inviting me.

And now, I open the buttons of his shirt, slowly, one by one, to reveal his broad chest, with its fine scattering of dark hair, and his taut, flat belly. I unbutton his cuffs and push the shirt away over his shoulders, and down.

Tracing the outline of his muscles with a finger, I follow the fine line of hair down his abs to where it vanishes below his belt. He bulges to the front, but as I move to his belt, he takes my hands, moving them away. "Not yet." he murmurs.

Then he slides arms under my torso and hips, and, eyes soft, crinkling at the corners, he lifts me, carrying me to the bed, lying me carefully down. Sitting beside me, he brushes my hair away, fanned over the pillow. His hands sweep over my body; my belly and breasts, my thighs, down my calves, as though trying to consume me, the whole of me. Fire jabs, exquisitely, through me, my core liquefying, and I sigh, arching, reaching for my Master with outstretched arms. Silhouetted against the candles, the dancing light makes a dark halo of his hair.

He takes one of my hands in his, our fingers lacing, and he kisses my fingers, but then releases the hand to bend, nuzzling the inside of my thighs.

His hand over the vee of my red hair, glistening with my juices, his fingers stroking me deeply, slowly. Sighing, I spread myself for him, my fingers tunnelling into his hair, as he opens me wide with swirling fingers.

He dips deeper, sheathing his tongue inside me and I gasp, shuddering. And now he is working me open, his tongue lashing inside me, driving me wild.

"Master. Please. I want you inside me."

He pulls himself upright, looking pleased. "As my Virgin requests."

Standing, he unbelts, doing battle with his own erection to release it as he unzips. I giggle.

"Don't laugh, Woman," he growls. "A man has to have some dignity."

"How do you have dignity, when you have body parts with a will of their own?"

He chuckles. "I'll show you...." and naked, he lies beside me, resting his face against my chest, I think, listening to my heartbeat.

I stroke him, his cock swelling further, filling my hand. The blunt head of his erection pressing my palm, I rub finger and thumb over the ridge, enjoying the twitch and jump of his response.

"Enough!" he says. "You'll finish me off." And pulling himself above me, resting his weight on his elbows, he teases at my pussy. "Ready?" he whispers.

"Mmm, yes."

"Thought so. You're very wet." He nuzzles against me, not entering. His movements are small, but my body responds, my heart pounding as he presses his flesh against mine, tantalising my swollen core.

My breath catching, I try to swing my hips, to take him inside me, but he withdraws. "No." he murmurs. "Remember who is Master here."

I relax, lying quiescent. "That's better. You can have a little more now." And he test-probes my entrance, pushing his cock-head slightly inside, stretching me open, but not penetrating deeply. He holds the position, his cock gripped by my palpitating pussy.

He sighs, dropping his head to my chest, his own breath juddering and I feel the shiver of his lean thighs as he fights for his own control.

"I *want* to fuck you brainless, but I'm not going to. We'll take it nice and slowly this time."

"Master, please."

"No. Do as you're told."

I obey, to lie quivering, as my Master penetrates me so slowly, only a little at a time, before withdrawing again. My pussy vibrates, trying to clench around him, but he holds himself free of me until I settle again. Then again, he teases inside me, making a couple of short quick thrusts, again winding me tighter, something coiling up tight inside me.

"Please...."

"Please, what?"

"Please, Master. Please get inside me..."

"Like this?" He plunges deep inside me, hilting himself, then again withdrawing.

Hips bucking, I convulse and moan.

"Like that?"

"Yes, Master."

"Want it again?"

"Yes, Master."

"Ask nicely then."

"Please, Master..."

"Please what?"

He's playing me, but I can feel him trembling. He's having difficulty restraining himself....

"Please, Master. I want you inside me."

He thrusts again, a single time and withdraws. Again, my hips jerk, and I thrash under him.

Two can play that game....

He's not expecting it. His weight is still on his arms, but I reach around to embrace him, pulling him down onto me. Now, he wraps his arms around me, and I make my move, heaving suddenly, to roll, taking him with me. I have just enough time to register the surprise on his face before he breaks into laughter as I scrabble for position. Now, he is on the bottom, and I straddle him.

"Yes, Master. I *do* want you inside me." And I writhe my hips over him, positioning his cock at my entrance before sliding down on him.

Will he let me do this?

My Master sighs, lying back as he looks up at me, laughter in his eyes. "Nicely done, Madam."

Winding my hips in slow circles, taking his shaft with me, I feel him hardening further inside me, enlarging. Slipping up and down on the cock deliciously within me, I take it just as slowly as he did, revelling in the feel of the head slipping in and out of my tight, but flooding pussy.

He gives himself to me, allowing me to take control. His eyes close, but his breath quickens as I increase the tempo a little.

"Good?" I ask.

For a moment he is silent, then, "It's like the Glory that was Greece and the Power that was Rome."

And, straddling my Master, speared by him inside, I collapse into helpless giggles as he gazes up at me, his smile broad and bright.

Seizing me by the waist, he starts to thrust upwards, taking me with him....

*****

Michael

Clicking the door quietly open, I hear laughter, Charlotte's. There is a rippling quality to it that can only mean...

The bedroom door is open. Glancing inside, unseen, nonetheless, I see them, she riding him.

Always you can see that she loves him, but seldom does he drop the mask, letting others see that he loves her. Right now, both their faces are alight, in rapt adoration of the other.

She looks fantastic. Straddling his hips, arms curved above her head as she displays herself to him, her thighs are spread wide, taking him inside. Her waist and hip and spine blend into a tight curve, her breasts lifted high by her upraised position, the nipples hard and puckered. And her hair is a vivid splash of red against her pale skin, a smooth cascade over shoulders, breasts and waist. Her eyes are lit with joy and lust and love.

Her skin glistens, slick with perspiration, and her lips are parted in a way that always makes me want to push my cock between them. Her grey-green eyes flash in an expression of sheer feral lust that makes my balls tighten, as I watch her rock and rotate over James' cock.

My own cock twitching into life, quietly, I retrieve a bottle of wine from the snow bucket outside, then, pouring three glasses, carry the tray into the bedroom.

They both look my way, faces welcoming.

"Ah, Michael," says James. "Good timing there on your part."

Charlotte simply flashes the smile of Eve at me, offering me apples....

I sit on the edge of the bed, sipping my wine. The glass is frosty, dripping with a chill dew.

Reaching forward, to her nearby nipple, I trace my glass over the puckered nub, and she gasps, flinging her head back. Simultaneously, James groans.

"Jeez..., go easy.... You're making her clench."

I laugh. "How to disable a man." And I trace the glass over her other nipple.

Again, she groans, and once more, James reacts, grunting, before pitching his head forward. He shudders, his hands grasping her hips, pulling her to him, jerking spasmodically as he pumps into her.

"If that's how you disable a man, how do you *enable* him?" I ask.

After a few moments, he relaxes back, his expression wry. "I had rather intended to keep that going a little longer," he complains.

"I don't think you've suffered much."

Charlotte still says nothing, but her eyes are alight with invite.

"Room for another there?" I ask.

In reply, she stoops to kiss James on the lips, then lifts herself away from him, kneeling on the bed, looking across at me.

Time for action....

I put my glass aside, but pass another to her, and to James. He sits up, pulling himself to the far side of the bed, setting himself to watch.

Charlotte simply kneels at the edge of the bed, taking a sip, then cradles her wine as she watches me undress.

As I look at her, naked, flushed and sweating with arousal, scented of heat and sex and James, her thighs shiny with her own juices and James' cum, my cock, already at half-mast, swells and hardens. And still, she simply watches me, with that wide-eyed/feral/little girl expression that makes me want to plant myself inside her, face or cunt, and fuck her 'til she screams.

I'm gonna make you scream now....

.... and I don't think you've come yet....

Pulling sweater and tee-shirt away over my head, kicking off shoes and jeans, my erection growing by the moment, I stand over her, offering myself to her.

She watches my cock, then, raising her eyes to mine, she parts her lips....

I push myself at her. Wrapping her mouth around the head, she licks me clean of pre-cum. As I knot my fingers in her hair, she works her mouth up my shaft. Dropping to all fours on the bed, she slides a hand inwardly, massaging my balls and the root of my shaft.

James reaches from behind her, between her legs, I think playing with her clit. Certainly, she responds, shaking and shivering, yelping occasionally. Not feeling entirely comfortable with her teeth around me just now, I pull away.

"Turn around," I say. "Head down, ass up."

Compliantly, she turns, dropping to rest her face on hands flattened to the sheets, and presenting me with her slick and swollen pussy, and her beautiful, pale rear end. James would leave that covered in his handprints, red on the white of her skin, but I can't bring myself to spank her....

Do I fuck you up the cunt or up the ass?

Let's have both....

Inserting a finger into her dripping pussy, I coat it in her juices, intending to open her up at the back, but she squirms and moans, her ass wriggling at me.

You really are feeling sensitive, aren't you....

I shove in a couple more fingers, aiming for her sweet spot. She cries out, semi-rising back onto all fours, but I push her down with the palm of my hand between her shoulder blades.

She wants it badly.

"You want to come, Charlotte?"

She nods, gasping as I work her g-spot.

"How do you want to come? With your clit? Or with me inside you?"

Her face pressed against the sheets "...inside me...." Her voice is broken, hoarse.

"Okay, but you're going to have me inside you both ways...."

With my juice and cum soaked hand, I insert a single finger into her back passage, opening her up, circling against the ring of muscle. With my other hand, I reach around to her clit, slipping between her lips to flick and massage at the small, hard nub.

At the back, I work in a second finger, stretching her further open. I want her ready to take me after she's come.

It won't be long. Her hips are beginning to judder, so, still working her clit, keeping her moaning all the time, I withdraw my fingers from her ass, instead plunging my cock, in a single movement, full length into her sodden pussy. She wails a response. And now I start to thrust.

Ahhh... she feels so tight, and her cunt clutches at me each time I withdraw...

Does she do that on purpose? Or can't she help it?

It doesn't matter. It feels great....

Grinding my hips against her, I circle inside her, working her from the inside. Her passage starts to judder around me, her climax rising...

With a scream she goes into orgasm, trying to writhe and buck, but pinned inside by me, she can't go anywhere. Still fingering her clit, I extend the moment for her as long as I can, before she yells, "Stop, Michael, please stop."

Immediately, I withdraw from her, but now it's my turn. My cock slick with her juices, I ease into her ass, watching her face from behind as I do so. James is watching too; her expression. I love taking her up the back, so does he; but always we are careful when we do so.

But she seems comfortable, her breathing short and rapid, eyes a little glazed, but okay.

"Charlotte, am I hurting you?"

She shakes her head, still with that same dreamy expression, and now, after a couple of short, slow test thrusts, I sheath myself inside her.

Her orgasm hasn't fully died away. She still pulses inside, and her hips are a-quiver....

Another one, Baby?

With easy slow thrusts, I fuck her ass, but reaching around again to her clitoris, I start to work her again. She's moaning softly. James, seeing what's happening, reaches in, tweaking at her nipples, rolling and pulling. And with each movement, she trembles and shivers.

And now, she comes again, this time rising back onto her hands, face upraised as she howls her climax.

And that's enough for me. Irresistibly, I cum, and balls tight, I shoot into her, slamming in my load as I bend close over her, holding her tightly at the hip and waist.

She may want me to be her 'Golden Lover', and for her, I will be, but still, I want to fuck my Charlotte.

*****

Charlotte

It is very good of Beth to invite me out, and Richard encourages her to be my friend, but I find shopping with her a bit surreal. It's great fun, but the shops she uses have sky-high prices and, although my Master always encourages me to buy something, still I don't like taking money from him or Michael. It doesn't feel right.

I buy myself a pair of pretty but cheap ear-rings, paying from my own account, and keeping my Master's credit card firmly in my purse.

And now it is time for afternoon tea....

*****

I sit, surrounded by twittering airheads; a dozen women, all newly introduced to me, and already, I have forgotten most of their names.

The topics of conversation involve how much their husbands are earning, hairstyles, fashion, who might be pregnant next, how much shopping allowance their husbands give them....

*Don't any of them actually **do** anything?*

None of them seems to have any life outside a procession of parties, entertainment and shopping. All live in the reflected glow of their husband's business or occupation, satellites to someone else's reality.

What do they do all day?

It occurs to me that Michael must make quite a bit of money out of these women. As I listen, it is clear that his Centre is a popular destination. They talk of gyms and make-overs, pamper days and manicures, who is the best masseur....

"The handsome, blond guy.... you know the one.... with the beautiful eyes...."

Mmmm....

I am bored rigid, trying to remain polite, and to at least *appear* to be paying attention to the prattling around me. Some of the woman are lovely to look at, or at least, perfectly made up and turned out, which often amounts to the same thing, and around us, I see male heads turned, looking in at the group, scanning the perfect faces.

Sitting, sipping tea from fine porcelain, exchanging meaningless chit-chat with these primped and preened ladies, nonetheless, I can't help but notice that Beth stands out among them. Noticeably, some of the surreptitious male admirers from around us are looking at her in particular. Although she is, like the others, perfectly turned out and spotlessly groomed, there is, in her eyes, a spark. She, like me, came from humble beginnings, and I know that she also had, in her own way, a fight to get to where she is.

And does she like it now, where she is?

Our eyes meet, and she sucks in a smile, rolling her eyes at the Barbie-like, conveyor-belt-produced beauty sitting next to her, whose current conversation centres around the best choice of polish to avoid chipped nails.

I begin to think that I may wear my roughened hands with pride.

The tea party disperses, one after another of the Stepford Wives making her excuses and leaving. Eventually, only Beth and I remain.

"Want something a bit stronger than tea?" she asks.

I sniff. "A glass of wine *would* be nice, wouldn't it."

We order a bottle of chilled rosé, with some nibbles to stop the alcohol sitting too heavily.

Beth looks at me. "Sorry about that," she says. "I forget that you're new to this. Dearly as I love Richard, having to keep company with the wives of his business associates can be a bit wearing."

"Mmm...." I try to be non-committal, to avoid being rude about Beth's friends.

"It's okay," she says. "I know exactly what you're thinking. It was just the same for me, as it became clear that Richard and I were more than just...." She looks at me closely now. "You'd better get used to it though."

I'm startled. "What? Why?"

"You're with James, and he's Richard's co-director now, his partner. You're going to have to rub shoulders with them too."

I'd not thought of that....

She laughs. "Don't panic. It's not all the time. Just put on your best bib and tucker when they have dinners and what-have-you, paste on your 'polite' face, and live your own life the rest of the time."

An hour later, the bottle is all but empty, and it occurs to me that I really do have a kindred spirit in Beth. She very much understands where I have come from, and she understands too, a lot of what is inside my head. With Beth, I can unload my worries.

"I have James telling me that he doesn't want me to go back to university next term; that it's too dangerous until they track down the gang members they are looking for...." I am almost in despair. "After everything I went through to get there, and now to be told I can't go back...."

"Have you agreed to not go back?"

"Um, no, not exactly...."

She gives my hand a squeeze. "Don't worry. It'll be fine. It's only going to be temporary. Perhaps some of your academic work could be moved around with your on-the-job training? That way it just changes the timing of individual parts of your work, doesn't it? Not the whole thing. If you like, I'll talk with Richard. I'm sure he'd help if he knew about it." She grins, wickedly. "And you *do* have compensations. After all, you've got *two* of them to play with, haven't you."

I laugh. She leans in, conspiratorially. "Don't they ever get jealous of each other?"

"No, not ever. It's never been a problem at all. The only time jealousy ever came into play was...." and I stall. How do I tell Beth that the single real outburst of jealousy came from my Master, over my meeting her own husband for the first time? Although, now that I think about it, his reaction to Daniel has also rung a warning bell. I change tack.

"After the auction, I met Michael on only the second day. It's been the two of them ever since."

Eyes wide, she stares at me. "So, when...." Her mobile rings. "Blast!" she mutters. Answering it. "Hi, Ross. Yes, sorry I'm late. I was just chatting with Charlotte. Yes, I'm coming now."

She looks at me apologetically, waving over the waiter for the check. "Sorry. Gotta go. Here, this is my treat." She pays the bill and leaves, smiling and waving back at me as she vanishes into the crowd, disappointed male faces following her.

*****

In Reception, having returned from my shopping trip with Beth, through the internal window I can see my Master talking with Richard. They're obviously busy so I pour myself a coffee and sit to read a textbook while I wait for him.

"Dendritic structures in the cooling of cast metals...." I settle to read, making occasional notes in the margins.

Concentrating on my book, I startle as a shadow looms over me. "Sorry," comes my Master's voice. "Didn't mean to make you jump." His head twists as he looks to see what I am reading. "You find the metallurgical side of things interesting?"

"Mmm, yes I do. It's very visual, easy to think about...."

We are interrupted as Richard exits the office. "Hello, Charlotte. Not waiting too long I hope?"

"No, just a few minutes." In fact, I have no idea how long I've been waiting. Long enough to work through a couple of chapters of my book.

He turns to my Master. "Anyway, we can finish it off tomorrow and...." His phones *pings*. "S'cuse me.... Oh, hello Ross. No, she's not here. I thought she was with you. No? Hold on a minute.... Charlotte, did Elizabeth say where she was going when you parted company?"

"She said that Ross was taking her home, and she was going to meet him."

A cloud passes over Richard's face. "When was that?"

"Er, maybe, three o'clock."

He checks his watch. "That's over two hours ago." There is urgency in his voice. He spins. "Francis...."

"Already on it, Richard." Francis is tapping keys, peering at her laptop screen. "Her phone is showing up as being in Berkeley Street."

Richard? She always calls him 'Mr Haswell'.

"Is that where you and she were shopping?" he asks me.

"Just around the corner, yes."

"Francis, give the exact location to Ross." and back to his phone. "Ross, did you catch all that? Yes, go and find her." Brow furrowed, he is pale.

"Richard, what's wrong?" asks my Master.

"Elizabeth was kidnapped once. Ever since then, I've always kept an eye on more or less where she is.... Part of Ross' job description is to be, essentially, her bodyguard. Charlotte, did anything odd happen while you were out with her?"

"Um, not odd exactly. There were men looking at her, but they were looking at all the women. I thought they were just.... well, looking at women."

"Did you say anything to Elizabeth about it?"

"Er, no." I gulp, hanging my head. "I should have, shouldn't I?"

Richard looks at me over his glasses. "You weren't to know, but for future reference Charlotte, be suspicious. It comes naturally to you anyway, and it's a skill you should hone, not damp down."

"Why was Beth abducted before?" asks my Master. "For ransom?"

"On that occasion, no. It was someone with a grudge against me, but ransom is always a possibility of course."

"How did you get her back?"

"Tracked her phone...."

Richard paces up and down. In less than five minutes, his mobile rings again. "Yes? No.... Oh, God! Yes, have a look around for anything else, then come back here to the office Ross, if you would."

He switches off his phone, looking sick. "Elizabeth's phone was in a refuse bin on Berkeley Street, along with her bag."

For a moment he almost sags, looking reduced. Then, swiping hands through his hair, he stands up straight again. "Francis, call Will Stanton would you. Report Elizabeth as missing."

My Master is shaking his head, unbelieving. "Richard, is there anything we can do?"

"Charlotte, these men you saw, 'looking at women'. Do you think you could identify them?"

"Um, I wasn't really looking at them, but I can try."

"You weren't looking?"

Feeling very awkward now, "When some guy you're not interested in, tries to eye you up, you look the other way...."

The office phone rings, Francis answering. "Richard, it's Will for you."

He takes the phone. "Hello, Will. Yes, yes that's right. Within the last two hours. Yes, she was with friends, Charlotte actually, out shopping. Charlotte's come back, but Elizabeth didn't get to her rendezvous with Ross...... Yes, that's right. Charlotte's here. She thinks she saw men looking while they were out, and that she might recognise the faces. Yes.... I'm sure she would look through the photos if you can bring them here...." He glances over at me, and I nod vigorously. "Yes, thanks. I'll be here at the office."

He passes the phone back to Francis and sits back on the desk edge, head back, breathing deeply with his eyes closed. My Master and I stand helplessly by. Then Richard stands again, pulling himself straight. "Sorry about that," he says. "I'm no good to her if I panic."

"What would you like me to do?" I ask.

"Will's sending an officer over with photos of known suspects for ransom, abduction and similar. If you could take the time to look through them...."

"Yes, of course."

"Shall I send out for something to eat?" asks Francis.

"Yes please, Francis. It could be a long night."

"I'll let Michael know what's happening." says my Master. "Don't want him panicking too."

Within fifteen minutes, I am sitting in the conference room, once more, scanning faces. This is becoming a habit.

An hour later I am still there, my Master sitting across from me, occasionally sipping coffee and ....

I freeze over a face. The police officer says, "Recognise him?"

The face is older, more lined, the hair receding and greyer, but...

"Yes, but not from today."

"Then where?"

"This man was at Blessingmoors. He was one of the staff there when I was a kid."

The officer checks the reference and taps it into his laptop. "He's an identified trafficker. And he's also known to be in this area now. We've been keeping an eye on him, but could never pin a conviction on him...." He taps more keys.

".... he has a number of known associates..." He keeps tapping.

Both Richard and my Master are bending behind over me, watching over my shoulder. The officer swings his laptop to me. "Could you look through those, please. See if any of them look familiar."

I click through half a dozen faces, then...." That's one of them. One of the men I saw today."

My Master straightens up. "Fuck!"

Richard drops a hand on my shoulder. "Charlotte, I'm sorry. It looks as though they took Elizabeth by mistake. They were after you. They abducted the wrong woman."

*****

The Virgin and the Masters

Part Three

A Continuing Tale of (Ex-)Virgin Erotica, BDSM and Ménage with Two Masters and *More......*

Part Nineteen Of
The 'Buying the Virgin' Series

Author: Simone Leigh

The Virgin and the Masters
Part Three

Charlotte

Richard turns to Michael. "Get her out of here, out of the City. Take her back to your mountain place. No-one's going to fall across that by accident. She should be safe there."

"Hang on." I protest. "I don't want to hide away. I should be helping here. And Beth's my friend too."

My Master swings a long finger in my direction. "*Go* with Michael. We have things to do here, and I'll work better when I'm not worrying about what's happening to you. If you're with Michael, I know you're safe."

"I'm not some kid to be packed off to bed. And I looked after myself quite nicely long before I ever met you."

"Charlotte. I'm not arguing. You're *going*. Michael...."

Michael takes me by the wrist, pulling me towards him. "Are you going to come without arguing? Or do I have to sling you over my shoulder and carry you out? Believe me, in this case, I will."

There is no way I can physically resist Michael. What choice do I have?

Reluctantly, I gather my dignity and leave with him. But I don't have to like it. As we drive up the steep mountain road, narrow and bending, I stare out of the passenger window, unspeaking.

"Are you going to keep that up all day?" he asks. "There's no point sulking at me just because you don't like the realities."

"And how would you feel in my situation?"

"It hardly matters. I'm *not* in your situation. He rubs my thigh with his non-driving hand. "Come on. I know you're not happy about it, but James really will cope better without you there. So will

Richard. So, why don't you make the best of a bad job and at least *try* to cheer up?"

He's right of course. And I shouldn't take it out on him....

I paint on a smile and turn it on Michael, full power, total dazzle.

He grins. "That's my girl.... Hey, how do you feel about picking out a Christmas tree from the woods at the back? We can at least get the place looking good."

"Great idea."

*****

Several hours later, our kitchen/lounge/living space smells pleasantly of pine and resin. The chosen tree did not put up much resistance in the face of Michael's axe, and now it has succumbed to my efforts to trim it up for Christmas.

We have no real decorations, and Michael refuses point blank to even consider going to buy any, so I have trawled through old cupboards, draws and hidey-holes in the hotel to see if I could find anything that would pass for Christmas decor. The result is odd, but colourful, as Michael, suddenly revealing a talent for origami, has shown me how to make stars and birds by folding paper. Using brightly coloured pages from old magazines has produced stars and birds the like of which nature never saw, but on our tree, they look great.

"No candles," he says. After all the work I've put in here, I don't want to accidentally set light to the place now."

*****

Michael

Sitting by the kitchen range that evening, its heat warding off the bitter cold of the December night, I watch Charlotte, happily making more paper birds, like some little girl at school.

"Why are you looking at me like that?"

"Like what?"

"As though you're trying to work something out..."

"Perhaps because I *am* trying to work something out."

She says nothing, simply gives me a questioning look, but her 'pretty and innocent' mask fades to her 'feral' face; that expression that says, this is who she is, and to hell with anyone who doesn't like it.

And James thinks she's a sub....

"I'm trying to join the dots.... make sense of you."

Now she looks surprised. "Me?"

"Yes, you."

"I don't follow." Suddenly, she looks worried. "You're not annoyed with me about something, are you?"

In my driest voice, "No more than usual."

She grins. "What then?"

"It's hard to put into words. I saw you, earlier, back in the offices, facing off me, James and Richard, over something you feel strongly about...." I point a finger at her.... "And by the way, I'm not fooled by your apparent surrender...."

"You threatened to carry me out over your shoulder...."

I ignore the comment. "I think about some of the things you've seen and experienced; the very worst of human nature. And you've come through it, for the most part unscathed. But I know it's marked you. You have nightmares sometimes, and I see your reactions when you are asked questions about your past. And I know you scare, but you don't let being scared stop you. You've got a core of solid rock...."

She is utterly silent, watching me, wide-eyed....

".... But then, I compare you to the Charlotte I saw just now, making paper birds. And the Charlotte I first met, that day when James had bought you only the previous day. And you had that look, the same one you've got now. James had taken your virginity the day before. You *behaved* like a young girl who had just surrendered her virginity.... I wasn't there, so I don't know exactly how it went with the two of you, but he was satisfied that you were the genuine article, that he was your first man; that you behaved like a girl who'd not been naked with a man before, especially an older man..."

"Don't you believe me?" she whispers. "After all this time, you think I was lying?"

"No, I don't think that. Because I met you the very next day, and you were.... so sweet...." I shake my head. "I'm having trouble matching up Charlotte-the-Almost-a-Virgin that I first met with the Charlotte-Been-Through-Hell that I only learned of much later. I can't connect the two. You must have seen assault and rape of all kinds when you were trapped in Blessingmoors, and yet, so far as I can see, when James.... took you.... you behaved like an innocent."

She shrugs, then stares at the ground. "Assault, beating... yes, I saw plenty of that. I was on the receiving end of some of it. Rape? No, actually, I didn't. As the kids began to grow up, they took them away ...." She pauses, apparently thinking. "I'd never thought about it until you just put it that way.... but, yes, sometimes the staff would feel up some of the children, especially as the girls got older, but it was never actual rape.......Perhaps there was an instruction on the staff? Not to touch them? Virgins bring a higher price don't they...?"

My stomach churns. How does she live with it? Her past?

She continues. "...and as for 'sweet'..." She beams a smile like a ray of sunshine.... "I'm glad you thought I was sweet. With everything that's happened, it brought the three of us together." Her eyes are shining as she looks at me.

Oh, God…. When you look at me like that….
"How do you feel about an early night?"
She throws her 'vamp eyes' at me. "I'd *love* an early night…"

*****

Even with the fire burning, the bedroom is not actually cosy, but the heat of the stove percolates through the walls from the kitchen, so it's not bad. And there's plenty of blankets on the bed.

"Get under the covers, quickly. Don't get cold." I say. She peels off her clothes with fast, economic moves and slips between the sheets, then, lying back on the pillow, framed by her long, red hair and one arm curved gracefully back over her head, watches me undress. Just seeing her do that gets me going, my cock twitching to life as our eyes meet. As I unzip and step out of my jeans, she grins broadly when she sees I am already erect for her.

I just want to push that in your mouth, Babe….
And you know it, don't you…?
As I step towards the bed, she opens her mouth, inviting me.
And how do I say no to that?
She teases me, offering her mouth, but not taking me in. Instead, she swipes her tongue over my cock-head, lapping away pre-cum, licking her lips and making a show of enjoying it. My breath shudders and my balls tighten, so I stare at the ceiling for a moment, reining myself in. When I look down again, she's still looking up at me, all big eyes and that little-girl-lost look she uses when she wants something, or when she's trying to pull the wool over my eyes.

But, when she's got her mouth around my cock, it's hard to resist….

She slides a hand under my balls, massaging and working them, pressing on the root of my shaft. And her mouth works up from the base, lapping and licking, working the ridge of the head, before she takes me inside, sucking gently, working the shaft with her hands.

I could just blow off right into her mouth right now, cover her tongue and watch her swallow, spray her face and tits with the last of it....

But I want to watch you come first, Babe....

I start to pull away. I want to work her, but she resists, mischief in her eyes as she grips my balls, holding me to the spot. I prise her fingers off me, and she giggles. "Straddle me," I say.

I lie down, and she swings a leg over me. "No, not like that. Over my face, and turn around."

She gets it, swinging around, crouching over me on all fours, presenting me with her thighs and pussy whilst, once more, wrapping her lips around my shaft

Her pussy, warm and wet, and so close to me, smells deliciously of her arousal. I love the scent of her anyway, and here, poised just above my lips, I have her pink, wet slit to enjoy, swelling and opening almost as I watch.

I *'Aaahhhh'* hot breath across her pussy and lips, and she twitches, the movement transmitting through her legs, where her thighs straddle my head.

It's not easy to move under her, so instead, I grab her ass in both hands, rocking her back and forth a little, just enough that my tongue can sweep both her pussy and clit in a stroke, and she wriggles and squirms, beginning to whimper.

And I *love* the noises she's making.

Parting her pussy lips with fingers, I spread her wide, opening and stretching her entrance. Planting my mouth over her, I swipe inside her with my tongue, her juices running down hot, as she shudders and trembles over me. Her salty, lemony-tasting, cunt pulses in my mouth, and as I release a hand to work her clit, the heat of her washes over my face and the still-growing pungency of her arousal fills my nostrils.

She is no longer sucking me. Instead, her head lies over my groin, her breath fluttering hot over my thighs and balls as her whole body shivers and vibrates. Her torso and breasts pressed against me, her heartbeat resonates through me.

She's very liquid now, and her whimpering turns to moaning. I lick circles through her cunt, and she spasms and jerks, her muscles trying to clench around me....

Oh God, Baby. I'm looking forward to getting my cock in here....

She's close to coming. The tension is building in her; just a little more....

Dipping fingers into her streaming cunt, coating them with her honey, I reach up and around her, easing one into her ass, circling inside the muscle as I do so.

She wails, and her entire body tenses, her breathing rapid and short, her heart hammering through me. She pauses for a long second and then her cunt goes into spasm above me. I plunge in my tongue, as deeply as I can, while she screams and howls, and her flesh pulsates around me. Pussy juices gush into my mouth, and her thighs, hard with tension, stretch and strain around me as she rides her orgasm.

As the moment passes, I push her upwards, rolling her from me, turning to prise her knees apart, get between her thighs, and fill her with my erection. As I plunge in, she is still trembling in the aftermath of orgasm, and she wails as I penetrate, spearing her.

Swinging her hips up, she wraps her legs around me, allowing me deeper entry. She takes me all the way in and I hilt myself, full length inside her. She's slick and ready, and fucking her is just pure pleasure as she howls my name. Clutching at my shoulders with one hand, she locks the other into my hair, rocking her body to match my thrusting, meeting me, our bodies colliding.

As my climax comes close, I seize her by the hips, pulling her hard to me. In the final moment, I press my face into her shoulder, spurting my load into her in a violent orgasm that wracks my body, leaving me shaking and panting.

I flop down onto her, my heart pounding. Kissing the side of my face, she strokes my hair, wiping away the sweat dripping from my forehead.

Gathering myself together again, pulling my weight up onto my elbows and looking down, she lies there in a tumble of wild hair, her face also running with perspiration, flushed with heat, her mascara beginning to run.

She looks amazing. She looks up at me, smiling and tracing the line of my face with a finger.

.... *I know what she's going to say....*

"My Golden Lover...." she murmurs.

"Any time you want me..." I reply.

*****

Charlotte

The dead of night:

Under heaps of bedcovers, our bedroom lit by the single candle we keep burning through the night, and the remains of the embers, glowing in the hearth, I lie, loosely entwined with Michael. I can't sleep at all, fretful with worry, and I simply rest there, watching his beautiful face.

In the dim, golden light, his features are a pattern of light and shade, finely formed; the defined line of his mouth set against a pale stubble where he's not had a chance to shave. My pussy is a little sore from that, but I'll not say such a thing to him. And his beautiful blond hair contrasts with oddly dark lashes, which, eyes open, frame their fantastic blue, but now, on his sleeping face, give him an oddly childlike look.

Never would I watch him like this waking. But now, free to gaze, I take simple pleasure in the beauty of my Golden Lover.

Outside there is a small noise, a splintering sound, as of breaking glass. Michael's eyes snap open, locking with mine.

He raises a finger to his mouth, pressing it against his lips, as he reaches under the bed, and pulls out his long-handled wood axe. He stands, naked, his breath a steam cloud, as he positions himself behind the door.

Holding the axe in one hand, he points to me, and thumbs me out of the bed, then points to the bolster and waves a finger pointing down the length of the bed. Moving as quickly and quietly as I can, I rise, push the bolster lengthwise under the blankets to resemble a human body and riffle the sheets over the top, so that it's not too obvious there is no head on the pillow. Then, as quickly as I can, I slip on the warmest clothes I have to hand, plus my steel-capped work boots, and gather Michael's clothes together, ready to pass to him.

There is a creak outside the door.

Michael stands, poised, the axe held with both hands supporting it, ready to swing at whatever comes through the door. I've seen Michael wield that axe, splitting wood. And our Christmas tree of earlier today barely resisted his blows. He knows how to use it.

I stand well behind him, keeping out of range of the blade.

The door opens slowly, grating on ancient hinges. From our vantage point, out of sight of the intruder, all we see is the silhouette of a handgun.

As the gun, and the hand holding it, come into clear view, Michael brings the axe down, at the last-minute twisting it so that, not the edge, but the butt of the head contacts the hand.

I'm not sure this is an improvement for the owner of the hand. There is a scream. The gun fires and the bolster and blankets jump under the impact of the bullet. The hand itself is not severed, but surely every bone is smashed. The gun drops to the ground and I snatch it up. For good measure, Michael brings the flat of the axe head against the gun owner's screaming head, and he falls silent.

"Come on," he says urgently. "We've got to get out of here."

"You can't go out like that; stark naked into two feet of snow."

"You're right." He grabs his boots, shoving his feet in, stuffing the laces inside for speed. "Bring those clothes."

He'll fuckin' freeze....

"Where do we go?"

"There's a walkers' shelter, only a few hundred yards down the trail. It's not far, but they won't find it in the dark without knowing it's there. Let's aim for there, and then we can take a breather."

How many are there of them?

Michael has only the boots he is wearing and his axe. I carry his clothes and grab my phone, stuffing it into a pocket, thanking all the powers that I'd thought to charge it up before I came home, At the last moment, I remember a couple of chocolate bars that are in a bedside drawer, stuffing them into my other pocket. And as we leave, I pull a blanket from the top of the bed.

We make our way, silently into the night. But as we leave through the back door, there are voices approaching us.

"Into the woodshed." hisses Michael.

Backed into the shadows, we stand silently, but the voices pass by. As we leave, for good measure I pick up a stout stick. It's not much of a weapon against a gun, but I feel better having it.

He had the axe under the bed....

"You were ready for them. You thought they might come here?"

"If I'd really been paying attention, I would have slept with some clothes on."

The night is bitter. Late December; Christmas only just around the corner and there is snow on the ground. There is only a cheese rind of a moon, but with the snow, reflecting shades of blue and purple into a velvet, spangled sky, we can see quite well.

"Which way?"

"Under the trees, into the shadows."

As quickly as we can, we slip through the darkness, from one blue shadow to the next.

How many are there?

Shivering violently, Michael says, "Don't hang around. If they find our footprints, we're in trouble."

"Here." I wrap the blanket around his naked torso, and he clutches it one-handedly at his neck, his other hand still holding the axe.

Behind us I hear can men talking; two voices I think, but I can't make out their words, *then*, there, right behind me, the sound of footsteps crunching in snow....

Michael hears it too, and whirling, he drops the blanket.... "Duck!" he says.... I drop to the ground, hearing the *whoosh* of the axe swinging above me, a soft and silken sound that cuts through the air and ends in a shriek, as the axe connects, flat-headed, with something above me.

There is a muffled scream as a body drops behind me, and I jump on it, pressing my hand over the crushed and splintered remains of a face, which tries to scream at me all the while I struggle to keep it gagged.

The neck below the face has a tie, so I unknot it and stuff it into the mouth, then pick up the gun which dropped into the snow beside the body.

Leaving the squirming body behind us, Michael and I run into the night.

In the walkers' shelter, Michael can finally pull on his clothes. He is badly chilled, and takes a minute or so to stamp the heat back into his legs, beating his arms about himself. I produce the chocolate, and we eat a bar apiece. We're going to need the calories.

It is very dark in here, and I can only just make out the white of his eyes as he says, "Well done, keeping a cool head like that. Most women would have gone into a panic when a bloody corpse dropped behind them."

"He wasn't a corpse, was he? I could see you took him with the flat of the axe. And he had a *gun*. They both did...."

"Still, you kept your head well, gagging him like that. If he's lucky, he might freeze first, instead of bleeding to death."

"Don't worry. I won't panic. I'll save the hysterical breakdown for later, when we're safe."

"Good girl." He kisses me on the head. "We'll head up the trail and take some of the side tracks. Under the trees, we should be able to avoid leaving too many footprints, and I'm not sure they'll follow us into the dark."

"Where are we heading?"

"There's another highway, six or seven miles along. If we can make it there, we'll be able to thumb a lift back to the City."

I wave my phone at him, flicking on the screen. Concealed in the shelter, the light cannot betray us now.

In the dim light, and with my night vision well-adjusted, I can see Michael's face clearly now. "Your phone!" His smile lights up. "I didn't realise."

"Well, I didn't dare try to use it out there. They could have seen it. I'll raise the alarm. We can have a welcoming party waiting for us when we get to the highway."

I tap in my Master's number.

"Charlotte? It's late to be calling. Is everything alright?"

Michael snatches the phone from me. "James. We were attacked. Not sure how many there are, but they're armed with guns. We've taken out two of them, but there's more, so we're taking the trail to Highway 427. It's several miles and we're travelling through the dark and the snow. Can you meet us there....?"

He listens, then grins. "Great. See you in a few hours.... "He glances over at me. "Yes, she's fine... No, neither of us is hurt. Yes, we're both fine, *really*. Yes, of course I will."

"He's bringing the cavalry...." He wraps his arms around me. "You okay?"

"Yup."

He stands back, staring into my face. "That's it? 'Yup'?"

"What else did you want? Some flapping female who slows you down, and goes all useless on you?"

He visibly swallows his words. "No, and I've never taken you for the useless type. C'mon. We'd better get moving."

"What should I do with the guns?"

"Do you know how to use one?"

"No."

"Safer without them then. Toss them on top of the shelter outside. They won't find them up there."

*****

We tramp through the darkness, Michael with the axe slung over his shoulder. At first, we pause every few hundred yards, listening for pursuit, but hear nothing. After the first mile or so, we simply walk at the best pace we can.

I start off, feeling well enough, but after a while, the adrenaline high that supported me during our escape, wears off, and in the intense cold, I feel dull and lethargic, my flesh chilling.

"You sure we're going the right way?" I ask.

"Pretty sure. That phone of yours got GPS?"

How stupid can I be?

"Of course it has."

I flick on the mapping app, then dim to night-mode as the screen dazzles me, knocking out my night vision. Michael peers over my shoulder, as the screen centres and displays our position. "Yup. Two or three miles that way." he points. "Come on. We're making good progress. If we walk quickly, we'll stay warm."

Walking quickly is easier said than done. The tracks are rough and uneven, knotted with tree roots that lie be-shadowed and waiting to trip the unwary. The last thing either of us needs is a sprained ankle.

We hear it before we see it, echoing through the pines; the wail of sirens. Then beyond the forest, through the trees, the flashing blue lights of many, many cars, an ambulance, and seemingly crowds of people; police, medics.... and finally, I see it, my Master's car. He is there, standing, leaning against it, his breath blowing blue clouds into the night air, scanning the tree-line.

Michael's eyes, glinting with amusement, meet mine as we survey the hubbub. "Well, he did say he was bringing help." Then he yells, waving as we emerge from the trees. "James! Here.... James...."

My Master *looks*, trying to follow the sound, his gaze swinging before he sights us, then, his face lighting up, he runs towards us. Flinging his arms around me, he pulls me to him, holding me tightly, too tightly, until I have to pull away. "Master, I'm okay, really. Please, I need air..."

He breaks free, but holds me by the shoulders, looking into my face. "You're alright? Really alright?"

"Yes, I'm fine. It was awful, but Michael...."

"Tell me later. Come and get warmed up."

He turns, slapping Michael's shoulder, who slaps him back. The two don't say anything, but men don't, do they?

Paramedics fuss around us with blankets and questions, apparently disappointed when we both insist that we are not hurt. Hot soup is thrust into my hand, steaming, savoury and fragrant in the night air. It is perfect, richly flavoured and herby, and just the right temperature for drinking. Warmth worms its way back down my frozen toes.

Michael and I return to the city in my Master's car, but we are flanked, front and rear, by a travelling wall of blue flashing cars.

"Where are we going?" asks Michael.

"Haswell Building." replies my Master. "We're taking the Penthouse guest apartment."

"That seems an odd place to go. You sent me away from there before." I comment, through a semi-stifled yawn. "Why there?"

My Master's face swings around to me. "It's defensible."

*****

There is a moment of bare consciousness as my shoulder is shaken. "Charlotte, wake up. We're here."

"Mmmm?"

"We're here." It is my Master. "Get out of the car. You can sleep as soon as we're in."

I stagger out of the car, walking in a semi-doze to the elevator....

.

.

..... and light streams in, through the windows over the bed. Blinking into brilliant sunshine, I sit up, trying to remember where I am.

Michael is lying beside me, still sound asleep, but I don't recognise the room. Still a bit confused, my only certainty is that my bladder is crying out for a bathroom.

My clothes are laid tidily on a chair next to the bed, along with a clean, white towelling robe, which I slip on. Barefoot, I pad out of the room.

I step out into a large and very beautiful apartment. We are high, very high, with a view over the City that ranges all the way to the mountains. Two figures, with their backs to me, are bending over a tabletop, discussing some large map or plan laid out on the table.

A bit awkwardly, "Ummm...."

The figures straighten up, turning to face me. It is my Master and Richard. My Master strides forward, hugs me and kisses the top of my head. "Good afternoon, Charlotte." Then he points. "Bathroom?" I nod.

When I return to the room, my Master is pouring coffee. "You said 'Afternoon'. What time is it?"

"About two pm," says Richard. "We let you both sleep. How are you?"

"Um, fine. I just haven't woken up properly yet."

"You want to go back to bed? Sleep some more?" asks my Master.

"No. Coffee's fine. Michael's still asleep though.... He saved my life you know. He saved both of us."

"We know," says Richard. "When you rang James here, the Police went straight to your mountain home, although they couldn't search the area properly until daylight. They found the two men Michael dealt with...."

"Are they alive?"

He sniffs. "Yes, but they're going to be hospitalised for a long time. The one they found in the snow is never going to be handsome again. His face is pretty much smashed up. What did Michael do to him?"

"They had guns. Michael caught the first one, who came into the bedroom, on his gun hand with the butt of the axe-head. I think it must have smashed all the bones. The other one, who came after us out in the snow, he caught in the face with the flat of the axe."

"Handy that he had the axe on him?"

"He had it under the bed. I didn't know about it until we heard noises. Then he used it to take out the one who came into the bedroom.... There was no time for anything. We had to escape out into the snow. All he had on was boots."

"*Only* boots? It was well below zero last night..."

"We didn't have any choice. There were at least two others. We just had to go. He had the axe, and I carried his clothes and a blanket. He couldn't get dressed until we reached the walkers' shelter.... Did the Police find the others? The ones he didn't get?"

"No. They'd left by the time the Police arrived."

"Will Michael have any trouble over....?"

"No. It was clearly self-defence, and defence of you. He'll have no trouble at all."

"Hello."

We turn. Michael is standing in the bedroom door, in a bathrobe similar to mine. "I heard voices." He yawns. "Is that coffee?"

My Master strides over, slaps him on the shoulder. "Charlotte was just telling us how you saved the day last night."

"She wasn't exactly helpless herself...."

*****

Cradling mugs, Michael and I start taking coffee on board. "Sorry," he says, "but where are we exactly? I'm a bit vague about what happened after we got into the car."

"You're in the top floor penthouse of my offices. Usually, it's used as VIP accommodation for visitors," says Richard. "But it's yours until the Police have the criminals who want Charlotte, safely locked up.

Michael casts around the room. "Pretty nice. I suppose there are worse places to be incarcerated."

"Why should you be incarcerated?" I ask. "It's not you they're after."

He looks me in the eye. "It's not me I was talking about," he says, his voice level.

"But.... it could take months to find them. I can't stay here all that time."

"I think you may have to," says Richard. He raises a hand as he sees me start to protest. "Look at it this way.... How did they know where to find you last night?"

"It's my home."

"It's been your home for a couple of weeks. Who else knew?"

"Um.... You and Beth.... Oh!"

The reality sinks in. They have Beth, and Beth knows all about me. She surely wouldn't betray me by choice, but she's not likely to be given choices by these men.

Richard shrugs, looking sick at heart. "I'm sorry Charlotte, but if it's something that Beth knew about you, then I think we can assume that they know it too."

I want to protest, but even I know that I mustn't inflict any more heartache on Richard. They have his wife. and it's because of me....

I'll try to make the best of it....

I wander over to the windows. "It's certainly a spectacular view...."

"Charlotte," says Richard urgently. "come away from the windows."

?

"They can easily afford to pay sharp-shooters. You mustn't stand by the windows where they might see you."

"I can't even look at the view?"

Richard stays silent for a moment then, "I'm going to leave you to it for a while. I don't doubt that the three of you want to talk. James, I'll be in my office when you're ready."

Richard heads out, leaving the three of us alone together. As he leaves, my Master almost sags. Taking the coffee mug from my hand, he pulls me upright and wraps his arms around me, his chin resting on my head.

"When you called me last night," he says softly, "and Michael told me there were gunmen after you... I didn't know how to react, how to deal with it...."

"You dealt with it the right way." chuckles Michael. "It looked like the circus had come to town as we came out of the woods."

"It was Michael who saved us," I say.

"Your own performance wasn't too shabby. When I saw you gagging that smashed up face with his own tie... There's not too many women would have done that...."

And of a sudden, it wells up in me. All the panic, and horror, and fear that I should have felt the night before, break free and I start sobbing, tears streaming down my face as my Master rocks me back and forth. I think he is comforting himself as much as me.

After a minute or so of this, Michael breaks in. "I like a woman who keeps her promises."

It is such an unexpected thing for him to say. My tears dry up. "Um, sorry. What?"

"You did promise me a hysterical outburst once we were safe."

Despite myself, I laugh. "So I did. Sorry about that. Just give me a minute, would you both."

In the bathroom, I splash my face, which helps. Then scrabbling through drawers, I find a toothbrush and paste. As I spit minty foam into the sink, there is a knock on the door.

"Mmm... Mmmmph." I reply through my mouthful of froth.

The door pushes open; Michael. "You okay?"

"Mmm...mmmphhh." I nod, spitting and rinsing again.

"Now there's a good idea." he smiles. "Is there another one in there?"

I rinse my brush and pass it to him. "Nope, but I think we're a bit beyond the niceties of oral hygiene wouldn't you say? Another coffee?"

"Please, yes."

By the time I return to the lounge with a tray of coffee mugs, Michael is back, stretched out, lounging on the couch He pats the cushion next to him, but as I move to sit there, he hauls me in by the waist to lie cradled back against him. From behind me, he strokes my hair, and reaches to kiss my neck; his warm breath, minty by my face.

My Master, his dark eyes soft, kneels in front of me, fingers caressing my face. "Thank you."

"For what?"

"Coming back to me. I was beside myself last night. I thought I'd lost you; both of you."

"Like I said, it was Michael who saved us."

"Yes, but I don't intend to thank Michael the way I'm going to thank you."

There is a huff of amusement behind me. "Er, no thanks, James. I'll pass on that one. No offence, but you're not my type."

Michael pulls me back against himself. "Lie back," he whispers, still stroking my hair. "Relax."

Easing back into the arms of my Golden Lover, I share the gaze of my Master, my Dark Angel. Leaning forward over me, he kisses me, softly, sweetly, pressing his lips against mine. Then he tugs at the belt of the bathrobe I am wearing, opening it up.

Mid-movement, he stops. "I'm sorry, but are you ready for this? Here I am, pushing myself on you, when last night you were running for your life...."

"Master, it's not the first time I've run for my life. And yes, I'm ready." I hold out my arms, welcoming him to me.

He says nothing, his expression thoughtful, but then sweeping his hands over my belly, and up to my breasts, he bends to suckle.

Last night took its toll on him too. He needs this as much as I do.

I wrap my arms around him, stroking. "Shhh... We came back. I came back. I will *always* come back."

He sighs, rests his head against my chest. "Master?"

"Mmm?"

"I want you inside me. I want both of you."

Michael stirs behind me. "Come on. That bed's plenty big enough for three."

My Master takes me by the hand, leading me to the bedroom, Michael following.

*****

Michael

He leads her by the hand into the bedroom, but once in there, she stops, turns and faces him.

She unknots his tie, unbuttons his shirt, sliding it from his shoulders, then leads him to the bed to sit.

Opening her robe, she lets it slide away, then naked, she kneels before him.

She unlaces his shoes and takes them off with his socks, then rubs his feet. James sighs, leaning back on his hands, closing his eyes and letting his head rest back. Then she unbelts and unzips him and kneels back, inviting him to take off his jeans......

.... Last night, I watched her gag a face from a horror movie, and yet, here she is; *she's* comforting *him*......

Jeez, Babe, what kind of life have you led?

James lies back, stretching out, allowing her to take the lead as she swings over to straddle him. He looks tired, worn, but nonetheless, his cock is tremblingly hard.

He really, really wants to be inside you, Babe

She meets my eyes, questioning. I simply smile back.

It's alright Babe. You look after him. He's my friend too, but I can't give him what you do....

Charlotte and I were the ones attacked last night, but we were running on an adrenaline high, stress, pressure and excitement. All he had was anxiety and helplessness.

She doesn't yet take him inside her. Instead, on all fours above him, she stoops to kiss him, his chest, his cheek, his lips, then using her long hair, she strokes him, trailing it over his skin in a cloud of red. Sweeping down the length of his torso, she washes him in a red tide, sliding it over his cock and balls. His head throws back, mouth opening in a gasp.

Then, pulling her hair free of him, she takes his cock into her mouth, sucking at it, fucking him with her lips. I see her tongue wiping over the ridge of his cock head and into the slit, before, quickly, she positions herself over him, nuzzles him to her pussy and, in a single movement, smoothly sheathes him.

You must be really wet to do that, Babe.

Sliding up and down his shaft, slowly she raises and lowers herself. She looks simply fantastic; her smooth curves a-ripple with her movement, and her hair flowing over her glistening skin.

James isn't going to last long. Already he's panting hard, his eyes glazed as he looks up, watching her as she rides him.

And then I'll have you Babe, but it won't be you riding me then.... I'm going to fuck you, and hard....

She ups the tempo, working his cock, working him. He's dripping with sweat and he's about to blow. Abruptly she changes her rhythm, to a circular twisting of her hips, winding him around inside her....

James groans and his eyes squeeze closed. Flinging his arms out, he seizes her at the hip, pulling her to him as he thrusts upwards, pumping into her. Back arched and muscles straining, he spasms into climax before, grunting, he relaxes back and opens his eyes.

The two gaze at each other before she leans to kiss him again, then kneeling upright again, she twists to look at me.

"Yes? "she asks.

"Oh, yes," I reply. "But don't think you're taking the lead with me."

She grins, unhitching from James. He rolls away, looking much more relaxed.

You needed that my friend....

I push Charlotte back and down, roughly, and she squeals. "I'm going to fuck you 'til you howl."

She goes all wide-eyed. I'm not usually ungentle with her, but I think it's what she wants right now, and I'm going to give it to her.

"Spread 'em," I say, pushing myself between her knees, squeezing up into her thighs and plunging my shaft into her already dripping cunt.

She yells, but not in pain. It's more a cry of triumph. "To the victor, the spoils," I mutter to her, and I start to pump her, ramming in. She tries to hold me, but I grab her wrists, pushing her arms over her head.

She looks great, stretched out for me, her body tensioned, tits riding high. And with my hands holding her like that, I have a bit more traction to drive my cock deeper into her.

She sings her arousal, wailing and panting with every thrust I make. Her tits are flushed almost scarlet, the flush running up her chest and neck, and down her belly. Her whole body glistens with sweat and her eyes are like wild jade, alternately looking at me, then James, lying beside her, and returning to me. She isn't smiling, exactly, but her mouth is open, lips parted as she pants and cries out.

My balls are tightening, pressure rising. I could just let go now and shoot her full, but I want her to scream for me first. I thrust harder, battering her inside. James reaches to finger her nipples, pulling and rolling, squeezing hard in time to my thrusts.

She draws still, her whole body straining as she quivers under me; the calm before the storm. Then her head flings back, eyes closed, and she howls her orgasm as her pussy clenches and pulses around me.

That's all I need, and I let go. Immediately, my own climax takes me, and I spurt into her, shooting her with everything I've got.

In the aftermath, we lie quietly together, James and I to either side of her. Finally, she says. "I'm going for a bath. I'll have a soak, so I might be a while."

I kiss her. "Enjoy."

Just the two of us now, James looks rough, though better than he did. "How are you?" I ask.

"Better now that you're both back and safe."

"She can be unsettling sometimes, can't she?"

"How do you mean?"

"Her comment about it not being the first time she's run for her life."

He glances up at me, then looks away, nodding.

"She's going to go nuts up here you know, not able to do anything."

"What do you suggest? She's going to have to deal with it."

"How did *you* feel last night? When you knew that we were running, but you could do nothing?"

He presses his lips together. Now I have his attention. "It drove me nuts too." But then, "You brought her back, but Richard's not got Beth back. How do you think *he's* feeling?"

How do I answer that?

*****

She paces up and down.

"You're going to wear a hole in the carpet." I'm trying to joke, lighten the mood, but it's not going down well.

"What else can I do?" she mutters. "I can't go out. I have no work to do. I can't even stand and stare out at the view...."

Her voice is savage, and what's worse, is that I understand exactly why....

I try to be patient. "What are you hoping to achieve with this Charlotte?"

"I want to *do* something. You can't all seriously expect that I'm just going to sit here and wait for the future to come to me. You won't let me leave. I can't go back to university. I'm not even allowed down in the lower offices in the same building, even my own office..."

"That's at least partly because no-one believes that you won't try to leave if you're let loose."

"What do they expect of me?" Her voice is rising to a screech.

She can't help herself...

"It's only been a day, and I'm bored stupid. It could be months. Michael, I can't *do* this."

"Charlotte.... "I step over, try to take her in my arms, but she brushes me off.

"You're as bad as them. You just want to treat me as something pretty to be protected. I'm *not* that person!"

I try again to hold her. "Don't touch me! Leave me alone!" She storms away from me.

We need to deal with this.

"I just need a word with James. I'll be back in a bit."

I take the lift down, nodding to Ross who is seated on 'guard duty' outside the elevator shaft.

In Reception, Francis nods me through to Haswell's office. "He's in there."

"Hello, Michael," says James. "Didn't expect to see you down here?"

"It's Charlotte...."

"What's wrong? Is she alright?"

"She's like a caged animal up there, and we need to do something about it."

Haswell shrugs. "She's going to have to live with it. Things as they are, there's no other choice."

I hesitate, trying to choose my words. This is James' co-director after all. "Richard. Charlotte is *not* like Beth. She won't just accept it. If we simply try to keep her caged up, she won't *stay* caged...."

Haswell scratches his chin. "She may not like it, but there's not a lot she can do. I've got Ross guarding the elevators up there. The stairwells to that part of the building are all locked, and for good measure, I've had the codes cancelled on her door and car passes. Like it or not, she *can't* get out."

Does he really believe that? If she's determined?

Hold your patience...

"Can I suggest that you give her something to do before she *finds* something to do?"

"What's stopping her getting on with her college work?" says James.

"Her mind isn't *on* her college work. She's been told she can't go back for now, and it could be months before she can.... She's not in a good state of mind, and I for one don't want to have to deal with her in the state she's in."

"What do you mean? Has she been rude to you?"

"She didn't mean to be. She's just lashing out at whoever's handy. It happened to be me."

James stands, a set to his face. "Whoa..." I say. "Take it easy...."

"It doesn't matter what's upsetting her. She has no cause to take it out on you." He turns to leave. "I'll be back in a while."

I know that look. And Charlotte's in for a lesson on good behaviour.

Should I follow? Keep it in hand?

Maybe she'll feel better for it... blow off some stress.... I'll give them a few minutes...

"Richard...." I hesitate, not sure how much I can say to James' billionaire partner.

"What?"

"I know you think...."

"Yes?" He sits back in his chair, hands clasped behind his head. "Come on. Out with it. If it's something awkward, it's better dealt with."

"I think that you and James both think of Charlotte as a sub. Intelligent and pretty, but just a sub. And she's not. There's a lot more to her than that. If she can't get what she wants by.... legitimate means, she's perfectly capable of taking matters into her own hands."

He says nothing, considering my words. I push my case. "I know she looks like Beth, but she's had a fight on her hands all her life. It's second nature to her. She'll not simply *accept* it."

"You think not?"

"She ran from the home half a dozen times."

"And was caught and returned every time."

"She was a *child* then. She not now. She's intelligent, devious and she'll follow through to get what she wants. For God's sake, bring her in on whatever's going on, or she'll take steps to do it herself."

He ponders, thoughtful. "Alright. You've made your point. I'll bring her in.... Um, right now is probably not a good time though." He casts his eyes upwards.

"Mmmm, no... I'll give them half an hour and then go up."

*****

Charlotte

I watch Michael leave, sorry, even before the door has closed behind him, for what I said.

He didn't deserve that. He's trying to help.

I follow him out to the lobby, but the lift doors have already closed behind him.

"Ross..."

"Sorry, Charlotte. I'm under orders. You're not going anywhere. He'll skin me alive if I let you through."

I wander back into the lounge, pacing up and down, unable to settle, unable to think straight.

What's wrong with me?

Maybe a glass of wine would settle me. I pour it, then realise that I really don't want it.

Tea then. I put on the kettle. As I'm waiting for it to boil, the click of the apartment door echoes through.

Michael! He's come back. I'll apologise to him. Tell him I'm sorry.

But as I go through to the lounge, it is my Master waiting for me, and he does not look happy. Arms folded, head tilted, he gazes levelly at me.

Oh crap...

"Anything you want to tell me?" he says, his voice cool.

"If it's about Michael, I know I owe him an apology. I thought you were him just then. I came out to say sorry."

"Well, that's a start I suppose." He does not look mollified. "And what had Michael done to deserve your being rude to him?"

"Nothing. It was my fault, not his." I stare at the floor, knowing what's coming.

He crosses the room to me, seizes my chin in his hand, forcing me to look up at him. "Things are difficult enough without you

throwing tantrums. Beth abducted. Gunmen coming after you....
Charlotte, Michael saved your life, and all you do is vent your temper
on him when he's trying to help."

My temper snaps. "I *know*. I've said I'm sorry. I was sorry almost
before he'd left the room, but he'd gone, and I *can't follow him* to
apologise...."

My voice is rising all the time. "I'm a prisoner up here. You can
wrap it up in nice furniture and good carpets, but I'm a prisoner in a
gilded cage. And I can't.... I can't *do* anything!"

I am shouting now; venting anger and frustration and I don't
know what else. "It wasn't meant to *be* like this."

My Master's face furious, "Don't you dare speak to me in that
tone!" And he slaps me across the face, hard, the blood rising where
his hand has caught my skin.

And I see red. I slap back, catching him on the cheek.

For a moment he freezes, as though he can't believe what I just
did, then grabbing both my wrists, he pushes me towards the
bedroom. "In there, Madam." he hisses. He doesn't shout, his fury
turned to iced words.

Do I fight this?

Is there any point?

"Alright," I say. "I'll go into the bedroom. I'll take whatever it is
you're going to hand out. but it doesn't change anything. It doesn't
change what's in my head."

I walk into the bedroom, and without being asked, bend over the
end of the bed, my face pressed sideways against the comforter. And
I wait.

My Master does not hurry. Instead, he stands over me, arms
folded, looking down. After a moment, he pulls me upright by the
wrist. "Alright then. *Tell* me what's in your head." His anger is still
there, but it is contained now.

"You've got me locked up here, for my safety as you say. But I'm not a child, and I'm not stupid. You all want to tell me what I must or must not do, and no-one asks me what I think, let alone what I want. Instead, you just want to run my life by .... diktat. Alright, I'm being hunted. We all know why. So, do I stop thinking for myself? Wait to be rescued by my knights in shining armour? Is that what you expect of me? Because I'm going crazy caged up here, and.... and I'm sorry I took it out on Michael. He really *did* do nothing to deserve it."

He faces me, arms still folded, face expressionless.

What's he thinking?

He stares at the ceiling, then looks away from me, then back at me.

Abruptly, he pushes forward, grabbing me by the shoulders, pushing me back against the wall, fastening his mouth over mine.

What...

He tugs at my tee-shirt, roughly, pulling it up over my head, then reaches around, unclipping my bra.

He points at my jeans. "Off," he instructs.

I remove the rest of my clothes. He strips off too but keeps his tie in his hand. As I stand naked before him, he pushes at my chest with the flat of his hand, propelling me backwards onto the bed.

Jeez.... hope he's going to give me time to....

His erection is huge, and he's not wasting time. He clambers over me, and, holding my eyes as he does it, ties my wrists, binding them to the bedhead. Then flipping me over, he rolls me onto my stomach, the tie twisting painfully tight.

"Master.... My hands...."

He reaches, unties and reties, allowing blood back into my fingers, then hauls me up at the hips, presenting himself with my ass....

Ah, I know where this is going....

...he slaps hard across my ass. It stings, and I gasp.

Is he angry still? Or just letting off steam?

He rubs the spot where he caught me the first time, then slaps again, in a different place...

.... Yeah... letting off steam....

And knowing now that he is not angry with me still, my nerves vanish and...

... my pussy floods.

Now, he slaps again, and again, but this time my gasp evolves into a cry of arousal. He plunges fingers inside me, briefly finger-fucking me, testing my readiness I think, and with a grunt of satisfaction, bringing his body atop mine, slams his cock inside me.

He rams home, arrested only by my inner walls, and I yell at the pain. But a part of me is dissolving, tension evaporating as my Master plunges into me, driving in hard again and again.

His own breathing is laboured, and our bodies are quickly slick with sweat as he rides me, taking me, claiming his due.

His hand snakes around me, fingers working down to my clit. Normally this would have been simply too fast for me to work to climax, but as the tension in me uncoils, orgasm takes its place, welling up in me, ready to explode against my Master's ramming of my insides.

My pussy erupts into climax, pulsing violently around my Master's cock. I'm not sure if it triggers him, or if he simply releases his control, but as I buck and jerk and howl my pleasure, he growls against me, grinding hard as he shoots into me.

With a gasp he rolls off me to one side, reaching to untie my wrists. I collapse next to him, and he reaches round to pull my face to his, kissing me.

"I think we both needed that," he says.

I nod, still panting. "Thank you, Master."

"Thank you?"

"I feel much better now."

He huffs a laugh. "I'll tell Michael, next time you start getting cantankerous with him..."

"*Cantankerous?*"

He laughs. "Feel free to substitute the adjective of your choice..."

"Well, okay.... how about 'grumpy'?"

"Look, I'm sorry. You were right. We shouldn't have tried to lock you in your ivory tower like some latter-day Rapunzel."

"Wasn't she golden-haired?"

"As you say, so you're clearly unsuited to the role. Listen..." he turns serious. "Despite our... um... personal de-stressing techniques..." he grins, "You can't just go wandering around. It really is too risky..."

"I want something to *do*. I'm never going to be the idle type."

"I know. And it was unfair of me to expect it. Leave me with it. We'll find legitimate work you can do to help with all this. Fair enough?

"Yes, Master. That's fair enough."

*****

Michael

"How is she now?" asks James

"She's a lot better. Seems to have found herself something to do.... Although I notice that she's not doing any of it sitting down...."

"Really?"

James tone is bland, but there is a glint of amusement in his eyes. Richard looks briefly over the top of his glasses, then looks away, smiling to himself.

"What is she doing?" asks James

"I'm not sure what it is exactly, but she has plans of the City spread out. Seems to be cross-referencing them to various websites."

"I gave them to her," says Richard. "We're trying to figure out just how they got Elizabeth out of sight so easily."

*****

Charlotte

Will Stanton is here. And the Commissioner of Police is not a happy man.

"And how long do you think it took them to figure out they've got the wrong woman?" demands Richard. "And how would they react then?"

Will looks sympathetic. "Richard. They're not going to simply kill her. Assuming that they didn't decide just to...." He swallows his words, obviously editing what he was about to say, "She has a value to them. Even if they don't know who she is; her value as a ransom hostage, they're *traffickers*. A woman who looks like Beth; they'll take the time to get a good price for her."

This is his edited and improved version of what he was going to say?

Will continues. "We have shots of them getting her into the car and driving across the City, but then they disappear into a parking lot and the car is abandoned. Clearly, they changed it for some other vehicle, and on the way out, well, hundreds of cars have gone past."

"Assuming they got out by car of course."

"How else then?"

Richard slams his fist against the table, rage and frustration writ large. "You're saying that we have no leads? None?"

Will hesitates, then, "I think the only way we are going to get a handle on where they are, is if we can entice them out.... some sort of lure...."

His eyes slide across to me.

My Master leaps up, eyes flashing, face furious. "Absolutely not!"

Michael speaks. "No. Richard. I'm sorry. Beth is a lovely woman, but you are *not* using Charlotte as bait to track her down. I know James is on your payroll, but I'm not, and I say 'No.'"

I've never heard Michael sound like this before: implacable, almost threatening, but he sits there, face set, lids half-lowered.

"Don't I get a say?" I ask.

"*No*, you don't," says Michael. "You're not doing it." His arms are folded as he stares me down.

"But...."

My Master interrupts. "*No,* Charlotte. You're not doing it."

Now I begin to be angry. "I'm not a little girl to have decisions made for me. We've already had this discussion, haven't we? You can't *tell* me what to do."

Michael looks thoughtful. "No? Watch me. In this case, Charlotte, just watch me."

I tick off on my fingers. "One; The Police think they know who the culprits are, but not where to find them. Two; They could have taken Beth by mistake, but they could just as easily have been intended to pick up both of us and they happened to get her first. Three; The Police have no leads of any kind on hideouts, car registrations, routes out of the City, or anything else. Four; I can't even go home right now, or back to university and Five......" My voice falters, tears threatening.... "Beth is my friend, and she's in trouble because of *me*..."

Taking a deep breath, I fight back the pricking at the back of my eyes. Tears don't help anyone. "And this isn't small trouble. They probably don't want to kill her.... me.... Otherwise, it would just have been a bullet in the head in a parking lot.... It's more likely they want to learn what she.... I.... know and then sell her on.... me on...."

All three men are watching me, jaws dropped. "Jeez, Charlotte. You sound cold-blooded when you talk like that," says Michael.

"It's about survival isn't it," I say, keeping my voice heartless. "Richard was right when he said that you're no good to anyone if you panic. Some things *have* to be done in cold blood."

My Master, watching me carefully, says "Like selling yourself to the highest bidder? Done in cold blood?"

I lift my chin, meeting his eye. "And how else do you think I could have done it?"

Richard interrupts. "Alright, Charlotte, you're a survivor. We all know that. But you won't help Elizabeth by getting yourself caught and trafficked as well. All that would mean is that we'd lost both of you. And while she may be your friend, you don't owe her that..."

I owe it to you though....

But I stay silent; keep my thoughts to myself.

I look at Will. "So, I'm happy to be corrected, but in fact, the police have *no idea* where Beth is? And no leads of any kind to follow? Please tell me if I'm wrong on this."

Miserably, he nods his head.

Richard looks sick at heart. His face is drawn, and he's lost weight over the last few days.

He loves her...

It dawns on me that I am flanked by Michael and my Master. "What's this then?" I ask. "You're my jailers again?"

Both men look askance at me. Michael says "Charlotte, take this as it's meant, but while James thinks you're his obedient little sub...." My Master looks startled. "....and will do as you're told, I don't. And frankly, I'm not willing to let you out of my sight just now."

"You think I'll try to do something stupid?"

"No. I think you'll try to do something clever. But that doesn't mean it wouldn't be dangerous in the extreme and.... I'm not letting you."

"We've discussed this. I'm not property."

"No, you're not. But you *will* be my wife, and that entitles me to a say."

Time to shut up. Let them think they've won.

I hang my head. "Perhaps you're right." I try to appear to have submitted. My Master appears to have swallowed it, nodding in apparent satisfaction. Michael watches me from the corner of his eye.

He's not fooled.

*****

Later:

"Promise me."

"Promise you what?"

Michael gazes at me. "You know what."

"I promise you I won't do anything stupid."

He tilts his head. "And will you promise me not to do anything clever?"

I remain silent. He looks distressed. "Charlotte...."

"I'm not going to make you a promise I'm not sure I can keep. Anyway, you don't need to worry do you? You've all got me locked up in here. What could I do?"

*****

Michael

"So, what is it you're working on, Charlotte?"

She leans over a large table surface, comparing various plans. "It was an idea Richard had, about how they might have gotten Beth away from the City. It's not as though I've anything better to do, so I said I'd help."

"So, what *are* all these?"

"They're all plans of the City, but in different ways and from different perspectives.' She holds up one of the plans. "This one's an underground map of the sewers and drains." She points again. "Access tunnels and electrical schematics for the subways." Then she waves over at another, covered in a mess of sticky dots and annotations. "That one's the roadmap, and I've been superimposing details of where all the cameras are, not just the official ones, but the private ones too where I can find them on webcam sites. And that one...."

"Okay. I get the picture. You're looking for the non-obvious ways that someone might have been spirited out of the City? And the ways that they might be spotted anyway?"

"Yeah, basically that's it. It's complicated because some of the networks tie up together and some don't. For example, the old nineteenth-century sewer system was built covering most of the City, as it was then, but when they started construction on the subway system..."

"Everything had to go around or over or under..."

"Yup. And then they needed the...."

"I get it. I get it." I hold up my hands, laughing, but scanning the pile of ragged maps and plans, the modern documents, the tabs open on webcam sites, the biro'd comments and yellow notes over everything... "You did all this manually?"

"Not all of it. I've scanned and digitised most of this lot so that I could superimpose the systems over each other. Uploaded them to the cloud."

"You've done a hell of a lot of work, Charlotte."

"Have I got anything better to do with my time?"

I shrug. "Oh, I nearly forgot. I picked up a couple of pieces of mail for you." I pass her the small padded envelopes. "What are they?"

She hesitates, but only briefly, feeling through the padding at the contents. "Oh, I got bored. Did a bit of online shopping."

"Shopping? You?"

"As I said, I was bored. Oh yes, this one, it's a necklace I saw, that I quite liked the look of."

She opens the packet, producing a small locket, the kind that opens to take a photo.

*She **must** have been bored. When does she ever buy stuff like that? If you can't read it, she's not usually interested....*

"Mmmm. Very pretty." I say. "We'll turn you into a society lady yet."

She smiles, but I can't avoid a nagging feeling of missing something.

*****

Charlotte

They think they have trapped me.

The concierge has been told not to let me out of the building. Ross sits outside by the lift. Cameras scan the corridor outside the apartment. And they think I don't know that my parking pass has been invalidated, so I cannot exit from the car park.

To Hell with this!

*****

My plans in place; my car keys are in my pocket, my Master's parking pass with it, exchanged with my own while he was showering....

"How's the work going, Charlotte?" asks my Master.

Standing up from a large map of the City, I explain my various markings. "I've been plotting out where all the public cameras are along through-routes. There are a lot of them online available for anyone to view. I thought I might be able to use them spot some kind of pattern for the route they could have taken with Beth."

I'm talking hogwash. My real reason for interest in those cameras is quite different.

My Master raises his eyebrows. "Good idea. Any luck with it?"

"No, not really. I've just not driven around the City enough to be able to read the map very well. Really, it needs someone with a lot more ground knowledge of the roads."

Will he take the bait?

"Perhaps Ross could help with it? He's Richard's driver after all."

Bingo!

"Of course he could. Should have thought of that myself."

My Master calls in Ross, from where he was standing in the corridor, guarding against my use of the elevator.

"Ross, Charlotte had an idea about checking the routes...."

The three men gather around the map, engrossed. I make a show of pulling up web-cam sites on my laptop as they trace out possible routes through the City. When their attention is thoroughly diverted, I slip out.

I send the service lift down first: it's a long slow trip, and hopefully, it will be several minutes before it can return. Taking the turbo-lift to the parking levels, using a fast-acting epoxy adhesive, I quickly attach a tracer under the wheel rim of my car where it shouldn't be noticed, toss my phone on the passenger seat where I have a good view of the screen, and *go*.

I reckon I have less than five minutes to get out before they notice, and I've used three of them coming down to the car. I need to get out of the parking lot before the alarm is raised, and the building locks down.

Trying to drive normally, not to raise suspicion, I drive up to the barrier, swipe my Master's parking pass and as the barrier raises, I join the stream of traffic.

A minute later, I tap the phone screen again to send my pre-prepared message.

*****

Michael

James looks up from the map, glancing around the room, then stands up straight, turning, looking wild. "Where's Charlotte?"

"Bathroom?" I ask, and rap smartly on the door. "Charlotte? You in there?"

No reply. I push the door open, checking inside. Nothing.

"The lift!" mutters Ross, dashing through to the hall, followed by me and James.

The turbo-lift is already way below us, twenty stories down.

"The service elevator?"

"She's sent that down too."

James all but bangs on the intercom, yelling at the answering concierge. "Lock the doors down there. Stop anyone coming in or out of the building until I or Richard Haswell instruct otherwise."

But I am watching the indicator. "She's not stopping at the ground floor."

"The car park?" mutters James. "In that case, she's about to discover that her car pass has been blocked." He picks up his phone, tapping briefly. "Francis. Is Richard there? Will you tell him please, that Charlotte's trying to leave the building. Can you make sure everything's locked down while we get her back. Yes, that's right. Thanks." As he hangs up he says, "Richard's on his way up."

"Or he will be, when there's an elevator to bring him," I say, nodding at the indicator. It stops at the parking level, then a moment later starts rising again. The service lift, much slower, is still descending.

James' phone rings. "Yes? Oh, hello Francis.... *What!* How?" His eyes roll upwards. "I see... Thanks."

He darts a look at me. "She's out. Security says her car just exited the parking lot using my pass...."

He stabs at his phone, pacing the room, mobile pressed to his ear. "Pick up the phone Charlotte.... Pick up your *fucking* phone."

Then he pauses, glancing up at me. "Answer-phone.... Charlotte..." he says, visibly hanging on to his self-control. "Listen, please come back at once. We're coming after you, but please, call me back...." He glances sideways at me. "Or.... call Michael if you're not comfortable calling me. Please. I don't know what you think you have in mind, but you're *not* safe out there and you *must* come back. Now, *please* call us back."

The lift *pings* and Richard steps out, his face like thunder.

"What happened? Are you seriously telling me that three grown men can't keep one little girl locked up?" He swings on Ross. "And where the hell were *you*? You were supposed to be standing guard over the elevator."

Ross, pasty-faced, starts to stutter. "It wasn't Ross' fault." interrupts James. "Charlotte diverted us all rather neatly."

I cast my eyes back over the map, considering.... "You know, she did divert us, but there's an awful lot of work gone into that map for a diversion...." I am interrupted.

My phone pings. Simultaneously, so do James' and Richard's.

We have all received an identical message, from Charlotte.

"Check your e-mails".

"What the hell?" mutters James. "Fucking wilful, infuriating, stupid woman...."

I interrupt him. "Wilful she may be. Infuriating she certainly is, but stupid she's not. She's obviously planned this, so perhaps we should start working around whatever it is she's up to. Let's do what she said, and check our e-mails."

Ruefully," You're right...."

"Richard. Can I get online somewhere?" I ask.

"Let's all go down to my office. We can see things more easily there."

As we enter Reception, Francis flags us. "I've just had a message from Charlotte..."

"You and we all," shouts Richard back at her as he sweeps by to his office. Get hold of a laptop for Michael to use."

James darts through to his office, returning with his computer. And Francis is already heading out of the office, returning moments later with her own machine.

James taps furiously away, then pauses. He glances up. "Just downloading now.... Ahh...." He taps again. Then he frowns.... "It's a password; 'Charlotte-01', and several links to.... to what?"

Simultaneously, I log onto my own e-mail. "Yup. There's something here from her, sent to me and James, *and* Richard *and* Francis. Looks like she was definitely going for belts and braces to get her message out...."

James taps and waits, then leans forward, peering at the screen. "The links she's sent are all to tracking sites of one kind or another. Fuck! She's set up tracers and she's using herself up as bait... The first one is a find-your-phone site for her mobile."

"There's no guarantee that she'll get to keep her phone," says Richard. "The first thing they did was get Elizabeth's off her."

"We'll still be able to see where it gets dumped," I reply. "And it's not the only link."

"The next link is to a different tracker site," says James. "Another provider. A different device."

"The third one too," I say.

"How many links has she sent?" asks Richard.

"Seven altogether, every one different."

Richard scratches his head. "Where's she got hold of so many trackers? Or *any* trackers for that matter?"

"Mail order I'll bet," says James. "She had several packages delivered over the last day or two.... I'll check her browser history when we have her laptop here..."

And a penny drops in my head. "She opened one of those packages while I was watching. It was a locket, the kind you put a photo in. I thought it odd at the time but didn't think it through. I wonder if she's wearing that locket, and there's a tracer inside?"

"Are all seven links working?" asks Richard.

I click between screens... "Hang on, I'm trying to watch too many things at once for a single screen...."

"Francis. Have a scout around would you," says Richard. "Pull in half a dozen laptops from wherever you can find them. And then try to get hold of Will Stanton for me."

James shouts after her. "And can you fetch Charlotte's laptop too, Francis. I want to check her browser history."

A few minutes later, the office is awash with computers, all displaying different screens; a couple with incoming e-mail screens, but most displaying some form of map or plan with a travelling point.

I follow the trail of the first screen I've opened, then realise what I'm looking at. Comparing it in my head with her webcam plan, "She's taking a route out of the City that is well-populated with webcams. She diverted us by talking about Beth, but it's herself she's done it for...." I yell through to Francis. "Sorry, but can you go back up there and bring down all those plans Charlotte was working on.... and then can you keep trying to call her, see if we get her attention..."

James looks at his screen, compares it to the map with Charlotte's pins, markings and annotations. His tone is acerbic. "She's set herself up as bait, and she's making herself highly visible, to them *and* to us. The Police will be able to see any car that follows her while she's in the area. But that's only going to last while she's somewhere with road cameras. There's a few on the highways, but mainly they fade off as you leave the City."

"She's doing a helluva speed," I comment.

"Is she normally a fast driver?" asks Richard.

"No, very much the slow and careful type usually. Her car was chosen for economy and reliability, not for racing."

Is she being pursued?

My stomach tightens...

"Where is she now?" asks Francis.

"Well away from the City now, and off the main highways... no more cameras."

Two of the points have stopped moving. Of the others, three are following matching trails, two are on different trajectories.

"One of the static signals is the one for her phone.

"So, they've got her and dumped her mobile?" The thought leaves me feeling queasy, panicky. "The other static one?"

His tone is grim. "No idea." He mutters something to himself.

"What was that?"

"She's not going to sit down for a fucking week when I catch up with her..."

"Keep your temper under control. It's not helping."

"Oh, and you're pleased with her?"

"No, I'm not. When we do get her back, I'll hold your coat. But we all know why she's done this. From her point of view, it's for very good reason."

"Where's the phone been dumped?" asks Richard. He is on his own mobile, talking urgently with someone.

I zoom in on the spot. "Um, a couple of miles off Junction 42 on Highway 593, Westbound."

James interrupts, "Hang on.... The phone signal's just died.... It's gone."

Richard continues talking, passing on the information, then turns back to us. "Will's sending over an officer to see this, but he also asks for the links and password, so he can see it himself."

"Gimme his e-mail address. I'll forward the original message to him."

James is still peering at one of the screens. "Okay, so assuming her phone's been turned off or smashed, why is one signal static, two of the trails going off in one direction, and the other three all match each other?"

"Suppose she's got a tracker on her car or the keys, and the other three on herself somehow? If she's been taken out her car, and they're getting rid of it somewhere...."

James is zooming in on the wayward trail. "You could have something there...."

Richard turns from his phone again. "Will says he's coming down here himself..."

I watch the three remaining dots move across their screens. "Wonder where she's got the other tracers?"

*****

Charlotte

Out on the street, amid the stream of traffic, again, still following my general trajectory, I take all the most visible routes. I want to appear to be heading out to my university, but I choose routes that are heavily watched and be-camera'd.

My phone rings, flashing up with my Master's avatar. I don't answer, letting it ring off, then when a few seconds later there is the *bing* of a left message, I tap it onto speakerphone.

As I imagined, my Master is not happy with me. He is containing his temper, but I can hear the suppressed fury in his voice. I smile to myself as he says that, if I am uncomfortable speaking with him, I should phone Michael back.

Think I'll pass on that... We can talk when this is over....

Guess I'll not be sitting down for a while....

Outside the City, I join the main highway traffic, watching carefully in my mirrors for any sign of pursuit.

My phone rings again, and again. Repeated bleeps of messages arriving become irritating. I would turn the phone off, but right now, it is fulfilling a valuable function: tracking me, reporting back as to where I am.

I finger the locket I am wearing, another tracer now inserted inside. Perhaps it will be discovered, perhaps not. I have others...

In the rear-view mirror, I see the anticipated 'action'. A car is gaining on the queue of traffic behind me, weaving between lanes as it draws closer. A series of cars are overtaking me on the outer lane, but two flank me, slightly to the fore and aft, and then slow down, matching my speed, blocking my exit to that lane.

On the inner lane, another car is hanging behind me, blocking the passage of any other vehicles that try to 'undertake' me.

I swallow hard. I did this entirely of my own choosing, and now the reality is upon me.

Go for broke.

I must make this look realistic. Slamming my foot down on the gas, I pull away with all the acceleration my little car can muster. She's sweet and small, and not intended for this treatment. Foot hard to the floor, I swerve to the inside to undertake the car ahead of me, only to find myself blocked by another, slower car, immediately before me. The blocker car behind me immediately pulls up close, tail-gating me; another exit blocked.

Horns blare around me, as 'normal' traffic is bullied out of the way. Drivers speed up, pulling away from this obvious trouble spot, doubtless happy to be on a journey elsewhere. In under a minute I am blocked front, back and outside by vehicles. Another pulls up on my inside, blocking my possible exit as we pass a junction.

As the next junction draws close, the inside vehicle withdraws, and I am herded onto the exit.

We're on a wild route here. In all directions, the roads lead deep into the wilderness. Very few people use this road.

Still being forced along at an uncomfortable speed, we are now some miles off the main highway. The car ahead of me abruptly slows, forcing me to stop.

For reality's sake, I flick on the central locking, knowing that it won't last more than a few seconds. Nonetheless, I start violently when a gunshot blows apart my driver's side door lock. I don't have to fake the trembling as hands haul me roughly out of my seat, dragging me away from the car.

My keys are snatched away, along with the tracker they carry. One of my captors gets in and speeds away, back the way we came.

"Get her bag. Dump it. And the phone."

My mobile is turned off and dropped to the ground, stamped on, repeatedly, until it is trash. My bag is flung far, dropping into the undergrowth.

I am hustled into one of the cars on the back seat. No-one speaks to me. Flanked to either side by men who clearly do not mean me well, I can only hope that the plans I laid in preparation are working as intended.

*****

Michael

Richard's phone rings. "Yes? Hello, Will. Yes?" His face falls. "Right, thanks for letting me know." He clicks off his phone.

"Will's got a patrol car out at the spot where the stationary signal is. They've found her bag, simply tossed into the scrub. It had one of the tracers in there, stitched into the lining. Her phone was on the ground, smashed to pieces."

"The car?"

"No sign of it. but he's got patrol cars following the two sets of diverging trails. I think we can assume one trail is the car, and the other is Charlotte herself."

"Will those tracers work everywhere?" I ask.

James sucks in his cheeks. "GPS, in theory, should work everywhere there's an open sky, but it can be blocked. The question is, will it occur to them that she's wearing tracers. If they get them off her, or block the signal...."

"And what blocks the signal?"

"It doesn't take much. RF interference sometimes from a computer. Tinfoil will do it, physically blocking the signal. A metal-roofed garage... sometimes even a tinted windscreen; metal incorporated into the glass.... At a push, wet leaves under tree cover can do it."

We watch the dots crawling along the screens.

Richard's phone rings again. "Hello? Ah, Will. Any more? Yes? Okay. I'll pass it along." He clicks his phone off. "They've found the car. It was parked up in a scrap dealer's lot, queued to go through the crusher. One of the tracers was under a wheel rim. Another on the keyring. They've arrested the owner on suspicion."

We sit there, watching three dots crawl over screens when, suddenly, with no warning, they blink off, the signal gone.

We have lost Charlotte.

*****

The Virgin and the Masters

Part Four

A Continuing Tale of (Ex-)Virgin Erotica, BDSM and Ménage with Two Masters and *More*......

Part Twenty Of
The 'Buying the Virgin' Series

Author: Simone Leigh

The Virgin and the Masters
Part Four

Charlotte

Sitting quietly, I look carefully around me, trying not to be conspicuous about it. I am inside, in effect, a tin box.

Will the tracer signal get through this?

Almost certainly, no....

We have changed cars twice, and now I am locked in the back of a truck. I still have three tracers with me, all different, but the odds are that, just now, no-one can pick up the signal from any of them.

Master, Michael, where are you? Are you looking for me?

At some point, presumably, I will be taken from the truck to.... who-knows-where? Perhaps the signal will be detectable then, at least while I am outdoors.

But it may be brief. Will someone be watching the monitor then?

And, when all is said and done, despite my anxiety, I need my captors to take me.... wherever they are taking me....

Don't give them trouble. Don't make them tie you up. Keep your hands free....

I am being guarded. A man with a gun and an unfriendly expression sits by the tailgate, blocking my exit. However, since the entire point of the exercise is that I be taken to Beth, I have no interest in escaping just now.

Sit quietly. Get them off their guard.

So, I remain, trying to behave like a model, terrified, prisoner; doing exactly as I am told and hoping that.... well.... hoping....

Fight the panic. It doesn't help.

Fear pooling in my stomach at what I have done, and the consequences, if my plans do not work as I intended, my tearful face is not entirely an act.

Have my Master and Michael received my messages? Detected the tracker signals? I have set a sequence of events in motion, and I can only hope that they play out in the way I planned....

Michael

Charlotte's signal vanishing from the screens, for a moment we all, James, myself and Richard, sit frozen, staring, trying to will the signal back to life.

Oh, God Charlotte. Where are you?

"Time to go." says James, swinging away from his computer. "We've done as much as we can from here."

"Yes. Which car?"

"Yours. It's more rugged than mine. We may need to go cross-country, or on poor trails."

"Okay. I'll drive. You handle the computers and concentrate on finding the signal again. You're better at the tech stuff than me."

"Fair enough.... *Francis*..." he yells out of the office, calling in Haswell's P.A.

All but immediately, she appears around the door. "Yes, James?"

"We need connectivity while we're on the move.... we could end up god-knows-where. I want you to get dongles for the laptops...." He starts jotting. "Here's the spec. I want you to get all different types and networks. If one network doesn't work in a given area, another might."

"Does GPS need an internet connection?" I ask.

"No, but the mapping programs it works with, *do*. There's no point having the signal, without the data to map it to."

"I'm coming too," says Richard. "Francis, send out Ross and whoever else is to hand, to get whatever James needs. Tell them I want them back *here*, with the equipment, within twenty minutes."

He pauses, obviously thinking. "Do you think we want the police in on this?"

"We should have them available," I say. "But if the area is suddenly flooded with police vehicles, someone's going to start asking how they know to look there. If Charlotte still has her tracers, we don't want them being taken away from her."

"Fair point. I'll have a word with Will and ask him to keep any police presence discreet for the moment."

*****

I drive at a crazy speed, following James' navigation from the previous path of the tracers. We pass the spot where Charlotte's assorted signals separated, where we now know that she was taken from her car; where her phone was destroyed, and her bag thrown away. We pass by, still pursuing the more recent trail.

"This is where we lost the signal," says James. Haswell says nothing, his face grim.

"You think we should just circle first?" I ask. "Try different areas to try to catch the signal?"

"Yes. You just drive. I'll keep an eye on the trace... Wait! There... it's back again...."

"Which way?"

I slam onto the gas. After only half a minute, James again. "Damn! It's off again..."

"Perhaps taking her out of a car and into a building?"

"Seems plausible."

"Did you see enough to get us there?"

"I think so, yes. Certainly, we can get closer. Keep driving. We're losing the light."

*****

Charlotte

The truck rattles to a halt, and the engine stops.

Are we here?

The door opens, from the outside I notice, and my guard thumbs me out.

It is still daylight, and we have pulled up in woodland, at the end of a broken mud track, much ridged and rutted. Only tough, overland vehicles would be able to reach here. There is a long, low, block-built shed. Overhung by trees, the shed would not be very visible from the air.

Fuck! The roof's made of corrugated iron....

The signal from my remaining tracers will almost certainly not escape the building, so I have only a few seconds out of doors for them to transmit freely and be spotted again.

I drag my heels, delaying the moment until I am in the shadow of the metal roofing, and my Masters will no longer be able to find me. All the while, I glance furtively around, looking for any detail that will help in my escape.... and Beth's.

Is she here...?

.... Am I in the right place?

But the guard seizes me by the arm, his fingers biting into the muscle as he drags me indoors. Without word or ceremony, I am marched through a main central room, then pushed through a side door, staggering to keep my balance as I am thrust inside. The door slams closed behind me.

The room is small and cheerless, with no furnishings barring a bucket in one corner, and bars on the window; a cell.

And Beth is here....

I've found you....

Sitting on filthy blankets piled in a corner on the floor, her face is tear-streaked, eyes red and swollen, her hair an unkempt red tangle around her shoulders.

She looks utterly lost.

"Hi. How are you doing?"

She looks as though she will burst into tears again. Her voice broken, "Oh, Charlotte! They got you too...."

I can't say too much. She needs to keep looking scared....

"Yeah, 'fraid so. If it's any help, it was me they wanted in the first place."

She stares up at me. "You? I thought they must be trying to ransom me."

I sit down next to her, and she shuffles up the blankets to make room. "They're connected to the people who ran Blessingmoors. It's looking as though they want to make sure I don't give evidence."

Her breath shudders as she resists weeping. "It's awful here. There's things living in the blankets. They keep getting into my hair."

We've been imprisoned by traffickers, and she's worrying about fleas?

Convenient though....

"Have these." I pull a couple of combs out from my hair. "I know what it's like when it gets out of control. I always use more of these than I need. Here, let me put it up for you, out of the way. You'll be more comfortable like that."

I plait her hair into braids, winding it up and pinning it with the combs.

*****

The cell door opens, and a gun jerks down at us, where Beth and I sit on the floor. "You two. Out."

I stand, then help Beth up as she struggles to rise.

Is she ill? Or just scared sick?

We are trooped into the main room....

.... and I meet a face I know; a face from the past, a face that once looked over teenagers as though they were cattle.

Tall, fair-haired, although silvering, his features sharp, well defined, he would be a handsome man were it not for the twist of cruelty to his mouth.

Walking slowly around me, he examines me from all angles, arms folded, face expressionless.

"You know me?"

"Yes. You're Lawrence Klempner."

He is older now, but not so changed that I do not remember him. He stares down at me, pursing his lips. His voice is chill, passionless, but there is something else in his eyes; a cold hatred....

Of me?

Why? Where's that come from?

"I wouldn't have recognised you from being a teenager you know. You're a lot better looking than you were then. Useful that." he says. "But I do see your mother in you. You are very like her, Jennifer. She was beautiful too, to begin with anyway."

My stomach churns.

He knew my mother? How?

He perches on the end of a table, legs outstretched, crossed at the ankle, arms folded. And clearly, he is enjoying himself, relishing my discomfort, but I say nothing. "Yes, I knew your mother; Michelle Conners. You want to know how? I ran her, with a string of other whores."

Still, I say nothing. He wants to bait me. I refuse to be baited.

"Looks like it runs in the family, doesn't it? You sold yourself too, *auctioned* yourself, and now you live with two men. I assume they *are* both fucking you?"

How does he know this?

"What I don't know though, is..." He points at Beth. "Who's she? You never had any sisters. I'd have known."

I hold my silence, staring him down. He glances contemptuously at her. "It hardly matters. I suppose you're bound to go looking for family. What is she then? A cousin?"

*They **really** don't know who Beth is? They don't know whose wife they're holding prisoner?*

"What do you want from me?" I ask.

His eyebrows arch. "What do I want from you? Well, let's see.... for a start, I want payback for what you did to Charlie Jenkins."

Who? Aaahhhh.... Jenkins....

Oh, crap....

Supervisor Jenkins; who chased me when I ran; a fourteen-year-old girl pursued by a man threatening to have me gang-raped, and he went under the wheels of a truck...

And Klempner.... was his friend?

So, monsters have friends too.

"I didn't kill him. He wasn't paying attention. Got run down."

"He was after *you* because you wouldn't do as you were told, wouldn't obey.... *just* like your mother. She didn't like doing as she was told either... usually had to be persuaded when I wanted to fuck her. Am I going to have to *persuade* you? Or are you going to do as you're bid?"

He sweeps his head back, indicating the other four, no five men in the room. "We're going to have a lot of fun anyway, you and me, and the others here. I gather you enjoy it, having a few of 'em going at you..."

Where is he getting this from?

"I'd rather like to keep you nearby for the long-term." he continues. "Run you with the other hookers. I'd enjoy that, seeing how much cock you can suck in a day. But I think you've got a big mouth, so instead, I've got a buyer for you. You're going where no-one speaks English, and no-one cares about what comes out of a whore's mouth... just what goes in it."

He surveys Beth, trailing fingers through her hair, over her face, lifting her chin with a finger. "And I'll get a better price now, selling you as a pair."

Beth's fear is visible. Trembling, her eyes are frantic, skin pale, and glistening with a cold sweat.

"I wouldn't do that if I were you," I say. "Handling her. You don't want to devalue your goods."

He doesn't stop; running his hands over Beth, her shoulders, her waist, one hand settling below a breast. Her breathing is shallow and rapid. "The buyer I have in mind for you two won't care." he sneers. "Quite the opposite. He likes to know that you've been brought to heel before he pays."

I force a laugh. "You're nuts. You *really* have no idea who you have there? Whose wife she is? She's worth far more to you for ransom than any third-world hustler's going to give you."

Now I have his attention. "What are you talking about? Who is she then?"

"That's Beth Haswell... Elizabeth Haswell.... *Richard* Haswell's wife...."

He looks at me blankly. "You know.... *Richard Haswell*... Billionaire.... Owns half the fucking city. And that's his wife you're pawing at. He'll pay a fortune to get her back, but he might not be so happy about it if he thinks you've been fingering his property."

He stares down at me, slit-eyed, doubt written large, but I have his attention. "You're lying."

"No, I'm not. Look it up. You should find photos of her on the internet easily enough. Go on; search for images, Richard and Elizabeth Haswell."

He jerks his head at one of the chimps in the background. "Do as she says. Look it up."

The thug taps in on his phone, staring at the screen, gapes and then thrusts the phone at Klempner. He looks at it, looks at Beth, comparing the two.

"Alright. She's worth a lot. That doesn't mean she's not joining in the fun..."

"Haswell is a *billionaire*." I drip contempt from my words. "He likes his goods pristine. If you mess with her, he'll probably not pay as much, or at all."

Klempner sucks in his cheeks. "Yeah.... I'd see it like that too.... Okay. Lock her up again." Then he turns to me. "Now, you...."

Oh, crap....

The group of men closes in on me.

*****

Beth

The door opens, and Charlotte is all but thrown inside, landing hard on the floor. She picks herself up slowly, rubbing her shoulder and hips, where they hit the concrete. Her face is swollen on one side, starting to bruise.

She's badly upset, wringing at her hands.

Her rings are gone....

"Those aren't the clothes or the shoes, you were wearing before," I say.

"No, they're not." and she won't speak after that.

*****

The day fades, and the temperature falls. As I start to shiver in my thin blouse, Charlotte shuffles up close to me, wrapping an arm around my shoulders. She rubs my arms, as though trying to warm me, but then starts talking, very quietly.

"They're taking us out of here, Beth, to the buyer they've got for us. We've only got one chance. Between being taken out of the building, and them getting us back into that truck, we have to *run*."

Nausea rises in the back of my throat. "A buyer?"

"Mmm... yes. Although I'm not sure he's so keen to sell *you*, now that I've told him you can be ransomed. But I don't know. He seems hell-bent on revenge on me, and I think he's got you wrapped up with me in his head. Either way, we have to get away from here...."

"But where? There's nowhere to go...."

"It doesn't matter Beth. Trust me on this. We just have to get *away*. When I say, you run, as fast as you can, with me. Now *shush* before they hear us."

*****

Charlotte

The door slams open, and the guard puts a tray on the floor: water, bread and what might be cheese. I don't fancy it much with the flies thronging around it.

"Hey, can I have my old shoes back?" I ask. "These hurt my feet."

The guard looks at me askance.

"They're just shoes," I say. "Check them out if you want to. If you're trying to sell me, it's not going to improve my price if I'm limping, is it?"

He looks back to where I see Klempner in the other room. He pauses, nods, and head-points the guard at my old clothes.

The guard picks out my trainers, feeling his way carefully through them for anything that doesn't belong there, and finding nothing because there is nothing *to* find. With a grunt, he tosses them to me in our jail and bangs the door closed again.

I sit and put on my own shoes, then, trying to be casual, pass the pair I had been wearing to Beth. "Here, change out those court shoes. I can see from here they're rubbing you sore, and the heels must be killing you by now."

She doesn't get it and for a moment starts to demur, but I widen my eyes at her, hoping she gets the message.

Saying nothing, she changes out of her high heeled fashion shoes. "Better bring those with you when we go," I say, raising my voice for the benefit of our captors. "No doubt they'll want us both to look our best."

*****

Keys rattle in the lock and the door opens again.

Speaking as quietly as I can, "This is our chance, Beth. We might not get another. Pretend to be really frightened, and do exactly as they say until...."

She nods, visibly gulping, fear raw on her face. "Pretend?" she murmurs

One of Klempner's apes, holding a gun on us, barks, "Out...."

Making a show of eye-rolling obedience, I stand. Beth joins me, and I hold her hand as we are herded out to the main room. The windows are dark, and I try to remember if there is a moon tonight.

Klempner grins at me, the smile not reaching his eyes. "Don't worry. We'll have our party later. I'm looking forward to it."

I drop my head, looking at the floor, trying to appear submissive. The worm of fear coiled in my gut tries to unravel, but I push it firmly down. This is no time for panic. A wrong move could cost both my life and Beth's.

Outside, the air is sweet with rain and, although the night is chill, the forest breathes fresh around us, the peaty scent of soil and damp leaves. Overcast, the night is a velvet deep, and the trees, a drift of welcoming shadows.

Still holding Beth's hand, I wait meekly, as one guard opens the back of the truck, another standing beside us, gun held loosely, not really paying attention. Looking briefly back inside, the interior brightly lit, all the others are doing one thing or another; packing up to leave, all distracted.... I turn quickly away, not wanting to destroy my night vision.

With a squeeze of my hand, I give Beth a half-second forewarning, then with my free hand, sweep the gun hand of the guard up and aside.

And, towing Beth behind me, I *run*....

The two guards who accompanied us out, yell an alarm, and there is shouting and cursing behind us.

"Where are we going?" gasps Beth behind me.

"It doesn't matter," I yell back. "Just away."

The two are right behind us as hand-in-hand, Beth and I run helter-skelter into the night.

*****

Michael

We sit, parked up by a diner, James with his eyes fixed on his laptop screen. I stare into space. He glances up at me.

"What are you thinking about?"

"What do you imagine?"

"Well, of course, Charlotte. Something specific?"

I stare up into the car roof for a moment, caught between embarrassment, the knowledge that Richard is seated right behind us, and the need to unload some stress.

"I was thinking about that noise she makes. You know the one, when she's good and aroused, getting close to coming, sort of a cross between a moan and a wail..."

His face twitches and he looks away. "Yeah... it's a good sound isn't it...."

"Shall we move on? See if a different area gives us a signal?"

"Yes, I think so."

*****

Beth

I can't believe it, but we have left our pursuers behind us under the trees. We are in the parking lot of a diner, closed now for the night, but just off the main highway. The forest closes behind us, but ahead, dissolves away to more open ground. In the night, I cannot make out any detail.

Bending over, clutching my sides against a stitch, I heave in great lungfuls of air.

"Don't relax too much," says Charlotte. "We're not stopping here. It's the first place they'll look, a parking lot like this. If we follow the highway, we'll make best speed. We can hide off-road if we need to."

She's bending over into a trash bin.

"Charlotte, what are you doing?"

"Looking for something to eat."

"Eat? Out of the trash bin?"

"It'll be okay. These places always empty the bins overnight, so this'll be today's. So long as it's still in the box so the flies can't get at it, it's fine. And you'd be surprised what people throw away...."

Appalled, but fascinated, I watch her; this girl, apparently so like me. But right now, she feels alien, as the depth of the differences between us comes home to me. "How do you know this stuff?"

Still searching through the bin, she says "When I was a kid, trying to run from the home, the first couple of times, I got picked up by the police when I was caught shoplifting for food. After that, I found other ways to eat...."

She roots among cardboard and greasy papers, then emerges with a box. "See, here you are. There's most of a meal in here. It's cold, but it will keep us going."

"I don't think I can."

"Do want to eat or not?"

"Is it good?"

"No, it's lousy. I hate junk food, but we've got to have something inside us. Your body can't run on empty."

Reluctantly, I reach into the box; deep fried chicken. I bite in, fighting my instinct to gag. She's right; the food is perfectly edible, but I'm eating *trash* and my stomach heaves at the thought.

There is a distant rumbling, the sound of car engines. "Come on," she says, grabbing my arm again. "Time to go."

*****

Michael

James jerks bolt upright, "There's the signal again! It's only a mile or so away, on the road, back the way we came."

My foot to the floor, I make a screeching turnaround, then accelerate, engine screaming, following the trace.

In under a minute, cornering, the headlights swing onto two figures, running ahead, one lagging behind the other, being dragged behind by the arm.

"Look there... running.... It's them, *both* of them, Beth and Charlotte...."

Drawing closer, the one to the fore - it's Charlotte, still racing away - twists her head around, red hair flying... She U-turns, now running away from us, still towing Beth behind her. Beth staggers and trails, but Charlotte pulls her along, gripping her by the wrist.

"Fuck! They don't realise it's us."

"Beth! Charlotte!" Richard hangs out of the window, shouting and waving. "It's us...."

Charlotte, her face swinging round again, slows, turns, still dragging the weary Beth behind her, and now running towards us. She's yelling something, gesticulating wildly with her free hand, trying to tell us something, but....

Headlights swing from the side and front. A car screeches in from the opposite direction, moving directly towards them, and a second drives in from off-road. Charlotte, head twisting, looks from one side to another; for the shortest of moments, indecisive.

Slamming on the accelerator, foot hard down, wheels squealing, I speed towards the two fleeing women.

The car coming in from the side will reach them before we can. The other may do so. Charlotte suddenly breaks loose from Beth, pushing her towards us, waving her arms and yelling instructions.

The two women split, going in different directions, Beth hobbling towards us, Charlotte dashing into the off-road darkness. One car swerves to follow her, the other keeps coming towards us and the frantically running Beth.

James pushes his laptop aside. "Shit! We can't follow both."

"Neither can they…" I concentrate on my driving, closing in on Beth.

Richard is still hanging out of the window, calling to his wife.

"Get ready to pull her in," I yell at James and Richard

"Richard!" Beth's voice is desperate, her face visibly tear-streaked even in the weird headlamp-lit darkness.

At the last moment, I brake hard, metal shrieking, gravel thrown up from the tyres. "Get her in!"

Richard slams open the door, reaching for her. The car is still moving, the on-coming vehicle screaming down on us. As Richard pulls Beth bodily into the car, lifting her off her feet, shots fire, the dust jumping by the wheels.

"They're going for the tyres…"

I slam onto the gas, and the car pulls away, slamming us back in our seats.

Charlotte…

I accelerate into the off-road darkness, scanning for her running figure, but there is no sign of her, and now shots are coming at us from two vehicles.

Driving crazily through the dark in pursuit of Charlotte, swinging the car from side to side as I go, so that the headlights have a chance of catching her, we give chase, but there is nothing. In the night, hiding, she could be anywhere; behind a tree, or a rock, or simply flat to the ground looking away from the light. The sound of gunshots follows us, bullets skittering from the ground.

James sounds sick. "We can't stay. If we lose a tyre, we've all had it, and we'll be no use to her then."

Incredulously, "You're saying we should go? If they catch her again, what do you think are her chances of escaping a second time?"

"We've got Beth. Let's get her to safety. We'll come back. How far away can she be? And if we come in daylight, with the police, perhaps she'll see it's us and come out of hiding."

"Can you navigate me to a road?" In the darkness, on the broken ground and trying to outrun our pursuers, I have no idea where we are, or where anything else is.

Richard is on the phone, talking urgently to someone. Tapping off, he says "I've spoken to Will. He's going to saturate the area with patrol cars. If we can get back to the highway, we'll have company very quickly."

"And perhaps Charlotte will break cover then," adds Beth.

"We're only a minute or so off the main road," says James, pointing. "That way, if you can."

Still being tailed, it's not easy to turn, but as we approach the highway, already, blue lights flash, uncanny in the black night, and our pursuers drop back. Some of the blue flashing cars pursue them into the darkness.

Surrounded by police vehicles, I slow down, pulling up on the verge. James is peering at his computer screen again. He sighs. "We're down to just the one tracer and it's travelling with us." He turns to the back seat, where Richard is cradling his violently trembling wife. "Beth, where have you got it?"

"Sorry, James. I'm not with you."

"We found you because Charlotte planted tracers on herself and her car. She didn't tell you?"

Beth shakes her head dumbly, eyes wide. "She set herself up? To find me?"

James' skin is pallid, his speech slow. "She started with seven trackers. There's only one left, and it's here in the car. It's got to be on you. Did Charlotte give you anything?"

"Um, yes, a couple of hair combs. There were lice in the room they were holding us in."

James and I meet eyes for a second. "I'm sure she found that convenient," he says. "May I see the combs please, Beth."

She removes them from her hair, which drops down in plaits, passing the combs to James.

He examines them closely, using the light from his mobile to examine them. They are standard enough fare; cheap plastic hair combs, set with fake plastic gems, of the kind that can be bought in any market or budget goods store for a few coppers. "Mmm.... she did a good job of disguising the tracer, at least to the casual eye. She replaced one of these pewter type gems with the tracer; slotted it into the socket. No-one would notice it on a casual inspection."

"Beth," I ask. "was she wearing a necklace when you saw her? With a locket? The kind you can put a photo in?"

"She was when they first brought her in, but when they made her change all her clothes, they took it off her."

"Changed her clothes? Was that before or after she gave you the combs?"

"Some time later."

"It looks as though they caught on that she had the tracers, but didn't realise that she'd already planted one on you."

"What now?" asks Richard. "I'd like to get Beth home."

"Perhaps one of the police cars?" I suggest. "Now that Charlotte knows we're here, and the police too, maybe she'll show up."

Richard vanishes with Beth, all but holding her upright as she sags into his arms.

Will Stanton leans in through the window. "You two happy to stay here, visible? I've got patrols out there, looking for her. I think it's best if *you* are where she can see you easily."

James and I wait....

And wait...

And Charlotte does not appear. Neither of us wants to suggest the obvious.

Eventually, my gut grinding, "Perhaps they caught her again."

James nods, looking down, fingers pressing the bridge of his nose. "Perhaps."

"Let's stay until daylight," I suggest. "If she is out there somewhere, and can definitely see that it's us...."

But as the sun rises, and the long morning light draws fingers over the wild land, there is still no sign of her.

Neither of us has slept, so Will assigns an officer to drive us back to the City. Richard is there, waiting, his jubilation over Beth's return over-shadowed by the loss of Charlotte. "You two need to sleep. I'll make sure that the phones are manned, and, you never know, so I'll keep someone watching the tracer sites."

As I collapse into a troubled sleep, my dreams are haunted by visions of my wild, green-eyed red-headed beauty....

.... James and I, ready to make love with her, her smile bright as she sees us, there to fuck her. She lies back, writhing and stretching while she stares up at us, parting her legs in invitation....

.... I hold her tightly in front of me, my arms hocked under hers, tensioning her for him. Her body strains as I pin her tightly, and he pushes her thighs apart to plant his mouth over her sweet pussy.... I watch as he laps at her, his tongue wiping through her folds as she runs hot and wet, her juices flowing as her arousal builds. Her body shivers against mine, and in the mirrors, she watches me behind her, her eyes wide and dark as orgasm claims her....

.... she wails and howls in climax, never holding back, simply riding the wave as she bucks and jerks against me....

.... her wicked smile, and her eyes, as her lips wrap around my shaft, working me with her tongue until I spill into her mouth....

.... her smile as, poised over her, I push at her with my cock, teasing her cunt. I hear her gasp, feel her clench around me as I ease inwards....

.... running in the headlights, fleeing from me, thinking I am her enemy...

I love you.

And you left me....

*****

Three days go by. We hear nothing.

James and I return to the area, still searching. The police report finding a small building in the woods, a couple of miles from where we first saw the running women, but it is deserted.

*****

James' phone rings. He glances at the screen, frowning at an unfamiliar number. "Hello? Yes, I'm James Alexanders."

A voice blarts at him over the line. James' eyes widen, and he waves me over.

"A red-head?" he asks....... "Yes, give her whatever she wants. Is she there? Can I speak to her? What? Fuck! No, *don't* hang up. I'll get you the card details.... Hold on...."

He waves towards his jacket, hung over a chair. "Michael. My wallet...."

Light-headed with relief, I listen in.

James reads out credit card details, pauses, then, "No, it's not a joke. She'll come back. Whatever she was asking for, *get it* and make it ready for use. I want you to put a SIM card in there, on an unlimited usage contract. You can charge it to this card. And get the battery charged up fully. I want the phone to be ready for her when she comes back. And she *will* come back. .... I don't *care*. Use the battery from your own phone if necessary. Charge me for it. But have that mobile *ready* for her to use, as soon as she has it. Did she ask for anything else? Apart from the phone....?"

He taps off the connection. "That was Domestic Electrics in Barnbridge. Charlotte's in there trying to buy a smartphone, and an expensive data package with it. Also, LED flashlights and batteries. The assistant said she kept looking over her shoulder and then disappeared."

I find myself taking deep breaths, trying to clear my head. James, concern in his eyes, slaps me on the shoulder. "Calm down. She's good. And she's operating."

I nod. "Barnbridge? That's, what? Ten miles from where we lost her? But it must be fifty miles away from here. We can only hope she does go back to that shop."

"If she doesn't return there, she'll try somewhere else. Keep your phone handy. Think we should set off for Barnbridge?"

I ponder for a moment. "Let's give it a few minutes. Why does she want a data package? She's still up to something."

Fifteen minutes later, both my phone and James' *ping* with an incoming message.

"I'm coming. Don't tell ANYONE but Richard. DO NOT tell Will Stanton or police. They have an informer. Beth back safe?"

I tap a reply.

"Yes, Beth here safe. r u ok? Where r u? We'll come 4 u"

"NO. Ur being watched. I'm coming to u at Hswl bldg. Yes am ok. Will msg when I can. Might take couple days. Gotta stay under cover. Love u both. Sorry disobeyed you."

"Watched? Who by?"

But there are no more replies.

We stand in awkward silence. "I'm beginning to understand why she got so frustrated at being locked up, not able to do anything...." says James eventually.

"Hang on to that thought."

*****

A few hours later, we both receive a single short message.

"On my way"

Then nothing for a full day, until:

"Almost there."

And again, nothing else for some time.

And we wait.... endlessly....

*****

Two days later, the alarms go off. Richard glances up and around "What the hell...? Francis, is there a fire drill going on they've not told me about?"

"No, not today Mr Haswell. I'm just calling Security now... They're reporting some kind of disturbance in the basement levels...."

"Well, get them to shut off that racket!"

The alarms die down. "Um, what were we talking about? Oh, yes, how Charlotte is returning. So, she's not told you any details at all?

Just a couple of one-line messages to say she's alright and still on her way?"

James is pacing up and down the room. Patience is not one of his virtues, and my own is wearing thin. We are both stretched to breaking point. "All we know," he says, "Is that she wanted a top-end smartphone and flashlights...."

"She planned to travel in the dark?"

Francis pokes her head through the door, streaming tears of laughter. For the first time in days, I'm looking at someone with real joy in their eyes.

"Er, you'd better all get down to the parking level. You're wanted there...."

*****

A blue boiler-suited plumber levers up a manhole cover with a crowbar. Heaving and puffing, he rolls it to one side. "Not had to go down here for years..." he comments, then, grinning, reaches down with an extended hand. "Come on, Love. Y'know there's a reason they call these *man*holes. Usually, women aren't interested in wading through three feet of shite.

He heaves, and up comes Charlotte, filthy, her hair hanging in stinking rats' tails around her, and coated in God-knows-what over half her body.

She stands there, breathing heavily, staring at her hands. "Oh.... *that* was fuckin' awful." Then she spies me, James and Richard. "Um, hi Guys. Sorry it took a while. The plans I had didn't quite match the reality down there, and I had to make some diversions. Got lost for a bit. Er.... I know you're going to bawl me out, but can I have a bath first? I had to come through the sewers part of the way, and there were places I had to wade...."

James walks up to her, arms outstretched. She grins, all white teeth under the filth, but apology in her voice. "For God's sake, don't try to *touch* me...." Then she pauses. "Beth's okay? Yes?"

Richard beams at her. "Beth's fine. Thank you, Charlotte."

*****

In the apartment, Charlotte charges straight into the bathroom, strips off, dropping her clothes to the floor as she vanishes into the shower. The clothes are disgusting. I scoop them into a plastic waste bag and dump the lot, hovering over the laundry chute, before settling for the garbage. She herself, even under the clothes, is filthy.

In the lounge, James and I wait together. "What's our line?" he says quietly. "How mad at her are we?"

How do I answer that?

The woman I love abandoned me and left me numb with fear for her....

"Hugs first," I say. "Mad later.... Mmmm.... I'm just going to take a look at her, now the worst of the dirt should be off. See what state she's in."

With the shower running, dousing herself from the head downwards, facing up into the water stream, she doesn't hear me enter. On her arms and shoulders, down her thighs, all over her body, she is covered with bruises, just fading to blue and purple. And clean, her face shows more bruising; over one cheek and eye.

Her shower has the look of ritual. She is cleaning off more than honest dirt.

"How did you get those?" I ask, nodding at the blue markings over her.

She startles, spinning to face me, then, for the first time since the day I met her, seems bothered by her nudity. She looks down, not speaking, wringing her hands together, looking down, trying to cover herself.

"Charlotte..."

She bursts into tears. I step into the shower with her, still fully clothed, wrapping my arms around her.

"I'm sorry. I'm sorry...." she cries.

I rock her in my arms. "Shhh.... It's alright. You're safe now. And so's Beth."

James appears at the door. I meet his eyes, head-pointing down her body at the bruises. A rainbow of emotions crosses his face: anger, pity, sympathy, horror... "I'll get a medic here," he says and vanishes back into the lounge.

He returns five minutes later. "Doctor's coming."

Charlotte is still weeping uncontrollably. "I'm a bit wet," I say. "Here, you take her. Get her into bed." I pass her to James, who enfolds her in a large towel, then carries her out. Stripping off my soaked clothes, I go in search of dry ones.

I find the two of them in the bedroom, James rocking her in his arms, kissing her wet hair. After a few minutes, her breathing steadies and she falls asleep, her head resting against his chest. Laying her back against the pillow, he pulls the covers over her.

We sit in the lounge but keep the bedroom door open a little.

"What do you think?" he asks. "Just beaten? Or raped too?"

"Raped too, I think. When I went in there, she tried to cover herself from me."

He snorts, a sound of bitter laughter. "What could possibly be funny?" I ask.

"She's gone out, against every protest and effort to stop her. She's achieved what she set out to do; Beth is back with Richard. She's certainly been beaten, perhaps raped. She got home, God alone knows how.... That's obviously what all her interest in the City plans was about, so she anticipated *that* too.... She's pulled up out of the sewers.... and *now* she cries..." He sweeps his hands back through his hair, his expression helpless.

"Did you ask for a female doctor?"

He nods. Mmm, yes."

There is a knock on the door. "Ah, that should be her." But instead, it's Richard, with Beth.

They stand, wreathed in smiles until they see our expressions.

"James? Michael? Is everything alright?"

"She's been beaten. She's covered in bruises. And we think she's been raped."

Beth brushes past us. "Here, let me talk with her.. ."

She returns after a few minutes, patting both me and James on the arm. "She hasn't been raped. But she is pretty much at the end of her resources. She's been running for days. She was beaten while we were held, and she took some more damage while she was running, and..." She gives James a long look. "She thinks you're going to punish her. She really isn't in any state for that right now."

He stares down at her, his expression blank.

"James isn't going to punish her," I say. James swings to face me, arms akimbo. "Are you?"

For a moment, I think we are going to argue over this, then his eyes soften. "No, she's been through enough. Perhaps it will have taught her a lesson."

"That, I doubt," I say. "Let me handle it.... when she's ready."

Beth nods. "Right now, I'd say that what she needs is the pair of you, and to sleep."

Richard stands. "We'll come back later. Give me a buzz, James, when you think she's ready to talk."

As Beth and Richard leave, James eye-points the bedroom. "'Hugs, then?"

As we enter, Charlotte is sitting in bed, finger-combing wet hair. She looks up at us, then looks away. "Are you very angry with me?"

James sits beside her, kisses her on the cheek. "Yes we are, but that doesn't mean we're not happy to have you back."

I can't quite bring myself to touch her, instead standing, watching her, my arms folded. She looks up at me, then drops her gaze. "I'm sorry," she mutters.

I nod, lost for words. "I'll leave you with James, eh." And I go in search of the wine bottle.

*****

Charlotte

I wake to find my Master sitting beside me in an armchair, long legs stretched out, working on his laptop. As I stir, he looks up and smiles.

"Hello. How are you now? Did you sleep well?"

"Do logs sleep? Yes, very well. How long was I....?"

"About ten hours. You were exhausted."

"Yeah... I'd not slept properly for a few days. I didn't dare sleep above ground in case they found me. And I didn't dare below ground either...."

"Why not below ground?"

"Rats. Hundreds of 'em. Not sure what they'd do with a sleeping human body, but you read stories...."

He says nothing, just looking at me. I can't gauge his mood, his expression. "What is it?" I ask.

His head tilts, but his eyes are soft. I don't think he is angry with me. Then he stares up at the ceiling. "Where do I begin?" His voice is almost a sigh.

"Are going to punish me? If you are, I'd rather just get it over and done with...."

He gives me a long look. "Believe me, it came up in conversation. What you did was brave and noble on the one hand, but reckless and inconsiderate on the other. Michael was beside himself, especially when we lost your signal. Even Richard was upset. He thought that we'd lost both you and Beth. And no, I'm not going to punish you. Looking at the physical state of you, I don't think it's appropriate. However, I believe Michael has something he wants to say to you."

"Oh...."

"Yes, 'Oh'...."

"Where is Michael?"

"I'm not sure. I believe he wanted some time to think. He's pretty unhappy right now about the way you behaved."

"But Master, there was no other way we were going to get her back. The police had no idea where...."

He eyes me. "Are you going to tell me where you got all that bruising?"

"Um, different places...."

"You've been beaten?"

"Yes, some, but it wasn't too bad. I thought it would be worse...." His eyes widen, but he says nothing. "Some of the damage, I took while I was running. It was dark, and I was just going pell-mell; couldn't see where I was heading, just *away*. I kept crashing into things, trees, rocks; I tripped and fell a couple of times. Then in the sewers, there was a spot; I had to cross the stream. I was trying not to have to wade, so I jumped instead. But it was slippery. I lost my footing, fell in, banged my head.... that was the *worst*...."

Still, he looks down at me, dark-eyed. After a moment, "*Was* that the worst?"

A bit disconcerted, "Um, yes. Not sure what you mean?"

He speaks quietly. "Beth thought you'd been raped? Michael too. But then you told Beth, no."

"Raped? No..." Suddenly it makes sense, his attitude, his quietness. "No, Master. I've not been raped.... Um... I'll admit it came close. for a while, I thought...."

"But Charlotte, Michael said that when he saw you in the shower, you tried to.... cover up. That's why he thought..."

"Master, look at me. I'm black and blue. I didn't want him seeing me like that... and... and..."

"And what?"

"They took my rings, Master. The ones you and Michael gave me. They *took* them."

Suddenly everything wells up in me, and the tears come again, but now he sits beside me on the bed, wrapping his arms around me, kissing my hair. "Shhh... It's alright. It doesn't matter. They're only rings, bits of metal. We'll get you new ones...."

"But they're *not* just bits of metal, Master... they're special... and they took them..."

He chuckles as he holds me. "Every time I think I've got the hang of women, I discover I'm still on Mars and they're on Venus... Charlotte.... The rings are *symbols*... That's all. If you come out of what you did with no more damage than that, you should be thankful, not crying... Now... just calm down. We can talk about things properly when you're ready."

All I want is to stay there, in my Master's arms, letting him rock me, but, "I'd like to do that Master, but there's things I need to tell you.... and Michael and Richard..."

"Yes, I know. There are things I want to ask you, but we can spare a few minutes." He holds me close, and I relax into the warmth of him, breathing in his wonderful perfume, musky and male.

After a little while he says, "Do you want to make love?"

"I'd like that, but...."

"But....?"

"Um, you'll need to...." I'm not sure how to put this. I have never had to ask it before.

He takes me by the shoulders, looking into my face. "Charlotte, what is it? Talk to me."

My face heating, "You'll need to use a condom, Master. I've not been able to take my pill for the last few days...."

"Ah.... Yes, of course.... I'd become used to the luxury of not having to worry about that with you." He kisses me on the top of my head. "Wait there. I'll be right back."

He returns five minutes later. "There are vending machines in the public bathrooms downstairs." He sits beside me again on the bed, pulls a small foil packet from his pocket, placing it on the side table. His fingers running down the side of my face, "You *are* alright?"

"Yes, Master. I'm alright, just very tired. You don't have to keep asking."

He pulls the sheets from me, eyeing my bruised body. "Actually, I do. You might try to brush off what's happened to you, but no-one gets into that condition without paying a price for it."

Abashed I look away, not wanting to meet his gaze, but he pulls me into his embrace. "Shhh..."

As I sit up into his arms, he kisses my mouth, softly, stroking my hair, then traces his lips down to my shoulders, and around to the hollow of my neck. The scent of him drifts over me and I sigh, not exactly aroused, more enraptured, by my Master's lovemaking. I want nothing more than to lie with him, close, my skin on his.

He cups my breast, his eyes drifting over a bruise which, starting on my chest, draws livid colour over the skin of the breast. As he stoops to suckle at a nipple, I see his eyes close. He does not want to look at me like this.

Standing, he unbuttons his shirt, stripping off his clothes. Unusually, he is not yet erect, his cock lying quiescent. But he slips between the sheets with me, pulling me down to lie with him, his arms encircling me again.

He begins to kiss me in earnest, almost with desperation. His fingers clinging into me, nails biting in, he pulls me in close at the hip, squeezing against me. And now his erection rises, hard against my thigh. His hand pressed, palm hard against my stomach, I part my legs, allowing him in. He strokes my belly, the soft skin of my thighs, his breath juddering and shaking.

For a moment he pauses, his forehead resting against mine.

"Master? Are you alright?"

His voice is thick. "When your signal vanished Charlotte, we thought we'd lost you. That was a hard moment. You must never, ever, do anything like that to me, to us, again."

"I won't, Master. You have my promise. I've done what I had to."

He raises himself on an elbow, looking down at me. "Had to?"

"I had to get Beth back, Master. No-one else could have done it. and...." I hesitate, knowing how this is going to sound...

"And..."

"I couldn't leave Richard like that. He loves her. And I owed him so much..."

"Richard? You did all that for Richard? Not Beth?"

"Well, it was sort of for Beth, but mainly for Richard.... I owed him," I repeat.

He rolls his eyes skyward. "Charlotte, what the hell am I supposed to think when you say something like that? Do you have any other perceived 'debts' you feel you need to repay?"

"No, Master. I've said. You have my promise. I'll not do anything else like that. Truly."

He says nothing, simply nodding, then stoops to kiss me again. "Lie back," he whispers.

Lying beside him, I tremble at his touch. He kisses me again, softly, sensually on the lips, then, "I understand that you did what you did for good reason. Sometimes life gives us only bad choices, and you had to choose."

"Are you still angry with me?"

"I was, but not now. I'm proud of you."

"Proud?"

"Yes, very proud." He slants his mouth to mine, our lips meeting as his hand moves over me.

"And Michael?"

"I'll talk with him. He's as pleased as I am that we have you back, more or less safe and sound, but he is still badly upset."

"He's very angry with me?"

"I'm not sure, but I think you can expect some hard talking from him."

He nuzzles at a breast again, taking a nipple between his lips. I find my breath holding, only releasing as he mouths at the nipple, chuckling softly as I react to him; a small gasp as pleasure takes me, his touch slight, but exquisite.

Fingers splayed, he teases open my folds, sliding over and around my clit. My breath hitches as he works my nub, and his dark eyes crinkle at the corners. Thumbing back the hood, he fingers my exposed clit, rolling circles around it, looking pleased as I begin to whimper. I want to stroke him, to fondle his cock which presses against me, but as I move, "No. Just lie back. I'm going to get inside you now."

He reaches for the foil packet, rolling his eyes again as he tears it open. "Always detested these things," he mutters.

"Sorry, Master."

He kisses me again. "Nothing to apologise for. I'm glad you thought to mention it."

Rolling above me, his lean, sinewy body, keenly muscled, atop mine, his body heat seeps into me. He pushes down, his knees between my thighs, spreading me wide, then teasing at my entrance, rubbing against me, not entering.

His face beside mine, his breathing is warm and heavy. Twining my fingers into his hair, my face reaching for his, our lips meet in a soft, drawn-out touch, our mouths caressing.

"Please, Master. I want you inside me."

He lifts himself a little, looking down at my face, his eyes locking with mine as, with his odd non-smile, he repositions himself, then penetrates me, slowly easing inside me, his cock hard against my softness. His hand cupping the side of my face, he glides smoothly inside me, barely thrusting, simply working me within. His gentle love-making calms me, and I think, calms him.

"Are you going to come?" he murmurs.

"I don't think so, Master. But that's alright, I just wanted to be with you."

Our gazes locked, neither of us looking away, we move together.

"Master?"

"Mmm?"

"All the time I was.... away.... I was thinking about you... the two of you. I was doing what I had to, but all I wanted was to get back to you and Michael."

"It's alright. I know." And he stoops to take my mouth in his.

I wrap my arms around his shoulders, holding him close to me, breathing him in, the taste of him on my lips. After only a moment or so, he shudders, letting out a gasp and a sigh. "Charlotte...."

"Master...."

*****

Richard sits with Beth, across the table from me, his eyes glancing across at Michael and my Master. My Master looks relaxed, almost happy. Michael is distant, cool, and has barely spoken to me.

Richard's gaze on me is warm. "Charlotte, um, I know you have issues with James and Michael here, over what you did. And I can understand that entirely. But for myself, I am grateful beyond words for what you did. I'll not forget it."

I nod as Richard pauses, letting his words sink in, then, "If you're feeling up to it now, can you tell us more about what happened?"

My Master speaks. "Charlotte, you said there were some things you need to tell us? And we all need to know why you didn't want us to speak to the police. Richard here wasn't very happy when I told him that he couldn't discuss with Will Stanton what was happening..."

"I'm sorry about that, but Klempner knew too many things that he shouldn't have..."

Richard interrupts. "Klempner? Who's Klempner?"

"Lawrence Klempner. There were others there, but he was in charge, when Beth and I were captured. I recognised him from Blessingmoors. He would visit sometimes, looking over the older kids, pointing out the ones he thought were interesting..." My throat seizes up as I struggle with my next words.

Michael passes me a glass of water. "Take your time, Charlotte."

I gulp down the water. "He said he wouldn't have known me from the home, but...." Again, my voice dries up and I gulp more water. "He said he recognised me because I look like my mother."

My Master and Michael look shocked. Richard keeps his face neutral. "Anything else?"

Do I tell them this?

Yes, I must...

"He said.... he said that he... he ran her with the other whores, and that it must run in the family because I'd sold myself, and now I live with two men.... He holds some grudge against me. He said it was because of Jenkins, the man that died when he chased me, but it felt like there was more to it than that..."

Richard keeps his face bland. "That must have been... upsetting... for you."

"Yes, but *how* did he know about the auction? And James and Michael? The only people who know things like that are either us or the police. *They* have my records.... And then later, he got a phone call..."

I finish off my water. "I'm sorry, but could I have a glass of wine, please. This.... isn't very easy..."

Michael vanishes into the kitchen, returning with a bottle and five glasses. He fills all five, but I notice that I am the only one drinking. I knock back a couple of mouthfuls, then continue. "I persuaded him to leave Beth alone...." I look at Beth and she nods confirmation.

"Yes, Elizabeth told me about that," says Richard. "You convinced them she was worth more for ransom if they didn't touch her...."

I blush, embarrassed. "Sorry about that. It seemed the best thing to say..."

"No apology needed, Charlotte. But they then put her in a separate room and she thought that...." He vacillates, losing his words.

What did Beth tell him?

"I thought I was in trouble then, that they were going to gang-rape me," I say. "They started knocking me about a bit.... that's where I got some of the bruises.... but Klempner said he had a buyer for me. For Beth too, though I'm not sure he wanted to sell her after what I'd told him about who she is. At any rate, I don't think they wanted to leave too many visible marks on me if the buyer was going to be seeing me...." I gulp more wine.

"Anyway, Klempner's phone rang. It was weird. He listened for a minute to whoever was on the other end, then he looked like he'd seen a ghost. He hit me across the face, knocked me down, and told me he knew about the tracers. He told the others to find some different clothes for me 'cause the ones I was wearing had to go. He took the locket that had one of the tracers.... and my rings.... Then he.... he told me to.... um, empty my body cavities... or he would do it for me...."

"You had a tracer.... inside you?" Richard's face is twitching. Michael looks at me askance. My Master stares at the ceiling, struggling not to smile.

"Mmm. Yes, inside a condom to keep it dry... Um.... it's a bit embarrassing, now I tell someone else.... Actually the whole changing clothes thing solved my biggest problem..."

"Which was?"

"Beth's shoes. She was kidnapped while she was out shopping, and she was wearing high heels. I knew we'd have to run to escape, and there was no way she could run in those, but when they gave me fresh clothes, it meant there was an extra pair of shoes."

"And by then you'd already planted one of the trackers on Beth?" interrupts my Master.

"That's right. Anyway, when Klempner knew about the trackers, they decided to move out immediately. I'd already warned Beth that we needed to run when they took us out of the building. If we could get out into the open, so the tracer on her could operate properly, you'd be able to find us again. I told her to behave very meek and mild, so that they'd let their guard down and we'd have the best chance to escape."

Richard interrupts. "So, this phone call to Klempner..."

"It could only have been from someone in the police, or someone getting the information from the police. Who else would know?

"Who indeed?" Richard rubs his nose, looking thoughtful.

"And I heard him giving orders to have this building watched. That's why I didn't want any of you coming out for me, and why I came in the way I did."

"What happened after you and Beth split?" asks my Master. "We picked up Beth almost immediately, but there was no sign of you."

"At first, I just ran, from them, trying to loop back to you, but you were being chased too, and I couldn't catch up. Then, I heard the gunshots. And there were all those police around, and I didn't know who to trust, so I just made my way in the dark back to the main highways, and to the nearest town. I wanted to contact you. That's when I went into that electrical store. I needed the phone so that I could download all those plans I'd scanned, to try to find a way back into the City, and here, without being seen. After that, I just took all the back roads and trails to get to the edge of the City, then went underground as soon as I could."

"How did you do that? What route did you take?" asks Richard.

"I went down through the sewers first to get onto the old Marlepits train line...."

They all look blank.

"It's an old railway track, from when the City was first built, and they needed construction materials. It doesn't operate now, or for any time in the last fifty years, but the tunnels are still there. I just followed the line into the heart of the Old City and then used the sewers again to get under this building.... *achhe*... that was just disgusting..."

After I finish speaking, all three men and Beth sit quietly, watching me. Michael watches me constantly but, unsmiling, there is no welcome in his eyes. And when I think of it, he has barely spoken through the entire discussion.

*****

Michael

Richard talks for some time to Charlotte. And how can I blame him? By any measure, she saved Beth. And Beth is *his*. But Charlotte's success is bitter-sweet for me. Now that we have her back, I find myself dwelling on the sheer abandon of her actions. She left James and I behind, apparently without a thought.

I need to talk with her, and I wait for my moment, for some privacy with her.

Richard leaves with Beth, James joining them to discuss what Charlotte has said, and what to do next.

"Charlotte, while it's just you and me, there's something I need to say to you."

She looks at me, pale-faced, her green eyes vivid. She knows I'm not happy.

"I understand that you did what you did for good reason. Beth's your friend, and you felt you had to help her, but she's not the only person in your life. James and I both made it completely clear that we didn't want you to do anything rash, and you simply ignored our wishes. What you did was horribly unfair to both me and James."

She says nothing, her gaze downcast.

"You and I may not be formally married yet, but you're my wife already in every way that counts.... I'm not going to build my life around a woman who endangers herself so recklessly. And much though I love you, I want you to understand that if you ever do such a thing again, for me, that would be the end of this. Do you understand me?"

She stares at me, all big eyes, tears welling, then looks at the floor again.

"I know that love isn't something you've had much of in your life, but you have it now, and you must understand.... it works two ways...."

She finally speaks. "I didn't think.... Please don't leave me. I couldn't bear it."

"I feel the same way, but that didn't stop *you* leaving *me*, did it? When I'd specifically asked you not to..."

"I didn't leave you. I just..."

"Your plan worked out, but if it had gone wrong, you'd probably be dead now or shipped out to god-knows-where to spend the rest of a short life in sexual slavery - real slavery, not the kinds of games you play with James.... I would never have seen you again. How do you think I felt, sick to the stomach with fear for you? My guts knotting that I might lose you? And then when I saw you in the shower, covered in bruises, thinking you had been raped. You can't treat people who love you like that."

She remains silent once more.

"Do we understand each other?"

She nods.

"I asked you for your promise before, and you wouldn't give it. Now I'm not asking. I am *requiring* your promise; that you won't do anything like that again, no matter how good your reasons seem."

She nods, still silent.

"Do I have that promise?"

She nods again.

"I didn't hear you."

She whispers, "Yes, I promise. I won't do it again."

"Now..." I point to the bedroom. "Strip, and lean over the bed."

She hesitates, brows furrowed.

You don't believe I'm going to do it, do you, Babe?

"Do I have to repeat myself? Strip and bend over. I'll force you if I have to."

Her eyes widen, her face turning even whiter. Without a word, she goes through to the bedroom, undresses and then, trembling, bends over the end of the bed.

"Ass up."

She shifts position, presenting her pale derriere. Normally, in this position her pussy would be glistening with her arousal, but not this time.

She's shaking....

"I didn't want you thinking this is about James and his sex games. That's why I refused to let him do this. I'm the one that is punishing you, and this is the real thing. I hate doing this stuff. You know that. But I'm doing it now because punishment is something you understand."

I strip off my jeans, pulling out the belt as I do so, feeling sick. "I need some relief, so I'm going to fuck you; then I'm going to punish you, and you're going to accept it. Yes?"

Her face side on to the sheets, she nods, her eyes streaming.

"Michael, you need to..."

"I didn't ask you to speak. Just to do as you're told for a fucking change.... Open your legs further."

She obeys, and I test her pussy. She's dry, so I find a pot of lube, work her over inside, and myself. "This is for me, not you, do you understand?"

She nods, silently, again.

She's crying and right now, I don't care. I just want to fuck her. And to make her feel the way I did the last few days, used and unwanted.

I plunge into her and she gasps, her fingers gripping into the bed covers.

Am I hurting her?

But I don't ask, instead, I bang her hard, trying to fuck away the tension inside me. She makes no attempt to either stop me or take the ride with me, just lying there while I pump her.

After only a minute or two, my balls tighten with climax and I ram home as I shoot my load into her, spurting cum and stress into her in equal measure.

As I finish, she tries to rise, but I push her down. "I've not finished. I told you. You get punished next."

"But first I need to..."

I force her back, face down onto the bed, then casting around for something suitable, I spot James' tie. "Put this between your teeth."

White-faced, eyes swollen, she opens her mouth, silently accepting the tie, clamping it between her teeth.

"Are you ready?"

Head pressed down, she nods.

I don't want to draw this out, so I strike at her with the belt, a single blow. She judders, her eyes welling, but I don't believe it is the pain that makes her cry. A second stroke, and her eyes squeeze shut. A third and she whimpers, her breathing turning heavy.

That's enough. I've made my point.

I pull the tie from her mouth. She works her lips, trying to speak.

I lean close over her. "What was that? I couldn't hear it."

Through tears, she speaks. "I'm sorry. I'm sorry."

"Stay there." I fetch a tube of analgesic from the bathroom, apply it to the welts on her rear.

"What's that?" she asks, from her prone position.

"Painkiller."

"What's the point of doing something like that, and then giving me pain-killers?" Her voice is a whisper.

"I wanted to make a point in a way that you *get it*. I don't want you permanently hurt or in pain for too long."

As I finish, she slips off the bed and drops to her knees in front of me. Her voice is choked. "Please don't leave me...."

"Charlotte. Stand up. I don't need you to kneel for me."

She doesn't move. Sighing, I drop down to sit on the floor beside her. "Charlotte, I love you, and believe me, I *never* want to leave you, but you mustn't make life impossible for me. So long as I have your promise that you will never do such a thing again, then we're good. Do I have that promise?"

"Yes."

"Look at me."

Her eyes are red, her cheeks wet as she looks up. I wipe her tear-streaked face and kiss her. "It's done. Come on, dry your eyes. Want to share a bath with me?"

She nods. "Yes, but I need to shower first." She vanishes into the shower room, and a moment later, there is the hiss of running water.

Several minutes later, she is still in there. "Charlotte, are you alright?"

Stupid question.

Did I overdo it? Perhaps.

There is no reply, only the sound of water, so I go in to find her with the showerhead directed inwards between her legs.

"What are you doing?"

"I tried to tell you, but you didn't want to listen. I couldn't take my pill the last few days. You should have used a condom."

Ah, fuck! Of all the times to risk....

Oh God, what have I done to you, Babe?

I don't run the bath too warm, so as not to sting her sore ass. As we step into the foam together, she lies between my legs, her back against my chest so I can hold her in my arms. Her tears have dried, and she seems a little better.

But I feel lousy.

Guilt?

Her chest heaves....

"What?"

"I thought you would never hurt me like that; that it wasn't in you."

"I didn't like doing it. But what about James? You enjoy it when he does it."

"I always knew it was in *his* nature. Right from Day One. And I took it on board when I came back after that first week."

"Then? But he's never hurt you like that, surely? Your first day..."

"Men with wholly sunny dispositions don't go buying virgins at auction."

*****

Charlotte

"How are you feeling now?" asks my Master. "Better now that you've caught up on some sleep?"

"Mmm, yes. Much better thanks."

"Come and sit with me." He holds out a welcoming arm, inviting me to the couch with him.

I join him, trying not to wince as, stiffly, I sit.

"Charlotte. Is something wrong?"

I bite back against the pain. "I'm fine, Master."

He watches me. "No, you're not. What's the matter?"

What do I say?

"Michael.... punished me...."

He stares at me, his expression unbelieving. "*Michael?* Punished you? What did he do?"

I don't know what to say, so I remain silent, trying not to chew my lip.

His faces changes, clouding over. "Stand up. Show me yourself." Still, I hesitate. "Charlotte! Do as I say. I want to see."

I try stagger upright, but my thigh and buttock muscles are bruised and stiff.

My Master stands, helping me up, then lifting my skirt, he pulls away my panties, looking at the raw welts, He draws a long sigh, his body stiffening. "Michael did that?"

"Yes, I did."

Michael leans against the door, arms folded. His stance says aggression, but there is something in his eyes.... Regret? Guilt?

"Charlotte and I had rather a long discussion. I think I've made my point well enough. How are you now?" He addresses the last question to me.

I shrug. "It hurts. What do you expect me to say?"

My Master, his expression furious, steps towards Michael. "I thought we'd agreed...."

"Master. Leave it. It's done."

The two glare at each other, and I know that it's not done.

*****

We sit together in awkward silence. I try to distract myself from the simmering pain in my butt by reading, but I have to do it standing.

Of a sudden, there is rumbling, a crashing sound. The building shakes.

My Master looks up and around. "What the hell was that?"

He and Michael look out of the windows and down, straining to see all angles.

I open my laptop, jabbing at the keyboard. My Master looks down at me, the question is his eyes. "The security cameras," I explain, blushing. I shouldn't be able to access them, but....

Mouth pursing in humour, "Forgiven." he says. "What can you see?"

"Looking now," I say, clicking through screens and cams. Then I freeze at the scene before me:

Gunfire, explosions, men in masks: "The building's under attack!"

His eyes widen. "Come on," he yells to Michael. The two dash from the room, but at the last moment, Michael turns, jabbing a finger at me. "You *stay* here. You understand? No excuses. You stay here. Yes?"

I nod. "Yes."

"If you try to leave, I'll know. The cams out in the hall...."

I bite my lip and nod again. He stares at me for a moment, then exits.

Alone in the apartment, I watch with growing horror at what is unfolding on my laptop screen. Smoke. The ricochet of bullets from walls. Bodies lying on the ground, unmoving.

The door bursts open. It's Beth. "Richard sent me up here. What's happening?"

"The ground floor is taken I think, but...." I peer at the screen....

Oh, crap....

"What?"

"The building's on fire."

*****

Michael

Smoke billowing up the staircase, we race down to the lower floors. Using the lifts is unthinkable.

Alarms are ringing, and there is chaos, as panicked workers try to escape the building.

Up the staircase, coming towards us, are firefighters in full kit and mask.

Shit!

We're on fire?

James sees me looking upwards. "Don't worry. You can be sure she's getting the hell out as fast as she can. She'll not sit helplessly by."

"But she won't..."

He skids to a halt, hovering between one step and the next. "What? Why not?"

Breathing heavily now. "I told her to stay put. And I *made* her promise to obey. I think she'll try to keep the promise..."

James rolls his eyes. "Fuck! What a time to disable her...." He stares at me, hard. "And you accuse *me* of treating her as a sub..." He pats his pockets. "Damn! No phone. Got yours on you?"

"No. I just ran from the apartment. You?"

"So, she's promised to stay put, in a burning building, and we can't contact her?"

"Yes."

Oh God, Babe. What have I done?

James turns heading upwards again, but above us, there is a crashing noise. A few seconds later, we meet a group of the firefighters, descending again. "Get moving downward." yells one of them as he comes past. "The floor above here's on fire. The whole building's coming apart. You can't go that way."

From below there is a rushing sound and the smoke turns black. Coughing, we keep moving downwards.

And will Charlotte try to keep the promise I forced her to make?

The Virgin and the Masters

Part Five

A Continuing Tale of (Ex-)Virgin Erotica, BDSM and Ménage with Two Masters and *More*......

Part Twenty-One Of
The 'Buying the Virgin' Series

Author: Simone Leigh

The Virgin and the Masters
Part Five

Beth

Charlotte dashes to the stairwell, but acrid, black smoke billows up from below. Quickly, she slams the door closed, coughing and spluttering. "No way out that way."

"Down the garbage chute?" I ask. "Like they do in movies?"

She gives me an old-fashioned look. "Not a chance. Too narrow, and it's anyone's guess what we'd land in."

"I don't mind a bit of dirt if it's to escape a fire...."

"How about landing in a compactor, or a waste recycler? You got any idea what's at the bottom?"

"Er... no..."

"Well then.... Having said that.... let's have a look at the laundry chute."

Smoke surges up, flooding the room, a bitter-sweet chemical smell, and she jerks her head backwards, hastily, slamming the hatch closed "Must have taken hold in the dry-cleaning stuff....".

She circles, looking for options, a way to escape. "Jeez..." she mutters, her face white, and for the first time since I have known her, I see real fear in Charlotte.

Her phone rings and she snatches at it.

"It's James," she says with it pressed to her ear. "Yes.... Master, we're trapped.... We can't.... Right? Wonderful! Yes, Beth's with me. Richard sent her up here.... Yes, I will."

She taps off the phone, then yells at me, "Out onto the roof. There's help coming...."

Grabbing a couple of mobiles lying on the desktop, Michael's and James' I assume, she stuffs them in a pocket, and we dash out to the terrace garden. Even as we burst out into the fresh air, a helicopter is descending to us, a harness winching down.

Other choppers are buzzing the higher floors, scanning windows, but there is no-one in view other than ourselves.

Charlotte clips the harness onto me, and immediately I am hoisted away and up. Within a minute, the harness lowers again, and Charlotte too is winched to safety. As she is pulled into the cockpit, the 'copter tilts, turns and sweeps away. "Where are we going?" she yells to the pilot.

He shouts over the engine noise. "Sorry, I was told not to tell you. Mr Haswell's instructions." he shouts back." Just, *away* from the City.".

And below us, a rush of buildings, highways and the river vanish, as we sweep along the coast and off.

*****

Michael

Will Charlotte try to keep the promise I forced her to make?

The Haswell Building on fire and she is trapped in the penthouse apartment. Does she even know yet that she is trapped?

Passing a firefighter, James snags him by the arm. "There's a woman trapped in the Penthouse. We're not sure she even knows yet, that she's trapped..."

The fireman whips out his two-way, talking urgently into it, then clicking it off. "There's helicopters coming in to help on the top floors. Can she get onto the roof?"

"Got a phone on you?"

The firefighter passes a phone to James, who stabs at the screen. Phone pressed to his ear, staring into space, he mutters. "Pick up your phone, Charlotte, pick up your.... *Charlotte*! Where are you? Yes, get the Hell out of there. Get out to the roof terrace. Helicopters are flying in.... What..?"

He glances over at me. "Beth's with her.... Richard sent her up there for safety...." Then, "Yes, we'll catch up with you. If you see mine or Michael's phones, bring them with you."

James and I descend the stairs at speed. At every floor, black smoke surges and curls on to other side of glass plating.

Outside is a chaos of police cars, armed officers, fire engines, medical workers and ambulances, but oddly, very few other people. Will Stanton, the Police Commissioner, is there, shouting instructions. A familiar face in a squad car, Corby, who first bungled the interview with Charlotte, looks to be relaying messages from the car, and a large area is cordoned off, police widening the cordon as we watch. Above us, is the clip-clip of helicopter blades moving in on the upper floors of the office block.

Where are all the people? The office workers.... Trapped?

Richard is here, by Will, phone to his ear. Seeing us, he gestures us over, then waves up at the 'copters. "There's help on the way to the girls. Don't worry."

"Where is everyone?" I ask. "I thought they'd be teeming out..."

Richard almost laughs. "There's almost nobody in there, Michael. With the holiday break, no-one's here."

"Holiday break?"

He stares at me. "It's Christmas Day."

Christmas Day?

With everything that has happened, I'd lost track of the date entirely.

Richard waves over the scene; the tower block, chimneying smoke upwards, the mess of emergency vehicles, the choppers high above us, now lowering winches to the roof-top. "If there's a blessing to be had in all this, it's that we and the women were almost the only people in here. Had it been an apartment block...." He shivers. "As it is, the only real injured party is going to be the insurance company..."

James, scanning the scene, "And the attackers? Where are they?"

Will looks sick. "They seem to have simply faded away. They attacked, did the damage and.... "He holds up his hand helplessly. "I've got units out searching, but there's been a breakdown of the central computer. No-one can coordinate...."

"A convenient time for a failure," comments James. "Sabotage? Hackers?"

"I think so, yes."

"Your spy in the camp again?"

Will nods, lips pressed white.

"Hey!" There's a yell from one of the fire-fighters. "Stretcher-bearers, over here, fast" He waves wildly at the green-uniformed medics waiting by the ambulances. "We've got one of them."

Will comes alive. "I'll be back." Then dashing over to where the fire-fighter is dragging an unconscious man out of the building, yells "Can he speak...?"

*****

He returns, ten minutes later, looking disheartened. Head-pointing us to a quiet spot, "Richard, James, Michael, come with me. Let's get some privacy."

"He's unconscious, suffering from smoke inhalation, but the medics say he should survive. It seems he was trapped in the chaos and didn't get out with the others. I'm having him taken to a secure medical facility and there, as soon as he's fit to speak, he'll be interrogated. I'll keep you informed." He takes a deep breath. "Did you get Charlotte and Beth away safely?"

"Yes." says Richard, "And right now, I and the pilot are the only ones who know where they are. "I've had them taken out of the City and, no offence, Will, but I'm not telling you where to."

Will nods. "I understand. I'll be in touch." Turning, he shouts out, "Corby! I want to know the minute we hear from the hospital...."

*****

Charlotte

We're safe, taken to some spot in the back-of-beyond, and simply delivered. "Mr Haswell said to tell you that the hotel staff are expecting you." says the pilot as he drops me, with Beth, off on a pad, then immediately, rises, wheels and flies off.

The hotel staff are nothing if not courteous, and everything is there, waiting for us. Warm and comfortable, in a lovely suite, with gorgeous views, bathed and fed, and with fresh clothes waiting for us, we could ask nothing more.

I pace up and down, caged again.

How much of my life am I going to have to spend like this?

The door clicks open, swinging back. Standing there are my Master and Michael, and Richard following. He brushes past, wrapping his arms around Beth, taking her into the next room. Doubtless, they would like some privacy.

My Master simply tilts his head at me, soft-eyed. "Hello again."

Michael looks ready to burst into tears. He sweeps forwards, embracing me. "Oh God, Charlotte. You're okay. I'm sorry. I'm sorry." He holds me, rocking me in his arms, his head pushed into my neck. "I shouldn't have said what I did. Please, whatever happens from now on, you must always do what you think is the right thing, whatever the reason. I'll understand. This won't happen again."

His arms are tight around me, his voice hoarse.

Oh, my Golden Angel. Please, don't be so upset....

"Hey, I'm okay." I try to keep my voice bright and uplifting. "It doesn't matter what I promised. You didn't think I was going to hang around when the building was on fire did you?" I laugh. "I was quite sure you didn't intend me to promise to stay and get roasted ..."

His face falls and I wonder if I've said the right thing.

*****

Our stay indefinite, but with no real outlet for the stress of events, the hotel feels like a trap. Michael, normally my rock, my anchor when all else is in turmoil around me, seems to suffer the most.

I'm not sure what his difficulty is, but after our initial meeting, he is distant, not exactly cool but *unengaged*....

Is it that I hurt him? Or that he thinks he hurt me?

He fucked me when I'd missed being able to take my pill for a few days. Perhaps he feels guilty about that? He doesn't need to. Nothing came of it. But I've not found the right moment to reassure him.

I want to put it right. I know that I upset him when I set off, against all his wishes, to find Beth He punished me for it, but we have put that behind us now....

.... haven't we?

*****

Backing me against the wall, my Master leans over me, fixing me with his narrow-eyed gaze, pinning my wrists above my head.

"This has gone on long enough," he says. "I know that you and Michael had issues with each other; he with your behaviour over Beth, you with how he punished you, but both of those are dead and gone. It's time to call it quits."

My voice chokes. "What do I do, Master? He barely looks at me, let alone speaks to me. I've tried to talk with him, but I'm not sure he wants me any more...."

"He does. But he's having trouble dealing with what happened, so *I'm* intervening."

"What do you want me to do, Master? I want things back as they were as well."

"The three of us are going to make love, and fuck together, as we always have done. I want to see *you* with that wide-eyed look you give him when he pushes his cock in your mouth. And I want to see *him* with that glazed expression he has when he watches you come."

I'd love that....

"I'd like that too, Master."

His eyes soften. "I'm glad to hear it. Now, go wait in the bedroom. I'll find Michael."

"No need. I'm here. And yes, that.... sounds good...."

Michael leans against the door, looking in at us, blinking a bit. "Wine perhaps? Something to eat? Soften the edges a little?"

My Master tilts his head in agreement. "Excellent idea."

The three of us, sitting on the bed together: we share cheese, bread and olives. The wine is crisp and cold, with that perfect edge of chill and aroma that takes you to Summer hillsides and views of the sea. As we eat and drink, we say little, but Michael's gaze wanders constantly to me before once more, he looks down again.

I hurt you. I didn't mean to....

Standing with my two Lovers, my Master takes me at the shoulders, kissing me, softly, open-mouthed. Tugging at my pullover, he lifts up and over my head, then, turning me, "Face Michael. Finish undressing."

Flushing slightly, feeling a little awkward, I turn to my blond, blue-eyed Lover. I meet his eye for a moment, but then glance down, embarrassed by the space that has grown between us. He tilts up my chin with a finger, compelling my gaze to his, and lips curving as his mouth meets mine, he reaches around me, unhooking my bra, releasing my breasts to swing pendulously into his hands. My nipples tighten as he thumbs at them, crinkling rosy pink against my white skin, and a heated flush of arousal rises up my chest and neck.

My Master retires, standing to one side, as Michael takes me, his arms around my shoulders and waist, eyes intense, and his smiling lips brushing mine; my Golden Lover returned to me.

My pussy is running warm, liquid, loose. I want my Lovers with me, both of them, inside me.

Michael breaks away, and, hands on my waist, turns me again, to face my Master.

My Dark Angel.

His black-eyed gaze on me, his kiss is also soft and leisurely. One hand cupping a breast, the other strokes my cheek. From behind, Michael sweeps my hair to one side, mouthing and nibbling at the soft skin on the nape of my neck.

My breathing deepens, my mood rapturous as my two Lovers seduce me. For too long we have not done this, but now....

Michael, behind me, unzips my skirt, then his hands sliding down and inside, he pushes skirt and panties down to my feet in one smooth, practised movement. "Step." he murmurs, and I lift my feet, freeing myself, to stand naked between them.

My Master glances over my shoulders. I know that look... he and Michael...

He stoops, picking me up; carries me to the bed, then lays me carefully down, head on the pillow. The two of them, still fully dressed, stand over me, smiling down. Exchanging a glance, again my Master withdraws, leisurely unbuttoning his shirt. Michael sits beside me, sweeping his hands over my body.

"What would you like?" he says.

"You." I brush blond locks from his face. "I've missed you."

"I never went away." He strokes the outline of my lips with a finger. "I'm sorry if it seemed otherwise." Then he stoops to kiss me again. His mouth is soft and warm, the kiss tender, and all I want is for this to continue.

Smiling, blue eyes crinkling, he bends further, to suckle at a breast, but one hand quests south. Winding fingers through my red and dampening curls, he eases to my thighs, pushing ever-so-slightly to either side. "Let me in." he whispers.

I lift my knees, parting a little, but now, my Master sits at the end of the bed, pushing my legs apart, spreading me wide. He watches as Michael fingers my clit, opening my folds, parting my pussy lips. Pleasure stabs, silver and bright, through to my sex as I mewl at his touch.

Panting, sweating, as arousal curls up from my heating, flowing core, I stretch, displaying myself for them. Michael, watching my writhing movements, smiles as he pushes two fingers inside me, my slick pussy shivering around him as he thrusts home; at first gently, and then harder as he tests my arousal. Gasping and quake, I arch my spine to meet him.

Oh God.... I want you inside me....

Their eyes meet again, and now Michael retreats, undressing while my Master clasps me at the ankles, pulling me to overhang the edge of the bed. Kneeling between my thighs, swinging my feet over his shoulders, for a moment, he locks eyes with me again, lips twitching. I know what is coming, and he is making me wait, enjoying my anticipation. Michael behind him, strips off his jeans, revealing his erection. It stands, glistening at the tip, and throbbingly tall against his stomach.

Breathing hot over my thighs, the skin already slippery over my heated sex, my Master pulls my pussy lips wide, stretching me open, looking inward; he has always enjoyed examining me. One finger circling inside the quivering muscle, I jerk and shake as the movement makes my pussy pulse, each motion drawing a whimper from me.

It's too much. My pussy is melting and hungry. I've waited too long for this. "Please," I whisper.

He smiles, and leaning forward, draws his tongue between my lips, full length, from cunt to clit.

Convulsing, I howl. He circles my clit, winding it into spirals as my pussy clenches and clutches, desperate to be filled. Then, dropping down, he plunges deep, his tongue dancing inside me as I wail and moan, spine and thighs straining as I arch up from his shoulders.

Grinning, Michael straddles me, nudging his cock to my mouth. "That's more like it. Now, let's hear you make that noise again." And as his shaft pushes towards my lips, my Master swipes out inside me, sending my inner muscles into spasms. I fling my head back, my mouth opening wide as I yell.

"That's just what I had in mind," says Michael, pushing his seeping cock-head between my lips. "Now, *look* at me. I want to see that expression James was talking about." Briny-sweet pre-cum trickles across my tongue, the musky perfume of his groin flooding my nostrils as my voice is abruptly cut off by the cock gagging me.

I want to buck and jerk as my Master tongue-fucks me. His mouth fastened around my pussy now, he laps and licks, cleaning me out as I flood scalding juices. The tension rising in me, in belly, cunt and thighs as, my orgasm coiled tight, it readies to spring loose.

Michael, using my mouth to pleasure himself, pushes his hard cock inside, almost to gag point, before withdrawing, he allows me to swallow, then pushes in again. My jaws stretched achingly wide, I can't work him. Instead, wrapping lips over teeth, I simply accept him, pressuring the ridge of his cock-head as he works himself on me.

He locks eyes as he face-fucks me. "Not today," he says, "But one day, I'm going to try deep-throating you, just to see how it works out. I'd really like to push my cock in all the way, hilt myself to your lips...."

Head tilting back, eyes squeezed shut, I bawl out my climax as my pussy goes into convulsions. My hips trying to buck as my Master pins me, he holds me tight as he rides my orgasm, my cunt shuddering into his mouth.

Michael stares down at me. "I love watching you come...." Then he breathes deeply, visibly containing himself. "I'd love to just spill myself inside you right now, but...." He groans.... ".... Oh, what the hell..." and hot cream floods my mouth, splashing to the back of my throat, before, pulling free, he spurts his last over my face. "I love watching you lick my cum off your lips too," he says. "Go on. Lick yourself clean."

His eyes are deep, intense, as I wipe my tongue over my mouth, sucking at my lips, revelling in the taste of him. Then as the moment passes, his face softens again. "I've missed this, you know; the sheer *fun* of being with you."

My Master has withdrawn and is now repositioning himself, his thighs between mine, cock nuzzling at me. Michael casts backwards, smiling as he sees. "I think your Master wants to fuck you now." I can't see him, but I hear a rustle, and the rip of foil.

Michael unstraddles me, sitting to one side and pouring himself another glass of wine. "I'll enjoy watching you fuck together," he says as, my Master, nudging inside, and then penetrating me, I swing my hips in and up, to wrap my legs around his waist.

My Master; my first man, and whom, I later realised, I loved almost from the day we met. He bought me at auction; he paid for me, and he took me, with my virginity, but did it so thoughtfully, and with such care, that I, without knowing at the time, became his from the first. I do not believe he knew then it either. But later, I understood that I had fallen in love with him, and he with me.

And I met Michael only a day later.... and in time, I fell in love with him too.

And now my Master, pressing in, begins to move within me, easily at first, thrusting only lightly, and I move with him, matching my rhythm to his as our bodies meet. Stroke for stroke, I rock with him, my hips angling to take him deeply within me. He doesn't smile, except behind his eyes, but his lips brush with mine as he takes me, claiming his own, his body dancing inside mine.

And now, he thrusts harder, pistoning me, his shaft slicking in and out of me, ploughing in, driving deep. His breathing is heavy, his forehead forming beads of moisture, chest glistening with sweat. Ramming hard, he gifts me this pain/ecstasy which I crave, and of which, I never tire.

His climax is violent. Stiffening, he erupts inside me as, every muscle tensed, shuddering and groaning, he pours himself into me. Head dropped beside mine, he pants, and gasping, flops atop me.

As his breathing slows to normal, looking up again, he blinks as Michael thrusts a glass of wine at him. "Um, yes, thanks. Just give me a minute."

He rolls away from me, staring at the ceiling, then his eyes slide across to mine, then Michael's. "You two good now?"

Michael meets my eyes, then, "Yeah, we're good."

"I'm pleased to hear it. I'll have that wine now."

We sit together, we three, simply enjoying each other's company again. This is how it is meant to be, with our shared warmth, love and companionship.

*****

Later, dressed, and the three of us sharing a meal together in the lounge, Michael has an air about him of.... what? He starts speaking, pauses, then starts again.

He's nervous?

"Charlotte, er.... with everything that's happened, Christmas has kind of been and gone without us. I wanted to give you a home for Christmas, and I've not been able to do that. And I didn't want to get you clothes or jewellery or perfume, because I know that things like that don't mean anything to you. But I *did* want to give you something special, something that counts for you."

Hesitantly, he slides an envelope towards me. "For you." There is.... an expectancy, about him.

My Master looks intrigued. I glance up at him and he shrugs. Whatever Michael's gift is, my Master is not 'in on it',

I open the envelope. It contains two pieces of paper, both scanned copies of an original. Staring at them, for a few moments, I don't understand what I am looking at.

Then the haze clears....

The first: *'This is to certify that on this day of 14th April 1992, Frank Conners did join in lawful wedlock with Michelle Kimberley.... by mutual consent before witnesses....'*

The second: "This is to certify the following record of birth.... *Name: Jennifer Conners. Sex: Female. Name of Father: Frank Conners. Maiden Name of Mother: Michelle Kimberley....*"

I stare at them, my eyes filling. After a minute, I gasp, finding myself releasing breath I didn't know I was holding, and I just sit there, not knowing how to react.

Michael looks worried. "Hey, I didn't mean to upset you. I thought you'd be pleased...."

"Oh, I am, I am." I stutter.... "How.... Where?"

My Master's voice is irritable. "Am *I* permitted to see what all this is about?"

Silently I pass the documents across the table to him. A brief glance and his eyes widen.

"I know that it matters to you, finding out where you come from," says Michael. "And after what Klempner said to you about your mother, I thought it was even more important."

Tears streaming down my face, I simply nod. He continues. "I had trouble tracking down the records because of course, all that area has been levelled, and I didn't know where old documents were being stored. And so old as that, they'd not been digitised either. But with Klempner dragging your mother's name into things, and his obvious interest in you, Will Stanton had good cause to, um, *assign resources*, to tracking down the information."

"One thing's clear from this...." says my Master. "Whatever the truth of the whole thing, Klempner lied. Your mother and father were married. I wonder just what it is he has against you? Or perhaps against your mother and father?"

"I thought about that too," says Michael. "A grudge against the parents, taken against the child?"

I finally recover my words. "Oh, thank you. Thank you." I fling my arms around him, and now, Michael's eyes flood.

The door buzzes, and without waiting for a reply, Richard enters, followed by Beth. "James, I just wanted to go over...." He pauses, surveying the scene; my tears, Michael's glossy eyes, my Master's frown. "Um, is this a bad time?"

"No," says my Master. "No, not at all. You've just caught us at, um, a bit of an emotional moment. Michael just gave Charlotte her belated Christmas gift...."

Richard, lips compressed, looks disapprovingly at my Golden Lover. "And she's crying about it?"

"It's alright," I say. "Really, it's alright. It's just.... Michael's found my birth certificate and my parents' marriage certificate."

He breaks into a broad smile. "Congratulations, Charlotte. I can imagine how important that is to you. Er.... May I look at them? Would you mind?"

"No of course not, Sir." I give him the envelope.

He slips out the two papers, quickly glances at one, then the other, and bursts out laughing, passing them to Beth. She, just as quickly, quickly glances over them, and again laughs out loud.

My Master and Michael look at him, baffled. I'm confused myself.

"What's funny?" asks Michael.

Beth is grinning widely. "What's funny...." says Richard, "....is that Elizabeth's maiden name was *Kimberley*."

I stare at him. "You're kidding...."

Richard is also smiling hugely. "Nope. I always thought the two of you looked too much alike for it to be a coincidence," he says. "Welcome to the family...."

Beth wraps her arms around me. Richard glances briefly at my Master (*asking permission*?). My Master holds up his hands in a 'How could I refuse?' gesture, and Richard hugs me too, giving me a chaste kiss on the cheek.

And for the second time that day, I burst into tears.

After we have all calmed down a little, Michael still looking bemused at the sheer impact of his 'gift', my Master says, "Of course, this all begs the question of why Klempner said what he did to Charlotte...."

I sober up quickly. "I felt as soon as spoke, that he had some kind of grudge against me. He said it was because of Jenkins getting killed, that he held me to blame for that. But it didn't feel right. I'm sure he was lying about that. If his grudge was actually with my mother, or my mother and father..."

Michael interrupts. "I should mention, Charlotte, that this isn't the only information that Will is trying to find. When these came to light, I also asked him, and he agreed, to try to have any other family connections checked. None came to light...."

"However," interrupts, Richard, "Now that we know there *is* a family connection, and we have a starting point, we can start a proper search on your behalf," says Richard.

"I was always a little surprised, Beth," says my Master, "That with such a similarity between the two of you, that *you* didn't ask your family if there might be a connection?"

Beth blushes. "Actually, I did. They were a bit close-mouthed, but eventually, I got it that my grandfather's brother, George, had a bit of a reputation for, er...."

"Climbing back-yard fences and bedroom windows?" suggests Michael, with raised brows and a winsome smile

"Er, yes," she chuckles. "Something like that. No-one really wanted to talk about it very much. There was a bit of a conspiracy of silence."

The three men burst out laughing. I feel a little indignant. "So, you thought I might be your er...."

"Second cousin..." interrupts my Master.

"Yes.... illegitimate second cousin? And you didn't say anything?"

She shrugs. "Well, I had no proof except that everyone says we look alike. Having those papers changes everything. I can ask my family properly now."

*****

Michael

Charlotte looks depressed. Chin resting on folded hands, she stares out of the window.

"What's wrong?" I ask.

"I should have been going back to University in a few days. Here we are, camping in a hotel.... I can't go back to college. We can't go home. You can't even go back to work on either the house or your fitness centre.... and...."

I wrap my arms around her. "It'll all work out. You'll see. And the house, the University and the Centre aren't going anywhere..."

Richard interrupts. "Don't fret about your studies, Charlotte. I've dealt with that on your behalf."

"You have?"

"Beth told me about the conversation you had a few weeks ago. Your academic work has to be interspersed anyway, with industrial and commercial training for your qualifications. We're shifting the order around so that you do a lot of the non-academic work now, and over the next few months."

"And how do I get industrial training locked in a hotel room?"

"You don't, but you also have to cover basic accountancy, company and commercial law and similar. You can do those from here."

"Aaahhhh...." Her eyes roll.

"You have a problem with that?" I ask.

"Mmmm.... Hadn't thought that things like accountancy were included."

"It depends what you want to do," says Richard. "If you end up working with a large corporation, such as mine, then you need to grasp at least the basics so that you understand the implications of your own decisions. And if you run your own company, then you certainly need to understand the bottom line; how to read a set of accounts, a balance sheet, how to interpret a profit and loss account."

Charlotte looks as though she's sucked a lemon.

Richard continues. "You will find it is very common for successful businesses to be jointly headed by the 'money man' and the 'technical man'. My own background is in finance. Which is *why* I took on James as my co-director. *His* expertise is on the technical and engineering side of things. But if *you* learn at least the fundamentals of the accounting and finance side of things, you will be stronger, and less dependent, for it in the future."

She sighs. "Fair enough. Where do I start?"

*****

Later, when we are alone, "It's very good of you, Richard, to put yourself out like this on Charlotte's behalf. I appreciate that it's in thanks for what she did for Beth, but nonetheless..."

Raising his brows. "Don't be fooled, Michael. Yes, it's partly in thanks. She craves education and training. I'll see that she gets it. *But,* I don't have to bring her into my company as a 'thank you'. It's mainly a cold commercial decision on my part."

"Sorry... Not with you?"

"Sooner or later, I want her on my Board."

?

"On your Board?"

"She's got intelligence, looks, a driving personality, and balls of solid rock. What more could I ask? Once she's trained up and knows what she's doing, she'll be a power to be reckoned with." He rubs his hands, almost gleefully. "Let's see the other shareholders stand in *her* way when she decides she wants something..." Then he sniffs. "On the whole, I want her working with and for *me*, not someone else..."

Despite myself, I smile at this. "I take your point, but suppose she doesn't want to follow that path? Wants to do something else?"

"Such as?"

"She might want to have a family, children."

He cocks a speculative eyebrow at me. "Well, you're the one marrying her.... Still, families grow up, and I suspect you may find that the adventure of family life will never be enough for that one.... She's spent her whole life living on the edge. I'm not sure she's capable of dropping to the same gear most people live in."

Is he right?

It's a dismal thought. Can I make Charlotte happy?

Richard looks at me sympathetically. "Michael, you said it to me yourself, and, at the time I ignored you. If you try to cage her, she won't *stay* caged. You might bear that in mind."

Arms folded, I stare at the ground. "Mmmm... you're giving me food for thought."

Cocking his head, he grins and leaves.

*****

Lying on the settee, Charlotte's head rests very comfortably on my lap. It's wonderful, feeling that everything is back to normal between us. There's stuff that needs sorting out, all kinds of problems, but it's not about *us*. Despite everything, life couldn't be better. My sky is blue, and the sun is shining.

She's reading a book, and clearly hating every moment of it. It's on the basics of accountancy, and every so often she emits a small sigh. Also, I see her fingers moving, as though, running through figures in her head, her fingers are helping with the counting.

I'm holding a book myself, a light novel, but making no pretence of reading it.

In the armchair opposite us, James has been listening, eyes closed, to some piece of soft classical music, but his glance slides sideways to Charlotte, then up to me. One eyebrow raises speculatively.

I'm more than willing.

"Charlotte, how about a break?"

The book drops instantly, her head tipping back to meet me. "Sounds good. What did you have in mind?"

I eye-point her sideways. "I believe your *Master* is trying to attract your attention."

Her body slides back against mine, stiffening and stretching as she looks his way. James slowly rises from his chair, moving to stand over her, gazing down.

"I believe, looking at him...." I murmur into her ear, ".... that your Master would like you to suck him off. And that he wants to cream into your mouth."

Her breath hitches. She doesn't speak, but her chest is heaving, and for a moment her face swings back towards me in question.

"Me? Oh, I'll think I'll get on top of you; push my cock inside and fuck you hard. Make you scream a bit."

Wrapping fingers into her long, red locks, I hold her head, controlling her movement, steering her towards James. He smiles as he sees what I am doing, unzipping himself, pulling out his shaft, so that it stands, already hard, waiting for her. From my sideways position, I can see her expression: a little-girl-lost mixture of devotion, lust, and adoration of James.

Come on Babe. Let's see you get really worked up....

"Your Master wants your mouth wrapped around his cock," I say, loud enough for him to hear too. "Open up."

Breath shuddering, she parts her lips, and I angle her face to take him as James pushes his cock-head at her lips.

"Lick," I instruct. "Get your tongue around him. And then we both want to see you taking him well in."

She mouths and licks at him, bringing up her hands to unbelt his pants. There's a tang to the air. She's wet already; the scent of her pussy pungent and sweet, and my own cock twitches in response.

Yeah... I'm gonna shaft you, then spill in there....

James eases in and out, between her lips, and my balls tighten. I love watching myself face-fuck her, and this is almost as good. He's streaming pre-cum, which she laps at, swiping it from the slit, where it trails in glutinous strands. He pulls free of her to wipe it, with his cock, glistening, over her lips.

"Clean your lips," I say. "Lick them clean. You mustn't have dirty lips when you are sucking off your Master."

She glances sideways at me, wiping her tongue over her mouth. "No, pay attention to what you are doing. Look up at James. He notices if you let your attention wander."

She gazes back up at him, eyes wide, enraptured.

Abruptly, he stands back, arms akimbo, still staring down, his lips twitching in a half-smile.

Still gripping her hair, twisting tight, "Stand up. Your Master wants you naked." Rising with her, she pants loudly, rapidly, as I pull her upright by her hair.

She starts to unbutton her blouse, but I interrupt her. "Did I tell you to move?"

From behind her, I unfasten the blouse, all but ripping it off her. Equally roughly, I take off her bra, then cup her tits, lifting and squeezing them, displaying her to James. He stoops to take one in his mouth and non-too-gently teethes at the nipples. She yelps, but another wave of scent tells me her pussy is flooding, and she is enjoying this just as much as we.

James chews at her breasts, wringing moans from her, and she shivers as I unzip her skirt, pulling it down, together with her panties. "Step," I instruct. I toss the clothes to one side. then again, with each of her sandals, 'Step'. She obeys, to stand naked and quivering between us, her thighs visibly glistening with her own juices.

Again, meeting eyes with James, together we strip off our clothes. I am already erect; he even more so. Wrapping an arm around her waist, I pull her rearwards onto the couch, to sit cradled back against me

James, kneeling, roughly pushes her knees apart. He doesn't bother testing her. We can both scent her arousal; she's sopping. Shoving his palm flat against her chest, pushing her back against me, he jams two fingers, hard, inside her. She moans and bucks, arms flailing, and I grab her by the wrists, pinning her. As James finger-fucks her, she writhes and struggles in my arms, but cannot move.

Again, James' glance, kneeling back on his haunches. Sliding back and down with her in my arms, I whisper to her. "Spread yourself properly. Your Master wants to taste your cunt."

Moaning, she spreads her legs wide, but James, holding her under the legs, lifts and swings her back onto me, and I finish the movement, seizing her under the knees, bending her, all but doubled-back on herself, thighs pressing against her own chest, pussy spread and displayed to James.

Panting violently, "Oh God, fuck me. Please, one of you fuck me."

Balls tight, and cock twitching, I reply, "All in good time. You know who is your Master here, and *he* decides when you may be fucked."

James says nothing, but smiles down at her, running a finger over her bright red slit. She twitches and jumps as he circles her clit, then delving in, stretches circles inside her. Her hips are shuddering, her heart hammering through her chest and through to me.

James pushes a finger inside her, and she moans and jerks. Then stooping, carefully, and touching no other part of her, he thumbs back the sheath, and wraps his lips around her pink, erect clit, sucking gently.

She yells and jerks, pitching and thrusting against me, all but breaking free of my grasp, but I renew my hold on her, pinning her immobile.

With his tongue-tip, he winds his way along and through the length of her vulva, from cunt to clit, and back again. Using fingers to spread her open, he probes and licks at her. She's flooding, and his face is wet with her juices as he delves into her with his tongue, wiping her out inside, then weaves upwards again to lap at her clit.

"Please," she says, pleading. "Please, get inside me. I *need* to come."

"Not yet," says James, breaking away momentarily, and stooping, fastens his mouth over her cunt.

And now, she *screams*, her whole body in spasm as James sucks her out, tonguing her inside.

"Oh, God. Oh, God. I can't...." and for a moment, she goes still. I feel her tension, her body poised against mine, bound in my embrace, straining against me. And then her orgasm breaks loose.

I wonder sometimes, what orgasm feels like to a woman. Certainly, it looks as though takes the whole body. Charlotte howls her climax, straining against my grip on her, almost battling against me. Her belly pulses against my hand and her fingernails bite into my skin. James tightens his grip on her spread thighs, his face pressed hard into her cunt.

Finally, she screams "Enough! Enough! I can't stand anymore."

Instantly, he retires, wiping his face, but now, repositioning himself, plunges his cock, full length inside her. There's no hesitation, no testing her. She's as open as it is possible for a woman to be, and he hilts himself, hard, into her. Our position is slightly awkward, but he rests his hands for balance on the settee-back, leaning over the two of us, as he fucks her.

He's not gentle, ramming home as she squeals and wails under him. And he is close to climax himself. He watches as he penetrates her, studies his cock moving in and out, glistening with her honey, her thighs flushed and wet, and her red curls soaked. His own breathing is rapid, face and chest sweating and his dark eyes, all but black with hugely dilated pupils.

Groaning, he presses home, grinding as he pumps into her. Head dropped to his chest, eyes squeezed shut, he grunts and then, with a gasp, withdraws, waving at me to take over as he seats himself back in his armchair.

"Charlotte, on the bed, on your back."

Flushed and sweating, she obeys me, walking through to the bedroom, then lies down on the bed to gaze up at me, hips swung upwards, knees a little akimbo. I am cock-twitchingly, ball-tighteningly, ready to come, and I'll not hold on more than a minute or so.

Standing beside her, looking down. "So," I say, "Do you want me to shoot in your cunt or your mouth?"

Again, in silence, she smiles with her eyes, opening her mouth, parting her lips in that inviting cherry-coloured 'O', that just begs me to shove myself deep inside.

I'd love to.... Would she like it? Could she take it?

"How are you feeling? Want to try something? I'd love to deep-throat you, but I'll not do it if you don't want."

Still, she doesn't speak, but she tilts her head a little more, parts her lips a little further. James, who has followed us, disappears from the room, returning a minute later with a jug of water and a glass. Sitting on the bed beside her, he strokes her face, holding her hand.

I say, "Charlotte, move so that you overhang the bed. Let your head drop back."

Standing by her, cock-head poised by her over-hanging face. "If this is too much, you bang the bed with your hand, or squeeze James' hand, and I'll pull out right away. Yes?"

She stretches her neck, reaching for my cock, which oozes over her mouth as I push inwards. James positions himself to watch her face, as best he can from where I press close to her.

Easing forwards, I rock, sliding in and out, gradually, slowly, a little deeper every time. She seems okay. I glance at James, who has a better view of her than I do. He is watchful but seems unconcerned.

You okay, Babe?

I think so, yes.

It feels great....

At first, she works my cock head with her tongue and lips, but then, as gradually I work deeper, she simply takes me. Pushing at the back of her throat, I am acutely conscious, that perhaps now, she might be uncomfortable, might gag.

But she doesn't.

"Just relax...."

Oh God, but she feels good. Penetrating further, as I squeeze into her throat, it tightens on my cock-head. And now, her tongue massages my shaft.

Ooohhhh...... wow.......

It is utterly, indescribable....

I'd like to extend the moment, but I'm already poised to come, my balls tight with pressure. Seeing myself, pushed inside her, my groin pushed against her face, cock sheathed in her mouth, it's too much.

Pulsing, I spill into her throat, shooting my full load deep inside. It's so tight, so good. And, groaning, I shoot once, twice and then a third time into her before it is too much and, with a gasp, I pull away.

As my head clears, she's not moved. "Good?" she asks.

"Oh...." I stroke her face. "You have no idea...."

*****

Charlotte

And yet again, I scan photographs, looking for faces. Not yet knowing who the police 'spy in the camp' is, Will Stanton, the Police Commissioner has provided the information to me directly, no intermediaries, and I am searching images of people known to be associated with Lawrence Klempner and his activities. Beth, keeping me company, is also looking. After all, captured by them herself for a while, perhaps she might notice something I miss.

Many of the photos are very old, drawn from files which have been collecting dust since the time of the original investigation into Blessingmoors. Some are taken from other investigations into similar criminal activity. Since Klempner and his gang have tendrils extending much further than simply the old Blessingmoors children's home, I am being asked, yet again, to scan some hundreds of faces, now from many parts of the world. The investigation has become international. I begin to wonder just how big this is, and how much money is involved.

And yet, with so much at stake, given that I am to be witness in a trial against some of the criminals, why was I not simply murdered? Why was Klempner so keen to capture me? Because he knew my mother? Or claims to have done so?

It seems bizarre.

"I'm hungry," says Beth. "How about you? We could go to the restaurant. It's not as though we'd be leaving the building. Would that be alright, Michael?" She glances around. "Where is he?"

"Having a shower, but I'd rather carry on with this, anyway."

"I could order something from room service then?"

"Sure, whatever you like."

Beth raps on the door of the bathroom. "Michael? You want to eat?" After a moment. "I don't think he can hear me over the shower." She orders a light meal for three, just sandwiches and a drink. "They said it shouldn't be more than ten minutes. I ordered for Michael as well."

"Fine." I don't look away, wearily watching face after face cross the screen.

Then, I see the familiar, and my stomach freezes. Jabbing at the pause button, I halt the slide-show, staring at the image in front of me.

And now I know who Will Stanton's spy is.

"Beth...."

And at that moment, the door buzzes. "That'll be the food," she says. As she unclicks the lock, the door slams open. men burst in, and before she can make a sound, Beth is seized, a hand pushing something over her mouth. She tries to scream, to fight, but after a few moments, goes limp.

And one of the intruders, I know; Corby, the 'police' officer' who bungled my first interview, and whose face now stares out of the screen of my laptop.

"Hello again, Jennifer." he snarls.

I stand, trying to back away, but trapped between the table and my chair, my legs tangle and they are on me. Screaming, I try to call out for help; "Micha...." but before I can get the words out, a soft pad is pressed over my mouth and nose, with a sweetish chemical smell.

Struggling, I try to not to breathe, but my vision blackens at the edges and eventually, my body, gasping for air, betrays me, forcing me to draw breath. Everything wavers and....

*****

I wake in some small dark place, being jolted by movement....

A car boot?

I have a thick headache. Nausea churns my stomach. And I can't move. My ankles are bound together, taped I think. My wrists too, behind my back. And my mouth is taped tight, I cannot scream or cry for help. Close by me is the heat and scent of another human body... Beth?

Trying to speak through my taped mouth, I can only make inchoate sounds, no speech, but there is a reply, and, yes, even through the gag, it is Beth's voice.

Bounced around in the dark, I can only lie helplessly, wondering what is to come.

*****

Michael

About to step into the lounge, just a towel around my waist, I remember that Beth is there with Charlotte, and take a minute to pull jeans instead. I've seen the looks she gives me....

No need to tempt fate....

Still towelling my hair, I step into the lounge, then stop....

Something's wrong....

The apartment door is open, swinging wide. Chairs, and the table, are knocked to the floor, and there is a faint, sweetish, chemical scent of.... something.... in the air.

The women are nowhere in sight.

Thoroughly alarmed now. "Charlotte? Beth?" Then shouting.... "*Charlotte? Beth? Where are you?*"

Jeez!

Jabbing at my mobile. "James. Charlotte and Beth are gone! Are they with you?"

"No. They're fucking not! I thought you were supposed to be keeping an eye on them?"

Pacing up and down the room. "I was in the shower. When I came out, about a minute ago, they were gone, and there's signs of a struggle. Where's Richard?"

"He's here.... raising the alarm as we speak."

"Oh, Shit!" I freeze in mid-stride as I register the screen of Charlotte's laptop. "James. We know who the police spy is. He's among the faces Charlotte was looking through. It's Corby."

"Corby? Who.... Oh, fuck! That police officer that interviewed her? The one that tried to go after me?"

"Yes, *him*."

*****

And helpless, James and I, and Haswell, must wait for news; any news.

"Wonder why Corby's first act was to try to attack you? Trying to get you prosecuted over the business with the auction?"

James shrugs. "Perhaps to take Charlotte's defender out of the picture?"

"She has *two* defenders, and they knew that...."

He looks at me, pointedly. "They came after *you* with guns. Discredit one. Murder the other. Isolate her?"

"*Why* is she so important to them?"

"Her testimony at court is likely to put a lot of people in prison, quite likely for good."

"Okay, so she's an important witness. But, that being the case, why haven't they simply murdered her? They've had plenty of opportunities."

Richard sweeps in. "Will's on his way. He says he has information for us."

*****

Beth

Wheel crunch over gravel and a pause. There is the whine of.... Hinges? A gate? Large doors? Then a brief movement and the hum of the car engine stops.

The *clunk, clunk* of car doors opening and closing, then the scrape of keys right by us. The boot opens and light floods, blindingly over us. Charlotte's eyes are calculating, her face white.

Roughly handled, we are lifted out and carried through from a shed-cum-garage area into what looks like a private house. It's rather old, with beamed ceilings, and cracked lime and horse hair plasterwork. But it is so ordinary. We could be *anywhere*. And it would all look perfectly normal, were it not for the reception awaiting us.

Still bound and gagged, wrists, ankles and mouths taped, we are carried through into a very large room, before being dumped down, sitting next to each other on a shabby couch. The room is huge, with a vast open roof-space, as though it has been a barn or shippon. Perhaps we are in some deserted farmstead?

Klempner is there, waiting and watching, arms folded. He is well dressed, in a suit, polished shoes and a clean white shirt. A cold smile playing over his lips, he is certainly pleased with himself.

There is a domineering edge to his stance; the man in charge, with a hard-wired arrogance that nothing is going to quench.

I can't put my finger on it, but something about him is familiar. *Who does he remind me of?*

It's irrelevant. I dismiss the thought.

"Hello, again," he says. "Nice to see you both. I was getting really quite annoyed at the trouble you've been causing me, but now you're back, we can all be friends again."

He nods to one of our captors. "Un-gag that one." He points at Charlotte.

With deliberate roughness, the tape is torn from her mouth, leaving her lips bleeding. She licks over her mouth but says nothing, simply staring at Klempner.

He arches brows. "Nothing to say?"

"Like what?" She almost spits the words. "Am I supposed to plead with you? I still don't know why I'm here."

"You're here because you've made my life difficult, and now you're going to.... *compensate me*, for it."

"I don't think that's it." Her voice is strident, insistent.

How can she be like this? She should be terrified. Instead, she's just angry....

"Is that right?"

They're playing some sort of.... game?

"You said you knew my mother," she says.

He doesn't move, except to tilt his head a little. His eyes are flat, lids hooded. After a pause, "So?"

"How did you know her?"

"I told you. She worked for me, with the other whores."

"I don't believe you."

He shrugs, saying nothing.

"What became of her?"

"She died...." His eyes stay cold, but there is... what? An eagerness for her to believe? ".... Heroin overdose."

"And what do you know about my father, Frank Conners?"

He laughs. "Conners? Your father? Don't fool yourself. You might have his name, but that's all. You're a whore's brat. Your father could have been anyone...." He pauses. "Could have been me..." he drawls.

She looks as though she has bitten into rotten meat. "Why do you hate me so much?"

"Hate you? Why should I hate you? I don't know you. You're nothing."

She tilts her head. "That's what I'm asking. You *don't* know me. So why do you hate me? If I was just a nuisance, for being a police witness against you, I think you would have simply had me murdered. So, there's more to it, and I think it's to do with my mother."

His lips curl into a sneer. "Really? Well, you're over-thinking it. You're simply goods, with a value. And so's she..." He points at me. "And despite what you told me about her husband and ransoming her, I've decided against it. You're being sold as a pair. Quite the exotic mix, two lookers like you. There's quite a market for that kind of.... novelty item.... in some parts of the world you know."

There is a ring-tone, and he glances down before plucking a phone from his pocket. "Yeah.... they're here. You did a good job. Are you joining us for the fun? Sure, we'll wait, there's no hurry. See you later." He nods at the men in the room. "Lock them up."

"Like that, Boss?"

"I need to pee," says Charlotte. "Are you going to take this tape off?" Klempner hesitates. "If you don't," she continues, "It's going to get smelly around here, pretty quickly."

He sniffs, nodding at one of the men. "Take it off her. And the other one."

The tape is stripped away from the both of us and we are thrust into a small bare room, where I collapse onto the floor in an agony of pins and needles. Even Charlotte dances around the floor, flapping her hands as blood pumps back into her fingers. Then she paces up and down, shaking arms and legs, stretching limbs and straining her neck backwards. "God, but that feels good," she says. "Thought I was going to seize up entirely like that."

She grins down at me. "Come on. Cheer up. Could be worse."

I struggle to sit up from my spot on the floor. "Worse?" I ask, unbelieving. "How?"

"We could still be tied up."

*****

Michael

We sit around the table, James and I, Richard and Will.

Will, sighing, says "As you know, since it is clear that *something* in Charlotte's family history, relates to Lawrence Klempner and this current situation, I've had good reason to be able to investigate old records which might otherwise not be deemed relevant, that I could not otherwise justify assigning resources to. You know about the first part, when, at Michael's request, I had her birth certificate located, along with her parents' marriage certificate. And now, with Corby identified, I have more of a free hand. It was difficult before, simply not knowing who could be trusted...."

"What makes you think he was their only informer?" asks Richard.

"Because, having identified him, with the benefit of hindsight, all the information we know to have leaked out, including how they knew you were *here*, can be traced back to some connection with him...."

"How *did* he know we here?" demands Richard.

"He was there in the aftermath of the attack on the building. It was probably no more complicated than listening in to you giving instructions to your helicopter pilot."

Richard rubs the back of his neck, distress on his face.

"Of course," continues Will, "We can never be one hundred per cent sure, but we *are* ninety-nine per cent sure, that, in terms of police infiltration, Corby was acting alone. Remember, he even manoeuvred himself into being the officer to interview Charlotte about Blessingmoors, then tried to use that, to attack James."

"So, you know who he is, or was?" asks James.

"He was essentially Klempner's right-hand man. Certainly, that was his role in the days of the original investigation. This was known at the time, according to the records, but was never provable, because witnesses either clammed up or vanished entirely. In time, Corby himself, or as he was then known, Elliot Bech, also vanished, and in truth, it was assumed he'd probably been murdered himself in some form of gang dispute. They're a violent bunch, and occasionally, what was left of them, would be found floating face down."

"So, Corby... what? Had a change of identity and joined the police force?"

"So far as we can tell, yes. He seems to have been there as a sleeper for years, positioning himself to be in the right place if there were movement on the Blessingmoors investigation or any of the other inquiries which we now know to be linked to it...."

"How did you establish those links?" asks Richard.

"Through Charlotte's identification of individuals known to her from Blessingmoors, but also known to us through other activities. It's a huge network, working internationally, and all on the general theme of trafficking vulnerable individuals; children, migrants, the dispossessed. The movement is typically from one country to another, where the victims don't speak the language, don't know the local laws and have no way of requesting help. However, large as the network is, Klempner is the king-pin, the common link. Take him out of the system, and a lot of it simply falls apart."

Will chews his lip, hesitates, then continues, "On the subject of Blessingmoors itself, I have to say that I am pleased that Charlotte is not present to hear this, although I suspect I am not going to say anything that she didn't actually know already.... The cellar that she led us to on the site: forensics have now had the opportunity to re-excavate, from where the site had been demolished over it, and investigate....

.... What they found is not good. The examination of the site is still by no means complete. Suffice it to say, that a number of shallow graves have been identified. The human remains within have been recovered, and there is an on-going effort to identify the individuals concerned...."

There is an appalled silence around the table. "Under the circumstances, "says Will, "I'm not going to dwell on this too much. All I *am* going to say is that there is all the motive in the world, for the culprits to try to remove Charlotte, as a witness to much of this, from the picture, and to prevent her giving testimony at court. All aside from the considerable monies made from the trafficking, she is effectively witness to institutionalised murder."

"So *why*..." I interrupt, "... have they not simply murdered her?"

Will raises a hand, forestalling me. "I'm coming to that." He glances around the table. "I have to say, that we are missing certain records. Corby may be responsible for that, or it may be that over twenty years or so, they have been misplaced or misfiled, and we have simply not yet located them. However, some things *have* come out, about which we are clear.... and there's no easy way to deliver this.... Charlotte's father, Frank Conners, was murdered, either by, or at the instruction of, Lawrence Klempner."

There is stunned silence, then, "Is it known why?" asks James. "He was involved with their trafficking trade?"

"We don't know the motive. Perhaps that was it. What is also unknown, as yet, is how Charlotte herself, or as she then was, Jennifer Conners, came to be in Blessingmoors at all...."

"That file you had on her, said she was placed there as a ward of the court; that her mother was unfit...." I point out.

"Yes, that's so." agrees Will. "However, here we have a discrepancy because what has also emerged, is that Michelle Conners was not, in fact, deemed unfit as a carer, as the mother of a young baby. When we cross-referenced to the court records, there is *nothing* there to support the content of the Blessingmoors file...."

I am about to interrupt again, but Will raises a finger, silencing me. "*And,* what we now know is that in fact, Michelle Conners was, at that time, given a new identity for her own protection. Her child should have been with her at that point."

"So, Charlotte's mother is alive? She has a family?" demands James.

"We don't know. We can't find her. We have had officers visit her last known address, but that is from over twenty years ago. She's dropped off our radar."

He is about to say more when his phone rings. He glances at the scene. "Excuse me a moment. I need to take this call."

He listens in silence then, "Yes? Good... and... Yes? I'm on my way." He taps off the mobile. "The attacker they dragged from the building has woken up. He wants to plea-bargain. He's ready to talk."

"Does he know where Beth and Charlotte have been taken?"

"I'll let you know as soon as I do."

*****

Ill at ease, barely speaking, we wait. And we wait.

James paces the room. Richard sits, drumming the tabletop with his fingers. I fight down the nausea that rises every time I think about what Will has told us.

And Charlotte is in the hands of these people.

Richard's phone rings. "Yes?" He covers the set for a moment. "It's Will. Yes? Yes.... What!" He jots something down. "We're on our way. How long before you can get there? Is that with back-up? Right!"

He clicks off. "Come on. We're going. We know where they were taken, and it's not far away. Can you believe it? We're almost on top of them. It's an old abandoned farm. I'll tell you on the way."

*****

Charlotte

I try to alternate between sitting and resting, and standing and walking about. When my opportunity comes, I need to be able to *go*.

Beth doesn't look so good. She's not handling this well. Will I be able to take her with me again? I'm not sure. How can I judge, when I have no idea where we are, and what I will find outside?

There is a click of keys and the door opens, and a man brandishing a gun enters, followed by Klempner. He smiles brightly at us.

"Good evening ladies. I just thought I'd bring you up to date on the news. My colleague, Mr Corby, will be arriving in due course, and we'll be starting our entertainments then...."

Beth cowers in the corner, where she sits on the floor, leaning against the wall, legs outstretched. Klempner stands over her, inserts first one foot between her ankles, and then the other. He does no more, but his implication is obvious as he pushes her legs apart.

Staring down at her, he says, "Corby wanted to fuck Jennifer first; show her how *annoyed* he is with her. But that's my privilege. He can have you instead. The pair of you look enough alike that he should be happy with that. When he's finished, the others can take turns with you... Or they might not take turns. That's up to them."

He waits, enjoying her fear. "Ever done that? Had a man at every hole? I know *she* has." He tosses his head across to me.

Beth says nothing, tears rolling down her cheeks, her breathing short and rapid.

He turns to me. "I'm having *you* first. Get some pay-off eh? Before I let the others at you? How many can you handle at once d'you reckon? We'll find out, shall we?"

"What payoff? What have ever done to you?"

He shows his teeth....

Is that a smile?

.... But he doesn't reply, just leaves the room, and his goon follows. The door closes behind him, followed by the rattle of keys in the lock and the slam of bolts.

The exit is locked. The two small windows barred. The only way out of this room is to be taken out.

I give it a while, but I can't wait too long.

How long have we got? Before Corby gets here?

I bang on the door. "Hey, I need the bathroom."

After a minute or so, and the sound of a struggle with lock and bolts, the door bangs open again, and one of Klempner's hoods sticks his head in the room. "You only just went."

"That was hours ago, and.... and I'm nervous. Please, I've gotta use the bathroom."

He rocks his head in an indecisive, "Should I.... Shouldn't I...." kind of way, then, gun trained on me, points me out of the room into a hallway, and at the next door. "In there. You've got two minutes."

In the five or ten seconds I have, between exited the one room and entering the next, I get a quick glance around the hall; several doorways lead off, and one of them looks like an outer door.

The window is not barred, but the tiny opener at the top would not be nearly large enough for me to squeeze out. Trying my luck anyway, I stand on the WC seat to open it, peering out.

It's dark outside, but there seems to be a courtyard and.... barns? Outbuildings? Yes, it's an old farmyard. If I can get outside, there should be plenty of nooks and crannies to lurk in while I get my bearings.

I've used at least half of my allotted two minutes.

How to get out?

Break the glass?

Nope - there are cross-bars on the outside, the perfectly normal kind, often used as anti-burglar devices in isolated buildings.

Perhaps....

It's the oldest trick in the book. Could I be lucky enough that he'd be that stupid?

There is a bang on the door. "C'mon. Time's up. Out you come."

Silently, I open the small top-light, leaving it as wide ajar as I can, then stand behind the door.

The banging increases. "Come on. Out of there. Or I'll come in."

I remain silent, and after a second or two, there is a crash as the door is kicked in, me standing behind it. I suppress an 'Ow!' as the door bounces in my face.

I can't see the man, but hear, "Fuck!" and he dashes back out, and I hear the bang of another door opening.

Darting out from my hiding place, into the hall where the outside door is swinging open, I dash out into the darkness. I hear other doors opening behind me, and yells and shouts or pursuit from behind as I run....

*****

Bolting out into the darkness, I duck into the cover of one of the barns, then halt. There's no point simply running. I *can't* outrun them, and Beth is still in there, so I can't just leave.

Watching figures dashing around the farmyard, running, searching, bawling and shouting, I back into the shadows, trying to think.

Hands reach out from behind me, one pulling me in tight by the waist, and the other clapped firmly over my mouth.

My blood pounds a single pulse, so hard inside me, that it makes my fingertips tingle. My heart racing, I try to *scream*, but....

"It's me. Shhh..."

"*Master?*"

"Yes, we're all here."

"Michael?"

"Yes, and Richard. The police are on their way."

"*Just* the three of you? How soon before the police get here?

Richard's voice from the shadows behind me. "Maybe thirty minutes. They're coming from the City. That hotel we were staying in; it's not far. When the police found out where you'd been taken, we were closer than they are."

I swivel out of my Master's grasp. "We don't *have* thirty minutes. They've got Beth in there, and Klempner wants to gang-rape her, and me. And they're *looking* for me." I gesture wildly around the yard where, bit by bit, all the hiding places are being checked. "We can't all stay here for thirty minutes and not be found. I'll distract them...."

My Master's hand whips out, gripping my wrist. "Like Hell you will..."

"If they don't find me quickly, they'll *keep* looking, and they're bound to find all of you. Better if I distract them, and then you're free to act.... There's too many of them for you, without having surprise on your side..."

"How many?" asks Michael.

"I've counted eight, including Klempner. "And I think they're expecting Corby."

And with that, I twist my hand from my Master's, and run out into the open, deliberately making enough noise, that the two thugs close by, hear me. As I dash across the courtyard, they yell, raising the alarm, and all of them give chase, following me into the darkness, and away from my would-be-rescuers.

*****

Michael

She slips James' grip, racing out into the courtyard, and away from us. James curses, reaching to catch her, but she dodges his grip and goes. *"Charlotte!"* he hisses. But she ignores him and keeps running.

He stands, holding his hands mid-air, in frustration, as though trying to shake her by non-existent shoulders. "When I catch her again, she is not going to sit down for a fucking week!"

I say nothing. I agree with him and can add nothing. After a silent pause, Richard says, "She had a point though."

James turns on him, finger raised, then halts. "Yes, she did. Let's...."

There is a yell from the darkness beyond the yard. "We've got her."

Flanked on both sides, pinned at the arms, Charlotte is marched back to the farmhouse.

Klempner leans against the side of the door as she is brought in, picking his teeth. "Back inside with her." he drawls. "It's party-time."

All the gang-members vanish inside, closing the door behind them. When it seems clear that all is quiet, James mutters "How many of them did you count?"

"Five out here chasing, plus I think I saw a couple more moving inside, plus Klempner."

"Okay, so we're agreeing with Charlotte's eight."

"Hold on, the door's opening again," says Richard.

A man exits, wandering over to large, wooden doors, an out-building or garage perhaps. As the doors swing open to a dark interior, dimly, cars can be seen inside.

"Back in a minute," I mutter, moving quietly through the gloom, to wait just outside the door.

The man opens the boot of one of the cars, searching for something, then re-emerges, some object in his hands.

As he moves past the door, I step out of the darkness, the man's eyes widening as he sees me at the last moment; far too late to prevent the crack, as my forehead meets with his nose.

Dazed, but not unconscious, he struggles, so I head-butt him again, and he falls.

James appears at my side. "Any rope in the back of that car?"

"Better than that," I say, holding up what the man was carrying. "Tape."

As we gag and bind the unconscious man, James murmurs, "It's probably what they used on the women."

"Or were going to...." mutters Richard. "You're a dirty fighter, Michael. That's not a fighting style from polite circles."

"I'm not interested in fighting. Just in taking them out."

He nods, then, "Looks like they're all safely inside now. Shall we take a look?"

We cross the yard, working our way quietly around, until, standing right outside a brightly lit window, just beside the entrance, we can see in.

Inside, there is a very large room. Klempner and his men are there, with Charlotte and Beth. Beth looks to be almost in a state of collapse, terror-stricken and weeping.

But Charlotte....

*****

Charlotte

Propelled back inside by my captors to the large central room, a gun is trained on me, and my arms gripped at either side, before they release me, to stand in the centre of the room. Klempner nods at one of his hoods. "Get the other one."

Beth is all but dragged into the room. I don't think she can stand without support, and released, she drops to her hands and knees, sobbing and shaking.

It's up to me then....

How much time can I buy?

Klempner glances down at Beth and seems to dismiss her. She's not doing anything interesting; not *entertaining* him.

Trying not to be obvious about it, I glance around the windows, but all I see is darkness.

Where are they?

Klempner stands close to me; too close, crowding me. I scent him, his breath, his sweat. His smile is cold; his pupils, wide.

Oh, he's enjoying this.

And I'm supposed to be intimidated....

Fuck that....

"So, what's next?" I demand, keeping my voice loud. "You rape me? Gang-bang me? You think I can't handle that?"

Klempner's eyes widen, but he says nothing.

"You think I don't know about men like you? Remember where I grew up. You know a lot about me, so you know that. You don't scare me."

"No? Let's see what we can do about it...." His voice cool, almost indifferent, Klempner glances sideways, either way. "Hold her."

My arms are seized again, outstretched, pulled taut....

Don't show fear....

Klempner knots fingers into the front of my blouse, tearing it apart, stripping it off me....

Master, where are you....?

My bra follows, simply tugged apart and ripped away.

"You think I can't handle you lot?" I scream at them. "Eight of you? Go on. Try me. 'Cause you don't fuckin' frighten me...."

"Strip her," says Klempner. From behind, my skirt is ripped away, my panties torn apart. "Whores belong on their knees. Down you go..." Reaching out, he backhands me across the face, knocking me to the floor.

"Okay, boys. Showtime." And they close in on me.

Master....

*****

Michael

James peers through the window, then quickly pulls back, cursing quietly. "Jeez... She's a fucking lunatic sometimes."

"What's she doing?" I ask.

"Winding them up, drawing them onto her. I think she's enjoying it."

Through the window, there is a shriek of a voice. "You fucking bastards! You think you can do me? Let's see if you're up to it...."

I quickly look through, followed by Richard. She's being held down, kneeling between them, and she's screeching like a banshee. Klempner, side-on to us, along with most of his men, looks down at her as though she's mad.... I don't blame him. Even Beth, who has clearly been crying, is staring, unbelieving, at my red-haired demon-child.

"You're not seriously suggesting that she's getting off on this?"

"*Look* at her," says James. "At her face, her *eyes.*"

I look in at her again. He's right. She's wild, eyes like saucers, face flushed. But this time, as I flash a look through the window, she sees me, and immediately looks away, drawing all eyes to her.

She looks utterly insane, running on adrenaline and fear, but she's not. She's playing the game, giving us the time, and the opportunity, to do what is needed....

Standing again, she paces up and down, light-footed, naked, almost dancing, red hair flying, as she points, and gestures, and raves at them. "C'mon... Big brave men. All of you with guns, on one little girl? You think you can fuck me? Let's see what you're *really* made of...."

"She's like a fucking wild animal," mutters Haswell.

James nods, brows raised. "That's our Charlotte."

Klempner brings his hand, open-palmed, across her face, hard, and she goes down again, dropping to the floor. But she doesn't cower, just stays there on all fours, glaring up at him, fire in her eyes, panting.

Richard winces. "What's her pain tolerance like?"

James tilts his head. "In that mood, sky-fuckin-high."

"She doesn't scare *at all?*"

"Oh, she scares. It just doesn't stop her."

"We need to get in there *now*," I say.

"Yes, but let's take the time to do this right. There's more of them than us and they're armed."

"You cold-blooded bastard." I hiss. "Are you going to let them just get away with that?"

James, with a touch of steel in his eyes, that arrogance that says he will always be in charge, says "She's playing for time. Let's not waste her efforts. And no, when we get the women out of there, I'm going to blow the bastard's head off, and enjoy doing it. She's spent her life being hunted, abused. This ends *here*, tonight." He locks eyes with Haswell, who nods.

He's right of course. And, he may be my closest friend, but even I know that James has a dangerous side.

Her 'Dark Angel' she called him?

Just so.

"What do we do? One's accounted for. It's seven against three."

"Five against three." murmurs James.

"Five? Why five?"

He nods towards the window again. "She's got her hands around the balls of one, and another's about to shove his cock between her teeth. What d'you think will happen to *them* when we burst in?"

Despite myself, I cringe inside. Richard flinches, staring upwards.

"You have a point." I concede.

"Stay there a minute," says James. "I'm going to see if there's a rear entrance. Klempner's got his back to a door there. If I can get behind him...."

He vanishes into the darkness. Richard takes another quick look inside and chuckles. "I don't believe it.... She's got them, quite literally with their trousers down and they've put their guns to one side."

"Mmmm... yes. James is going to knock her sideways when he gets his hands on her, but she's done what she set out to do...."

"As always." murmurs Richard.

James reappears, holding a crowbar, a large spanner and a hammer. "Yes, there's a side entrance. I can get behind him. You want these?" He keeps the crowbar but offers the other tools. "They were in a shed to the rear. Can I suggest that you two go for the pair over by Beth, keep them from taking her hostage. I'll take Klempner...."

"And I think we can rely on Charlotte to do as much damage as possible...." I say.

James flashes his brows, clicking his tongue, then, "As soon as you see me appear behind Klempner, get in there, and we'll take out as many as possible while we have surprise on our side."

Poised by the entrance, I wait. Half a minute later, the door behind Klempner opens and James appears, moving carefully, the crowbar in his hand.

Charlotte, naked, on her knees, but watching, sees him and....

There is a shriek: two shrieks.

The man face-fucking her drops, screaming. His companion drops too, curling in on himself, clutching at his groin. Charlotte scrambles up, spitting blood.

For the smallest of moments, the tableau freezes as her would-be rapists, clearly not believing what they have just seen, hesitate. Everyone is staring at her, standing naked, her mouth dripping red.

Then chaos breaks out....

James, swinging the crowbar, brings it squarely across Klempner's head. Klempner screams, reeling, but turns to grapple with his attacker, knocking the bar from James' hand, to clang to the ground.

Richard and I burst through the door. Caught off-guard, my mark, a spanner smashing into his temple, shrieks and falls. Richard's puts up more of a fight, trying to go for a gun, but Beth sweeps her legs past his ankles, and as he falls, Richard, seizing him at the throat, smashes him backwards against the wall, where he drops, unconscious.

James and Klempner are still struggling, hand to hand. Stretching to reach James' throat, Klempner's face is contorted, twisted with... what? Hate? Fear? James' is cold, impassive.

The two are all but evenly matched, but Charlotte breaks into the fight. Snatching up the crowbar, now she swings it, bringing it down on Klempner's outstretched arms with the crack of breaking bones. Klempner howls and falls, writhing in agony.

Now, the surprise gone, the remaining three gang-members are scrabbling for their weapons. A gunshot whistles past my face, smacking into the plaster behind me. Another shatters through the window....

.... there is the wail of sirens, many sirens. In the darkness outside there is the flash-flash of blue lights and the squeal of brakes.

The three remaining gang members pause, looking at each other, then, the first holds up his hands, dropping his gun. The others hesitate, but....

"It's over," says Richard. "The police have come armed, and half the City force is here. You can't win now, and you'll not escape."

Two more weapons drop to the floor. Quickly, I kick them to one side.

Charlotte flashes a smile at James, but his gaze is furious. Eyes flashing. "Get some fucking clothes on."

Her face drops. Quickly she gathers her clothes, much torn, pulling them on as best she can.

Uniformed police, firearms at the ready, burst into the room, but the scene is already played out. Hand-cuffing both the conscious and the unconscious, the traffickers are either marched or carried out.

*****

Beth

Police work their way around the room, searching the building. White coveralled men appear.... Forensics?

"Charlotte!" James calls her, fury in his voice. "*Here*. Right now!"

Her eyes roll towards him, then to Michael, who shrugs, folds his arms, looking at her with a 'Well, you've got it coming.' expression. Certainly, there's little sympathy there.

"He's really mad at me, isn't he?"

"Yes, he damn well is, and he's not the only one."

Glumly, she turns and slowly, makes her way to James, standing at the end of the room.

He is livid. "What the *Hell* do think you were playing at there, Charlotte? *What* does it take to get you to behave in a reasonable fashion?" he hisses at her.

Michael is listening in. Pacing the room, arms folded, he stares at the floor. Richard, holding me in his arms, is, just as clearly, paying close attention.

James' raised voice echoes through, furious. Charlotte is subdued, quiet.

"I'm sorry."

"Are you? What *exactly* are you sorry for?"

"For what happened outside. I knew you wouldn't like it, but there was no time..."

"You *say* you're sorry, but would you do it again? Running off like that?"

She hesitates. "Yes, I *would* do that again. I couldn't leave Beth in here by herself. And I had to stop them realising that you were here."

His face softens. "Beth is not your responsibility...."

"But she is. She's my friend. It matters what happens to her. If you're going to punish me, then get on with it. I'd rather not wait, and I'm sorry for upsetting you, but I'm not sorry for what I did."

"I haven't decided yet if I'm going to punish you. Astonishingly, I'd like to hear what you have to say."

Her voice is all but a whisper.

"I didn't want Beth to get hurt."

"And what about *you*? What about you getting hurt? Michael was beside himself when he saw what you were doing. ."

"They were going to gang-rape her."

"And what about *you*? Your solution is to goad them into gang-raping you instead?"

"I'm tougher than Beth. And it doesn't matter for me the same way." Michael's head jerks up. Richard, turns, disbelief writ large over his features.

"Doesn't matter?" James' voice is incredulous. "Doesn't *matter*? Charlotte, we're not talking about fun and frolics at the clubs, with Michael and I close by, watching to make sure things don't get out of hand. It would have been violent assault, and there's a fighting chance you wouldn't have survived it. Have you no idea...?"

She cuts him off. "No idea? Of course, I have an idea. You know how I grew up. I know exactly what could have happened."

James is quiet for a moment, then in a calmer voice. "Yes, of course you do..... But, I can't believe you could be so unthinking."

"I wasn't unthinking..."

Michael interrupts, "James, let me.... Charlotte, tell me exactly what was in your mind when you did.... what you just did. And what do you mean? It doesn't matter the same way for you?"

She is quiet for a moment, then, "I was thinking that I didn't want them to touch Beth. For me, it would be just.... just, one more thing that's happened. You two, it wouldn't upset you that there's been other men.... But it's not like that for Beth. You've seen her friends. They're all polished nails, expensive hairstyles and gossip. If it got out that something like that had happened to her, she'd be humiliated. And there's Richard too...."

Michael's voice is cold now. "Richard? Charlotte, I know you felt you had a debt to him...."

My husband drops his head, nestling his face in my hair. "Oh, God..."

Michael is still speaking. "…. but that debt is *paid*. And more than paid. Do you understand me?"

Still staring at the floor, she says, "He had to have her back unhurt.... Caesar's wife...."

"…. must be above reproach?" Michael expression is bitter as he finishes her sentence. "But *you* count for something too, Charlotte."

James stares at her, swiping his hand through his hair. His dark eyes slit, an outstretched finger pointing at her, "This discussion isn't finished...."

In my peripheral vision, there is a movement. Michael yells a warning, and runs.... and I scream.

Like some nightmare scene from an old movie, the world goes into slow-motion....

Framed in the doorway is a man with a gun, pointing across the room, directly at Charlotte. It's Corby, his face, cold and impassive, as he aims.

Michael, still running, throws himself bodily at Corby, in a desperate bid to take him down, to prevent the inevitable.

James and Charlotte both turn, see Corby. Charlotte's eyes widen at the gunman as the pair turn, looking for cover. But, framed against the blank wall at the end of the room, there is nowhere to go, nowhere to hide.

James, almost calmly, seizes hold of Charlotte, swings and turns, places his body between her and Corby.

As Michael tackles the gunman, bringing him down, the gun fires. Corby's aim has been knocked, and he fires low, but the bullet smashes into James and, crying out, agony on his face, he falls....

There is the hammer of bullets from all directions, and Corby drops, his body jerking and jumping, as one round after another punches into him from police weapons. Lying still, blood pools around him.

Charlotte is on her knees by James, tears streaming, shrieking denial, screaming as, her hands covered in blood, she scrabbles at him. But unconscious, he lies there, unmoving, blood spurting.

*****

'The Virgin and the Masters'

Part Six

A Continuing Tale of (Ex-)Virgin Erotica, BDSM and Ménage with Two Masters and *More......*

Part Twenty-Two Of
The 'Buying the Virgin' Series

Author: Simone Leigh

The Virgin and the Masters
Part Six

Beth

A scene from a nightmare....

Corby fallen, lying in an expanding pool of blood, dead, under a hail of police bullets. Police in every quarter fired at him, bringing him down, jerking and jumping as he fell, but too late....

Michael, blond hair plastered to his skull, chest heaving, eyes wide in shock; not having been able to move fast enough to prevent Corby's shot ....

My husband, Richard, yelling down his phone for urgent assistance....

James, protecting Charlotte with his body, deliberately taking the bullet meant for her, lying unconscious on the ground, brought down by the single round Corby managed to fire. And his blood; so *much* blood, spurting, even through the small bullet-hole in his clothes, to a pulse-beat from his thigh.

And Charlotte.... dropped to her knees, besides James, her clothes soaked in his blood, more blood splashed over her face, weeping and shrieking denial, scrabbling at him in utter, hysterical panic.

And now, Michael is *there*. "Charlotte, don't fall apart now! This is *not* the time."

She keeps screaming, tears streaming, drawing trails through her blood-spattered cheeks.

Michael slaps her, hard, across the face. "He's just taken a bullet for you," he says, his voice cold. "An artery's been cut. If we don't stop the bleeding, he's got *minutes*. Through everything that's happened, you've kept your head. *Don't* lose it now. Keep thinking straight, *for him.*"

As though a curtain draws over her face, she calms, her breathing rapid, her stare, blank.

Face immobile, voice empty of expression, "What do I have to do?"

He takes her hand, pressing it against James' thigh. "Press *there*, hard, and keep pressing." He turns to Richard. "We need medical help *fast*."

My husband, phone still pressed to his ear, nods. "There's an air ambulance on its way...."

"He's cold," says Charlotte, touching James' face with her free hand. "Clammy almost."

Michael nods. "Shock," he mutters, checking James' pulse. "His heart's racing.... and his breathing.... Jeez...." He swings back to my husband. "Richard, how long for that ambulance?"

"Five minutes. I'm talking with the medics on board. Talk to me. They've got questions. I'll relay them."

"Shoot..."

"They're asking what medical training you have?"

"I'm a first-aider for a fitness centre. I'm not trained for *this*...."

The two keep talking, Michael tersely answering questions between instructions to Charlotte and others.

Charlotte, normally pale, is white, her own breathing rapid and shallow. Michael strips off his shirt, ripping it apart, folding the shreds and passing a pad of fabric to Charlotte. "When I say, lift your hand. I'll push this in there, and then press down again *hard*."

She nods. "What is it I'm doing?"

"Blocking the flow of blood to the wound, from the side nearest his heart. One, two, three... now!"

She lifts her hand and he pushes the pad into place. "Press again, *now*. As hard as you can."

Michael scans the room. "That chair. Yes, that one... bring it over." I fetch the chair, and Michael lifts the unconscious James' feet up onto the seat....

"Two minutes," says Richard.

A tension-ridden silence falls, the blood-ridden Charlotte staring at Michael. Her tears have dried, but her voice is weeping. "Don't let him die...."

His eyes meet hers. "He's my friend too."

And.... at last.... the sound of rotor blades outside.

Richard charges out, to guide in the medics. Two immediately attend James. One tries to fuss over Charlotte, but she brushes him off irritably.

"It's not her blood," explains Michael, voice curt.

*****

Charlotte

He just lies there, eyes closed, unconscious.

He's normally so alive. Everything about him is alive. Even when he's angry with me, I love it that he's always on the move, in motion; thinking, talking, being *him*. To see him like this, so reduced....

Please don't leave me. Please....

I miss you.

Wake up, Master. Come back to me....

Please wake up.

*****

"Would it help to hear our voices?" I ask the doctor. "*Can* he hear our voices?"

The doctor shrugs. "We don't know. Odd things happen in these cases. People who we believe are deeply unconscious, later report hearing conversations around them."

Perhaps I could read to him?

"It can't do any harm."

*****

I sit in the armchair by his side, reading aloud from .... I struggled to choose what book to read to him, since it occurred to me, belatedly, that I have no idea what my Master reads for pleasure.

I try to choose something classic instead, something appropriate; but 'Wuthering Heights', with Cathy, Heathcliff and Edgar, and their doomed love triangle, isn't right. Neither is 'Gone with the Wind', with Scarlett, Rhett and Ashley. 'Pride and Prejudice', 'Jane Eyre', 'Anna Karenina', all dwell on the failure of three lovers to make their situation work.

In the end, I choose something very different, 'Time Enough for Love', an old 1970's Sci-fi novel, in which the characters make their polyamorous family *work*.

Is it right? I don't know, but it's a long book and gives me something to read to my Master.

*****

Michael

The couch is narrow; the kind that gets used in waiting areas and receptions, but she's there; positioned to watch James' face, pale, red-eyed, exhausted.

She looks like a little child, sitting by him, crying, her face almost whiter than his, except where her eyes are swollen and blotchy.

I wish I could wave a magic wand, Babe.... Make it right for you.... .... And him.

But this one is out of my hands.

Richard and Beth call by. "How is he? Any change?" she asks.

I can only shake my head. "The surgeon says they've done everything they can. Replaced the lost blood. Repaired the artery. Found the bullet and removed it.... They say his chances are good, but we have to wait."

Beth is close to tears. Richard doesn't look much better. He lays his hand on my shoulder. "I wish I could help. There's so little I can do. But.... don't worry about medical bills. That's all taken care of. Whatever it needs...."

"Thanks. I appreciate that."

"Never under-estimate self-interest," he says. "I need my co-director back." He's joking of course, trying to lighten the mood, and it shows in his eyes. "How's Charlotte?"

"Not good. Cries half the time, and sits staring at him the rest. I don't think she's slept in the last two days, and it doesn't help that I can't get her off that chair. If I could get her to lie down...."

"Ah." Richard raises a finger. "On that then, I can help. Should have thought of it before. Let's get a couple of extra beds into the room for the pair of you." He marches down the corridor. "Nurse!"

*****

Beth

We return a few hours later, Richard wanting to check that his instructions have been carried out and that the threesome are comfortable.

As we enter the room, the scene would make a statue weep: James, still unconscious. Michael and Charlotte, both asleep on a single bed beside James'.

"We shouldn't disturb them. They've had little enough rest. Let's go and have a coffee. We can come back in a while." says Richard.

"Yes, and we should bring them something to eat."

"Good idea. I'll call Ross. Get him to put something together for them. They'll need better than vending-machine snacks at a time like this."

*****

We return a couple of hours later with Ross' meal. Miracle-wise, in the short time, he's put together a hot casserole, salad, fruit and cheese, juice and coffee; all in picnic-style containers, for easy eating in difficult conditions.

We hover at the room door. Michael isn't there, but Charlotte is sitting on the edge of the bed, her back to us, holding the unconscious James' hand, kissing his fingers.

She's talking to him, and even though I can't see her face, I hear the tears in her words.

".... I know you always worried about being older than I am.... But I still thought we were going to have years and *years* together.... Now.... What am I supposed to do? With you like this? I love Michael too, but it's supposed to be the three of us. Don't leave me, Master. Please don't leave me...."

She starts sobbing. It's a gut-rending, heart-broken sound. Richard and I exchange glances. Even his eyes are filling.

We sit either side of her on the bed. I wrap my arms around her. Richard holds her hand.

Where's Michael?

He appears at the door, towelling damp hair, sees us, with Charlotte, and visibly curses under his breath.

"Oh, Charlotte. I thought you were asleep...." Then to me. "Gotta use the bathroom sometime...."

"We brought food for you."

"That's great, thanks. Charlotte. C'mon, eat."

"Ross cooked it. It's his mother's recipe chicken-casserole...." I say.

Her voice is numb. "I'm not hungry."

"Yes, you are." insists Michael. "You just think you're not."

She makes no move towards the food, which even I, accustomed as I am to Ross' good cooking, have to admit smells wonderful.

Charlotte won't look at it. Her face works, as though she's suppressing the urge to vomit.

Michael pushes the casserole at her insistently. "Charlotte, eat." Still, she doesn't make a move. "Charlotte. James would want you to eat it."

That finally does it. She picks up a fork and takes a small mouthful, chewing endlessly, forcing it down.

Richard catches Michael's eye, gesturing him out into the corridor. Michael looks across at me. "I'll stay here," I say.

He nods, following Richard.

After a few minutes, they've not returned, but Charlotte is drooping. "You should sleep." She nods but doesn't speak.

"Let me get you into bed. You're right next to him. You can watch him from there." She nods again.

I help her into bed, fully clothed still, tucking her in like a little girl. Almost instantly, she drops off. I wait for a minute or two, to be sure she's asleep, then look out into the corridor. Michael and Richard are there, talking quietly.

"You think we should get her sedated?" asks Richard. "Or perhaps away from here? It can't be doing her any good, seeing him like that."

Michael shakes his head. "I don't think sedation is the answer. Whatever happens, she's going to have to deal with it. I think it's better just to have the people she loves around her. As for taking her away; I don't think you'd get her out of there with a bulldozer.... Beth! You've left her alone?"

"She's asleep."

He looks angry, pushing past me, back into the room.

Charlotte is still there, sleeping, but is now in James' bed, lying next to him, one hand resting against his face.

A doctor arrives, white-coated and efficient looking. He spots Charlotte in the bed, and for a moment, surprise, then disapproval, washes across his face.

"You want us to get her out of there?" asks Michael.

The doctor hesitates, then shrugs. "Strictly, I should say yes, but on the other hand, if he can feel or hear *anything*, I don't know of a better way to remind a man what he has to live for."

*****

Charlotte

I'm trying to sleep, but can't. Michael has his arms around me and drifts between sleeping and waking. From his breathing, I'd say he's sleeping right now.

Blurry-eyed, my head aching from too much crying, I watch my Master. He's close, all but next to me after Michael pushed the two single beds together.

His eyes blink open.

He's not focussed, his stare glazed, not fixing on anything.

But he's *waking*.

I push back to my sleeping lover. "Michael! *Michael!*"

Michael's voice is confused, groggy. "What? Charlotte? What was that?"

"He opened his eyes. He's waking up."

But as I look back, and Michael sits up to see, my Master's eyes are closed again.

It doesn't matter. He's *waking up*.... He's getting better.

*****

I sit in the armchair by my Master's side, reading to him.

".... The way to live a long time—oh, a thousand years or more—is something between the way a child does it and the way a mature man does it. Give the future enough thought to be ready for it—but don't worry about it. Live each day as if you were to die next sunrise. Then face each sunrise as a fresh creation and live for it, joyously. And never think about the past. No regrets, ever...."

His eyelids blink open, dark eyes staring aimlessly at the ceiling. They close again, but a moment later, flick back.

I lean forward in my seat. "Master?" I whisper. "Master? Can you hear me?"

He blinks again, then his eyes slide sideways towards me. He tries to speak, and fails, mouth and lips dry. Quickly I dip fingers in the water jug, pat his lips damp. I pour a little into a glass, and supporting his head, holding the glass carefully, I help him sip a little, wet his mouth. "Master? Is that better?"

This time his eyes meet mine. "Charlotte?" His voice is so weak, but he's speaking. He's with me again.

I take his hand in mine. "Yes, it's me. I'm here, Master."

He smiles, still struggling to speak. "That's good, Charlotte. That's good."

*****

"How are you feeling?" asks Michael.

My Master, lying flat on his back, fingers pinching the bridge of his nose, "Err.... terrible, actually. I've never felt so knocked out."

"Mmm.... That's a good sign actually."

My Master looks up at him doubtfully. "It is?"

"Ah-ha. It means you're *alive*."

*****

"How long have I been here? I feel dreadful."

"Four days," says Michael. "Do you remember what happened?"

"Um.... no, not really. I was blasting Charlotte for behaving like a maniac." He frowns at me, but his lips are puckering to a smile. "Then.... er.... it's a bit hazy after that...."

"Corby was there, with a gun, aimed at Charlotte. I tried to get to him, to stop him from firing, but I couldn't move fast enough. I only knocked his aim off. You grabbed Charlotte, and shielded her with your body; took the shot instead."

My Master blinks. "I did?"

"You did. It was either the bravest or the most stupid thing I've ever seen. You dropped like a stone, and I think you were unconscious before you hit the ground. The bullet severed your femoral artery. You lost a *lot* of blood. You're very lucky to still be here, to be *able* to complain about how you feel."

My Master swallows, digesting this. "But Charlotte wasn't hit?" His eyes swing back to me.

"No Master. It didn't touch me. I'm fine. And even if you don't remember doing it, thank you. I'd be dead if it weren't for you; for the two of you."

*****

A day later, pumped with painkillers, my Master is much more himself. He is still very weak but is sitting up in bed, propped up with pillows. With me and Michael, Richard and Beth, sitting around him, he is happily talking, with the air of one giving court.

While he and Richard discuss plans, Michael sitting, silently watching, taking everything in, it all feels so much more normal....

Whatever that means....

"So where do we work from now, as a base?" asks my Master. "With the old offices burned out. What has actually been lost?"

"Oh, it's by no means a disaster," says Richard. "All the information that mattered was stored in the cloud anyway. And, as you know, it was always the plan that we would move to the new headquarters as part of the City Project. I've simply brought forward that phase of the works. The offices are going up as we speak. We should be in there within three months."

"And until then?"

"Until then, I've rented out one of the old warehouse blocks down by the docks. It's not ideal, but it will do as a temporary fix..."

Beth has brought some more of Ross' delicious food. Ye gods, but I'm hungry!

I polish off a dish of chicken and vegetables and, without asking, Michael shovels more onto my plate. I down that too, and, with an air of satisfaction, he pushes an apple into my hand.

"On the subject of temporary fixes...." continues Richard. "I was going to suggest, that since the renovations are not complete in your own home yet, and...." he nods to Michael, ".... you could do with a free hand to get on with the work, why don't the three of you move back into the beach house for a few weeks. It will be much easier for you to complete your renovation works that way, and your mountain home really isn't a suitable place for a recuperating man right now."

"Thanks, that'd be great."

*****

It is very late at night, almost early in the morning. The light is eerie, just the glow of dials and displays on medical equipment. The only noise is the hum of air-con.

Michael spooned behind me, he and I sharing the single bed beside my Master, as, unable to sleep myself, I watch him sleep.

I had thought Michael was sleeping too, but he moves, lifting my hair away with one hand, to kiss the nape of my neck. The other hand sweeps the curve of my waist and hip.

"How are you feeling now?" he murmurs.

I turn to face him. "Much better, thanks. I'm.... I m sorry I've been so awful the last few days. I didn't know what to do, how to cope."

He kisses me again, softly on the lips. "Sorry? For being upset when the man you love, is hovering between life and death? I don't think so."

"And what about the other man I love?"

He smiles, moving to wrap his arms around me. "You want to *make* love?"

"Mmm.... Yes."

Hands around my shoulders and waist, he pulls me in close, his mouth open over mine. My Golden Angel is feeling lusty, and already his erection presses against my belly.

It's been too long. With all the panic and the fear and the upset of the last few weeks, our lovemaking has been interrupted. But now, with my Master, if not well, at least on the mend, my libido surges. Desire for my Golden Lover blooms warm; curling and winding up from my core. Trembling and sighing, I stroke his beautiful face.

In the dim half-light, he smiles. "Ahh.... that's better. *That's* my Charlotte again."

He drops his face to the soft skin of my neck, nibbling and nuzzling. "You smell wonderful," he says. "It's good to see you smiling again." His hand skims my waist, wanders up to a breast, which, stooping, he cups to his face. The nipple between his lips, his mouth is warm over my skin. And now, my breath catching, arousal flushes hot over me.

Arching my spine, flexing my body against his, I fling my head back, then looking sideways, see that my Master has woken, and is watching us calmly. A smile plays across his lips. In the half-lit room, his dark eyes are depthless pools.

"Master? Do you want....?"

"I don't think I'm up to it right now." he smiles. "But don't let me stop you two. I'll enjoy some vicarious love-making this time."

Michael pulls himself up beside me. "Kneel up." he murmurs. "Face him."

Turning on the edge of the bed, Michael kneeling behind me, I face my Master, he watching as Michael runs his hands over me, over my body. His hands, flat-palmed, press against the slight curve of my belly, smoothing over my waist and hip, sliding up to cup and support my heavy breasts. One-handedly, he plays with a nipple, the other hand slipping down to the vee of my thighs.

My Master silently watches; Michael displaying me to him. As fingers work through my foxy curls, I part my thighs further, inviting the fingers more deeply in. Michael reaches inwardly, scissoring between my labia, opening me up. "I want you good and wet," he says, loudly enough to be heard, and my Master smiles.

His eyes follow the movement as my clit is fingered awake, his eyes crinkling at my small gasps, electricity jabbing through to my sex. I'm sensitising now, growing moist and slippery, and my bud is stiffening, small and hard under Michael's expert manipulation.

He alters his grip, one hand swinging around my waist, pulling me tight, the other coming in from behind me, to push into my slick pussy. "Play with your tits." he murmurs. "Display yourself. Your Master wants to watch you show yourself."

Michael finger-fucking me from behind, my breath judders as I dip into the water jug by the side of the bed, wetting the pads of my fingers to tweak my nipples hard. They crinkle to tight nubs, and I raise my arms skywards to lift my breasts, displaying them to best effect. My hair, long and loose, cascades to my waist, but Michael sweeps it back over my shoulders, clearing the view for my Master.

Fingers rubbing hard at my g-spot, a thumb working into my ass, I'm close to coming. I *want* to come. I want my Master to be able to watch me come. Flushed and sweating, I drop a hand to my clit, then use the other to stretch my lips apart, opening myself fully. Rubbing and working the tip of my bud, I find just the spot where....

My pussy tenses, coils and trembles. Streaming hot inside my thighs, my sex shudders and quivers as my climax builds. Watching me, mesmerised, my Master follows my every move until, suppressing my urge to scream, I come....

Shaking and bucking, I might fall, but Michael supports me as orgasm wracks me. "Shhh...." I can hear the smile in his voice. "Remember where we are. Try to keep the noise down."

My climax waning; "Master, um.... are you hard?"

"Err, a little, but I don't think I can...."

"I'll do the work Master if you want me to."

"I'd like that...."

The hospital air is very warm, easily comfortably enough for me to pull back his sheets, at least for a few minutes. "You'll tell me if I hurt you?"

"I don't think you'll hurt me, Charlotte."

Michael sits beside us, stroking his own erection while he settles to watch me pleasure my Master. Occasionally he sweeps my hair away where it interferes with my movement, or to give himself or my Master a better view.

Gulping, I try not to look at the bandaging and bruising on the leg where the bullet smashed in. Instead, sitting beside him on the bed, I bend to kiss him, my lips brushing his; skin on skin, soft and warm. His breath is sweet, and a little minty, and as I deepen the kiss, his hand curves around into my hair.

Tracing the outline of his teeth with my tongue, one hand caressing his cheek, with the free hand I stroke from his temples and cheek to his ear, down to his shoulders, and the tender skin of the base of his neck. The fine dark hair of his chest ripples under my touch, and as I glide down his arm to meet his hand, our fingers mesh. Lifting his hand, I kiss the lace of fingers.

He sighs as I draw my hair over his chest and stomach, trailing it along the length of his body, teasing at his nerve endings as it sweeps south over his groin. His semi-erect shaft trembles as my copper tresses flow and spill over him, stroking his balls and the delicate inner skin of his thighs.

Slipping inwards a little, I run my fingers inside his thighs, then upwards and inwards over the crinkling tightness of his balls, cupping them into the palm of my hand, rolling them with my thumb. Eyes closing and breath deepening, his head drops back.

I don't want to go any further down his legs, towards his injury. The bruising is too widespread; the wound too raw. Instead, I take the twitching tip of his penis between thumb and forefinger, rubbing gently, sliding back and forth, as the shaft swells and stiffens in my hand. Ringed around the shaft, I glide up and down his length with one hand, work the head with the other.

He is beginning to tremble, his breath to judder. His eyes open again to meet mine as I '*aaahhhh*' warm breath over him. I love to arouse my Master, and my pussy liquefies and flows as he responds to my touch. I would love to take him inside me, but, so recently hurt, I don't think he is ready for that.

Still holding his gaze, I drop to take his beautiful cock in my mouth, which now is hard and ready for me, firm and sensitive, a dewdrop on the head, which I tongue away. One hand still working the shaft, the other fondling his balls, massaging the root of his cock, with my lips, I pleasure the head. Circling with the tip of my tongue, I insert, ever so slightly into the slit, enjoying the salty-bitter pre-cum that seeps out. He quivers as I take the whole of the head in my mouth, giving him my heat, sucking gently as I swipe my tongue around the ridge.

But my Dark Angel is ill and exhausted. Sighing, he strokes my head as I love him with my mouth. Is he going to come? I don't know. But I want him to know that I'm here for him. As I look up, he's watching me, his eyes holding mine.

His breathing grows heavy and slow. "It's wonderful Charlotte, but I'm sorry. I'm not ready yet."

"That's alright Master. You want me to stop?"

"Mmmm.... I know you and Michael want to make love. I'd like to watch you."

Michael reaches across, pulling me to himself across our conjoined single beds, and underneath as he rolls atop me.

"Spread those thighs, Madam." he laughs. "Your other lover wants to fuck you."

On strong arms, he holds himself above me, as he presses between my legs. I'm warm and wet... ready for him. And my pussy pulses as I gaze up into my Golden Lover's smile, and across to my Master, where, propped on an elbow, he watches us.

Michael is beyond aroused. Perhaps watching me pleasuring my Master has readied him for me. Rock hard, his cock, always large, is huge, stretching me open as he penetrates. And of course, we have not now made love for some time.

I gasp as he fills me, his thick shaft widening my passage with its girth, and he grins down as he squeezes inside me, his deep blue eyes brilliant with desire, intense with lust. "That feel good?"

"Oh God, yes...."

"How do you want it? Soft or hard?"

I chuckle. "It doesn't come much harder.... but I'd like you to start soft, then work from there...."

He brushes lips over mine. "My pleasure..."

He pulls out of me, then pushes in once more. It's tight enough that my pussy sucks at him, and I find myself, hands around his neck, pulling up close against him, swinging a leg around his hip, as I try to ride this colossal fucking.

He knows he's testing me, and loving it. Mouth open over mine, he revolves his hips, working my g-spot, wringing helpless moans from me. He's holding me tight, not letting me move. Michael doesn't often 'take charge', but when he does, his sheer physical power is a turn-on. His well-muscled body is tremendously strong, and when he decides to pin me, as he is doing now, I simply can't move. He can do whatever he wants, and he knows it.

"That's enough baby-play," he says. "Let's take it a bit harder." He ups his tempo, repeatedly impaling me with his cock, still holding me so that I can't even squirm, only puff wordlessly, as the breath is knocked from me with each thrust.

Oh.... God.......

My igniting pussy is about to combust, as with ever-increasing cadence and energy, my Golden Lover pistons into me. My gasping turns to wailing, and he claps a hand over my mouth. "You're in a hospital, Charlotte. Let's not upset the nurses." But still, he rams into me, ever harder.

And finally, he lets rip entirely, pounding relentlessly inside me with all his strength, wrenching strangled screams from me as my battered cunt goes into liquid meltdown. There is nothing subtle about this. It's simply a good hard fuck and I, and my body, love it.

There's no warning, no gentle spiral upwards. Orgasm strikes, rampaging through me.

Gagged by Michael's palm, gripped immobile in his grasp, my body can only jerk and spasm as he steamrolls into me, my muffled shrieks, perhaps, contained within the room.

He's watching me, as he always does when I come. And as my own seismic climax subsides, Michael stiffens and pauses, dropping his face down to my shoulder. Then hips bucking, he spurts into me. Once, twice, and a final juddering pulse before, relaxing, he releases his grip on me and rolls onto his back, breathing heavily. He gives me a quick smile and then lies back, gazing upwards.

I turn to my Master. "Are you alright?"

"I'm fine, Charlotte. I'll be back on form in a few days."

Michael rolls to face him. "James...."

"I know. I know. It could be longer."

"You were very badly injured, Master...."

He blinks. "I'm sorry. I don't mean to be irritable. And.... that was good to see. The two of you."

I kiss him. "I promised you that I would always come back to you, but this time, you had to come back to me."

He strokes my cheek. "Always."

*****

The following day, Richard and Beth come to visit. "Got everything you need?" asks Beth.

"Yes, everything except the magic wand it needs to provide overnight healing for a strong, arrogant, bad-tempered patient," comments Michael.

"That bad?" asks Richard.

Michael shakes his head. "You have no idea...."

"Um, by the way...." says Richard, rubbing the side of his nose, "Er, there's no non-embarrassing way to put this, but when you're um.... *busy*.... in the middle of the night, you might want to keep the noise down. The matron down there...." He cocks his head at the door. ".... was laughing, but a bit indignant."

I've never seen Michael blush before, but he flushes scarlet, looking anywhere but at Beth and Richard.

"Was she very annoyed?" I ask.

"Richard chuckles. "What if she was? Oh, by the way...." He fishes in his pocket. "Will Stanton asked me to give you these. They were taken off Klempner." He holds out his hand, dropping something into mine....

... Two somethings: my rings. The two beautiful rings, in red and gold, and white and gold, gifted to me by my Master and my Lover, drop into my palm.

And as I slip them back onto my finger, to sit, interlocked as one piece again, the sun is shining, and my sky is blue.

*****

I sit at the table, a screen dividing the room, separating us, as Klempner seats himself at the other side. His body language is all arrogance, insolence and 'Why am I bothering with this?'

Two guards are here, one on either side of the screen, impassive but alert.

Michael stays in the background, leaning against the wall, silent, purse-lipped, arms folded, watching.

Klempner glances across at him, dismissively, then back at me. "That'd be Michael then? Where's the other one? James, is it?"

Michael tilts his head, but impassive, doesn't speak.

"Yes, this is Michael," I say. "And James isn't here because he's recovering in hospital from when your friend Corby shot him."

Klempner's eyes widen.

Surprised?

"You didn't know about that?"

He sniffs. "No, they'd not told me that." He hesitates....

So, what do you think of that then?

".... What's his condition?"

"He'll live, but it was touch and go for a while."

"And Corby?"

"Dead. The police took him down."

He nods pensively, then the sneer is back. "And why are *you* here? For that matter, why am I here?"

By God, but you're an arrogant bastard....

"Will you talk to me?"

Let him think he's in control....

He leans back in his chair, arms folded, shrugging. "I don't know. It depends on what you want to ask. I don't have a lot of incentive to co-operate, do I? They're going to lock me up and throw away the key. And you'll be testifying against me."

*It's **all** about control with you, isn't it?*

Who do you remind me of......?

Michael comes up behind me, touches me on the arm. "You want to go? You're going to get nothing from this one."

I shrug him off. "No, not yet."

Klempner looks at Michael, his hand on my shoulder. "So, how does it work then?"

"How does what work?"

"You, with two of them? How does *that* work? Two men with one woman." He sounds genuinely curious. For the first time since I met him, some of his naked hostility has faded. "Okay, regardless of what I said when we met before, I know you're not a whore. So, how does it work?"

Flushing, "I don't see that's got anything to do with you."

He sits back in his chair, coolly watching me. "Oh, you might be surprised.... You going to answer my question?"

Why would you be interested?

"No, because I don't see that it's any of your business."

His eyes glaze over, the aggressive stone-walling returning.

"What's your grudge against me?" I ask. "You said it was because of Jenkins, but I don't believe you. There's more to it than that. It's not really me at all, is it? It's to do with my mother and father?"

"You're going to testify against me. That hardly fills me with warmth."

"I don't believe that either. If that *was* it, you would simply have had me murdered. You wouldn't have gone to all the trouble you have, to capture me, hurt me, make my life miserable...."

He sits back in his chair, regarding me, one finger pressed to his lips. "Alright, Jennifer..."

Who *do you remind me of...?*

"It's Charlotte...."

"Alright, *Charlotte*. Quid pro quo. I'll talk to you if you talk to me."

?

What...?

"What do you mean? You hate me. Why would you want to talk to me?"

"I want to know about you, and how you make it work with two men."

What the Hell...?

Uncertain, I glance up at Michael. He shrugs. "Your call."

"Alright. I'll talk to you." I say. "If in return, you'll tell me what I want to know."

Arms folded, face non-committal, "Okay. Shoot."

"How did you know my mother and father? What were they to you? I know you murdered my father."

His eyes drop.

"Did I?"

"I'm told by the police that you did. And I believe it."

"Okay, I killed Frank Conners, yes; if you're determined to call him your father...."

"Why?"

"He was my friend, or I thought he was. It turned out I was wrong."

"So why did you think he was?"

"We'd go out together, drinking, chasing women. You know, the things men do.

"What was he like?"

He sniffs. "The reliable type. Solid, dependable...."

"Was he.... a good man?"

His head tilts, eyes narrowing. "What sort of question is that?"

"Did he know you were a trafficker?"

He doesn't reply, folds his arms, stares me down.

I gulp. "And my mother? What about her?"

"She was a hooker."

"I don't believe you."

"He sighs. "Jennifer....

"Charlotte...."

"Charlotte, you don't *want* to believe me. But I assure you, she was a hooker, and rather a good one. She enjoyed what she did; worked at the top end of the market. Charged a *lot* of money."

I swallow hard. "You said you 'ran her', with a string of other women...."

"Yeah, well, I lied about that. I *was* running women, but your mother wasn't one of them. Frank and I were in one of the classier hotel bars downtown. Some of the call girls would hang out there, looking for rich marks. She hit on us there...."

Please let him be lying....

He sees my expression. "You still don't want to believe me? She was *very* good at her job. Good enough that, at first, we didn't realise she was a professional. We thought she was just being.... friendly. And I'll admit, when I set eyes on her, I thought she was the most beautiful thing I'd ever seen...." He pauses, looking long at me. Michael's grip on my shoulder tightens. ".... So did Frank. We took a room for the night and.... well, *you* know the script from there. You've had two guys together often enough I'm sure...."

Don't let him bait you....

"So, what then?"

"She was fun to be with. Not just a good fuck, but actually good company. We both liked her. And she seemed to like us.... *Really* to like us I mean, rather than just pretend to because that's part of the job description. In the morning, we took her number, and later, we called her back. It went from there. We'd meet up with her a couple of nights a week. It became regular. And then...."

Michael's voice is soft. "And then you realised, that you'd fallen for the woman you thought you'd just bought."

Klempner looks at him from under hooded eyes. "Which of course, is something *you* know about...."

Michael shrugs, non-committal, then takes the seat next to me. "So, what happened then?"

"Conners was crazy about her. Never stopped going on about her. Talked about marrying her.... She was a whore.... A high-class prostitute."

"But a whore *you* were in love with too...."

Klempner's face freezes. The arms fold again. The aggression is back. I'm not sure where to go from here. I try another tack.

"So, *quid pro quo*. What did you want to ask me?"

"I told you. I want to know how you make it work. And why? Two men sharing you? I know all about you up to the point I had you shipped out to that farm, up north. After that, I lost track of you for a while. When Corby first told me *you* were testifying, I gave him instructions to find out as much as he could about you from the last few years. He tracked the records; told me about you auctioning yourself, living with two men. I thought at first, you had just grown up into just another whore. But that's not it, is it?"

How do I answer that?

So, I don't answer, just wait for more.

"*Why* did you auction yourself?" he asks. "You've grown up looking just like her. You're beautiful. You could have had men throwing themselves at you; throwing *money* at you."

"I didn't want to be some man's property. If I did that, I really would be a whore. I wanted to be myself, to go to university, have a life I chose. But I needed to raise money for the fees."

He frowns, looking bemused. "You sold yourself for a week, no holds barred, just to go to college?

"*Just* to go to college? I needed the education it takes to get somewhere in my own right. Yes, I've got looks, but a woman who relies just on that always ends up as property at some level. And looks fade in the end. What happens later? I want more than that."

He ponders this. "So, you had your week with them. Then what?"

"I had the money. I started at university."

"And later? What? You went back? To the man, the *men*, that bought you?"

"Yes, I did."

He's shaking his head, disbelief written large. "*Why?*"

"They'd been good to me. Better than anything else I'd had up until then..."

Klempner looks sceptical.

I lean forward, as far as I can with the screen separating us. "Remember where I grew up." I hiss. "You dumped me in that hellhole at Blessingmoors. Two guys being good to me, and paying me well for it, felt like Heaven."

Michael's head swivels to me, but he doesn't speak.

"So, you went back because they were paying you again?" says Klempner, still looking confused.

"No, they weren't paying me. I went back because I wanted more of it. And later, I realised .... I wanted *them*."

"You wanted them? Or you'd fallen in love with them?"

"Yes."

"Both of them?"

"Yes, in different ways."

"You didn't choose between them? They didn't try to *make* you choose?"

"Choose? Why would I choose? I love them both. They both love me. They get on together. Why *should* I choose?"

Michael breaks in. "*That's* what happened, isn't it? With you and Conners. You both fell in love with Charlotte's mother, and you made *her* choose between you. She chose Conners. And you murdered him for it, and took revenge on her."

My heart pounding.... Of course, that's it.... It's so obvious when someone else sees it first.

My Golden Lover. You see it every time, don't you....

Klempner's face is a study in .... what? Regret? Self-loathing? Grief?

He stares at the desktop. "Yes, that's what happened."

"Did *she* know what you were? A trafficker? A slaver?"

"No, of course not. She only learned that later, after...."

"After she'd already rejected you? Chosen Conners? What did you do? Threaten revenge by enslaving *her*? Like you did with Charlotte? Ship her out to some godforsaken part of the world where she had no hope of rescue, or of anything but a short, miserable life?"

Klempner is silent, his expression sick.

"The two of you paid for her in the first place...." Michael continues, relentlessly. "You *knew* that you didn't have to have a conventional relationship with her; that there can be other ways of living. But when it came to it, you forced her to decide between you...."

Klempner gazes down at the table-top. "When she learned what I was, what I did, she said I sickened her. She wouldn't look at me."

"Well, most people *don't* like the idea of slavery...." Michael's voice drips disgust. "So, for the sake of a convention you didn't really believe in, you threatened and drove your lover into hiding, murdered your best friend, and have spent the years since trying to convince yourself that you did the right thing.... to the point that you continued your revenge against someone who was completely innocent in all of this.... Charlotte, probably Conners' child, but *possibly* yours."

My gut clutches. I'd tried to convince myself Klempner was lying when he said he could be my father, but if all this is true, then....

Oh, God....

"And your final revenge on her was to steal the child, to force *her* to grow up into slavery herself.... To fit your idea of...."

Michael is sputtering his words, shaking his head in disbelief. "And when you found she'd grown up to look like her mother, you became obsessed with it again, determined to have the daughter forced into a life that the mother had already told you repelled her...."

Still struggling with his words, looking sick. "Is she alive? Charlotte's mother?"

Klempner turns away, won't meet Michael's eye. "I've no idea. The police gave her a new identity, hid her from me. I couldn't find her, and I've not seen her for over twenty years. But if she's not still alive, it's nothing to do with me." He shakes his head. "Don't the two of you get *jealous* over her?"

His tone acid, Michael replies, "He's my *friend*. Friends share things. They don't go to war over them."

Klempner stares at him, then at me. "I thought you were a complete lunatic with that performance you gave, you know. *Daring* us to rape you. I know what you were doing, keeping us off the other one... Whatever else you are, you've got balls." He glances at Michael. "No wonder it takes two of you to keep her in line."

It is such an unexpected thing for him to say. Both Michael and I burst out laughing. "I'm glad you think we do." he snorts.

Klempner gazes at me, eyes wide. It's disconcerting. I shift in my chair, uncomfortable.

"What? Why are you looking at me like that?"

"I've never seen you laugh before."

"You were always threatening to have me raped or assaulted before. Why would I be laughing?"

He looks down.

Is that.... regret....?

"You *do* look like your mother."

I don't know how to react, and I'm becoming a little nervous. Michael's fingers creep around mine. Klempner notices. "Looks after you, doesn't he?" Then, glancing at our hands. "Nice rings. Are you getting married? To this one? What about your James then? Where does he fit in? I see you have your *two* rings back. Is he wearing one too?"

I ignore the question. "So, what happens now? I testify against you and your.... gang. You keep the dogs set on me.... 'Cause I don't doubt that even though you're in here, you've still got contacts out there...." My voice chokes.... " .... Everything I've done, and gone through, to make something of my life...."

... My voice is rising, growing louder, and I don't care. "... Right now, it's wasted, isn't it? I can't return to my college, because if I step outside I'm hunted, kidnapped, assaulted. You've made my life impossible; threatened and endangered my friends. You took my mother from me. Murdered my father. You tried to murder Michael. Corby shot James, even though he was aiming for me. He barely survived. Your men set an office tower aflame. It's sheer luck that no-one died there. You were going to gang-rape my friend, and me. Where does my life go from here? Everything I did to drag myself out of the hole that you dropped me in as a baby has been trashed. And all because you're obsessing over something I had no hand in. I wasn't even born for most of it...."

My eyes are welling. Michael's hand squeezes mine.

Klempner watches me. "Obsessing?"

"What you would call it?" The tears stream down my face.

"And *now* you cry?" he says. "Not over threats to enslave you, ship you out, gang-rape you? But because you can't go back to your university?"

"What the *fuck* have you done to my life? I never hurt you. And my mother really did nothing either. No-one chooses who they fall in love with. But she might have stayed with *both* of you if you'd let it happen.... But it's all about *you*, you selfish, evil bastard.... And with what they've got on you now, my testimony isn't even going to make any difference. You're in here to *stay*, but you've got me in prison too...."

I'm crying hard, sobbing, Michael's arms around my shoulders, but as I look up, Klempner is watching us, his expression unreadable.

It becomes embarrassing. I wipe my eyes on the back on my hand, my nose on my sleeve, before Michael, from somewhere, produces a tissue.

Finally, from out of the silence, Klempner speaks. "Jennifer.... Charlotte. Go get your life back."

I gulp down, hard. "What?"

"I said, get your life back. You're right. You appearing in court, no matter what your testimony, isn't going to make a difference to me at this point. Go home. Go back to your university. Go find your mother if you want to, if she's still alive. You won't have any more trouble or at least none that I'm responsible for."

Incredulity dripping from every word. "You're kidding," says Michael. "Just like that, it's all different?"

Klempner stares up at the ceiling. "Yeah... just like that. I suppose you won't believe me, but, for what it's worth to either of you, you have my word. Whatever else happens in your lives, I won't be behind your problems.... But there's a price...."

Ah....

"Which is?"

"I'm going to be locked away for a long time. Probably for good. Come and visit me."

I stand, my chair grating backwards. "You *cannot* be serious."

He sucks his lips. "I'm perfectly serious. Come and visit me... Talk to me sometimes."

"You murdered her father, tried to destroy her mother, enslave her.... And you want her to *visit* you?" hisses Michael.

"What harm can it do?" says Klempner. You think they're going to let me near her?"

"What I have to get past...." says Michael, "...is that I'm looking at a man who kidnapped, assaulted, and intended to rape and sell, my wife-to-be, and to crown it all, suspects he might be her father, suddenly turns into Father Christmas and says that everything's suddenly okay?"

"Yes, I did all that. But that was then. And.... I've already lost the game."

*****

Michael

"I don't know what the two of you said to Klempner, but he's changed his plea."

"Sorry?"

Will Stanton scratches his head. "He's changed his plea. He's saying that he'll give a full statement and plead guilty."

"Does he say why?"

"Yes. The other thing he says is, that he doesn't want Charlotte to testify in court. If she makes a written statement of anything considered relevant, he will comment and confirm whatever is there."

"What does he get out of this? A shorter sentence? A plea-bargain?"

"Hardly. We have him for murder, attempted murder, trafficking, assault; the lawyers are still arguing over exactly what the charge is over the business of the attack on the Haswell Building, but since he's confessed, in writing and on tape, to being responsible for it, that hardly matters. With what we've got on him now, regardless of Charlotte's testimony, he'll not be coming out of prison again for a very long time, if at all. He'll probably be sentenced to life-long imprisonment. In other times and places, he would certainly get a death sentence. Mind you, his lawyers are trying to argue that he's not of sound mind and shouldn't be tried at all. Or that he should be judged as not guilty by reason of insanity. But even if they got away with that, which I doubt, he'd still end up in a high-security psychiatric institution."

Is this for real? Can it possibly be for real?

"So, why then?"

Will's voice hovers between bafflement and misgiving. "He's making the sounds of remorse...."

"Go get your life back."

"You believe him? That Klempner's trying to make amends?"

He shrugs. "Perhaps. But whatever the reason, if he does what he says, we don't need Charlotte's testimony."

"You mean, she doesn't need to appear in court? She can go home? We can all go home?"

"It's looking good, yes."

*****

"Do you think he could *possibly* be sincere? After everything he did, you think he would simply give up? Forget his revenge, just like that?" James, sitting up in bed, radiates scepticism.

"I've got to say, no. But.... if we don't at least consider taking him at face value, what are our alternatives? We all have to disappear, like Charlotte's mother? Change our identities? Give up our lives?"

James sits, silent. Lips pressed together in a hard, white line. Then, "We can take precautions of course."

"Of course. I'm already on it. And this time, it's more than just keeping an axe under the bed."

"Oh?"

"The house is a complete renovation anyway. While it's stripped to the foundations, it's as good a time as any to install any extras we might think of."

"Such as?"

"Cameras, security protection, fences, pressure detectors *around* the fences, vibration sensors on the windows...." James stares at me. ".... And since we were digging out the cellars anyway for your....er.... 'Play Room'...." James grins. ".... I've extended the excavations somewhat to give us some extra options for getting out undetected if we need to."

"You're kidding? Some sort of secret door?"

"More than that. A tunnel. A literal bolt-hole, in case we ever have gunmen turn up again in the night. Personally, I don't want any more midnight escapes through the snow."

"Does Charlotte know about all this?"

"I've not gone into details.... She knows I'm doing something, but I think she's trying not to think about it too hard right now.... Listen, one other possibility *does* occur to me, about Klempner's motives. He changed his mind when it was pointed out to him that he was retaliating against someone who was completely innocent of what had happened. Even if taking Charlotte from her mother as a baby was part of his reprisals, her mother wouldn't know anything about everything that's happened since.... What kind of revenge is that?"

"So...?"

"So, Charlotte wants to know about her mother, probably to find her, and Klempner knows that. He's in prison for God-knows-how-long. Suppose he intends to simply sit tight, and let Charlotte do his work for him, track her down? With everyone trying to help her because she's the long-lost daughter, rather than the psycho she's hiding from?"

"And then pick up where he left off? Sheesh.... that's an uncomfortable thought.... you think he's mad enough for that?"

"Yup. In fact, 'mad' is an interesting way of putting it. I'm told by Will Stanton that he may not end up in prison at all. He's got doctors arguing that he's psychotic, criminally insane; and lawyers on both sides saying he should be locked up for the good of the rest of the human race, but in a secure hospital. Personally, I think he's just an evil bastard.

"So, we go for it? Try to get back to a normal life, but remain vigilant?"

"Eternal vigilance is the price of liberty? Yes, I think that's about it...."

*****

Charlotte

I'm sitting in the lounge, reading, keeping my Master company. Michael is on the phone, chasing up on-going work in our mountain home renovation.

Glancing up, my Master's eyes are on me. His injured leg outstretched from his armchair, nonetheless, he looks relaxed and comfortable. Chin resting on his fist, he watches me.

I know that look....

Smiling, "How are you now, Master? Feeling better?"

"Better? Yes, you *could* say I'm feeling better." His deep, satin voice is slow and measured, and there is no mistaking his intent.

I put down my book, kneel by him. His hand brushes my cheek.

"What would you like, Master?"

Leaning forward and down, he kisses me but winces slightly with the movement.

"Just sit comfortably, Master. I'll come up to you."

I stand, to perch myself on the chair arm, twisting around to allow him to kiss me, and to have my breasts within easy reach for him. I've been waiting for this moment, and for the last few days, have made a point of wearing blouses that either unbutton rather easily or which have long laces, to dangle invitingly.

A pair of these now hang by my Master's hands. He smiles, knowing exactly what I am doing; happy to play the game. Running a finger along my face, down over my lips and neck, he drops towards my slightly exposed cleavage and the trailing laces.

As he tugs at them, his eyes slide up to meet mine, warm with desire.

Michael, entering silently, sits by us on the couch, hands behind his head, watching. The laces unravel, and as my blouse falls open, I lean in closer, bringing my breasts close enough to feel the warm wash of my Master's breath.

He inhales deeply. "God, you smell good...."

"Would you like to go into the bedroom, Master? I think it would be easier for you in there."

"Mmm... yes."

As he moves to stand, Michael offers him a hand up, but he brushes him away irritably. Michael backs off, palms upright. "Sorry. Only trying to help."

"You're right." says my Master, apologetically. "I'm not dealing with this very well, am I?"

Stiff legged, he rises, limping through to the bedroom.

"Would you be more comfortable standing Master? Then you don't have to bend your leg too much."

He's embarrassed....

To save him having to reply, I simply bend over the end of the bed, presenting myself.

Nice, easy access....

With me in this position, he should be able to reach everything easily. Michael sits close by, calmly watching.

My Master is grinning. "God, I've missed this...."

I twist back to grin back. "Anytime, Master. Just say the word. We'll just do things the easy way for a while."

He flips up my skirt, hands massaging my butt-cheeks through my panties. "Now there's a view to make any man happy." Slipping hands inside my panties, he tugs down, but as he pulls, his injured leg buckles, and he staggers.

Michael is there, catching him, preventing his fall....

"Leave me alone. I don't need any fucking help...."

"Yes. You *do*." snaps Michael. "You took a bullet. It cut your main artery and caused a lot of muscle damage besides.... For God's sake man, I don't think you've taken on board yet, just *how* close you came to dying. And there's no shame in taking time to recover from that.

Now, if you would cut out the stiff-necked pride, and let us help you, we might *all* enjoy this a bit more."

My Master whips around, momentarily set to snap back at Michael, then he pauses, shrugs and laughs. "You're right of course, both of you. I'm sorry."

"Master, the doctor said that it will take you a few months to properly heal. You'll be yourself again, but you *do* need to take it easy for a while."

He nods, sheepishly. "What do you suggest?"

"Just lie down, Master. Let me do the work. If you exercise every day, you'll soon be stronger, and then you can slap my butt to glowing any time you want...."

He bursts out laughing. Even Michael chuckles. "That's about the size of it, isn't it. Alright. You win. I'll lie down. I'm sure you can work your magic on me."

Flinching slightly as he swings up onto the bed, he rests back against the pillows.

"How about a glass of wine?" suggests Michael. "It'll relax you a bit, and take the edge off that ache."

"Excellent idea."

"Back in a jiffy." Michael vanishes off to the kitchen.

My Master smiles at me. "Sorry to be so grumpy. I'm not used to being disabled. I'm afraid I make a poor patient."

"It'll be fine, Master. You're better every day...."

"I just want so much to be able to make love to you properly again."

"You always make love to me, Master. Just by being you. The sex is the cream on the cake, not the cake itself."

His eyes drop. "Of course it is." he murmurs.

I undress, not too quickly, allowing him time to watch me as I release my breasts, to swing pendulously as I move; to see me slide down skirt and panties, leave myself naked for him.

Then he holds out his arms to me. As I snuggle against him, he kisses my face, nuzzling into my hair, but there is a tension in him. He truly is upset.

Michael returns with bottle and glasses, glancing approvingly as he sees me nestled into my Master's embrace.

He pours, passing a glass each to the two of us, then sits on the edge of the bed to sip his own. He watches as my Master drinks half his glass, then eye-points me to move.

I'm ahead of him. I was also waiting for my Master to drink a few mouthfuls. Putting down my glass, still with his arms around me, I stroke his chest and stomach, kissing his shoulder and neck from my slightly awkward position. His breathing slows as he relaxes.

Running fingers through the scattered dark hairs of his chest, I circle his nipples with a finger, bringing a smile to his lips. He puts down his own glass, then leans back, eyes closing.

Tracing his body with my hand, I follow the fine line of hairs south down his flat belly, to his groin, where his cock lies quiescent. Trying not to look at the white scar on his thigh, I softly massage skin and muscle. I don't venture too far in yet, avoiding his cock and balls. This should be slow and gradual. Exchanging glances with Michael, he is soft-eyed, approving. He thinks I'm taking the right approach.

I need to move. Sliding out from my Master's embrace, I straddle his legs, but over the knees, not the thighs or groin. His eyes opening as I position myself, he follows my hands as I stroke my body, displaying myself for him, outlining the curve of waist and hip.

There is movement; Michael settling himself to kneel upright behind me, also straddling my Master's legs, but with his knees between mine, pushing my legs further apart. His arms curve around to cup my breasts, fingers pulling at my nipples, elongating them. He nips and twists at them, sending *frissons* of electricity skipping down through my belly to my growling pussy. I whimper and yelp as he repeatedly tweaks and pinches; my Master's cock twitching to life.

My Master's eyes follow every movement as Michael gently torments my crinkling nubs, plucking harder each time, drawing louder cries from me with each movement. I know what he's doing of course. This show is for my Master, and I respond with moans and yelps that will please and arouse him.

His shaft, hard now. "Down on all fours," says Michael from behind me.

Obediently, I drop, reaching with my mouth for my Master's cock, but Michael, knotting fingers into my hair, jerks my head back. "Not yet."

"Ass up." He pulls me up at the hip, then brings his hand across my naked butt cheeks. It's not a hard slap, though noisy, more a warning I think, of what's coming, but my Master's cock twitches in response as I yelp.

Michael slaps harder, really stinging this time. The sound of the slap is loud, and now I yell.

My Master's pupils are wide and dark. With every *Smack!* across my rump, with every holler from me, his cock jumps and trembles. Pre-cum oozing, quiveringly stiff now, he is ready for me, but still, Michael does not release me. Again, he brings his hand hard across my ass, and I know that his fingerprints are glowing against my normally pale skin.

Then he plunges fingers inside me, thrusting hard. "Time to open you up." he says, "At the back too I think." A finger inserts into my rear passage, circling against the ring of muscle. I'm going to fuck you up the back, but *you're* going to suck off your Master. And I want to see plenty in your mouth. And you're going to ride him…. James, do you want to come in her pussy or her mouth?"

He's panting, face flushed, chest glistening with sweat. "Oh, what a choice for a man…. Pussy I think. I still get a good view that way."

"Sounds good to me.... Charlotte, you heard him. Onto your Master's cock. Let's see him up you." He pulls me upright by the hair, then propels me forward on my knees, all but lifting me. "That's right.... In it goes.... All the way.... Now, ride him."

Speared by my Master, Michael with his hand twisted tightly into my hair, I raise and lower myself, sheathing and resheathing the lovely shaft inside me. For all his slow start, my Master is throbbingly hard now, filling my slick pussy as I revolve and gyrate my hips over his.

Michael's spare hand returns to a nipple, pinching and nipping in time with my movements, and I wail in response. "That's a good sound," he says. "I like that sound. What about you James?"

"Oh, I like that sound too."

"Thought so. Let's hear more of it." And his hand drops to my thighs, inserting inwards between my lips. He pauses, "This is going to hurt...." he says. "Just thought you'd like to know that."

Barely have I taken his words on board, when he pinches hard on my clit. Blissful pain ripples through to my pussy, and I scream.

"That's good...." mutters Michael. "That's what we want to hear. You, screaming." He thumbs back the fleshy sheath. "Let's see if we can improve on that, shall we." And he pinches again, now on my hard and exposed bud.

The pain ricochets to my cunt, and it convulses into orgasm, pulsing and clenching around my Master's shaft, deep inside me.

He grunts and jerks, and, head flinging forward, he comes too.

His hips bucking and grinding, he pumps into me. I am howling in climax, Michael continuing his torment of my clit.

Finally, I can take no more. "Stop. Oh, God, stop Michael.... I can't...."

He pulls away, relaxing his hold on me, but his face snakes around my neck to kiss my cheek.

"Good girl," he whispers. "Just what he needed."

My Master does indeed look very relaxed, now again leaning back against the pillows, his expression, mellow.

He lets out a slow sigh. "I don't think I'd realised how much I needed that. Thank you. Both of you."

"My pleasure, Master."

Michael chuckles "We aim to please.... Now then Charlotte. Back on your hands and knees. You've taken care of your Master, but now your Lover would like your attention."

I shuffle back a little, but as I drop down on all fours, my Master leans forward, taking my face in his hands. For a bare moment, he simply looks at me, then mouth open, he kisses me, before releasing me to my Golden Lover.

"Think I've changed my mind," comments Michael. "I'm gonna save your ass for another day. That pussy of yours is looking far too pink and inviting to be ignored." And with that, nudging into my entrance, he slowly impales me.

His movements are smooth and gradual, in complete contrast to the wild ride of the last few minutes. "A change of pace, eh? Let's finish off nice and slowly."

He holds me at the hip, pulling me to him to match his rhythm, and his easy penetration of my now wide and slippery passage is sheer honey and cream. Sighing, I rock with him, and rapturously, climax bubbles up again in me, my fluttering pussy quaking around him. Michael feels it coming I think, and as orgasm blooms through me for a second time, he releases his grip on my hips to slide massaging hands over my waist and shoulders, drawing his nails down along my spine. I luxuriate in his caresses as climax, dark and sleek, takes me again....

.... but now, so differently. The glow of orgasm smoulders through me, in lazy ripples that run through my core and belly and thighs, leaving me sighing and whimpering in pleasure. It is a sweet, ecstatic moment that, as the glow fades, is overtaken by Michael, gasping, to drop down behind, his arms tightly around me as he trembles and spills into me.

After long seconds, he raises himself from me, gently withdraws and sitting back on the bed, offers me my glass of wine.

"Think you can cope with that for a few months?" he says to my Master.

"Oh, I think so, yes."

*****

Michael

"Do you think he'll be alright?" she asks.

"I think so. His wound is healing. It'll just take time, that's all."

"I didn't mean that. I meant...."

"What?"

"I mean.... Do you think he'll be.... *alright?*"

"For sex, you mean?"

What's going through your head, Babe?

"Yes."

"Yes, I think he'll be alright.... Would it matter to you if he wasn't? Make a difference to you, about how you feel about him?"

"No of course not, but, I wonder how important it is to him?"

"Charlotte, when James won that first contract with Haswell, it was worth millions to him. Most men at that point would have bought themselves a flashy car, a boat, even a house. *He* went out and bought himself a virgin. What does that tell you?

*****

SIMONE LEIGH

Charlotte

"What's the problem, Charlotte?" asks Richard. "You look upset."

"Oh, the university isn't very happy about the way my course is being moved around, or at least, the way I'm moving around it. It's getting a bit uncomfortable trying to talk to my tutors."

Richard peers at me over his glasses. "That's supposed to be all sorted out. I dealt with it myself.... *Francis*...." he yells through the door. "Get me Chancellor Wilmore on the phone, would you. Tell him I'd like to meet up for a chat about the donation they're asking for towards that new library wing."

He winks at me. "When you've got them by the wallet, their heart and minds will follow."

Despite myself, I grin.

*****

Michael

"I don't think I can add much to this," I say. "I'll go for a walk down by the river while you're all in there. Give me a call when you're done, and I'll meet up with you."

When I re-join them, a couple of hours later, James and Richard are sitting at a table, each nursing a beer.

"Where's Charlotte?"

"Gone shopping," says James.

"*Shopping*? When did Charlotte ever go shopping? She hates shopping."

"It's a university town," says James wryly. "She's just discovered the street with all the second-hand bookshops...."

"Ahhh... Right.... Might as well get a beer then."

"Several beers I should think."

I order myself a drink. "How did it go? Got her course details sorted out?"

"Yes, and we're both quite pleased with the result," says Richard. "James said, and I suspect you agree, that, for her own safety, he'd be happier having Charlotte close at hand, rather than away for long periods...."

"Yes, I *am* happier with that...."

"Good. So, we've arranged with the university, that she can cover a lot of the material by distance learning and online training. So long as she can pass the exams, that covers all the academic material. And the practical experience presents no difficulties. I'll make sure she works her way around everything that's available in the industry within fifty miles. James here can handle that. He has a better grip on that side of things than I do."

"Sounds ideal. And the university is okay with that?"

"I'm making sure they're okay with it. They lean on the Haswell Corporation for a lot of favours. I've called some of them in this time." He looks smug, sips his beer.

"You like getting your own way, don't you?" I comment.

"Privileges of wealth." he smiles. "I can recommend it."

"I imagine you can. And by the way, you've not pulled the wool over my eyes, about at least one of your reasons for wanting Charlotte close by...."

He eyes me. "Meaning?"

"Charlotte is *not* Beth's bodyguard."

"Mmmm.... She's done a better job of it than Ross. On his watch, Beth has been kidnapped twice, and Charlotte herself escaped when he was supposed to be guarding her."

"That still doesn't make it Charlotte's responsibility to look after your wife...."

James watches us, narrowed eyed and silent.

Richard nods, musing over his beer. "Are *you* going to explain that to her? Or would you like me to try it?"

He has a point.

Let it go....

"And Charlotte, is she satisfied with your arrangements with the university?"

"She seems to be, yes," says Richard.

I glance across at James. "You're unusually quiet. Do *you* think she's happy with it?"

"She's happy enough," he says, dryly. "And for once in this, she's going to do as she's damn well told. She'll get what she wants this way, so she has no good reason for arguing about it."

I fall silent, sipping my drink as they discuss future plans, the re-timed plans for the City project, the move to the new headquarters....

He's feeling better.... The arrogance is back....

.... though you're a good man, my friend.... even if you have sharp edges...

But what if you weren't......?

You had a failed marriage and it didn't turn you.... You simply found an outlet....

Did Klempner go wrong because of what happened with Charlotte's mother?

No.... He was already a trafficker.... He turned her stomach....

There were two of them, and she was made to choose....

My thoughts are interrupted.

"Ah, Charlotte, there you are." James eyes the bags she carries, weighing her down. "I see you have enjoyed yourself."

Her eyes are sparkling, jade-bright against her pale skin. "Oh, yes. What a great place...."

"Mind if I look at what you've bought?"

She pushes her bags towards him, James working his way through her book stack, raising eyebrows at some of her choices, muttering to himself as he does so. "'Modern Cosmology and Philosophy', 'The Chronicles of Narnia', 'The Mythology of the Ancient Greeks', Asimov's 'The Gods Themselves', 'Fundamentals of Physics: Mechanics, Relativity, and Thermodynamics', 'The Complete Sherlock Holmes', Lovelock's 'Gaia', 'Pride and Prejudice'.... An eclectic mix. Have you considered specialising?" He is laughing quietly, despite the implied criticism.

"Specialisation is for insects...." she sniffs.

James' brow furrows. "That's a quote, isn't it?"

Her eyes slide up to his, "Yes Master, it is."

He looks out of the window, scratching the bridge of his nose. "I *know* the reference, but for the life of me, I can't think where from."

She stares at him. "It's from 'The Notebooks of Lazarus Long.' taken from Heinlein's 'Time Enough for Love.'"

He still looks puzzled. "That's an old nineteen-seventies science fiction novel, isn't it? I don't think I've ever read it. Why would I know the quote?"

"You might not have read it Master, but you've had it read to you, in the hospital.... while you were unconscious...."

"While I was unconscious?"

Charlotte's eyes are brimming. "You were just lying there, dead to the world, and I was talking to you, hoping you could hear me. And when I couldn't think of any more to say, I read to you.... and you *did* hear me."

*****

Charlotte

It's getting a bit embarrassing, my Master emotional and I'm on the edge of tears. Richard, I think deliberately, shifts the conversation to something more routine.

"How's it going with the spa-hotel development, Michael?" he asks. "'Life and Beauty' was it? That's what you're calling it? Plans on track?"

Michael looks relieved at the change in subject.

"For the most part, yes," he says. "Just the usual snags and hitches you expect with any sizable project..."

"Such as?"

"Um... such as trying to get a swimming pool installed. I've got all the permissions in place to convert one of the out-buildings, but the bank isn't willing to extend the finance any further until I've got three years' trading accounts."

"But you've been running 'Life and Fitness' in the City for years.... and turning a healthy profit, surely?"

"Yes, but you know how it is since 2007. All the banks have tightened up the rules."

"Umm...." Richard rubs the back of his neck. "Take this the right way, but I'd be happy to help."

Michael stiffens, his voice cool. "Thanks, Richard, but I'm not a charity."

James chuckles. "Now, who's suffering from stiff-necked pride?"

Michael glares at him, but my Master is unabashed.

Richard is equally cool. "It *wasn't* a charitable offer, Michael. I'm a businessman. It was a proposal."

"Ah. My apologies." His voice contrite, "What did you have in mind?"

"I've been watching the reaction of Elizabeth's friends to this ever since you told us about your ideas, and I know they're queuing up to visit, especially since most of them already use your City Centre...."

"So?"

Richard scratches his chin, rubs the back of his neck. "Okay, my cards on the table. Michael, I've been *itching* to find a way of getting in on your project. And it seems to me that this might work for both of us. I'd like to fund whatever's needed to get the spa-hotel project up and running, as it should be, from Day One, in exchange for a shareholding.... How would you feel about that?"

"What size of share are you thinking of?"

"Got your figures to hand?"

"No, but I've got them in my head.... Anyone got a pen and paper?"

The barman produces a pen. A paper bag from my book purchases is commandeered. Michael jots down figures on it, *'Hmmm's* for a minute, stares into space, writes some more, then passes it over to Richard.

Richard works his way through, staring at the notes and numbers thoughtfully. Then *he* gazes into space for a minute, fingers twitching.

Counting on his fingers? Working a calculator in his head?

Then he scribbles more notes and annotations.

Finally, he writes a one-line sentence under the lot, glances at Michael for a second, then, against Michael's raised eyebrow, and my Master's barely suppressed amusement slides the bag across the table to me.

"Let's see how your accountancy's coming on, Charlotte. What does that lot mean?"

I scan the hieroglyphs in front of me....

I set out to study physics and learn the secrets of the universe. Then I changed to engineering, so I could learn how to build a city. Now, I'm being asked to.... cost it?

"Um.... Michael's put down the value of the site from a surveyor's assessment, along with what he paid, plus the mortgage from the bank. There's the value of the work done so far, and what's still needed. There's an estimate of numbers of clients, income and expenses over the next three years.... Michael... you hold all this in your head?"

He sucks in a smile. "You run a business, that's what you do, at least if you expect to *stay* in business."

"Keep going, Charlotte," says Richard.

"Okay, um, Richard's over-written some of the estimates on income and expenses, some upwards and some down. Err.... you've scrubbed out interest payments entirely, but added in some legal fees...."

"If I put cash into the project to replace bank funding, there won't *be* any interest payments," comments Richard.

Of course, yes....

I work my way through the rest. "You're offering to cover all the building and development costs, plus some marketing, in exchange for a thirty per cent share?"

"I think thirty per cent is a bit steep, don't you?" says Michael calmly.

Richard sniffs. "Well, that's open to negotiation isn't it.... but you've not stopped talking to me...."

The two lean across the table towards each other, Alternately taking the pen from the other, scribbling amendments on the paper bag, crossing-out previous notes and over-writing them. Richard is clearly enjoying himself. Michael, for all his restraint, is also, I think, enjoying himself.

I glance at my Master, who, lips pursed, is suppressing a smile. In a low voice, he says, "They've already decided they're going to do it. It's just the thrill of the chase now...."

Men....

The pen is tossed to the table-top. Richard and Michael stand, shaking hands. "Done!" says Michael. "Charlotte, meet your new shareholder."

?

"*My* new shareholder?"

He rolls his eyes. "Didn't you read any of those papers I showed you? About the purchase of the hotel and house?"

"Er... well, I scanned them quickly, but it all seemed a bit...."

He looks at me, face blank. "Boring? Is that the word you're looking for?"

I hang my head. "Yes."

Richard laughs. "You'd better start taking an interest in these things now, Charlotte. It's a bit odd that I should know already that you're a shareholder in 'Life and Beauty', but you don't."

Blushing. "Sorry. I didn't realise."

Michael grabs me under the chin. "We're getting *married*. Of course you're a shareholder."

"On that subject...." continues Richard, "Have you set a date?"

Michael goes very still.

Waiting?

"Er, we'd not really discussed it," I say. "With everything that's happened...." I glance at my fiancée.

He still doesn't speak.

What's he waiting for?

My Master breaks in. "I was rather hoping that I'd be asked to be Best Man." He swings to Michael, who is suddenly wreathed in smiles. "You can take that as a heavy hint."

"Who else would I ask?"

All eyes fix on me. "So, when were you thinking of, Charlotte?" My Master gaze is level.

That's what Michael's waiting for....

He still remembers that I only ever said 'Yes' to marrying him, under pressure....

....and he wonders if I will commit to a date?

I throw my arms around Michael's neck, pulling myself up to kiss him. "How about the Spring? You should have the house and the hotel ready by then. We could have the reception on the mountain."

His face lights up. "That would be wonderful."

"There's one other thing though...."

His face falls. Voice tense, "And what would that be?"

"Who's going to give me away? I don't have a father. But since it looks as though Beth and I are related.... somehow...., the nearest thing I've got is, a sort-of brother-in-law." I look at Richard.

He beams. "Charlotte. I would be *honoured*. And Beth could be your bridesmaid?"

"I'd like that very much."

My Master smiles as he watches me, and Michael is a man walking on sunshine.

*****

Three months later....

Spring is here on our mountain. I sit on grassy slopes, cradling a mug of coffee. Beside me, sitting on a blanket, one leg outstretched, stiff from where it is still healing, is my Master.

The sun is shining, and there is the mood of a whole new start. From behind us comes the bang and clatter of the last of the workmen in the house, with occasional yelled instructions from Michael. His spa hotel is ready for guests and has a planned opening date for Easter Weekend, and thanks to Beth, lots of pre-bookings from well-heeled ladies.

Eyes slanted sideways to me, my Master asks, "You're not too upset about not going back to college this year?"

"No, I'm fine. Doing it this way works just as well as actually attending. So long as we have a decent internet connection, I'm good."

He still looks concerned. "You *are* sure of that? I don't want any more sudden disappearances."

I kiss him on the cheek. "I'm sure. Truly."

Michael strolls down the lush hillside to join us, his blond hair, a bright halo, and his blue eyes, brilliant in the sunshine. "Room for another one?"

"Oh, I think we can spare a bit of turf." says my Master. "Everything going well up there?"

"Really well, yes. Even the house is beginning to look more like a home and less like a building site. We could move back here from the beach house anytime we wanted now."

"I'd like that," I say. "You promised me my home, months ago. And now it's here."

Michael, restrained as ever, says nothing, simply taking my hand, kissing my knuckles. Then, "I wanted to ask you something, Charlotte...." He hesitates.

Choosing your words?

"Yes?"

".... All through your life, you've had everything thrust upon you. Even meeting James and me, you chose to enter the auction, but you did that out of necessity. I'd like to know what you want. Now that you are free to choose for yourself, what is it that you *want?*"

He sits, watching me, chin on his knees, arms wrapped around his legs, quietly waiting for my reply.

What do I want?

I look around: this beautiful place, my new home behind me, my Master to one side of me, my Golden Lover to the other.

Below us, a breeze ripples the lake and sunshine dances over the water. The air is sweet and warm and wild flowers nestle in short, sheep-clipped turf. It is Paradise.

I hold out my hands. "What more could I want? We're all here, at last, together. I have you both. I have what I want.'

I see it pass between them; that locked eye glance....

Oh.... Oh....

Michael kisses me softly on the mouth then, standing, takes my hand. "I think I'm going to ask you to prove that." he grins.

At that moment, there is a bang and a crash from the house, followed by loud swearing.

"Oh hell!" spits Michael. "What now?" He shrugs apologetically at us, then goes back up the hill to see what the problem is.

My Master chuckles. "You know, it won't be that long before all the workmen go home. We could, um, prepare things for when Michael is free...."

"Sounds nice, Master. Here, let me help you up...."

*****

"I thought we were supposed to just be preparing things...." I say.

My Master raises his head. "Yes, quite. I'm preparing you. I wouldn't like Michael to find you *non-prepared* for him.' He returns his attentions to my inner thighs, where he is kissing and nibbling at the soft, delicate skin. Thus far, he has not strayed much further, but already my core is melting.

"Please, Master."

"No, we're waiting for Michael. Don't be impatient. And besides, I enjoy watching you like this. I can see you arouse, watch your pussy open, *unfurl*. Let's see if I can help it along a bit."

He doesn't, as I expect, open me with his fingers. Instead, he laves my outer lips with long, languorous strokes of his tongue.

Aaahhhh......

"Yes, there you go, see. Beautiful.... Opening up all by yourself...." And as his tongue laps at my inner lips and beyond, I wail.

Ohhhh.... Godddddd......

I'm trying to flex, to arch my spine, but since my hips are already pillowed up, my arms and legs outstretched, I can barely move.

"Now *there's* a pleasant sight." Michael is leaning against the door, looking down at me, grinning.

My Master glances up from where his mouth is fastened around me. "Didn't see you there...."

"You were occupied. James, you look like a man enjoying oysters.... Love the starfish look, Charlotte. Nice ropes those."

"Mmm... Oysters? Not too far wrong there. Succulent lemon and brine.... Thought you were still working in the hotel?"

"They've all gone. Then I heard Charlotte's siren call. And *that's* a noise that's going to pull me in every time, like a starving man to a feast."

"Siren call eh?" says my Master. "If I recall, in the original tale, it was Odysseus who was tied up, not the siren...."

"Er... guys.... I'm still here you know. Listening. I can hear every word you sayyy.... *Aaahhhhhh....*"

My Master raises his head from where he is licking out the inside of my pussy.

"That the noise?"

"Yeah, that's the one.... You know, I've got a humongous hard-on now, and a deep urge to put it somewhere...."

"My dear chap, don't let me stop you. Here, do take over."

"Just keep her busy for a minute would you, while I strip down for business."

"My pleasure." My Master circles my clit with his tongue-tip, then sucks at my flowing pussy. "You're right you know. Oysters.... You want to....?"

"No, don't disturb yourself. I can see you're having fun down there. I'm just going to feed my cock to the top end."

Michael, naked now, and with his shaft as humongously large as advertised, straddles my chest, pushes a pillow under my head and wipes his cock-head over my lips.

"You can start by licking me clean. You got me started off early."

He's already streaming pre-cum, which trails in glutinous ropes from my lips. I lap it away, and he wipes the re-forming droplet around my mouth again. "Keep going. I love shoving my cock in your face, and in about a minute you're going to get the lot. Sorry if that seems quick, but I think James is going to tongue-fuck you to coming this time, and I want to watch *that* when I know you've already had a mouthful from me.... Now, open up."

The streaming cock-head prods at my mouth, then, as I part my lips, pushes inside, fat and warm and slick. Michael chews his lip as, looking down at me, he pushes in. "Wrap your lips around me. Tighter.... that's it. Do as you're told...."

My molten pussy is flooding, my Master plunging in deep with his tongue, swiping out, then withdrawing again to suck on my clit. He pulls back for a second. "She's going to blow anytime. You want me to let her come?"

"Mmmm.... tempting. Just hold on a little while yet eh? What do you think? Should I spill in her mouth or over her face?" Michael continues his slow face-fucking.

"You're not doing either 'til I'm there to watch...."

As my Master rises, his leg still a little stiff and slow, Michael, pupils huge in his amazing eyes, deep blue, dark-lashed, pushes in again, pulls out once more. "Jaws aching?"

"Mmmfff..." I agree.

"Thought so. Open up again, let's see how much I can make 'em ache...."

My Master seats himself beside us. Michael, not ceasing his movement, glances towards him. "So, mouth or face?"

"Best of both worlds? Most in her mouth.... finish off over her face...."

"Great idea...." And with that, he groans, shuddering his climax between my lips. Hot cream pulses over my tongue, jetting to the back of my throat with its salty tang and, at the last moment, he jerks outwards to spray, stickily, over my nose and eyes and cheeks.

"Now, I call *that* a pleasant sight." says my Master from under arched brows. "Something for me to think about while I'm finishing off the other end."

"Off you go then. I'll keep an eye on things up here, now that I can watch her come, all prettily coated like that."

As my Master returns, to push his tongue back into my pussy, Michael sits, just watching me. He trails a finger over my spattered face, wiping up his cum, and pushing the finger into my mouth. "Clean it up," he says.

I suck at the finger, then wail as my clit is thumbed free of its sheath and gently nibbled. His mouth hot over my nub, my Master teethes gently, oh so gently, at me, but, lightning striking through to my sex, it burns through to where my orgasm bubbles and seethes, ready to boil over.

He drops to suck at my pussy, laving away hot juices, and lapping back upwards through my lips. Tensed against my restraining ropes, every tendon taut, I shudder and writhe, trying to find a place to explode into.

And it bursts free. My orgasm boils and spills, breaking through me in spasms that wrack me with excruciating pleasure. Shrieking against the sheer violence of it, I strain against my own body as my volcanic cunt erupts pulse after pulse of heat, through heart and body and soul.

"Stop. *Stop*. Please, stop...."

Instantly, my Master pulls away to stand. Michael darts over, helps him upright, and he plunges deep into my still vibrating core. He's on the brink himself, and my continued howling as he rams into me, sheathing himself against me, again and again, takes him to the edge.

Wild-eyed, sweating, he drops almost over me, deep inside, but supporting himself on outstretched arms. A final thrust, and he comes, juddering and shaking as he spills into me. Groaning and grunting, eyes squeezed closed, his body tensioned in climax, he remains poised for long seconds before, at last, with a gasp, relaxing. Eyes opening, he stands, withdrawing from me, before flashing me a smile, then another to Michael.

"That was *intense*...."

"Let's share a glass," says Michael. We both nod and he disappears out of the room whilst my Master unties me from my spread-eagled position. With a towel, smiling as he does so, he wipes my face clean, then kisses me. "You look beautiful."

Michael returns, bearing a bottle and three glasses. Pouring he says, "A toast I think." Seated to one side of me on the bed, holding up his glass, "To my future Wife, and my Best Man."

My Master raises his glass. "To my Best Friend and my Wife-de-Facto."

And mine: "To my Master and my Husband-To-Be."

*****

*This is the concluding episode of "The Virgin and the Masters".
However, you can meet up with Charlotte, James & Michael again in
"The Virgin's Wedding"[1]
You can see them also, along with Richard and Beth,
in a special one-off episode of the
'Bought by the Billionaire' series:*

---

1. *https://books2read.com/the-virgins-wedding*

"The Master's Wife's Birthday"[2]
After that, they return in,
"Charlotte's Search" - Box Set One (Free Download)[3]

2. https://books2read.com/masters-wifes-birthday

3. https://books2read.com/charlottes-search-box-set-one

Free Audiobook
'Friends'
'Mastering the Virgin' Part One

4

The Boys are Back in Town....

James is a Dom. Michael loves women.

When the two become unlikely friends, they form a team, working the clubs and enjoying a carefree bachelor existence.

Until, one day, James is offered an unusual opportunity: to Buy A Virgin...

The First Part In A Tale of BDSM, Ménage Erotic Romance.

---

4. https://www.simone-leigh.com/books/

friends-mastering-the-virgin-1-audiobook/

CLAIM 'FRIENDS'
THE AUDIOBOOK

[5]

'Her Master's Wedding'
'Charlotte's Search' Part One
FREE DOWNLOAD

When you Marry Two Men What Happens Next?

As Charlotte's wedding day approaches, will her marriage to one of
her Masters affect her relationship with the other?

Has her old enemy forgotten her? And will the past return to reveal
its secrets?

A BDSM Ménage Romance and Thriller

6

DOWNLOAD
'HER MASTER'S WEDDING'

7

'Mastering the Virgin' Box Set One
FREE DOWNLOAD

You've read 'Buying the Virgin'? Told from Charlotte's point of view? Now read 'Mastering the Virgin', where James and Michael get their say.

8

The Boys are Back in Town....
Two Friends
One Virgin
One Week

8. https://books2read.com/mastering-virgin-box-set-one

It was all supposed to be about sex – a bit of fun.
No-one mentioned Love....
A BDSM, Ménage Erotic Romance

9

'Triad'
'Mastering the Virgin' Part Thirteen
FREE DOWNLOAD

10

The Past Returns....
She sold herself, and then she returned to him, her Master, and to her Lover
Now, the Three believe her past is behind her.
But Dark Forces are moving....
A BDSM Ménage Erotic Thriller

---

10. https://books2read.com/triad

DOWNLOAD
'TRIAD'

[11]

See The Book Trailer
'Mastering the Virgin' Box Set Three

12

13

See The Book Trailer
'Triad'

14

TAKE ME TO
THE TRAILER

15

---

14. https://youtu.be/VNvBbVujTCE

15. https://youtu.be/VNvBbVujTCE

Suggested Reading Order For the 'Buying the Virgin' Story

The story of 'Buying the Virgin' started out as a simple little story of a week of auction erotica frolics told from the point of view of Charlotte 'The Virgin', with James, her purchaser and Master, and his friend Michael. This was five episodes making up what is now 'Buying the Virgin' Box Set One

The tale has however, grown in the telling and has expanded to Four Box Sets (with more coming) of 'Buying the Virgin' (BTV), the current four Box Sets of 'Mastering the Virgin (MTV), with more coming, new characters introduced in 'Kirstie's Tale' and it has absorbed 'Bought by the Billionaire' whole.

Understandably enough, I am receiving an increasing number of requests for a suggested reading order for the books.

So, I've put together a guide in this blog post[16] It's by no means set in stone. Much of BTV and MTV can be read interchangeably, but for those of you who are perhaps new to the story or who have encountered it half-way through, perhaps with a free download of 'Triad' or similar, here's a suggested reading order for you.

---

16.   https://www.simone-leigh.com/suggested-reading-order-for-buying-the-virgin/

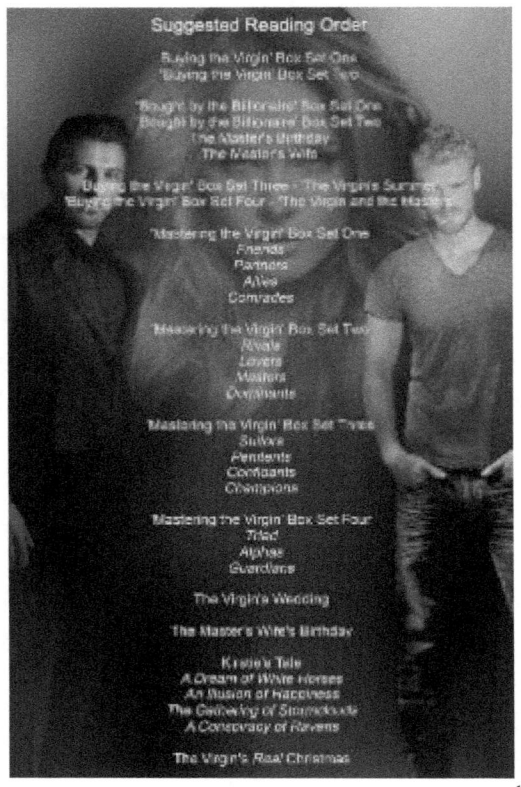

17

18

17. https://www.simone-leigh.com/suggested-reading-order-for-buying-the-virgin/

18. https://www.simone-leigh.com/

suggested-reading-order-for-buying-the-virgin/

Free Resource
'Buying the Virgin' Timeline Infographic

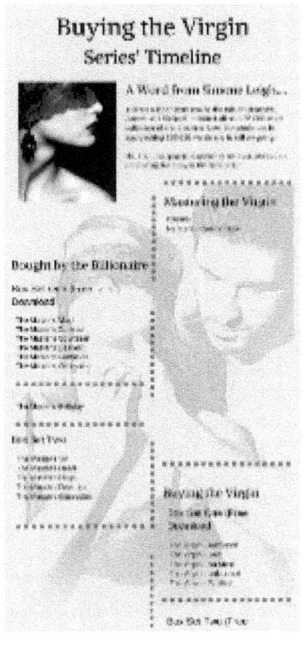

19

'Buying the Virgin' started out as a bit of fun erotica. My original intention was to write a series of five short stories that would give readers a 30 minute 'helping' of erotica over a cup of coffee.

But the story has grown in the telling. With four Box Sets out and more to come, side stories, extra characters and.... well.... Spoilers.... Lol!

So far, the tale is up to around 700,000 words and is still growing.

So, for those of you who would like to check in what order to read the books, I have an infographic for you. I update it regularly, and at some point, when I get my 'tech-head' screwed on, I'll produce an improved version with the book links built in.

Hope it helps ?

---

19. http://www.simone-leigh.com/timeline-infographic-for-buying-the-virgin/

[20]

Free Download
'Red as Blood'
Book One of 'Tales of Blood and Darkness.'
Little Red Riding Hood?

21

*Belle is eighteen and should be a woman. Terrified that she may be
barren and have no future, she confides in her Grandmother.
But as the moon waxes full, she learns that her family has a secret...
Darkly erotic re-telling of an old fairy tale.*

___

21. https://www.instafreebie.com/free/2pLV2

DOWNLOAD
'RED AS BLOOD'

22

Want to Read Where It All Started?
Free Download
"Buying the Virgin. Box Set One"

23

She Auctioned Herself and Her Virginity

The penniless Charlotte dreams of a bright future, but she has nothing to sell but herself and her virginity. She chooses to auction both to the highest bidder.

What will happen when her owner takes her away?

23. https://books2read.com/box-set-1-the-virgin

24

Who is Richard Haswell?
Free Download
"Bought by the Billionaire. Box Set One"

25

Elizabeth is a student working in a dead-end hotel job to makes ends meet, but dreaming of a better life. When she foolishly decides to shower in the penthouse bathroom of one of the hotel guests, it has consequences she did not expect.

A BDSM Billionaire Erotic Romance

26

25. https://books2read.com/bought-by-the-billionaire-box-1

26. https://books2read.com/bought-by-the-billionaire-box-1

Free Download
'Enslaved'
Book One of 'Submissive to Her Master.'
Dying of Boredom?

27

What has She to Live for?

Martha is jaded with life to the point of suicide. About to end it all, she encounters a stranger who takes her on a wild ride of passion, convincing her that she has something to live for.

'Submissive to Her Master' is a story of Master and Slave, BDSM erotica.

---

27. https://books2read.com/enslaved-submissive-to-her-master

DOWNLOAD
'ENSLAVED'

28

Free Download

'Freedom'

Book One of 'Call of the Wild.'

A Perfect Life?

29

Anna is a writer, making her living on the move and living her life as free as a bird.

---

29. https://books2read.com/freedom-callofthewild

She seems to have complete freedom and a perfect life. But is everything as it appears?

DOWNLOAD 'FREEDOM'

[30]

About the Author

Simone Leigh is English but has lived in Spain for the last few years. Here, she divides her time between working on her tan, renovating her beautiful villa, writing erotica and swimming naked in her swimming pool.

Visit Simone Leigh's Website[31]

http://www.simone-leigh.com/

32

Romantic, Intelligent, Erotic Fiction

---

31. http://www.simone-leigh.com/

32. http://www.simone-leigh.com/

Contact Me

Simone Leigh

If you would like to get in contact, with comments, questions, reviews or even requests the kinds of stories you would like to read in the future, I'd love to hear from you.

Follow Me

Website: https://www.simone-leigh.com/
Facebook page: https://www.facebook.com/
perfumepetalsandthorns
YouTube: https://www.youtube.com/channel/
UCLa1RTmTBXwOKCxRb-WU69Q
Twitter: https://twitter.com/SimoneLeigh_CBE
Instagram: https://www.instagram.com/simoneleighauthor/
Newsletter Sign-Up: https://www.simone-leigh.com/
my-newsletter/
Bookbub: https://www.bookbub.com/profile/simone-leigh
GoodReads: https://www.goodreads.com/author/show/
15454039.Simone_Leigh
BookSprout: https://booksprout.co/author/2791/simone-leigh

My Newsletter

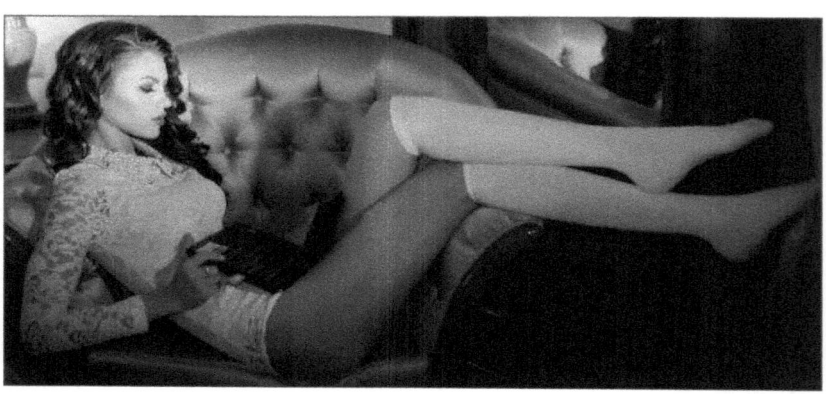

If you would like to receive my newsletter, you can click the link below to subscribe. I send it out, typically once a week on Fridays. In it you will get news, offers, free books, competitions and sweepstakes, and my random musings direct to your inbox. And I'll also send you a free book as a welcome gift.

If you would like to see a sample newsletter, you can click the button below to see a recent example.

And of course, you can unsubscribe at any time.

SHOW ME A SAMPLE
NEWSLETTER

33

SIGN ME UP TO THE
NEWSLETTER

34

33. https://preview.mailerlite.com/y8i2p3

34. https://www.simone-leigh.com/my-newsletter/

Don't miss out!

Visit the website below and you can sign up to receive emails whenever Simone Leigh publishes a new book. There's no charge and no obligation.

https://books2read.com/r/B-A-AXDD-TEDO

BOOKS 2 READ

Connecting independent readers to independent writers.

Did you love *Buying the Virgin - Box Set Four - The Virgin and the Masters*? Then you should read *Mastering the Virgin - Box Set One* by Simone Leigh!

The Boys are Back in Town....

James is a Dom. Michael loves women.

When the two become unlikely friends, they form a team, working the clubs and enjoying a carefree bachelor existence.

Until, one day, James is offered an unusual opportunity: to Buy A Virgin...

A Tale of BDSM, Ménage Erotic Romance.

Explicit adult content. For mature readers only

This Box Set contains the following stories, previously published separately

Part One: Friends

Part Two: Partners

Part Three: Allies
Part Four: Comrades
Total approx 63,000 words
Read more at https://www.simone-leigh.com/.

Also by Simone Leigh

Bought by the Billionaire
The Master's Maid
The Master's Contract
The Master's Courtesan
The Master's Desires
The Master's Fantasies
The Master's Obsession
The Master's Sin
The Master's Heart
The Master's Rage
The Master's Wife
The Master's Wife's Birthday

Bought by the Billionaire Box Set
Bought by the Billionaire. Box Set One. Books 1-6
The Master Series. Box Set 2. Books 7-10

Buying the Virgin
The Virgin Auctioned
The Virgin - Sold

The Virgin No More
The Virgin Unleashed
The Virgin Fulfilled
The Virgin's Holiday
The Virgin's Christmas
The Virgin's Valentines
The Virgin's Master
The Virgin's Lover
The Virgin's Fantasies
The Virgin's Choices
The Virgin's Summer - Part One
The Virgin's Summer - Part Two
The Virgin's Summer - Part Three
The Virgin and the Masters - Part One
The Virgin and the Masters, Part Two
The Virgin and the Masters - Part Three
The Virgin and the Masters - Part Four
The Virgin and the Masters - Part Five
The Virgin and the Masters - Part Six
The Virgin's Wedding
The Virgin's Real Christmas
The Virgin's Summer - Part Four

Buying the Virgin Box Set
Buying the Virgin - Box Set One
Buying the Virgin - Box Set Two
Buying the Virgin - Box Set Three - The Virgin's Summer
Buying the Virgin - Box Set Four - The Virgin and the Masters

Call of the Wild

Freedom
Thralldom
Retribution
Revelation
Redemption
Call of the Wild - Box Set

Charlotte's Search
Her Master's Wedding
Her Lovers' Touch
The Sin of the Parent
The Daughter's Manumission
The Father's Betrayal
The Shadow of Obsession
The Loss of Innocence
Her Mother's Love
Her Enemy's Promise

Charlotte's Search - Box Set
Charlotte's Search - Box Set One
Charlotte's Search Box Set Two
'Charlotte's Search' Box Set Three

Kirstie's Tale
A Dream of White Horses
An Illusion of Happiness
The Gathering of Storm Clouds
A Conspiracy of Ravens

Mastering the Virgin
Friends
Partners
Allies
Comrades
Rivals
Lovers
Masters
Dominants
Suitors
Penitents
Confidants
Champions
Triad
Alphas
Guardians
Hunters
Saviours
Family

Mastering the Virgin Box Set
Mastering the Virgin - Box Set One
Mastering the Virgin Box Set Two
Mastering the Virgin - Box Set Three
Mastering the Virgin Box Set Four: A BDSM Ménage Erotic
Thriller
Mastering the Virgin - Box Set Five

Submissive to Her Master
Enslaved
Enthralled
Entranced
Enticed
Submissive to Her Master - The Box Set

Tales of Blood and Darkness
White as Bone

The Master's Child
Target

Standalone
Hearts of Fire. Poems of Love, Romance and Erotica
Kirstie's Tale - The Box Set
Trio - Three Short Stories
Mastering Charlotte
Buying Charlotte - The Complete 'Buying the Virgin'

Watch for more at https://www.simone-leigh.com/.

About the Author

Simone Leigh is English but has lived in Spain for the last few years.

She divides her time between working on her tan, decorating her beautiful villa, writing erotica and swimming naked in her swimming pool.

According to one internet troll, she is 'beyond redemption'...

Read more at https://www.simone-leigh.com/.

www.ingramcontent.com/pod-product-compliance
Ingram Content Group UK Ltd.
Pitfield, Milton Keynes, MK11 3LW, UK
UKHW040807140725
6875UKWH00016B/191